OVER HER DEAD BODY

A B MORGAN

Happy reading
Best Wishes
Ali Morgan.

HOBECK

This edition produced in Great Britain in 2021

by Hobeck Books Limited, Unit 14, Sugnall Business Centre, Sugnall, Stafford, Staffordshire, ST21 6NF

www.hobeck.net

A CIP catalogue for this book is available from the British Library.

ISBN 978-1-913-793-20-3 (pbk)

ISBN 978-1-913-793-19-7 (ebook)

Cover design by Jayne Mapp Design

Printed and bound in Great Britain

❦ Created with Vellum

This book is dedicated to my beautiful daughter who planted the seed for this story by making the legal business of death so intriguing. I will always be grateful for her knowledge as she guided me through the weird world of the undertaker.

I'M NOT DEAD

I reached out for the oval brass knob of the Yale lock, wedging my mobile phone to an ear with my shoulder. In need of repair, opening the front door had become a source of intense frustration, requiring both hands to budge it from the frame. Ordinarily I would have ended the phone call before answering the doorbell, but I was not prepared to lose my place in the queue to the call centre.

'All of our customer service operatives are currently busy. Please hold and we will deal with your enquiry as soon as possible. Thank you for your patience, Moorline Telephone Banking Services values your custom.' Once more the message was repeated, followed by a few bars of Vivaldi. After some determined wrenching with my teeth clenched, the door freed itself and opened to reveal two men in ill-fitting suits standing on the doorstep. One had a clipboard clamped to his chest.

'Yes?' In no mood for salesmen that morning, I was curt.

The man nearest to me cleared his throat as I scanned

him, trying to determine his reason for being there. Polka-dot tie worn askew; the top button of his shirt undone to accommodate a fleshy neck. 'Sorry to disturb you, madam,' he said, handing me a laminated card, passing it off as a warrant of some kind. 'The local authority sent us to recoup monies for a funeral.'

He glanced down at his paperwork while I checked over his job title and contact details. Being addressed as 'madam' hadn't gone down well, and only good manners prevented me from closing the door before he could finish his opening remarks. A half-hearted smile was all I could muster as I handed the card back. From what I could gather, he was some sort of debt collector. 'Gabriella Dixon. Does the name ring any bells?' he asked.

'It ought to,' I replied. 'But you've made a mistake. My mother's funeral costs were paid in full. I should know, I paid them.'

He looked at his more lightweight, silent colleague and again at the form, then took several steps backwards and checked the house number. 'This is number six Derwent Drive.'

'Yes, that's correct.'

'Your mother was Gabriella Dixon?'

'No, *I'm* Gabriella Dixon. My mother died less than a year ago – she used to live here. I've just moved in.' My neck was aching, so I juggled the phone across to the other shoulder, still holding onto the edge of the door and speaking around it. 'It's a long story. Now what do you want?'

I wasn't normally this impatient, but the morning hadn't been going well and their intrusion was preventing me from dealing with more pressing matters. My ears vied for attention, caught between *The Four Seasons* in one ear and a council debt collector telling me some claptrap about an outstanding bill on the other. 'I'm desperate to speak to my bank, so can you come back another time?'

When he showed no sign of retreating, I looked at the ID badge slung on a lanyard around the man's neck, checking it corresponded with what I'd read on his so-called business card. 'Paul, is it?' He nodded, staring at me with a frown. Then he started running his chubby index finger across lines of typed information on the clipboard. His sidekick, whose name I hadn't bothered to find out, craned his neck to see the form and provide back-up for a bewildered colleague.

'Well, Paul, whoever sent you can be reassured there's no money owed in respect of my mother's funeral. I paid the bill at Castle and Wyckes in full and on time, just as she had instructed me to. I paid everyone, even the dreadful caterers. My mother's name was Eileen Brady, and she's buried at St Ninian's. Got that? Want me to sign anything?'

Paul's eyes widened, and he handed me the sheet he'd been referring to. Reading it, I grinned as the truth dawned. 'Oh dear, someone's got their wires crossed. I should trot back to the office if I were you.' Perhaps it wasn't the most suitable reaction, but I laughed. 'Whatever your piece of paper says, it's wrong. I can't be dead, because I'm here talking to you right now and I'd know if I'd popped my clogs.' With a condescending nod of my head, I handed the paperwork back to Paul, who stood pulling at the knot of his dreary tie. 'A simple case of mistaken identity, I would say.' Smiling thinly, I closed the door and made my way back to the lounge. 'Dead indeed...'

When a human voice unexpectedly cut into the loop of music and recorded announcement, it broke through into

3

my amusing thoughts about who had attended my funeral and wondering what I'd died of; I was still tittering.

'My name is Yasmina. Before I deal with your request, can I take your name and the first line of your address, please?'

Moorline Bank, at last.

'And the first and third digits of your PIN.' There was a considerable delay before Yasmina at the call centre spoke again. 'Can I ask the nature of your enquiry?'

I was still very embarrassed after having a debit card payment declined by the local garage the day before, and further irritated that the card had been swallowed by the ATM on the forecourt. By chance, I'd had a credit card from another provider to use, saving me from total ignominy. Nothing like that had ever happened to me before. No matter how confidently I'd tried to brush it off as a bank error, the cashier at the garage had continued to stare at me as if I were attempting to commit a heinous crime.

Consequently, I was short with the girl on the phone. 'Simply put, Yasmina, I can't access the money in my account, and my online banking isn't working for some reason.'

'Can you please confirm your identity for me again, caller?'

This time I distinctly heard a note of misgiving in her polite tone. 'Why are you asking me these questions again?' I queried, but as I uttered the words I panicked. Had I dialled a scammer by mistake? I quickly held the phone in front of me so I could check the call display on the screen, only to find the usual number; the one logged into my phone, the one I always used. Whether the chipper-voiced Yasmina was being obstructive or overzealous, I wasn't sure, but since she was putting questions to me twice I suspected something was awry. 'Look, I've told you my name, address, and my mother's maiden name. I know my PIN, and I'd like you to tell me why I'm unable to access my bank account online, or anywhere else for that matter. Can you sort this out?' With concerns beginning to creep up on me, my throat closed off, resulting in a squeak at the end of my plea.

As it turned out, Yasmina couldn't help me. 'Caller, I'm required to inform you that you do not have permission to access any account in the name Gabriella Louise Dixon. We have suspended these accounts.'

I scraped back my hair with one hand and held my astonishment in check at such an outrageous statement. 'Suspended? Do you mean they're frozen? On whose say-so? These are my accounts and I need to access them.' Flabbergasted wasn't the word. Incredulous barely covered it. 'Can I speak to your supervisor, please? There's been a mistake. I start a new job soon, I have a mortgage to pay any moment now, and I need a functioning bank account.' It was becoming harder for me to remain composed.

Again, there was a delay before the response from Yasmina, but this time there was no getting away from the truth. 'Caller, the bank has received notification that the holder of these accounts is deceased. Therefore, I suspect you of trying to access money to which you are not entitled, and I must pass on your contact details to the police.' Sweet Yasmina appeared to be reading from a script. She ended the call by informing me that if I wanted to take the matter further, I must make an appointment at my local branch to provide valid ID.

'Don't you worry, I bloody well will!' I shrieked. Cheeky little madam, who was she to be accusing me of trying to steal my own money?

Side-stepping an empty tea chest, I sank into the musty upholstery of my parents' ancient sofa. A vacant expression on my face, I stared at a faded family photograph. 'Whatever next?'

I cross-checked the time on the old wall clock with my watch. 'Shit.' The last hour had flown by, and like it or not, I would now be late for an important meeting. The late Gabriella Dixon.

2

THE WILL

I ran the last few yards from the car park, and spotted Laura, all piercings and cheesecloth, waiting for me outside the office building. Coils of blue-green batik held a dark mass of undulating Medusa dreadlocks away from her face. She no doubt considered it a stylish look, when in fact she resembled a grubby market stallholder selling incense sticks and hubble-bubble pipes. My sister hadn't the slightest sense of occasion, turning up looking like this. Poor dress sense aside, it delighted me to see that neither of her children was in tow. The last appointment had been an awkward demonstration of how not to conduct business affairs, when one bawling baby and a stroppy toddler took precedence over the legalities.

In shabby espadrilles, Laura beckoned for me to hurry while hopping from foot to foot. 'Where've you been?' she asked. 'I was panicking when I couldn't get hold of you. Try switching your phone on.'

'Sorry, I got held up. Some monstrous blunder at the

bank. I'll explain once we're inside.' Time and breath were in short supply.

'You made it. That's the main thing,' Laura said, giving me the once over. 'I see you left the house in a hurry. Perhaps we should have waited for you to settle in. You look frazzled.'

I caught sight of my reflection in the nearest window and set about tidying myself up. 'Frazzled and then some,' I said, as I tucked the tail of my white blouse into the waistband of a pair of tailored trousers. It had been a poor decision to wear linen trousers, which were now more crumpled than the matching jacket. Much to my annoyance, I hadn't had time to reassemble the impressive bun on top of my head before stepping out of the car. The wind had taken its toll, and as I marched towards the glass entrance doors of Bagshot and Laker's solicitors, more wild wisps freed themselves. I must have looked frightful for Laura to pass comment.

Our appointment was with Bernard Kershaw, a little full of himself in the typical public-school manner, a partner in the firm and as dull as he was thorough – I rather liked him. As we stepped inside the front office, Mrs Fiona McFarland, his secretary, ushered us straight through.

'I think we've made it in the nick of time,' I said to him, one hand outstretched in greeting.

'Five minutes late actually,' Bernard Kershaw replied, as he shook hands with polite words of welcome and then did the same to Laura. We took our seats opposite his desk. Without conferring, I sat to Laura's left as I did each time we saw our solicitor. 'Right, down to business,' he said. 'Time is money. Yours not mine.' He was short on charm and this was as near to humour as he ever came in our presence. 'Both your wills have been drawn up as we discussed at your last appointment.'

He handed over copies for inspection. 'Read them through and then I'll ask Fiona to witness them unless you have any objections,' he said, nodding his rounded balding head. 'Then we shall proceed with the last remaining issues regarding your mother's estate.'

Unable to resist, I smiled across at my scruffy sister as we silently shared a private joke. It was Laura's fault for referring to Bernard Kershaw's secretary as "Fiona McFatarse". And all because the woman wore her Scottishness with pride in the form of tartan skirts, with her centre of gravity set low and wide. Fiona didn't really deserve the unflattering epithet, and I reminded myself of this as I pulled my face straight again.

Today I was to pay Laura half the value of our mother's house in exchange for sole possession of it. It was part of a fresh start after Mum's death. With an unpleasant and damaging divorce recently behind me, I'd returned to Bosworth Bishops with a plan to renovate the old family home, such as it was. The property itself, although tired and dated, was a decent-sized Edwardian semi with a massive garden suitable for development. By using the proceeds of my divorce settlement, I only required a small mortgage to manage the building costs and would eventually bag a handsome profit. It was time to draw a line under a spectacularly stressful year, and I looked forward to completing the final legal requirements and embarking on my new life.

Laura and I were the joint and equal beneficiaries of our mother's will. Except for the dispersal of a few personal items, and a bequest to my best friend Stella, who spent most of her teenage years at our house, our mother's instructions were simple enough.

Bernard Kershaw looked from me to my sister. 'On release of the agreed funds to you, Laura, we will request the Land Registry to reassign the deeds to Gabriella. Then the terms of your mother's will are met to my satisfaction.' He shuffled some papers. 'I sent a directive to the bank for release of funds as per the completion documents, but as yet no monies have arrived.' Bernard seemed unperturbed by this. I wasn't so calm.

'Oh, dear,' I said with a gulp, realising what could have caused the hold-up. 'I was afraid this might happen.'

'No need to panic, this isn't unusual. Mortgage lenders can be a little reluctant on occasion.' The unflappable solicitor tapped his pen on the desk and put a cross against an item on a list. 'I'll chase them up.'

Engrossed in reading her last will and testament, Laura visibly perked up at the mention of the money. I knew why, and if I was in her position, I too would be thrilled at the prospect. The windfall would free her from the burden of debt, leaving her, husband Curtis and their two young children in enviable circumstances. 'Don't worry, Gabby. I know you're good for it,' she said to me with a ready smile. Her local accent made her sound like a yokel in contrast to Mr Kershaw's cut glass English.

Leaning towards him, I tried to clarify the situation. 'I wanted to check my account this morning but the app on my phone didn't let me in, so I called the bank to make sure the funds were either there or with you, Mr Kershaw.'

'You can't control everything in life, Gabby,' Laura said, throwing me a wry smirk. 'Mr Kershaw knows what he's doing.'

Fidgeting with my hands, I continued, 'This is serious, Laura. Please let me finish.' Even to my own ears I sounded more of a stroppy headmistress than usual. My sister always had that effect on me. 'There's been an error at the bank. There's some confusion about Mum's death and I can't access my account because they've been notified that I'm the one who's died.' I wasn't expressing myself very well and shook my head to clear my sluggish, sleep-deprived mind. 'I'll make an appointment with them to get the mess sorted out.'

When I looked up, Mr Kershaw wore the same impassive expression he had moments ago, but Laura was staring at me with open amusement. 'That's hilarious!' she said, confining a guffaw to a snort of laughter. 'You don't look dead to me. Shall I come with you to the bank in case they need proof you are who you say you are?'

Seeing the funny side, I managed a smile in return. 'I may well take you up on that. The way my life is going, I need all the help I can get.'

'There's irony for you,' Laura said. 'It's normally the rest of the world asking for *your* advice.' Slumped in her seat, she shimmied both eyebrows and flicked wayward dreadlocks back over her shoulders. 'At least it explains the weird text I had from Phil at the weekend.'

It shocked me to learn that my ex-husband, who refused to speak to me these days, had been in touch with my flibbertigibbet of a sister. 'What? Why did he contact *you?*'

There was a playful twinkle in Laura's eyes. 'The text said he was sorry to hear the sad news and hoped I was doing all right in the circumstances.' She shrugged and gurgled, 'I thought he'd sent a message to the wrong number, but I guess he must have heard about your untimely demise.'

Bernard Kershaw interrupted. 'Ahem... ladies, I suggest

11

we make another appointment to finalise the matter of the house when we are able. In the meantime, are your wills in order?'

I didn't hesitate. 'Fine. A straightforward change of executor in my case. Now that I'm back living in Bosworth, it's much easier if you undertake all my legal matters, Mr Kershaw. Nothing has changed since I wrote my most recent will: Laura and Stella still get the whole shebang between them. I hope you spend it wisely, Laura.' I reached out and squeezed her shoulder. 'Apart from keeping the bloody taxman happy – who'll do you for death duties, inheritance tax and anything else they can dream up – and paying Mr Kershaw and his partners their well-earned cut, you'll be rich.'

'Stella? Why are you leaving half to her when she's got enough money already?' Laura said. 'And what if she dies before you? More importantly, what if I die first?' she asked, sounding genuinely pained at the thought of having to share; a trait obvious in her from childhood.

'Stella is my best friend, and I'll leave her whatever I like, thank you very much. If you die before me, then Leo and Alice will reap the rewards. Anyway, that's not very likely.'

Laura was much younger than me. I'd left for university when my sister was four years old. It was my one and only escape route. After that I rarely trekked back to Derwent Drive, and when I did it was out of guilt. I only returned for Christmas dinner, special birthdays, or a flying visit at Easter. I'm sure Mum and Dad assumed I'd be an only child, so when Laura appeared, in the year my father turned fifty-eight, life for all of us had been turned upside down and had to be reshaped to account for her existence. The months leading up to and following her birth were the most disrupted of my life until this dreadful year.

A series of unwelcome events had conspired to drag me back to number six Derwent Drive, Bosworth Bishops; somewhere I thought I'd never return to. Perhaps I never should have.

3

BLUNDER AT THE BANK

'*S*orry to mess you about,' I sighed, looking to Laura and then across at Mr Kershaw. 'I'll trot along to the bank and see if I can get this straightened out as soon as possible. Shall we at least get the wills signed, in case I really am dead?' Even Bernard Kershaw cracked a smile at that comment.

Within a matter of minutes, we were back outside on the pavement and, after a peck on the cheek from my wild-child sister, I headed towards the High Street. Moorline Bank was so close it would have been a foolish waste of time to phone first. I strode purposefully to the enquiries desk where a helpful lady, in a navy-blue uniform several sizes too big, made an internal call to a colleague. They asked me to wait.

After what seemed like an age, but was probably no longer than fifteen minutes, two members of staff approached with serious faces, leading me to expect a rapid resolution. They ushered me politely but firmly into a glass-walled office in one corner of the bank. I took a seat as indicated by a lofty gentleman who stooped over a buff folder, as if embarrassed by his own height. He had more teeth than his mouth could reasonably cope with, which did him no favours when he spoke.

The badge on his jacket bore the name William Jordan and informed me he was the branch manager. The lady with him, squat and flushed, was labelled as Dina Moss, Investments Adviser. William Jordan fingered the cover of the file, moving rubbery lips over his protruding front teeth, he said, 'How can we help?'

A salvo of spittle narrowly missed my face when I drew myself taller in the chair. 'Well, as I explained earlier to the call centre, I can't seem to access my account. There seems to have been an administrative error.'

The curious-looking branch manager glanced sideways at his companion. She sat with a narrow smile fixed in place, not committing herself to an exchange of looks with her senior. 'Do you have any forms of ID with you, Mrs Dixon?' William Jordan continued.

'Yes, of course,' I replied, unsurprised by the request and willing to oblige with my driving licence, tucked into the leather cover of my mobile phone. He seemed to scrutinise this for some time. 'Do you have any household bills?'

'Not with me, no. You see, that's my old address, I rented a flat while my divorce was going through. I'm sure I have utility bills in a box somewhere, but I've just moved house. I moved in yesterday.'

'So, this isn't your current address?' William Jordan gave me what could only be described as a disbelieving look, making me flustered.

'No. I haven't had time to… Please allow me to explain; I have a mortgage with you… or at least I will have.'

'Not at this branch you don't.'

'No, in Crewsthorpe where I work... the branch there. But don't you hold a record of letters from my solicitor here in Bosworth Bishops? He's only a ten-minute walk away.' With a wave in the vague direction of Bagshot and Laker's I hoped to convince him of my legitimacy as a longstanding customer.

William Jordan drew a breath, shuffling in his seat. 'I don't know what to say. You see, Moorline have been informed, in the correct manner, that Gabriella Louise Dixon is deceased. The paperwork is in order and relevant steps taken as outlined in our policy.' He stared at me with uncertainty. 'I shall have to ask police to intervene.'

'The police? But I've said who I am. I'm not... dead. I'm sitting right here, breathing, talking, thinking and speaking. I'm not dead in the slightest, so whoever told you otherwise is wrong.' Heat rose from my neck to my face and I could feel myself reddening.

'According to our records, Gabriella Louise Dixon died four weeks ago and so far you've only produced a driving licence as proof of identity. Not good enough in these circumstances, I'm afraid.' He handed my licence back.

With a rapidly increasing heart rate and sense of unease, I slid to the edge of the seat. 'Well, what would be good enough? Passport? Copies of bills? A sworn statement from my sister or my solicitor to vouch for me? I'm sure they'd be more than willing to—'

'Please, Mrs...'

'Dixon. Gabriella Dixon. I don't have another name. Well, I do. My maiden name was Brady, Gabriella Louise Brady. No doubt your paperwork confirms this.' Affronted by the constant insinuations of dishonesty, I took to my feet.

The nod from William Jordan was meant for his

colleague, but I saw it; an unmistakable confirmation that I was, on paper at least, officially dead. At once my legs gave way, and I sagged back into my seat. 'What am I supposed to do?'

A pseudo-sympathetic grin came from Dina, the investment adviser, who until this point had said nothing. 'We suggest you report your problem to the police. We must do the same. Attempted fraud is extremely serious.'

From somewhere I managed a spark of sarcasm. 'I can't be accused of trying to obtain money by deception if it's my own bloody money, now can I?' Pulling a lengthy sigh from deep in my chest, I asked again what I should do.

'That's not our problem, Mrs Dixon. That will be for you to take up with your solicitor, I would imagine.' William Jordan spoke with expanding eyes; he seemed to have something more important to say. 'If you are genuine, you won't mind leaving your address and contact details. Your current ones.' Emphasising the last words, he handed a pen and paper across the desk.

'Fine,' I said, scribbling wildly. 'No problem, nothing to hide. I just want this resolved. I'll go to the police station today and save you the bother.' Dragging myself to my feet, I lurched unsteadily from the see-through office, acutely aware of the eyes watching me. I made it out into the street, not daring to speak another word to any of the bank staff. What could I say?

The man I bumped into barely acknowledged my apology for stumbling into him, which irritated the hell out of me. I flicked two fingers at the ignorant berk as he strolled on, tugging the collar of his suit jacket upwards, Elvis style. 'No... I'm fine. Thanks for asking. Twat.' Scowling at his back, I caught sight of Dina Moss staring after me from the glass frontage of Moorline Bank and I was sorely tempted to aim two digits at her, the unhelpful wasp.

Intending to call Laura, I pulled my mobile from my handbag only to find I had no signal. Looking again, there was no phone service, no 4G either, nothing but seventy-four percent battery power. A dead me and now a dead phone. This was too much. Tipping my head skyward, I let rip to the clouds. 'What the fuck is going on?'

Across the street was a Currys PC World advertising a Carphone Warehouse within. Without thinking about alternatives, I made my way there to seek technical help.

The sallow-faced lad at the desk didn't look old enough to have a job, but he had a certain gawky charm. 'Can I help you? Having a problem with your mobile?' he asked with the Bosworth burr evident in his accent.

'Good guess,' I replied. 'What gave me away?'

'Your expression and the way you're holding your handset.'

Relaxing my extended arm, I congratulated him on his powers of observation. 'You couldn't be more right. The bloody thing seems to have gone on strike, and I'm having a stressful enough time as it is. Can you fix this?'

The lad prodded a few buttons, then took down the identification details of the phone. He cross-referenced it on his computer and called EE. And although I could only hear one side of the conversation; I prepared for grim news.

Looking me in the eye, the assistant said, 'The bank suspended your direct debits, so the contract's cancelled. Looks like you must take this up with them.' He gave an apologetic wiggle of his lips. 'On the upside, there's nothing wrong with your phone.'

The humiliation didn't stop there; my credit card was rejected, reducing me to some pitiful negotiations for a pay-as-you-go SIM and handing over precious cash. By this stage, tearful exhaustion was taking hold. When everything was arranged regarding a usable phone, as far as it could be, it was as much as I could do to thank the assistant before making my way back to the street again. 'I give up,' I whispered, and aimed my feet in the direction of the car park in the hope my tired body would follow.

Why was this happening? Which fool had pressed the wrong keys on a computer and convinced the authorities, and my bank, that I was dead?

4

LIMBO

*W*ith further advice from Bernard Kershaw needed, I popped back to his office. This couldn't wait. After I'd spoken to him, I would report the issue to the police and then return home to hide among the storage boxes. With luck, Mr Kershaw would be the man to unravel the mystery, even if it would cost a pretty penny in legal fees.

'Are you all right, Mrs Dixon? You look wiped out,' Fiona McFarland observed, rising from her desk when I arrived back at Bagshot and Laker's. 'Come and sit down for a minute, I'll get you a drink.'

I sank inwardly as the large ornate mirror on the wall told its tale. If it were at all possible, my hair was in greater disarray than before. Pale and haggard because sleep had eluded me for a fortnight, there was a furrow etched between my eyebrows. Worse than that, I was visibly shaking.

'Hot sweet tea?' Fiona asked.

'That would be lovely. My blood sugar levels must have dipped. Is Mr Kershaw in? I've got a real problem.'

Dashing towards a plain door marked "Staff Only", Fiona halted. 'He's with a client. Have your tea and I'll see if he can fit you in again for a few minutes. I won't be long. I may even find a wee slice of my homemade shortbread.'

I gave her a grateful thumbs up. 'That would be lovely.'

*A*s he strode back and forth in front of the Georgian sash window, Bernard Kershaw shook his head. The movement allowed daylight to catch his impressively large ears. They glowed a sunset red. 'I'm rather stumped, Gabriella. I must say, this is the first time I've ever come across such a thing. I can certainly contact your bank and check their position. I would also advise you to report this matter to the police.' The puzzled expression on his ruddy face deepened as he continued. 'If this turns out to be true, and you have been registered as deceased, then the will you signed today isn't valid in the eyes of the law. At least, I assume that's correct. I'm not sure there's ever been a legal precedent.'

Plodding towards the window once more, he stared out onto the street below. 'In these circumstances, your previous will still stands. It was sound advice from your divorce lawyer James Diamond for you to change your will as soon as divorce proceedings began.' This stunned me. Until he'd mentioned the wills and my divorce, I hadn't considered this problem with the bank to be anything other than human error, something easily rectified.

'You mean, this is identity fraud?' I exclaimed.

'It's possible, although somewhat extreme, I have to say,' Bernard boomed. 'Because without a body, no one would find it easy to register you as deceased. Not unless they could lay their hands on a medical cause of death certificate.'

This left me with one possibility.

Because I'd made use of a law firm much closer to my place of work during my divorce, Bernard Kershaw hadn't handled it and wasn't familiar with all the details. It fell to me to break the news. 'My ex-husband is a GP,' I said. 'Dr Philip Dixon. Bodies and death certificates are not hard to come by in Phil's line of work.'

Bernard Kershaw turned and cocked an eyebrow. 'Well, that's certainly...'

'Oh, come off it. There is no way... it's got to be a data-inputting mistake somewhere, but where do I go from here?' I asked, throwing my hands open wide. Phil faking my death in revenge for our marriage slamming into a wall? It was preposterous. 'What will the police do?' I asked, determined to find a way forward.

'Not a lot, I would say. So far, no crime has been committed, but if this is a deliberate act, there has to be a motive behind it. Money tends to be the biggest one. I'll get in touch with the bank, make enquiries and check with the local authority to see if the problem stems from there.' He looked at me, frowning once more. 'While I explore the legal route to have you resurrected, as it were, you must think carefully about how this may have happened. Who had your bank details, for example? If it is a wilful attempt to defraud...'

His voice trailed off, leaving me with a heavy weight settling in the pit of my stomach.

5

NOT ABSOLUTE

*U*se of a phone turned out to be a mixed blessing when I rang Bernard Kershaw for an update the next day. 'This is a humdinger,' he said gravely. 'I can confirm your bank received a copy death certificate, which would lead me to believe your death has been formally registered. Positive news in one respect.'

'Is it?'

'Yes, at least we know it's not an administrative cock-up by the bank.' I heard him breathing as he pondered for a moment, delaying the next piece of news. 'On the back of that, I can also confirm the monies you were expecting from your divorce settlement were not in your account. They remain with your husband's solicitor. I do hope you're sitting down.'

With my heart taking an extra beat, I perched on the upholstered arm of the settee. 'I am now.'

Mr Kershaw inhaled loudly before daring to tell me why this might be. 'Your divorce lawyer should have been through this with you. James Diamond's usually very thorough, so I'd be surprised if he wasn't crystal clear,' he said. 'To be explicit, just because you and your husband eventually came to a financial agreement, and he released funds to his solicitor and a *decree nisi* was granted, *doesn't* mean you are legally divorced at this point. You should have told me the *decree absolute* was still pending.'

Something in his tone warned me this was hugely significant, and somewhere along the line I hadn't paid proper attention. 'It dragged on for months,' I said. 'I assumed when the court order was made, the rest was a mere formality. I was expecting... I was told the final lump sum would be in my bank at the end of last week. It wasn't there on Friday and I've been so busy with the move I didn't have time to check until yesterday. I assumed it would be there.'

'Never assume, Gabriella. You know what Albert Einstein said: "Assumptions are made, and most assumptions are wrong."'

'Does this mean I don't get the money?' The implications didn't bear thinking about and I tensed for the answer, my sweaty hand slipping as I pressed the phone ever closer to my ear.

'James Diamond was informed of your death on Friday. For that reason, he retained the monies payable under the terms of the divorce and returned them to your husband's lawyer together with his sincere condolences. In the eyes of the law, you are not divorced, so...'

With my world crashing around me, I could barely move my tongue to speak. Only the day before I'd found out about my frozen bank account, and now I'd discovered I was not divorced and not entitled to any financial settlement because, allegedly, I'm a pile of ashes.

'Gabriella? Are you still there?'

I replied weakly, asking him to explain how any of this could have happened.

'I've been on to the local authority and your apparent cremation took place last Thursday. A local funeral service is seeking recompense for the balance of disbursements over and above the deposit paid for your final send off. Your husband declined to cover the outstanding bill and the undertakers have made use of a private debt collection company to recover costs and seek out other relatives before resorting to your executor. Probably why they turned up on your doorstep this week. In my opinion, we urgently need to trace the person or persons responsible for registering your death. How did you get on with the police?'

There was a sickly fluttering in my belly as I began my story. 'Bloody marvellous,' I said, letting out a sigh. 'The desk sergeant practically laughed me out of the station. No crime committed. No report necessary. He said people sometimes faked their own death, but he'd never come across anyone registered as dead who looked so well and was making such a fuss about it. He made me feel like a complete idiot.'

'Sounds like he didn't take you too seriously?'

'Correct. I overheard him describe me as a local nutter to his colleague.'

After a poignant pause, Bernard outlined his proposed plan of action. 'I'll need formal proof of your identity, which shouldn't be too difficult. Once I have those vital documents, I will request a court hearing to overturn your status as deceased. How long that might take is anyone's guess. The courts are in an almighty muddle these days.'

'Can't you take the information to a judge straight away?' My voice sounded almost childlike, and it annoyed me that I couldn't control my mounting anxiety. It was hard to get my head around being a victim of a calculated plan.

'If only life were that simple, Gabriella,' Bernard replied.

'Well, from where I'm sitting, death seems more complicated than I'd previously given it credit for. And while I remain a non-person, I've no access to my own money,' I protested. 'How am I supposed to manage?'

'That's a very good question.' With his tone moderated and manner sombre, Bernard Kershaw tied up the situation in a few concise sentences. 'Prepare yourself for a rough ride, Gabriella. In my view, you are in need of specialist assistance.'

'Why do I need a specialist?' I asked. 'What sort of specialist?'

Bernard's mellifluous voice never wavered. 'On occasion, I employ a private investigator for problematic situations such as this. The chap I use is well versed in the business of death. Want me to instruct him?'

Uncertainty prevented me from making a hasty decision. 'And have my personal life rummaged through by a complete stranger,' I said. 'I don't think so.'

'Gabriella, please listen. Consider my advice very carefully. Involvement of the Coroner isn't out of the question.'

'Can the Coroner overturn my registration?'

'If she's given enough evidence to demonstrate a miscarriage of justice, then after an investigation and an enquiry I would say... yes. But we must be certain this is not a human error or an administrative oversight. We need evidence. I'll give you details for my private investigator. You can look him up and let me know later. Got a pen handy?'

Not wanting to appear rude by dismissing the idea out of hand, I trudged to the console table in the hall. Despite having no intention of taking up his proposal of using a private detective, I took down the details. I didn't need a private detective to tell me who was behind this, I could work it out for myself.

Firstly, I had to shake the idea that Phil was involved somehow. He wasn't usually the vindictive type, but the divorce process had turned us against each other more than the collapse of our marriage had done. With undue haste, I determined to confront my not-quite-ex-husband. One way or the other, I had to know.

There was an anti-climax when I was forced to leave Phil an answerphone message, although with hindsight it was probably wise. I recounted the facts before accusing him of maliciously ruining my life. An hour later he called me with his infuriated response.

'You're not dead then? What fucking game are you playing this time? I asked you to stay away from me for good reason, Gabriella. I can barely comprehend what I've heard you accuse me of. Expect me to accept this wanky-pants nonsense, do you?' There were many inventive expletives coming from the phone. 'What do you expect me to say? We were married for twelve years and you think I would do something this outrageous. Break the law? For you?' He was fuming at such a rate I had few opportunities to interject. 'What do you take me for?' he yelled. 'You're the one who excels at deceit, not me. You're the one who lied about wanting children.'

It was plain I hadn't considered carefully enough before making such serious allegations. Uncertainty caused me to stutter. 'I… I couldn't think who else it would be…'

'Really?' The indignation in his familiar voice was hard to miss. 'Try a bit fucking harder then.'

'I'm sorry, Phil. I really am.' This was going very badly. The man I had already hurt so much had taken another battering at my expense. 'I've apologised. There's no need to keep swearing at me.'

'Oh, I have no qualms about telling you exactly what my views are. I'm being hounded for funeral costs and you're not even dead! How the hell do you think that makes me feel? I'm not the only victim of your lies. Even Laura had a visit from debt collectors chasing for a payment. Didn't she tell you?'

'No, she didn't. I don't know what you mean,' I said. 'Two men called here yesterday. That's when *I* found out.'

'And you expect me to believe you? You're just sick enough to have done this to yourself and, given your history, I wouldn't put it past you.' He sniffed, loudly. 'I haven't killed you off, Gabriella. Although, God help me, I could happily throttle you at this very moment.'

'But I haven't done anythi—'

'Let me make myself clear. I'll say again, stay away from me. I want nothing more to do with you. Goodbye.'

His words continued to echo around my head as I absentmindedly unpacked boxes in the kitchen, but the more I considered them, the more they rankled. I may well have been wrong to accuse him of such treachery, but had he really suggested I'd done this to myself? I thought he still held some affection for me.

When I was married, Phil and I always shared so much, and he gave me the confidence I needed in life and in my career until I blew it by deceiving him. Not with another man, not even with another woman. The destruction of my marriage came from denying him the one thing he wanted; children. That and never being entirely honest about why I didn't want them.

Without his companionship, his love and close friend-ship, I felt very much adrift in a sea of acquaintances. We had so many good times together, and we were such pals it was tough to come to terms with his ultimate rejection. I understood it. I just couldn't accept it.

I looked around, seeing for the first time how incongruous my belongings were in a house where I didn't feel at home. Tears formed on my lower eyelids because the smell of the house brought back awkward emotions which I struggled to swallow down. The idea of returning had seemed so attractive a few months ago, but in reality had only dredged up a past gladly left behind.

6

THE MURDER HOUSE

*C*aught up in a frantic day of unpacking and dealing with my solicitor, I'd forgotten to call Stella. Usually she and I spoke several times a week, especially since being separated by geography and no longer able to indulge in girly chats over a long lunch with too much food and laughter. What a horrendous wrench it had been to say farewell at the airport as Stella left for a life in Spain.

My only remaining anchor in life, Stella had abandoned me to live in sunshine and flowers with husband number three, the very rich Carlos Cortez, or Chaz as I preferred to call him because it irritated the heck out of Stella. I didn't begrudge her a happy ending because it gave me hope of a brighter future once I'd cleared up the little matter of being dead and having no access to money.

'Scooby-Doo, I'm sorry to call you at the wrong time. I've so much to tell you...'

It was one of the strangest phone calls. 'Run that by me again,' she said.

'I know the date that I died and when I was cremated,' I said, realising how ludicrous it sounded.

'You sound pretty good for someone burnt to a crisp.'

'My body is the same shameful state as usual, but my head is reeling with it all. And as for my finances...'

Stella phoned back immediately, saving me the cost of the call to Palamos. 'So, let me get this straight,' she said. 'Your divorce settlement is back with Phil. The mortgage you needed to fund the renovations has not materialised because you're dead, but you still have a roof over your head. Half a roof. How is Laura taking the news?'

'I haven't told her yet. To be honest, without access to my bank accounts, I've been more worried about basic day to day living.'

When she heard about my lack of immediate funds, my amazing friend offered to send emergency cash via her brother. 'I'll ping it to Graham's account, he's not too far from you, he can always drive over. Three hundred be enough for now? Get the essentials in... alcohol, for example.' If it wasn't for Stella's lifesaving offer at the end of a phone, I would have been at a complete loss.

For a good few minutes, Stella and I debated whether Phil was the one behind an underhand revenge attack on my life, despite his protestations. In the end, like me, she decided it was unlikely.

'It sounds like you're back to square one. It must be a computer glitch or something,' she said. 'I'm sure your new solicitor will resolve it in no time.'

'He's suggested I make use of a private investigator.'

'Goodness. Well, if you think you can afford it.' This was something I hadn't considered. I hadn't even asked Bernard Kershaw how much one would cost. Did they charge a daily rate? I made a mental note to check out the facts.

While we chatted, I looked out of the front window, and my eyes were drawn to number seven. 'Perhaps it's him at the murder house,' I said, with conviction. 'Kenny. Laura hates the man; you should hear what she says about him. He's got to be a psycho. He even looks like one.' I peeked through the net curtains. Personally, I detest the damned things, but they have their uses when spying on neighbours.

'The murder house?' Stella asked.

'Across the road, the spooky bungalow, you know the one. Don't you remember it?'

'Vaguely… The last time I was there was your mum's funeral, so I wasn't really paying much attention to the neighbours.'

Number seven Derwent Drive was an eyesore, architecturally speaking an insult to the other properties lining the otherwise respectable road. It lay on the opposite side to number six, squeezed onto an infill site, and for as long as I could remember, it had looked like the scene of a crime; hence being called the murder house by Laura. On the wrap-around drive there were a total of seventeen motorbikes, all protected by black and silver covers. In front of the garage was a black Mercedes estate with a personalised plate. It had been there so long the tyres had perished and the paintwork was bleached by the sun. Moss had taken root in the rubber window seals.

Most disconcerting of all was the view inside the undressed bay windows of the bungalow. Metal racking lined three walls of the front room and on the shelves were bundles wrapped in black plastic, taped but not labelled. Body parts, most likely, I told Stella.

She didn't know Kenny and didn't recall much about the bungalow because, four years after my departure for university, Stella had left Bosworth Bishops too. Neither of us had reason to stay.

'He visited yesterday.'

'Kenny the Murderer? Where's he been all this time, prison?'

'I've no idea. A car turned up, a crimson saloon, and Kenny got out, a lot older and fatter than I remember him. He went to each of the bikes, lifted the cover a foot or so, then moved on to the next one. Got himself into a terrible stew, biting his nails, and chuntering to himself. I felt quite sorry for him.'

'That doesn't sound like a psycho murderer to me,' Stella said.

'Perhaps not, but he is *very* strange. You should have seen him. He was in his pyjamas, satin ones at that.'

But Kenny at number seven seemed an unlikely candidate for the person who was trying to ruin my life, especially as I'd never really spoken to the man. 'I can't remember his full name. He never speaks to anyone on the street and we all pretend we haven't seen him, apart from Laura. She just flicks him the V-sign.'

After a brief discussion on the delights of living opposite a crank, it was back to discussing my predicament.

'What are the police doing about it?' Stella asked once she'd got her head around the outrageous story.

As I was about to respond, three long rings on the doorbell saved me from the pain of repeating the story. The bell chimes preceded the sound of the stiff front door being unlocked and rattled open.

'Sorry, Stella. Got visitors. Call me tomorrow? And thank you.' I blew her a loud kiss down the phone.

7

GOING DOWNHILL

'*C*ooeee! It's only us. Thought you'd want some help.' It was Laura, and she wasn't alone. She was entitled to walk into the house without waiting for me to answer the door, I supposed, but it still vexed me when she did it. From now on this was to be my house; not my parents' old home, not her old home, *my* home. When she barged in without so much as a by-your-leave, it was as if she was asserting her rights as co-owner until I came up with the money to buy her out.

'Aunty Gabby? What you doing in Nana Brady's house?' A moon-faced toddler thundered towards me for a hug, caught his feet in a neatly folded pile of newspaper and fell headlong in a sprawling heap, painfully bashing his head on my shin. The resultant racket was almost enough to shake dust from the cheap chandelier above my head.

'Goodness me Leo, are you alright?' I said, picking him up and settling him onto my lap as I took a seat on a threadbare footstool. Giving his head a gentle rub, I tried not to sound irritated by the intrusion, and shouted a hello to Laura who was releasing baby Alice from her pushchair.

'Any sign of Kenny at the murder house today?' she asked from the hallway.

'No, nothing. I was just telling Stella about him when you arrived. Was I expecting you?'

'No, it's what sisters are for though. I'll sort out your recycling.' This was typical of Laura. She was more interested in saving the planet than easing the pressure of a stressful house move. 'Here's your post. Bills by the looks of it,' she said with a snap as she made her way across the room, slinging Alice onto her hip. 'All those trees cut down, and for what?'

Ignoring the inevitable reference to the rainforest, I held out my hand. 'Redirected mail. Just the usual guff, I set up direct debits for most of the—' I stopped. 'Oh, no... if my bank accounts are closed, things won't get paid.' Up went the marker on the frustration meter once more. At every turn, there was another obstacle.

'I had a visit from your friendly neighbourhood debt collectors this morning. I told them to do one because you're not dead.'

'And what did they say to that?' I took the small pile of letters handed to me by Laura, who watched as I rifled through them. Leo had settled and was giving me the hug he'd intended on arrival.

'They said they needed something in writing. They had a form for me to sign to say I wasn't in a financial position to contribute, but when I told them you weren't even dead, they gave up with the form. I'm expecting someone from the funny farm to turn up next.'

More interested in what my letters contained, I wasn't listening to what she was saying. 'Off you get, Leo. Let's go to the kitchen and put the kettle on for a cuppa, shall we?' It wasn't tea I needed; it was privacy in which to read the contents of an envelope franked with a familiar logo. The university where I was due to commence as a lecturer had sent plenty of information already, but this was the letter to finalise the timetable.

Laura must have seen it. 'How many weeks in your current job before you leave?' she asked from the relative comfort of the old sofa where I'd placed a fluffy throw and new cushions to cover up the faded upholstery.

'Seven weeks, then I have a two-week break before I start my career as a university lecturer in early September. I'm looking forward to the change.' I made my way into the kitchen, ripping at the envelope. 'This letter is the thumbs-up.' I let out a quiet sigh. Everything was in order. With a new job and a new bank account, I would be up and running again in no time.

Placing the open letter on the kitchen table, I filled the kettle while Leo watched. 'Shall I open another letter?'

'Yes, Aunty Gabby, but Leo have biscuits?' His finger aimed unwaveringly at a biscuit barrel on a shelf near the kettle. 'Nana!' he shouted, stretching out the words, calling for his grandmother. 'Nana... biscuits!' The tin had remained empty for months, but he wasn't to know. 'I go find her.'

'No, Leo, Nana Brady isn't here anymore. She's... gone to the angels.' I cringed as I said this. Laura was adamant that referring to angels was the best way for Leo to accept his grandmother's death, but as he had no concept of angels, let alone heaven and hell, it was not having the desired impact. When I showed him the inside of the empty biscuit tin his confused face contorted.

'The angels? They did eat the biscuits?'

'Something like that,' I replied. Putting the tin back where it came from, I spied another, much smaller one, wedged in the back corner of the same cupboard. It was my mother's rainy-day stash of cash, and I was compelled to look inside. 'Now let's see what's in here,' I said, making a game of "find the tin and open it, only to be disappointed". Leo wasn't interested in the contents of another potentially empty receptacle, and he tottered back towards the lounge to tell his mother how cross he was with the greedy fat angels who'd eaten his grandmother's biscuits.

There was a depressing lack of rattle as I shook the battered enamelled container, but on popping the lid a ready smile lit up my face. 'Thou shalt not go to debtors' jail quite yet,' I whispered. Pulling out a roll of notes, with no delay or guilt, I tore the elastic band from it and began counting the precious find. Five ten-pound notes, two fivers and a two-pound coin. Strictly speaking, I should have shared it with Laura, but brushed aside the thought as I hid the money inside the tin again, vowing to seek out other places where I might find a pound or two.

Until I had the house to myself again, this would have to wait. Instead, I refocussed on the letters, waiting for Mum's old kettle to boil. A plain white envelope contained a hand-written note, which I guessed had come from a zealous congregation member at St Ninian's; the local church where my parents had worshipped. Whoever it was, had a strange idea of suitable words to welcome a new parishioner and encourage them to join in the praying. In neat writing was a reference to a passage in the Bible. As soon as I read the brainwashing nonsense, I screwed it up and threw it onto the table. 'Bloody God-squad – I'll give you a sodding eye for an eye...'

Turning my thoughts to the next letter, I noted the business address. It was from the human resources department at work. Assuming it was about my forthcoming departure and the usual complex calculations regarding pay, pension and annual leave, I scanned the first line, initially not comprehending the meaning.

'Oh, for pity's sake,' I moaned when the words sank in.

'What's up?' Laura's question could barely be heard above the insistent whining from Leo.

'My HCPC registration's been voided.'

'Your what?'

'My Health and Care Professions Council registration. I can't see any patients without it. I have to phone them straight away. Give me a minute.' The phone call wasn't productive, forcing me to search my temporary office space for the documents needed for proof of my registration status.

'Do you have to go now? This very minute?' Laura asked, opening her arms wide to show how much unpacking there was still to do. As if I didn't know. 'I could stay and tidy up,' she offered.

'I don't mean to offend, and it's a kind, thoughtful offer, but...'

'Understand. Not to worry. We like a trip on the bus, don't we, kids?'

Not convinced by this show of tolerance, I found myself making excuses for not wanting to leave my sister and two small children to their own devices. I should have been honest with Laura because frankly, I wanted her to bugger off and leave me alone. 'I have my own way of doing things. You know how fussy I am.'

There was no arguing with that statement. Laura and I were like chalk and cheese when it came to organising a home. She knew that as well as anybody. 'Besides HR won't accept faxes, my email isn't working, so I've got no choice. If I drive over there today, perhaps they can sort this out before I go back to the office on Monday.' Exasperation was evident in the way I scooped up my car keys and slung my handbag onto one shoulder. 'My diary is completely choc-a for the next month at least... God, I don't have time for any of this.'

Fortunately, Laura didn't pick up on the double meaning. The endless fall-out from the death certificate arriving at the bank was bad enough, but I could have done without uninvited disruptive visitors. As much as I usually enjoyed seeing the children, today had seen me fail as a fun-loving aunt. Even so, I had to smile at Leo's attempts to delay their departure. Wittering on about how bored he was, little Leo was ignoring his mother's attempts to lure him out of the door. 'But Mummy, the angels did steal my toys. Where they gone?' Belligerent, he stood hands on hips staring into a space where previously a toy box had lived. Baby Alice, so quiet on arrival, joined in with some mewling of her own and Laura was valiantly trying to pacify her and settle her back into her pushchair.

I was no help at all. 'Sorry to shove you out, but I've got to go,' I said, flapping paperwork above my head and shooing them through the doorway. 'I'll catch up with you all soon... promise.' I waved them off. 'Have a lovely time on the bus, Leo, be a good boy for Mummy.' The sigh escaped my lips at about the same time as the uncharitable thought about Leo being a stroppy little bugger at times. 'Rather you than me, Laura,' I mumbled as I yanked at the door handle of my shiny Nissan Nismo and swung my handbag onto the passenger seat. The car was a divorce present to myself, in anticipation of a handsome settlement from Phil.

Before starting the engine, I glanced over the registration documents, so vital for my job. Renewal wasn't due for over a year, so it could only be the direct debit causing a hiccup. Moving house twice in rapid succession was bound to result in one or two problems, but this week had been dire.

A ninety-five-mile round trip, wasting precious time and using up expensive fuel, was on the cards. I briefly regretted not being more sensible about the car I'd purchased. Despite being recommended by my friend Stella, who loved to shop, the Nissan had a serious lack of luggage space, but I loved its power. For a change, I'd decided for myself what car to buy; no nagging parents and no Phil dictating practicalities above fun. I rubbed my hands around the steering wheel and breathed in new leather. The Sat-Nav was top of the range and had taken some knob-twiddling before I found the setting to turn off the voice commands. I can't abide being told what to do by a robot voice.

About to leave the drive, I noticed a BMW parked on the kerb, three or four doors down. I'd seen it several times since moving in and assumed it belonged to someone on the street, but it struck me as odd that every time I saw the car the driver was in it, sitting there. If he lived on the street, then why not get out?

I watched in fascination as he took aim, with what looked like a camera, through the open driver's side window. It was pointing towards number seven, the murder house. Perhaps Kenny was a serial killer after all – The Silk Pyjama Killer of Derwent Drive. This random thought made me smile for a second or two before I started up the car, satisfied I had solved a minor mystery.

Barely out of Bosworth Bishops and with the road ahead clear of traffic, I accelerated smoothly and relaxed enough to sing along to the car radio, buoyed up by Stella's offer of a cash loan to get me out of immediate difficulty. Giving Elton John a run for his money, I was enjoying the freedom of the countryside when blue flashing lights came into sight in my rear-view mirror. Glancing at the dash, I was thankful to see I was not speeding, but when the police car didn't make to overtake, the nerves kicked in. I was being pulled over. I drew up to the kerb and waited, window down, engine turned off.

The traffic officer who strode up to my car seemed pleasant enough, and he was accompanied by a tantalising waft of aftershave. 'Good afternoon, madam. Is this your car?'

'Yes.'

The officer stepped back to look over the bodywork and down at the tyres.

'Can you tell me why I've been stopped?' I thought immediately of Moggy. Years ago, police had ticked me off for driving my faithful old banger with the clattering exhaust barely attached. I was told to take immediate steps to make her roadworthy. I can still recall the sense of disgrace. Since then I'd been a model citizen; or at least I hadn't been caught for the occasional breach of the highway code and the Road Traffic Act. My expensive and sporty Nissan was almost brand new and most definitely roadworthy, so it threw me.

'ANPR picked you up a mile or so back there.' My bewildered expression must have registered with the officer who kindly filled in the blanks. 'Automatic Number Plate Recognition.'

'Right, yes. Is there a problem?' I was still confused.

'I'm afraid so, madam. According to our records, this car

is untaxed and uninsured. Do you have your driving licence with you by any chance?'

'Yes, I do, but... I know the tax and insurance are in order.' I was unsettled by his manner. 'I've very recently moved house and I haven't had a chance to change the address on my licence and registration documents yet but...' When I handed the officer my photocard licence it flapped in my hand, despite me having nothing to feel guilty about. When he asked me to get out of the driver's seat and follow him to his vehicle, my mouth dropped wide open in pure astonishment. This happens to nasty little toe-rags who hammer the streets of Manchester in stolen vehicles, or drunk drivers who weave across traffic lanes and put people's lives at risk, not to respectable law-abiding professionals. 'What for?' I asked, staring up at him.

'Just come with me, please. It'll be so much easier for my partner to run checks from our vehicle. Can you confirm your name again, Miss—?'

'Mrs. Mrs Gabriella Dixon.' There was no reason to feel ashamed, I was innocent of any wrongdoing. But, however hard I tried to convince myself all would be well, shivering tension crept up each limb, rendering them weak as I unfolded from the car. There was no let-up of nerves as I shuffled into the rear seat of the police vehicle.

'I'm Sergeant Roy Mace and this is Officer Dan Tawanda. We have reason to suspect that the vehicle you're driving is not insured or taxed in accordance with legal requirements. Bear with us.' He called up on the radio to request a PNC check for my driving licence, and none of us had to wait long for a response. With my heart thumping, it was as if I could foresee what was about to happen next.

'Don't tell me, my licence is invalid too,' I said with a

croak. Screwing up my face as the news came floating over the airwaves, I must have looked a blameworthy sight.

Officer Dan Tawanda and the fragrant Sergeant Roy Mace angled themselves to see me better and deliver their verdict. 'So, madam,' the sergeant began, 'How do you explain this?'

'I can't.'

'No, I don't suppose you can.' He wriggled to the right more and eyed me with blatant suspicion. 'The car was registered to a Mrs Gabriella Dixon at the address on the driving licence, but... note my use of the past tense if you would... here's the thing. The licence is invalid because Mrs Gabriella Dixon is sadly no longer. She's dead, departed, gone. If I'm right, Dan, this would strongly suggest the lady keeping us company in the back of our vehicle is not who she's pretending to be.'

8

WHO THE HECK IS PEDDYR QUIRK?

$\mathcal{F}$eeling rather foolish, I stared at the gleaming brass door handle of P.Q. Investigations and prepared for what was beyond. I couldn't quite believe my life had come to this.

The police eventually accepted that, in all probability, I was telling the truth. Although it took assertions from Laura, Bernard Kershaw, and a phone call to Ingrid, my senior manager at work, before they listened. This didn't prevent my car from being seized but did cause a problem when it came to prosecution for driving without a valid licence, insurance or road tax. As I was dead, they had nobody to prosecute. Bernard Kershaw said I would have that to look forward to when this business was resolved, and I'd have to pay my car loan back even though I no longer had a car to drive. More debt, more misery and more lucrative work for Mr Kershaw.

. . .

*A*fter careful perusal of the BBC Valley Radio website, the police officers at the station finally conceded I bore a striking resemblance to Dr Gabriella Dixon, the resident expert on child behaviour issues.

'They call me up for phone-ins. Like I keep telling you, I'm a therapist, I have a PhD.' Unable to charge me with anything, because I'm dead, they advised me to ensure my death was unregistered to avoid further problems with the law. 'Such as?' I ventured. Looks were exchanged and the female officer leading the questioning heaved her shoulders upwards.

'Council tax avoidance, non-payment of utilities, squatting...'

'Squatting?' I repeated in alarm. 'In my own home? My mother left me and Laura that house in her will. I own half of it, for God's sake.' Feeling Bernard's fingers around my upper arm, I pulled back. The policewoman looked sheepish, and I realised she'd been joshing and that things were bad if my sense of humour had abandoned ship.

'Sorry, but you did ask,' she said.

'It's me that should apologise. I shouldn't have snapped at you, but nobody I've spoken to can suggest how bringing me back from the dead might be achieved in a hurry. Meanwhile, I'm getting closer to insolvency.'

On our way out of the police station some time later, Bernard Kershaw persuaded me it was time to accept help from his private investigator. 'I'll make an appointment for tomorrow,' I promised.

· · ·

P.Q. Investigations wasn't one of those large national companies with a website making promises to find missing loved ones or catch the cheating husband. Instead, it lurked unobtrusively up a flight of stairs behind the varnished wooden door of number 220a Dyer Street in Bosworth Bishops, which to an outsider represented the most genteel part of town. In the vicinity were no fewer than three funeral directors, a monumental mason, a wedding dress shop, a dentist, a café and two florists. Almost all eventualities catered for except medical emergencies.

I located the entrance to P.Q. Investigations sandwiched between Clouds – who promised a more enlightened way of dealing with death – and Lily Fields, the well-named flower shop. I'd arranged an appointment for a free thirty-minute consultation and was told I would meet a man called Peddyr Quirk, hence the P and the Q, and I'd asked for a spelling of the unusual first name. 'But if I go over the thirty minutes, how will I pay him?' I'd asked Bernard, my well-meaning solicitor. Given the uncertainty of my finances, his response was not hugely comforting.

'Don't worry. I'll add any expenses to your bill.'

The tiny oriental woman who greeted me was effusive and rather peculiar. She was a whirlwind of activity and of cheerful chitchat, and the severe fringe of her shining black bobbed hair shimmered as she spoke with only a hint of Chinese inflection. 'Everyone calls me Connie. Connie Quirk is so much better than Fen Fang Wong, don't you agree? I tell everyone my husband bought me for my brains and beauty. He doesn't have either. Take a seat, you're early.'

For a second I thought I'd misheard her. 'He bought you?'

'It's a joke. I married him by mistake...' Connie's slender frame vibrated as she laughed at her own witty reply. 'Like my new cactus?' she asked. 'Tina in the florist's up the road promised me I wouldn't be able to kill this one. She even gave me an instruction book.' Connie Quirk proudly turned the spiky plant in its pot, left and right, showing it off to its best advantage. 'Mr Quirk gives it less than six months.' It was hard not to smile, despite my misgivings about making use of a private investigator.

Looking around, I settled into what I did naturally; observation. What I saw made me question the validity of Bernard Kershaw's recommendation because, from where I sat, P.Q. Investigations resembled the office of a theatrical agent and not that of a private investigator.

Sure enough, there were certificates on the plain walls showing Mr Peddyr Quirk's accredited membership of The Association of British Investigators, and SIA licence. Another provided proof of public liability insurance. But these important documents vied for space between huge photographs and posters in frames, mostly of actors. Autographs added a personalised touch and when I peered at the ones closest to me, they all mentioned Peddyr with a "thank you". I wondered what he'd done to become so popular and why he had such an unusual name.

Scanning around the white-walled room, I pieced together Peddyr Quirk's former life. Motorbikes seemed to feature heavily and, although I didn't have a clue who some people were, Peddyr Quirk revealed himself as the common denominator in the photographs. I could pick out a couple of familiar TV series. *Midsomer Murders* was straightforward to spot, and so was *Morse*. There was a shot of an Oxford university building in front of which Peddyr posed with Kevin Whately in a chummy embrace.

Evidently Mr Quirk had a fascinating past. As for his present: his office reception area was spotlessly clean, comfortable and cared for, which somehow instilled a sense of confidence in me. I presumed he would be fastidious and fascinating, and eased myself into a more comfortable position on the hard chair as I waited for the man himself. The next few minutes had me doubting my solicitor's ability to judge character. Peddyr Quirk was not what I was expecting.

I heard loud clumping footsteps as someone climbed the stairs, and heavy breathing reached a crescendo. 'Feckin' fags'll be the death of me,' the man said, as he lolloped towards Connie. The first thing I noticed, apart from his Irish accent, was the man's smell. He exuded a strange fug of stale cigarette smoke, alcohol and damp mouldy corners.

Connie nodded in my direction. 'Your nice lady is here.'

'So she is,' said the scruffy man in a grubby brown suit, a grimy baseball cap rammed low over his heavy brow. 'Peddyr Quirk. Nice to meet you.' Barely acknowledging me, he turned back to his wife. 'And I suppose you gave her that old tripe about me buying you from a Hong Kong back-street slave trader, but...' he continued, wagging his finger, 'did you tell her they refused to take you back once I discovered what a gob you have on you.'

With my illusions shattered, I flashed a quick look up at a photograph to remind me of the handsome and much younger Peddyr Quirk in action slacks and a black roll-neck sweater being toasted by Pierce Brosnan. Looking back at the man as he was now, disappointment sank like a stone in my chest. 'What happened to the accent?' I asked, surprised to hear the Irish brogue replaced by an unfamiliar inflection I couldn't place.

'It comes and goes,' Peddyr said. 'Depends what mood

I'm in or if I want to be the affable Irish drunk in the corner of the pub, picking up the gossip. It's surprising how long I can make one pint last, especially if I chuck half of it down my trousers so I smell like a brewery. Look like I've pissed myself into the bargain.' He stepped back and cast his eyes over the front of his suit. 'Look at the tide marks on this fella.'

Connie grinned at him. 'These days he's forced into having a ciggie outside with the puffers and the wheezers. They know everything...'

'Can't be a proper wino if you don't smoke, don't cha know.' With a special Dublin emphasis on the last phrase, he handed Connie a vaping pen. 'Thank Christ I don't have to suck on the genuine articles. Disgusting habit.'

At a guess, Peddyr was in this mid to late fifties, although Connie seemed somewhat younger. Given her lively nature and youthful features, it was hard to make an educated estimate. The so-called detective made for a door marked "Private".

'I stink to high heaven,' he said, sniffing at a lapel pulled towards his nose. 'Give me five minutes to get out of my best suit.'

Connie was quick with her retort. 'Don't take too long over your hair, the lady doesn't want to be kept waiting.' Catching the mischief passing between the couple, I wasn't sure what I'd let myself in for. Was the man a buffoon, or was he merely adept at pretending to be one?

'Coffee would go down well if you can drag yourself away from your stupid pot plants,' Peddyr Quirk chirped.

'Yes, master... Would you like me to drink it for you as well?' Connie bowed in blatant mockery, but she never once stopped smiling and I found I was drawn to her. She came across as sharp-witted and cheery, with the air of someone who felt supremely confident in her own skin.

Peddyr Quirk was another matter. He was nothing like his photographs. The lithe, sleek, handsome man in the pictures had gone to seed in the intervening years. His mop of mousey brown curls was mown into a short crop, and his once chiselled features had filled out and rounded.

'Has he always been a detective?' I asked Connie as I searched the walls and shelves for hopeful signs. How the pictures fitted together escaped me, but at last I spotted one of him in police uniform being awarded a medal.

'Not always. He used to train actors and policemen to ride motorbikes, among other things.'

'So I see.' That was interesting but didn't answer my burning question about his qualifications. Around the room there were nods to Connie's previous life in Hong Kong; paintings of the cityscape, and even the ubiquitous fortune cat waving like a metronome from a bookshelf. My face must have reflected my thoughts about it being tacky.

'It's a Maneki-Neko. Japanese,' Connie said with a tut. 'Stupid thing, I hate it.'

'But why—?'

'Present from our accountant. Don't like to offend the woman. She's great.' There had been no real answer to my initial question about Peddyr's professional experience. We left it hanging there, unattended and unanswered because the phone rang, leaving me to my thoughts. A potential customer was making tentative enquiries.

Several minutes passed by before the door to the Quirks' private apartment opened again.

'Come into my inner sanctum. The place where the real investigators hide,' Peddyr said, directing me to his left.

Without optimism, I begrudgingly took to my feet, gave

a non-committal smile to Connie, and entered her husband's office through a part-glazed wooden door, taking a note of the time. Thirty minutes to waste my breath on the plonker who couldn't even bother to stay sober for the benefit of his clients.

Without realising it, I was staring at the man closing the door behind me. 'You scrub up well,' I said, speaking the thought out loud. It popped out of my mouth, and there was no taking it back. Face flushed with the embarrassment of an unguarded moment, I tried to cover up my mistake. 'Very neat. Clean... is what I meant.' This wasn't quite true. Smelly Mr Scruffy was now masquerading as Bosworth Bishops' answer to Bruce Willis, proving how wrong I was about him running to fat. The white tee-shirt and snug jeans covered a muscular body, sturdy rather than stout, with a broad chest and strong neck.

Peddyr Quirk gave a lopsided grin. 'Bernie tells me you're dead.' His mouth curled at the corners like a dolphin's, giving him a permanent smirk. It occurred to me that if he had been drinking, it certainly didn't show in his speech or the way he moved, and oddly he no longer smelt of anything other than soap. Bright eyes scrutinised me as I replied.

'Bernie? Oh, you mean Bernard Kershaw?'

Peddyr Quirk's office was like stepping onto the set of Sam Spade, or a Mike Hammer episode, I couldn't think which; amber wood, button-backed chairs, black-and-white photographs, and etched glass. A complete contrast to the reception area outside. Even the phone was retro Bakelite. 'Bernie and me go way back,' he said matter-of-factly in that strange accent of his.

'You do?'

'Years. He's a good man to have on your team. Tough as

old boots Bernie is. Take a seat and tell me how you died.'
Moving to perch on the edge of his polished desk he
reached for some papers and a pair of unflattering reading
glasses, while I made a dash for a tatty leather armchair
placed against the opposite wall. As far away as I could get.

Before setting off from Derwent Drive, I had liberated
one of my smarter work suits from the pile of clothes
looking for a decent wardrobe to hang in. Wearing a neatly
pressed outfit and a crisp cotton blouse, I'd hoped to give
myself some much-needed confidence. But now I wished I
hadn't. The chair was spongy, and I struggled to remain
composed as both knees rose far too high for me to cross
my legs in a ladylike fashion. The shortness of the skirt was
regrettable too.

'I've no idea how I died,' I said, squirming around to find
ways of maintaining dignity without flashing my knickers
at a man I'd only met minutes ago. The best I could do was
to sit sideways as I recounted the arrival at my front door of
two men from the local council offices, informing me I was
apparently dead. I followed up with the story of a frozen
bank account, a cancelled mobile phone contract, a run-in
with the police, loss of my beloved car and most recently
the forfeiting of my professional registration.

Listening intently to the answers, Peddyr asked a few
questions about who might benefit from my death, who I
might have upset, and my divorce. While he listened he
barely moved.

'Do you have your birth certificate? Passport? Driving
licence?' he asked finally.

'The police took my licence, but the others are at home.
My important documents are in a box in the dining room.'

'Good, then I suggest you take them to the registrar's
office and plead your case.'

'Simple as that?' Appalled at the unhelpful response the last ounce of energy used to keep a civil tongue in my head drained away. 'Are you fucking kidding me?'

'Yes, I'm joking. No need to get uppity,' he replied, as if I had amused him.

'Uppity? You'd be bloody uppity if some half-wit started joking about your life going down the toilet. Have you any idea what this is like?' Pushing down on the arms of the chair, I intended to storm out and march smartly back to Bagshot and Laker's to do some venting of spleen over Bernard Kershaw's expensive walnut veneer. However, defeated by the saggy upholstery and the look of amused disdain on Peddyr Quirk's face, I gave up, wilted, and let him continue.

'If it were that easy everyone would be resurrecting the dead left, right and centre, now wouldn't they?' He rolled his eyes at my idiocy. 'From what you tell me, you have money in the bank. Not as much as you would have if your car wasn't impounded or if your divorce had gone through before you died... but we'll come to that later. No one has stolen the money from your accounts, so nothing bad has happened other than inconvenience at work and for your sister who will have to wait for her pay-off.' He gave a short snort. 'I can't see what the big deal is. I mean... nobody died. Or did they...?'

Leaning across the desk, he picked up the phone. 'Connie, can you get hold of the register office? I need to pick the brains of someone experienced. See if Angela is there. Good girl.'

This confused me. 'I thought you were throwing me out.'

'Not yet. You've got a few more free minutes left on the clock, so it's only fair I check how the land lies.' On hearing

Connie's voice again, he raised his bold chin. 'Mighty, put her through.'

Looking at him, I was put in mind of a puffin. Drooping eyelids created angular eyes, and life's wrinkled creases formed at the temple. Although he exuded affable reliance, there was a deceptively sharp undercurrent to his enquiries. Peddyr Quirk seemed to have absorbed every detail of my sorry story and was recounting it, almost verbatim, to the person in the other end of the phone line. With neat eyebrows dancing, he listened to the information being fed back to him. 'Thanks, Angela. I may have to come down to look for myself if that's okay. This sounds fishy. Bless you. Speak to you soon.'

Placing the phone back on its cradle, Peddyr Quirk straightened and slid from the desk. He moved to the door and opened it. 'Connie, do I have another thirty minutes to spare?'

After closing the door, he made his way to sit in his office chair, which was when I spotted an uneven gait which hadn't been obvious until then. More blatant was the way he flexed his right hand, holding it at the wrist as if it was causing him pain. Something else struck me in that moment; his easy-going, dismissive manner had evaporated, replaced by a thoughtful, focussed intent.

'A woman by the name of Gabriella Louise Dixon was registered as deceased on the fourteenth of May. The person who registered her death took with them the relevant paperwork required for subsequent funeral arrangements.' Seeing my mouth open, he raised a hand to stop me from interrupting. 'The place of death was given as Worthington Court, Pinny Road. I know it well. A set of twelve low-rise flats inhabited by the elderly, with one or two exceptions.'

'So, they got a dead body with the wrong name?'

'We'll find out in due course.' Peddyr swivelled his captain's chair gently and rhythmically as he spoke. 'The medical certificate for cause of death would have to be signed by a doctor. Because death occurred at home, that doctor would have to know the deceased and have seen them very recently in order to sign the certificate. Not only that, but there would need to be a reasonable cause of death documented. One that didn't raise suspicions.'

'Did your source at the register office tell you what I died of?'

Peddyr nodded. 'Heart failure exacerbated by pneumonia, from the sounds of it. The records are not in dispute as far as that goes. Of interest to me is the person who did the registering. Mr Bird, who lives in the flat next door and witnessed the death, was the person who subsequently registered the death of Gabriella Louise Dixon; same date of birth as you, same name as you, but different address...'

'Then if it wasn't me, which it wasn't...' I said, tapping on my sternum '...who died?'

A thick silence fell over the room and the eyes of several fictional detectives stared at me from pictures hanging on the wall behind Peddyr Quirk's antique desk. Peter Falk as Columbo seemed to be winking at me. Ironside stared menacingly. After a long minute, the real-life detective in the room coughed. 'Start from the beginning again and this time I want you to work backwards.'

9

PEDDYR GOES TO SEE MR BIRD

Why do old people's homes always smell of cabbage and piss? Peddyr wondered as the paint-peeled door to flat number fourteen eased open. 'Mr Arthur Bird?'

'Who wants to know?' croaked the elderly man. Heeding Crime Prevention advice always to use the safety chain, only his rheumy right eye and part of a sallow cheek showed in the gap between door and frame. A sensible precaution, Peddyr thought. Although the old man was right to worry about the identity of his caller, he should also have asked how he got in through the main door security. When there's nobody about to tailgate, it's what the trades button is for.

'I'm investigating the death of your neighbour at number fifteen,' Peddyr said. Today he was wearing a decent suit, polished shoes, and an air of authority. With law-abiding old codgers like Arthur Bird, it worked every time.

'You'd better come in, officer,' the man said, making to

close the door a fraction, unlatch the chain and welcome Peddyr into his humble home.

'You should really ask to see some identification, Mr Bird. I could be anybody.'

'You're a detective, aren't you? A police detective?'

'I used to be with the police a long while ago and not round these parts. Nowadays I'm a private investigator, here's my card.'

Arthur Bird reversed on his slippered feet and opened the door. 'You seem very genuine to me. Do come in. Excuse the state of the place. My Florrie's poorly, you see, and I'm not too clever when it comes to housework. Come in, come in, make yourself at home, young man.'

'Who is it, Arthur?' A weak but echoing voice came from behind a closed door to Peddyr's right as Mr Bird herded him up a short hallway. 'Is it the nurse?'

'No, luvvie, it's a gentleman enquiring about 'er at number fifteen.'

'But she's dead. Died weeks ago.'

'Yes, luvvie. He wants to ask a few questions to help the police.'

Peddyr had said no such thing, but that's what Arthur had understood, so he let it ride. It wasn't too far from the truth. 'I won't keep you long, Mr Bird. It's just that there's a discrepancy with the registration of your neighbour's death.' Peddyr sat down on an unforgiving settee and took out a pen from a leather document case; a useful prop to add a soupcon of authenticity. He balanced a writing pad on his knees. 'The information I have here, states she died on the twelfth of May.'

'Yes, that's right,' Arthur said, sitting gingerly on what appeared to be his favoured chair; the arms were worn, the cushions soiled with use. 'That's when the doctor certified her as being dead. She actually pegged it seconds before midnight, so on the eleventh, if you want to be accurate.' Arthur nodded enthusiastically as he spoke.

'Can you tell me your neighbour's full name, to confirm I have the right details?' Calm on the outside, Peddyr prepared himself for big clue number one. The mystery body, registered as Gabriella Louise Dixon, was about to be dignified with a name and a past.

'Miss Josephine Dank.'

'That's her full name?'

'As far as I know,' said Arthur. 'You could ask her cousin. He'd know better than I.'

Peddyr licked his lips. 'Mr Bird, the reason I'm making enquiries is that Miss Dank's family have proved hard to trace. I don't suppose you have contact details for this cousin of hers.'

Arthur Bird aimed a quivering bony finger at a wooden writing bureau, the sort with a roll top. 'I might have his number somewhere. I'm not sure it works though. I tried.' Getting unsteadily to his feet, the old man shuffled to the bureau, slid the lid upwards, and reached inside to produce a battered black and red address book. There were a variety of small pieces of paper wedged inside the front cover, and he shakily fingered them. 'Ah! Here it is – Dave Smith's mobile phone number. He never even let us know when the funeral was. Sad, really. She lived alone for years. Never saw a sign of any family until the night she died, when he appeared out of the blue.'

Internally, Peddyr was smiling. This would be an easy interview. Arthur was so keen to be involved, he was gushing information. 'Dave Smith, right... yes, we'll follow that up. Thanks.' Taking the folded paper from Arthur, he tucked it safely into the document pouch. It was getting rather stuffy and hot inside Mr and Mrs Bird's flat, so Peddyr took the opportunity to remove his jacket. 'I know it might be upsetting, but do you think you could talk me through what happened?'

Arthur ran a hand through his grey forelock. 'Where do you want me to start?'

*A*ccording to Arthur Bird, Josephine Dank had lived at Worthington Court for seven years. He described her as being painfully shy, but always pleasant. However, he knew very little about her private life. 'She kept to herself,' he said. 'We used to see her at the doctor's sometimes. Then we spotted her in the waiting room at the cardiology department. Last year, I think.'

'October,' Florrie Bird twittered from the bedroom in thready, reverberating tones.

'That's right, luvvie,' Arthur said loudly with his head aimed at the far corner of the room. It took Peddyr a moment to work out what was going on, but when he did, he gave credit to the person who'd thought up the idea. By the nest of tables, he spied a baby monitor plugged into a double socket. 'Clever,' he said, aiming at it with his pen.

'Yes, ingenious, isn't it? Two-way, so Florrie and I can have a chat even when I'm not in the bedroom. It used to be exhausting traipsing back and forth every time she rang her little bell. Now she just has to ask, and I can reply. Saves a lot of to-ing and fro-ing.'

'Get on with the story, Arthur,' Florrie said, giving a gentle cough to remind her audience she was there and listening in. 'Tell him about her being a nun.'

Arthur gave an embarrassed shrug. 'Florrie made friends with Josie. Not bosom buddies, but they would pass the time of day at the door when she brought the milk in, when she was stronger. That's right, isn't it, luvvie?'

'That's right, Arthur.'

'She never married, said she'd devoted her life to the Lord, but then, a year or so before she moved here, she lost her faith. Gone. All of it. Can you imagine?' Behind a pair of thick-rimmed glasses, he flicked his wrinkled eyes to the ceiling. 'She suffered a terrible depression, they carted her off to the madhouse, and she never went back to the nunnery.'

Peddyr let Arthur meander his way through the story to begin with. Hurrying either him or his wife too much could be counterproductive, but he needed to get answers. 'Did she ever mention a cousin?'

'Never.' Florrie's voice was much stronger now. 'Not once. I told Arthur he was a con man. He asked for our full names and everything.'

'Tell me about that night,' Peddyr said. 'It could be vital for our investigation.' Ramping up the level of importance did the trick. Arthur cleared his throat and began speaking as if he were a witness appearing in court. It was devilishly difficult for Peddyr to remain deadpan.

'Miss Josephine Dank had been very unwell and was under her GP for antibiotics. We'd called him out the week before. I made it my business, as a good neighbour, to pop in. Fetch a bit of shopping for her.' At this point he paused and lowered his head. 'On the night in question, I had cause to be more concerned than usual. She'd taken a turn, and fearing the worst, I called an ambulance. Her breathing was laboured and...' He searched for the right terminology. 'Rattling.' Checking for approval from Peddyr he continued.

'By the time the ambulance arrived, it was too late. She'd gone. Nice and peaceful, mind. They radioed for an on-call doctor to confirm. He came. It was getting awful late by then, but there was nobody else to do it, other than the nice doctor – foreign fella, he was; Eastern European. He said to call the undertakers and arrange for the body to be collected, and he told me it would be a sensible idea to find details for any family. I had a rummage through her particulars...'

At this turn of phrase, Peddyr put his hand to his mouth, disguising a smile. Moments later, having composed himself, he asked, 'Did you find anything?'

'No, not really, the usual bills. Letters from a friend in Turvey Abbey. Photographs of her parents. They passed away last year, one after the other, bang, bang. I found her passport. She went to Lourdes twice. Didn't do her much good, did it?' He shook his head sadly. 'The doctor fella had another visit, so he left me with a dead woman. He seemed to think I'd have to deal with the paperwork. Apparently, he couldn't sign the death certificate because he didn't know the patient, but said he'd write a report for Josie's GP which could be picked up from the surgery... or something along those lines. I wasn't paying much attention. Getting weary by then, I was.' Arthur looked around, as if fearing judgement for what he was about to disclose.

'Before I knew it, I was alone with her. Coo-er. It was unsettling, her being so young. Too young to die, really. But I'll tell you, son, she wasn't the first dead body I've had to deal with.'

As he sucked in a deep breath, Florrie interrupted via the baby monitor. 'This is no time for a trip down Memory Lane. My Arthur was in the army, mister. And if you've got any sense, you'll tell him to shut up and get on with it. You need to hear about that Smith fellow. Dave Smith.' She repeated the name with contempt.

Whispering and mouthing the words, Arthur said, 'Northern Ireland. Two tours. Bloody nasty business.'

Putting one thumb up, Peddyr gave him respectful acknowledgement, being mindful to keep his voice down. 'Good man.' In his normal voice he returned to the matter in hand. 'So, Mr Bird, what happened when you rang the funeral directors, how does that work late at night?'

Sitting to attention in his favourite chair, Arthur's eyes twinkled. 'They have an on-call system. I phoned Castle and Wykes. We used them for my sister last year. Very professional.'

'I know them,' Peddyr added. 'They've made a respectable name for themselves. Did you use the Bosworth branch?'

'Now, I couldn't tell you that, son. I just phoned the number and got through to a pleasant fellow who took all the details.' Arthur used his fingers to remind himself of what he'd been required to tell. 'Josie's name and address. The doctor had her date of birth on his computer thingy. Only forty-three she was. Shame.' His thoughts wandered off for a moment. 'Now, where was I? Oh, yes. He wanted to know the name and address of her GP; same doctor's surgery as us, so I knew that one. Dr Prasad and his wife. Lovely they are. Do wonders with my Florrie.'

'Yes. Wonders.'

Sometimes Peddyr would forget Florrie was all ears in her bedroom until she reminded him with a comment. When she did, it was disconcerting to hear her disembodied voice coming from the far corner of the room accompanied by the echo of her proper voice, barely audible, drifting from the doorway.

Arthur ignored the interruption. 'Then I had to give my name and all that. Lots of details and stuff, you know. It was a good hour before they turned up. So, I had a cup of tea and told Florrie not to worry. I stayed with Josie, keeping her company.'

'I quite understand,' Peddyr assured him. 'What paperwork were you asked for by the undertakers?'

'Nothing. They said they had the information needed. They confirmed me as the person who'd phoned and such like... and I signed the form to say the details were in order. Two youngish men. Thorough. Knew what they were doing. One was an ex-Para. We had quite a chat.'

'I bet you did,' Peddyr said, arching one eyebrow. 'Then what happened?'

'Well, not long after they'd gone... Oh, I'd say within ten minutes of their van pulling out of the car park, the doorbell goes.'

'The main door intercom?'

'Yes. It *was* the intercom, as it happens. The man said his name was Dave Smith, and he was Josie's cousin. Now, son, this is where it gets suspicious because he told this cock-and-bull story about living in the Bahamas and Josie phoning him the previous week to say she was very ill and asking for help. He said he'd rung her flat and got no answer so he was sorry to disturb me late at night, but could I let him in. I did. Well, I had to, didn't I?' He looked again for approval.

'Someone would have to tell him, if he was a relative,' Peddyr offered. 'What did he look like?'

'I'll tell you what he didn't look like. He didn't look like someone who lives in the Bahamas. Tall and pasty, he was. Like he rarely saw the ruddy sunshine. Glasses. Wire rimmed. Wore jeans, not scruffy though. Had a coat and jumper on. It was on the chilly side. Wore one of them silly woolly hats. Rude bugger never took it off.'

Perking up at this morsel, Peddyr gave a half-smile. 'Did he ask much about Josie?'

Giving this question some thought, Arthur clamped both arthritic hands onto his knees. 'Yes, he did, as a matter of fact. That was a surprise in one way.'

'Oh? Why do you say that?'

'Well, he didn't seem upset. Strange fella. I told him they'd already taken her to the chapel of rest, so he asked if I could describe how she looked. I told him she was peaceful, which didn't seem to satisfy him, because he asked if I had a key to her flat.'

Peddyr second-guessed what Arthur said next. Dave Smith, if that really was his name, had encouraged Arthur to stay with him while he searched Josie's flat for a photograph of her. 'Said he wanted a keepsake. Hadn't seen her for years, apparently. All very odd if you ask me. I thought he was sifting through her drawers to find a will, but he said he was taking paperwork so he could deal with her affairs.'

'Florrie said this Dave Smith chap asked for your names and contact information. Why?'

'Tell him, Arthur. And tell him you think he stole your passport. Tell him.' Judging by the volume, Florrie was becoming rather agitated. She clearly hadn't trusted Dave Smith. Whoever he was.

A doubtful frown appeared on Arthur's forehead. 'I never thought nothing of it at the time. He asked if I had a letter or something with my name and address. He came into the flat. Sat where you are now. I went to the bureau and found a phone bill. Pleased him no end it did. He said he'd be in touch about funeral arrangements. Made him feel at home with a cup of tea as well, I did.'

'Why did he ask you to register the death?' Peddyr asked, cutting to the heart of the matter.

With his eyebrows shooting upwards, Arthur stammered a reply. 'Me? I didn't do any such thing. I told him where to pick up the death certificate and gave him the address for the register office. Handed the key to her flat and every responsibility over to him. He was the only relative. As far as I knew.'

Peddyr scratched at his right brow. 'And your passport is missing?'

'Only noticed it last week. Gone. Can't find it. And let me tell you, sunshine, I keep it in the same place, next to Florrie's in the bureau. Not that we need them now. Not going anywhere.'

So, Dave Smith had lifted the passport while Arthur was making the tea on the night Josie Dank's body was taken to the undertakers. Peddyr was chuffed with the progress made. Whoever Dave Smith was, he'd gathered the right information to present himself as Arthur Bird and register a death. But – and it was a big but – how had he forged a medical cause of death certificate? 'You have been two of the most helpful individuals in the course of my enquiries. I can't thank you enough.' Placing notebook into document case, Peddyr struggled to his feet, his knee giving out as he did so.

'Old war wound?' Arthur asked, inclining his head.

'Something along those lines, but fewer live rounds.'

'Aha! I knew it. I could tell.' Arthur sounded delighted with himself. 'Shoes polished. Ramrod back. Eyes that tell a story of battle and steely bravery… What regiment?'

With a grin, Peddyr shook the old man's tremulous hand. 'Can't tell you, I'm afraid, Mr Bird.' He tapped the side of his nose twice and winked.

Arthur Bird winked back. 'Thought so…'

10

WHO TO TRUST?

*N*ot having use of a car was proving to be an inconvenience I could do without. I now planned journeys into town well ahead of time, to allow for a lengthy walk, because I couldn't afford to get a taxi back and forth each time. Ready cash was perilously low. Consoling myself that the exercise would do me good, I strode out on my way back home from my first meeting with Peddyr Quirk. Walking gave me time to think, and I decided, on reflection, the Quirks were quirky. Mismatched and yet perfectly suited, but whatever I thought about them they were keen to help, for a fee. A fee I couldn't pay until resolution of this messy business.

Power walkers did not wear high heels, for good reason. By the time I'd pounded the pavements all the way home, my toes were complaining bitterly. Rounding the last corner into Derwent Drive, I imagined the blissful feeling of bare feet on carpet and of changing into less constricting clothes to continue the draining task of de-cluttering the house, removing Mum's trinkets and collectables and donating them to charity. The thought of achieving some semblance of order was spurring me on, despite running desperately short of time before facing the return to work on Monday.

'Oh, no. Who the hell is that?'

There was a truck parked on the driveway. I wracked my brains to remember which local tradesman I had invited to survey the property and give an exorbitant quote that day. I thought I'd cancelled them all. But when I got to the house, I didn't find a builder. It was Laura at the front door, standing on the threshold, one hand to her mouth. On hearing my heels clipping on the driveway, she turned.

'Thank God you're here. I wasn't sure whether to go in or not,' she said, perturbed.

'What do you mean?'

'Well, the door was open. Ajar.'

Thinking back, I couldn't recall when I'd pulled it to. 'Maybe I didn't shut it properly when I left. You know how it sticks. Anyway, why are you here again? Where are the kids?'

'With the M-I-L.' Laura regularly used acronyms for the most common of expressions, why she couldn't simply say mother-in-law was beyond me. 'Curtis's mum likes to see them once a week. It gives me a break. I came to help you get rid of your boxes and I need to talk to you about something.'

Glancing back at the battered truck on the driveway, I registered who it belonged to. 'Is he here?'

'Who?'

'Curtis. Is he with you?' When Laura shook her head, it pleased me no end. I'm not a fan of my brother-in-law. The B-I-L.

'Nah,' said Laura. 'I just borrowed the van.'

67

There was nothing wrong with Curtis Churchill per se, but he was so annoyingly cock-sure and arrogant. I couldn't take to him. Full of entertaining stories, Curtis Churchill never took himself too seriously as he bumbled through life with his pally backslapping antics, barely making enough money to cover the mortgage and feed the family. Laura should have thought of that when she married him, I mused, but what she saw was a loveable Devonshire rogue who she fell for, brick-dust and concrete mixer.

With a pushing gesture, I ordered my dithering sister to enter the house. 'Whatever... I've got to take these bloody shoes off. My feet are kill—' I stopped dead. Sheets of creased newspaper were strewn about, packing cases upturned, suitcases left opened where previously they were stacked neatly, closed. 'Someone's been in here.'

There was no need for Laura to ask how I knew this. My organisational skills are legendary, as is my requirement for a list and for things to be tidy. Before the move, I had labelled each cardboard box, detailing the items inside and which room they were destined for, but because of the tight timescale before I returned to work, I'd only liberated the immediate essentials. Someone less caring had been in the house.

Silent for a moment or two, we absorbed the scene.

'Why not nick the lot?' I muttered. 'Why turn the place upside down and not take anything?'

'How do you know they haven't?' Laura asked.

I pointed at the mantelpiece over the fireplace and said, 'Cut glass champagne flutes neatly in a row. And why leave an expensive set of Mum's silver napkin rings on the carpet?'

The rings lay in their polished wooden box, untouched on a velvet lining. These were the meaningless trappings of the life my parents had once spent entertaining friends for dinner, showing off their wealth and social standing. On first inspection no real damage was done, but as we made our way through the downstairs rooms, the dining room gave me the answer I was looking for. 'Shit, bugger and bum,' I said with a low groan. 'My laptop. It's gone. I had everything on it.'

A hand to my throat, I picked up the sheet of paper lying on the dining table where my laptop had been. Three letters were scrawled on it. "RIP". Followed by a familiar phrase, "Show no pity to the guilty. A life for a life." A cascade of prickles made their way down my spine as I turned to see Laura's lips parting to release a quick gasp.

'Fuck. This is getting creepy now,' she said, her head moving left to right, eyes darting to the doorway. 'And it most definitely isn't anything to do with Phil.' With a clenched jaw, I refrained from giving my opinion. She did not understand how cruel I'd been to my undeserving husband.

Needing comfort and protection from the jitters, we held hands as we searched the rooms upstairs which, it turned out, were eerily silent and reassuringly empty. On the way back down the creaking stairs, I willed the loss of my expensive laptop and the death threat to be the only unpalatable discoveries. Instead, my underlying fears were realised when I noticed the concertina file containing my passport was missing too.

'What else was in there?' Laura asked.

'Everything,' I whispered, intertwining both hands against my midriff. To keep rigorous order and store important paperwork in one place, the file had also contained my birth certificate, marriage certificate, school certificates, premium bonds, NHS medical card – everything that defined me was in there or scanned onto the stolen laptop.

Laura attempted to ease the intensity of the moment. 'You must have saved everything to a cloud account.'

'Yes, I have.' Grateful for the reminder, I gave her a diluted smile. 'It's all backed up. I've got passwords saved into my phone, but I'm not sure the bank or anyone else will accept electronic copies as proof without the originals.'

'Whatever is going on, we'd better report this to the police.'

The suggestion was sensible, and yet I laughed bitterly. 'The police? How? I'm dead, remember. The bastards won't even let me have my car back.'

'I could do it,' Laura prompted. 'We still own the house between us until this is sorted. I'll report it as a break-in and ask them to add it to the evidence for identity theft.'

After making a call to the police, we sat in the kitchen, opened the back door and let the outside warmth take the chill from the room. The rear of the house didn't catch the sun until the evening, leaving it shaded and cool in the summer months. Clutching a mug of tea, I reviewed the situation. It wasn't good.

'If someone doesn't commit an actual crime soon, I'm in the shit. The police won't act otherwise.'

'They said they'd look into it.'

'Yeah, right,' I said, bobbing my head shoulder to shoulder to ease the tension in my neck. 'Until then I've got no way of getting to my money, and work have asked me to provide them with an alternative bank account. They can't pay my salary until I do, but I can't open another account because I'm dead and now I haven't enough proof of ID. Brilliant.' I released a pent-up moan. 'I hope Bernard

Kershaw can pull a rabbit out of a hat soon. Because if not, I'm pretty much screwed.'

'Yeah, good old Big Ears,' sniped Laura. 'Let's see what he can do. He charges enough.'

Instinct told me I could rely on Bernard. Sadly, the same could not be said of Laura. Sitting across the Formica table from me was the sister I barely knew, the sister with whom I had nothing in common apart from genetics, the sister who had no job and no money of her own until I paid her what she was due from the house we were sitting in.

Tapping her fingernails against the mug she was holding, Laura asked, 'How did you get on with the private dick? Was he mean and moody?'

'Not exactly. Although I thought he was a dick to start with.'

'Tall, dark and handsome?'

'No, far from it. Tallish and solid. Not handsome, but not ugly. He's a bit of mystery but strikes me as intelligent and determined enough. That's the best I can tell you, apart from saying that either he must be short of work or owe Bernard Kershaw a favour because he's on the case already.'

'He won't work for nothing.'

'No, but he'll get paid as long as I pay Bernard Kershaw's bill. Which means he has to solve the problem and get me my money. If he doesn't, he won't get paid and I won't either.'

'And that leaves me well and truly skint,' Laura said. 'This place is the only asset I have; the rest is debt.'

'Let's not be too negative, Laura. With any luck, things will be straightened out soon enough.'

'So you say.' My sister rose from her chair, looking morose, and wandered toward the window. 'But if matters don't get sorted soon… I have a family to think about.'

Dropping an uncalled-for barb into the mix, she switched on Mother's dilapidated radio; the one wedged on the windowsill where it had lived for at least a decade, its aerial bent at the top. 'This'll cheer us up,' she said. Plainly she had avoided pushing the subject of money any further and used the radio to end the stilted moment.

The peace didn't last long, because when I heard the inane chatter from BBC Valley Radio advertising up-and-coming events, I took a sharp breath. 'Oh, no. What day is this? Friday tomorrow, isn't it? No, that's today. God! I almost forgot.'

A phone message had arrived the day before, asking me to confirm my usual attendance for the phone-in on BBC Valley Radio's monthly Lifestyle Show. Grabbing my mobile, I made to reply but caught myself. 'Laura, can I use yours? I'm rapidly running out of credit.'

'Sure, there's nothing more vital than your adoring public,' she replied, handing over her mobile. Noting sardonic undertones, I shot her a quizzical look, but allowed her to continue what she was saying. 'While you're at it, why don't you ask Talbot Howkins to do a feature on your untimely death? Ask the listeners for help.'

Biting gently at my bottom lip, I considered what sort of fiasco might ensue if I disclosed my own death on air. Would a public appeal help? Or would it provide more ammunition to whoever was behind this? I didn't know what to think, insomnia and stress were undermining any ability to problem solve. 'I'm not sure I want the world and his wife to know my business,' I replied, rustling up a grin of sorts. 'But thanks for the idea. I'll save it as a last resort.'

'I was joking.' In typical Laura fashion, her tone was tetchy. I put this episode down to annoyance at having her plans to recycle my packaging material interrupted again.

This was the second time she'd ostensibly come to help me settle into a new life, and the second time those offers of help had been side-lined by another drama. Dismissing her reaction as a temporary blip, I carried on with the call to Valley Radio. What I discovered had me fuming.

'They've only gone and asked Justin Parks to stand in for me. What a flaming cheek!'

Fiddling with her hair, Laura remained distracted by whatever was on her mind. Even so, she feigned some interest in what I had to say. 'Why? And who's Justin Parks?'

I tried to moderate my thoughts. Disturbing ones were pushing their way to the surface, and I had an urge to forget about being a mellow, forgiving therapist. I was livid. The need for a rant was tempered by counting to three and readjusting my watch before I could reply without use of expletives. 'Justin Parks is a colleague from work. I would say "esteemed colleague", but he's not. He's a slippery sycophant who wants nothing more than to take my job – which he's applied for, by the way – and to slide neatly into my spot on local radio. He can't wait to see the back of me.'

'Why did they think you wouldn't be there tomorrow?'

'Because as my email isn't working, they phoned my office number to chase confirmation. Slimy Justin took it upon himself to tell them I was unavailable.'

Laura shrank back in her chair. 'I wouldn't want to be him when you get hold of the man.'

'Wouldn't touch him with a bargepole,' I said, sticking my tongue out and shuddering at the thought. 'He has the looks all right, quite the James Bond in fact, but the way he smarms about makes your skin crawl. Slimy toad.'

'Are you going along anyway?' Laura asked.

The producer of the lifestyle show had been most apologetic and suggested I attend the studio as originally planned. 'Damn' right I am,' I replied to Laura's enquiry. 'Justin will make a right twat of himself and I wouldn't miss that spectacle for the world. They'll think twice before inviting him back.' In a childish reaction, I rubbed my palms together several times. 'He's a homophobic bigot and Talbot will eat him for breakfast. Hoo-bloody-rah.'

A wave of satisfaction gave some much-needed respite from the endless pressure of being dead. However, I had to address reality again if I was to get on with life, so I asked Laura to use her phone once more. 'Only to see if my emails are working again or not. I'm so sorry to have to ask you, but I don't have enough data and I cancelled the broadband and TV contract. They were booked for installation today.' I sighed inwardly. 'I've been going to MacDonald's for a ninety-nine pence coffee and use of free WIFI.'

Handing over her phone with the vaguest semblance of a sympathetic smile, Laura asked, 'How much money do you have left to keep you going?'

'You don't need to worry; I'll get by somehow.' Her interest in my money was too intrusive for my liking. Luckily the next problem arose, changing the subject. 'Shit. My Google mail has been completely deleted.' Putting down the mobile, I looked across at my sister. 'This is really beginning to get to me.' Clasping my hands over hot cheeks, I said, 'I think I'd better let Peddyr Quirk know about the break-in. Can I make another quick call?'

The phone was answered almost immediately. 'P.Q.I. Connie speaking.'

'Connie? It's Gabriella Dixon. I know I only just left your office, but can you tell Mr Quirk I've been burgled? Someone has taken everything that identifies me as me.'

On any other day I would have been factual, practical, and self-contained, but saying the words out loud triggered an uncontrolled response. My voice was strangled by my tightening throat. Turning my back on Laura, I left the kitchen; not breaking into a run, but trotting as far away from her as I could. I never cried. Not where anyone could see me, at any rate.

11

TRUE COLOURS

*L*aura found me about three minutes later in the bedroom. I'd commandeered the spare room, once reserved for friends and other visitors. It was hardly ever used. The large, sparsely furnished floral room contained a double bed, two bedside cabinets and a series of cardboard wardrobes on loan from the removal company. I had wiped away stinging tears and was staring down at her phone with a mixture of anger and bewilderment.

'You shouldn't have replied to Phil. It was none of your business,' I said, hearing Laura approach, each squeak and crack of the floorboards giving away her position.

'And you shouldn't have looked at the messages on my phone. They're private.' No longer the sweet voice of a young earth mother, Laura's response was unusually harsh. Raising my head to gauge her expression, I was unsurprised to find her propped in the doorway, arms folded, scowling.

'I still think you should explain yourself. I have a right to know what you and Phil are up to. What's going on between the two of you?'

The question resulted in a stiffening of her body. 'If you must know, he wanted me to hear some home truths. In fact, he said I was in danger of being ripped off by my own flesh and blood, and that you cared more about yourself than anyone else.'

'You spoke on the phone as well?'

'We did. It was… educational.'

The reason behind Laura's sullen mood and need to discuss money had become apparent. 'Well, he would say that,' I countered. 'He's just trying to inflict more divorce damage.' Defiantly, I stared hard at Laura. 'He must have closed my Google account because he's named as my legacy account manager, which fits neatly with his insistence that we sever all contact. He's hoping not to pay the divorce settlement.'

'That makes no sense at all,' Laura scoffed, rounding on me, her dreadlocks swinging. 'I'm not as stupid as you make me out to be. And just because you're the clever one, the bright spark, the intellectual… doesn't give you the right to blame Phil for things going wrong in your life.' She peeled away from the doorway and reached out for her phone, sending me a fierce look.

'Perfect Gabby… the sister I had to spend my life trying and failing to live up to. You're not dead and when you're legally alive again, poor old Phil will have to pay your settlement all the same.' She flipped the leather case closed and wedged the phone into a deep pocket hidden in the baggy folds of her patchwork Harem trousers. 'It's not his doing, all this. He'd be better off having you murdered. Then he really won't have to pay, and he'll have a claim on your money too because you're not properly divorced. I'd watch out if I were you.'

It was a strange sensation, like a coldness making its way

through my arteries, resulting in my chest clamping painfully. 'Now who's being bloody ridiculous, Laura?' I couldn't imagine anything so farfetched as being bumped off by a hit man paid for by my soon to be ex-husband, and yet the hypothesis had some weight to it. Shrugging it off as nonsensical words said in the heat of the moment, I said, 'Whatever Phil told you is bound to be skewed in his favour. Saying I'm selfish and money-grabbing makes him appear hard done by. Why listen to what he's telling you?'

'Because I like Phil. I always have. He's a decent man,' Laura said as she stared toward the window briefly before facing me again. 'He told me why he stopped loving you.'

'Oh, yes?'

'You shouldn't have lied to him. He didn't deserve it. Why lie?'

Not wanting the conversation to continue along the same path, I tried to convince her how convoluted these private matters were. 'In other words, butt out. It's complex.'

'Is it complicated? He asked you to consider adoption, and you strung him along. Then you drop a bombshell like that. How do you think he felt when he found out you were perfectly capable of having his children, but too selfish to want to? Those constant comments about infertility being a matter of rotten luck. Telling everyone you were not destined to be a mother.' Laura tossed her wild mane with an upward thrust of her head. 'The fact is, you were too caught up in your career; the adulation, the praise. It's heartless, Gabby. It nearly destroyed him.'

'Now, Laura…'

'Don't Laura me.' With another swish of her Medusa locks, Laura barracked me. 'We felt sorry for you. Poor, childless, barren Gabriella. She's only got her work to console her. Blah, blah, fucking blah… All rubbish.' She threw both index fingers in the air before aiming them at my chest. 'And you know what else Phil is right about?' Leaning in, Laura said with a reproachful look, 'With what you've got in mind for this place, you'll make a killing. I saw the plans for the other house you're going to build out there.' One hand waved towards the extensive garden. 'Doubling your money at least.'

Laura backed up and seemed to grow in stature as she continued her protest. 'I get my share of the value of this place, fair enough, but Phil's right: you used me to get what you wanted.'

I remained seated on the edge of the bed and placed my hands back to back between both knees. 'Say what you think, Laura, you obviously need to get something off your chest. It's better than letting it fester.'

'Don't patronise me,' she snarled back. 'You're not so wonderful. You're not as caring as you lead people to believe either. You were the daughter who couldn't be bothered to come and see Mum more than three times when she was dying, but you rocked up soon enough once she was dead, to play the grieving daughter. I did all the hard work,' Laura spluttered, elbows bent, hands on hips. 'I sorted out the funeral arrangements just as Mum had wanted, but they weren't good enough for you. No. Best black outfit on, you bowl into Castle and Wyckes with that stupid cow Stella, and take over. I'm done with your bossy self-righteousness.'

'Now hang on a minute—'

'No, don't stop me. I've been bursting to tell you this. I tried to be nice and let it roll off my back, but I can't. I'm sick to the back teeth of you treating me like an inferior being and it isn't right you should make a massive profit from this place. You only lived here four years. What gives you the fucking right to profit from it?'

I wasn't about to let Laura throw any further insults my way. I'd heard enough. 'It's my risk. My bloody money, Laura.' Standing to face her and force her to retreat, I reminded her of the basic facts. 'You still inherit when I die, so what's your beef? When you get your share of this place, you and work-shy Curtis get to live mortgage-free. More than most families ever get the chance to.' I slapped a hand to my chest. 'I give you the money now for your share of this place and I'm the selfish one?'

When Laura smiled, it wasn't the response I was expecting. I soon learned why when she reminded me who held the upper hand.

'What money, Gabby? You don't have any... you're dead.'

12

WHO SIGNED THE DEATH CERTIFICATE?

*T*he best and most obvious lead was Dr Prasad's surgery in Lime Grove, so Peddyr made his way there. It was a bright cloudless day, and he took his time sauntering along the tree-lined streets where the wealthier residents hid away behind wrought-iron gates in executive homes for the pretentious. Connie had been a source of interesting insights about his latest client, and as he strolled through the waving shade of the linden trees, he mulled over her observations about Mrs Gabriella Dixon. They had sat on the roof terrace to eat dinner the previous evening, a nightly summer ritual which often paid dividends. A cold beer would free up Peddyr's mind to wider possibilities, and Connie could contribute to his hypotheses, whatever they were.

'April 1978. That makes her a horse.'

'Oh, I don't know, she's not so bad looking,' Peddyr said, a grin spreading across his face. 'But now you come to mention it, she has quite a long nose and a heck of a mane.' Beaming at his wife as she swatted his forearm for being flippant, he popped an olive into his mouth. 'Sorry, I am listening, honest. Go on, Lao Po.' He didn't hold with Connie's horoscope obsession, but now and again it was a useful framework to hang traits from.

In the Chinese horoscope, Gabriella Dixon was born in the year of the horse. This didn't mean a lot to Peddyr, who couldn't care less if she'd been born in the year of the pygmy hippo. But to Connie it was a vital clue as to Gabriella's central personality. 'She's an earth sign in her Chinese horoscope, but a fire sign in the western one. She's an Aries.'

Peddyr shrugged at her, as he always did when she held horoscope and yin-yang discussions. 'Right. So, she's a ram and a horse,' he said. 'Interesting combination.'

'I'll cut to the important stuff,' Connie said, getting the message. 'She's a free spirit who needs space for herself. Must have her own life. Has a powerful belief in chasing dreams and the determination to achieve what she sets out to do. She's a work fanatic. Big ego. Easily bored, you know… impatient. But – and this is important, Lao Gong – she can be totally blind to her own faults.' Connie captivated him with her special knowing look; the one delivered with sincerity and a wrinkled nose. 'You be careful. Gabriella Dixon has hidden depths. She can be fiery too, but not like a red-head or an Italian. More like that gigantic snake in *Jungle Book*.'

'So, when she hypnotises people with her charm and her therapist's nonsense, she's doing what?' Reaching for a slice of ciabatta, Peddyr considered Connie's words carefully. 'Are you saying she's passive aggressive, or are you insinuating she's manipulative?'

Connie dabbed at the side of her mouth with the corner of a paper serviette before replying. 'I'm sure she's hiding something, and she covers it well. She was too hesitant when I asked for her story: "What brings you here, Mrs Dixon?" Way too controlled, as if I was impertinent to even ask her a straightforward question. She wore her smart suit like armour. Her hair is worn up because she never lets it down, not in public. You see what I'm getting at?'

Peddyr took what his wife said seriously. She was never too wide of the mark, horoscopes or no horoscopes, because she had a magical gift for reading people. If only their clients knew how clever she was, most of them wouldn't be so forthcoming with information. She'd perfected the dutiful wife performance, and when necessary she even played the dim receptionist, fooling many into divulging secrets they wouldn't otherwise reveal. Connie was far from stupid, she'd mastered several languages and often took on translation work for the Foreign Office – Mandarin and several Chinese dialects. All hush-hush and secret squirrel.

When they'd met in Hong Kong in 1985, it was a physical shock for Peddyr to discover there was such a thing as love at first sight, and for once in his life he didn't deny himself. It was a battle to win her trust, and the objections from the family had been a test of their commitment to each other. Having a relationship with a foreigner was bad enough and at the time he was a British officer in the Hong Kong Police which only served to alienate her parents even further. But never doubting she loved him too, he persisted and pestered until she agreed to marry him. It was the best thing he'd ever done before or since. He knew her better than anyone and they were a team in the true sense of the word, yin to the other's yang.

· · ·

*T*urning onto Lime Grove, he pressed an internal reset button and focused his mind onto his task for that morning. Arthur Bird had been precise in what he'd told Peddyr. Josephine Dank, the deceased, was registered at Dr Prasad's surgery and he would be the one who would have written the death certificate. Therefore, Peddyr reasoned, whoever had collected it would be the same person who went on to register the death. He'd worry later about how on earth the person responsible had changed the name and date of birth without a beady-eyed registrar spotting it.

The surgery was a purpose-built single-story building of grey brick and green window frames, nested in a spacious car park surrounded by well-chosen shrubs and trees. Plainly, minimal maintenance was the key aim of the person who designed it. The waiting room was spacious and airy with an appropriate distance given between patients speaking to reception and those awaiting their turn.

He'd picked a bad time. The number of prams, pushchairs and buggies was the initial giveaway, compounded by the cacophony that nearly had Peddyr turning on his heels before he got anywhere near the stony-faced receptionist. She looked in need of treatment for a headache, which was not surprising in the circumstances.

'Don't any of them come with volume controls?' he asked, sweeping a look at the three screaming babies who engaged in a competition to perform the most ear-splitting screech. Their respective mothers were frantically jiggling the red-faced bundles in their arms in a vain attempt to pacify the beasts.

'Sadly not. An off button would be a better idea,' the woman behind the counter offered with a grimace. 'I usually pinch some of my husband's ear plugs, but for some reason I thought it was Thursday today.' She rolled her eyes. 'Baby clinic, and we're running late. What can I do for you?'

'It's rather a delicate matter.' Raising his voice above the din, Peddyr appealed to her sense of discretion. 'A death...'

'Oh, I see.' She glanced over her shoulder. 'Samantha, be a dear and hold the fort for a few minutes. I need to take this gentleman into the back office.' A much younger woman in her early twenties, with sleek fair hair, smiled willingly and got up from a computer terminal. Peddyr was directed to a door to his left. Once closed, it was decidedly quieter.

'Thank goodness for small mercies,' the woman said, leaning against the wall for a moment. 'Now then, you said you'd had a death in the family. I'm so sorry.' She looked across at a long work surface where wire trays made a neat row. 'Can I take your name, and I'll see if we've had formal notification.'

Putting one hand in the air, Peddyr stopped her. 'No, Karen. Not in my family. I'm enquiring about a death certificate for Josephine Dank.'

Karen Hooper was the name on the receptionist's badge. Strange how that seemed to prevent people from introducing themselves properly, Peddyr thought. Deliberately engaging in friendly banter, making use of her first name, implied that he knew her already. It was working well, and she continued to act as if he were familiar to her.

A query creased her brow. 'Oh, now that name... give me a moment.' Checking the database on a screen, she quickly found what she was looking for. 'Goodness, that was back in—'

'May,' Peddyr said swiftly. 'The twelfth to be precise.'

Karen looked up from the screen. 'Correct. So...? You're here because?'

'Because I'm trying to find out who collected the death certificate.'

A shadow of doubt swept her features. 'Have we met before?'

'Very possibly. I do a lot of work with the police, and other services in town. Missing persons. Tracing relatives of the deceased, in this instance. If I remember rightly, you were enormously helpful when I asked for assistance with a tricky case six months ago. Although,' he said, tapping a finger to his chin, 'we only spoke over the phone.'

'Helpful, was I? Oh, that's nice to hear.'

Her shoulders relaxed as she returned to the information on the screen. 'Here we are. Dr Emil Prasad completed the paperwork because the on-call doctor didn't know the patient. We contacted the coroner's office to be on the safe side, because she was relatively young. But with her cardiac history and recent illness the all clear for a cremation was given. A Mr Arthur Bird collected the cause of death certificate, after lunch the same day.' Looking again at Peddyr, Karen raised her eyebrows. 'Any use to you?'

'Sort of. Did you deal with Mr Bird by any chance? I could do with a description.'

'I believe I did. And it stuck in my memory.' She rested one hand on the shelf of her waistline. 'He didn't look like an Arthur. Said his name was Arthur Bird, which to my mind isn't right. If I was his age, I'd have called myself Art. Like Art Garfunkel. Something more trendy.' She nodded her head several times.

'Young chap then?'

'In his late forties, I would say. Not young, but not old enough to be an Arthur.'

'Notice anything about the way he dressed? Any distinguishing facial features, perhaps?'

Karen Hooper had a way of expressing herself Peddyr admired. She didn't bother with niceties. 'That flipping hat,' she said reaching out an arm, palm facing down. With the other hand still on her hip, she resembled a little teapot, short and stout. 'A black woolly number. A beanie hat,' she said, allowing her spout arm to fall back to her side. 'I'm not too old-fashioned, but I still find it rude when men don't take their hats off indoors.'

'Perhaps he was a baldy,' Peddyr said, rubbing his velvet scalp.

'No. I could see from his sideburns he had short wiry hair. Greying but dark originally, I would have said. I'm almost sure he wore glasses, but don't quote me on that. He was tall. I remember looking up at him, annoyed by his dratted hat.'

Pleased with her astounding powers of recall, Peddyr thanked Karen and handed her his business card. 'If you think of anything else, would you call me? I'd appreciate it.'

Lips pressed tight, she examined the card carefully. 'Is that it, Mr Quirk? He's the one you're after?'

'I don't know yet,' Peddyr replied truthfully. 'He could well be. I've got a puzzle on my hands and he's part of it. The other mystery involves the medical death certificate itself.'

Karen Hooper flicked her eyes to the door. 'Use me while I'm here,' she said. 'I'll give you 'til the end of baby clinic. Anything to save my eardrums.'

Grateful to whichever screaming infant had taken it upon themselves to let out a piercing bawl at that very second, Peddyr smirked at her. 'Seems a fair exchange. Tell me, where does Dr Prasad keep such certificates?'

'Locked away. The same as the prescription pads they take on domiciliary visits. If he gets a call to verify a death, he takes the pad with him. There's a counterfoil, leaving a strip on the side as a corresponding record, and we scan the certificates onto our database if it's being collected from here.'

Thinking hard about what he might want to know, Peddyr pushed his luck. 'I don't suppose I could see a blank one?'

With a sideways glance, Karen Hooper only partially relented. 'No, but you can see the scanned copy of Josephine Dank's certificate. It's right here.'

For an important document, it surprised Peddyr to see how vague it was. Apart from the name of the deceased and the place of death, it required the date of death "as stated to me" and age "as stated to me". There were a number of options for identifying who was signing the certificate and Dr Prasad had circled the one which said, "Seen after death by another medical practitioner, but not by me". In Josie Dank's case, the form showed that a post-mortem was not being held. The important section headed, "Cause of Death" required the completing doctor to identify the main medical disease or condition, and any subsequent illnesses which may have contributed.

'Karen, could Dr Prasad have accidentally torn off two certificates and left a blank one attached to the one handed to Mr Bird?'

'No. One of us would have noticed as we scanned it in. Also, the doctor has to tear it from the pad very carefully and complete the counterfoil. Emil – Dr Prasad – would have noticed it if there was a blank counterfoil.'

'How many in a pad?'

Karen tapped at the side of her head. 'Twenty... maybe twenty-four. They have serial numbers, sequential.'

'And is the pad ever left unattended?'

'Not while it's here at the surgery. We gave Arthur Bird the certificate in an envelope. He couldn't have got anywhere near the blank certificates, if that's what you're asking.'

Peddyr smiled at her. 'It was.' He held his hand out. 'I'm grateful for your help, but it looks like the answers to the mystery lie at the register office.'

They both looked at the door and in unison breathed out on noticing the drop in volume. 'Baby clinic's done and dusted by the sounds of things,' Peddyr remarked.

'Until next week,' Karen said ruefully.

'I must make a note never to rock up during baby clinic again,' Peddyr said as he strode through the door back into the now peaceful waiting room. He waved a cheerio at Karen and a serene-looking Samantha. It crossed Peddyr's mind that Samantha may be deaf. It was the only reasonable explanation for her unruffled, smiling features.

13

THE SATURDAY PHONE-IN

*N*ever one for being late, I ensured an early arrival at BBC Valley Radio, looking as composed and professional as I could. The argument with Laura had unsettled me almost as much as the outrageous state of affairs concerning my finances. Another night of tossing and turning left me with jetlag, so I wasn't at my best. Far from it. Having said that, things had felt more positive when Stella's brother Graham delivered much-needed cash late the previous evening. The crisp notes were a joy to hold in my hands, connecting me with Stella. I think I chatted to Graham for far longer than he wanted me to, purely for that same reason.

Fearing a return of my burglar, I squirrelled the money away fifty pounds at a time in plastic sandwich bags, taping some to the underside of drawers. Others I hid in vases and trinket boxes around the house.

After Graham left, I had a quick tot up of cash assets. Remaining in my purse after a trip to the nearest super-market was nineteen pounds and eighty-six pence exactly.

Three hundred pounds from Stella, plus fifty-seven pounds from the secret tin and six pounds twenty-three pence in loose change found in the old three-piece suite, was an impressive total. It gave me nearly four hundred pounds to live on, unless I could persuade NHS Finance to pay in advance with notes. Highly unlikely, given my reported death in service.

On the back of the generous cash loan from Stella, I treated myself to a taxi to get me to the BBC studios in Crewsthorpe. It was worth the extravagance; I avoided getting a thorough soaking when the British summer served up a damp drizzle followed by a veritable deluge that Saturday morning.

Talbot Howkins, the show's host, was effusive in his welcome. 'Gabriella, darling, so immensely wonderful to see you. A month is always too long.' He placed one hand in the small of my back to guide me to his studio. 'Come, tell me all about your move. When's the housewarming?' On shutting the studio door, he transformed. 'Sit. I need to know about Justin Parks. I've been on Google and he looks such a dish. Tell me he's gay, darling.' There was a lecherous look in his eye.

'I don't think so...'

'What? Why don't you know?' His pouting lower lip made the gregarious Talbot look like a naughty child.

'Because I've never thought about him being one way or the other, he's just a colleague.' With a mocking sneer I ventured, 'Was it your idea to get him on the programme?'

A gifted presenter he may be, but he was a hopeless liar. 'My idea? No, whatever makes you think that?'

I huffed. 'After two years on your show, I can read you like a book. I didn't confirm, so you and Randy Andy panicked, looked up to see who you could rope in from my department and copped an eyeful of Justin Parks on our web page.' Circling a finger in the air I added, 'And bingo, your underpants took on a life of their own.'

A coy look gave him away well before his confession. 'Very good, Jessica Fletcher. You got me.' He tipped his head and gave a bashful grin. 'Forgive me. When he said you weren't available, I naturally…'

Lowering my glasses in mock dismay, I tutted. Most of the time through sheer vanity, I avoided wearing glasses, but at work and in the studio I needed them for reading. They gave an added professional gravitas into the bargain, and now they worked as another means of teasing Talbot.

'What's the plan?' I asked. 'I take teenage issues and Justin covers the rest of childhood mental health problems?'

'What a lovely compromise, darling. I knew you would be magnanimous in sharing the spotlight with Mr Handsome.'

Unable to help myself, I grinned. I was looking forward to seeing Justin squirm in his seat at having to cope with blatant flirting from Talbot and awkward questions from the public, but when Justin turned up late, he scuppered my free entertainment.

'Emile's arrived, bless him,' Talbot said, taking up his place behind the console and adjusting his microphone. 'And there goes Vic.' He waved through the glass partition into the next studio from where Vic Yarbury was ending the early morning Saturday show and handing over to the local news desk. 'Right, we kick off at nine fifteen, so take your seat, madam.' At that very second Dr Emile Prasad entered the studio, kissed me on the cheek and shook hands with Talbot.

'Any juicy questions this month?' he asked, taking his seat.

'They've been coming in thick and fast this morning, Doc. Glue ear, verrucas and a skin condition for you so far. Gabriella has a couple of teenage corkers, and we've saved the best naughty child ones for our new panellist Justin Parks, if he turns up.' Placing the headphones on, Talbot checked the clock again as Dr Prasad settled himself and pulled his microphone to the best height for his head. He and I chatted for a few minutes, listening out for the end of the news and watching Talbot shuffle notes and pick up social media information as it came through to him from his producer.

'Where's your laptop?' Emile asked me, noticing the pad and pen I had at the ready.

'My work one is at work, because I'm officially on leave. My personal one was stolen… yesterday.'

On hearing of my dilemma, he offered to share use of his iPad in case I needed to check a reference. 'You scribble it down, I'll search, and vice versa when it's my turn. Deal?' he asked. I was so thankful he was there.

A swaggering Justin Parks was ushered into the studio as the weather report was being announced with a short jingle. 'Here I am,' he said, reaching out to shake Talbot's hand, apparently not noticing the look of displeasure and a curled lip. 'Couldn't find where to park the Maserati.' At the sight of me, sitting opposite the radio presenter, he almost fell over his own feet.

'Justin…' I drawled, elated to witness his smug expression slipping away.

'Gabby. I didn't think you'd be here…'

'Justin Parks, meet Dr Emile Prasad resident GP,' Talbot said with a wave of one hand. 'Take a seat and brace yourself, we're on air in about ten seconds.'

There was no mistaking his irritation. Good looks and a

flashy sports car may have swung it on any other occasion, but tardiness never impressed Talbot. 'Do what the others do, and you'll be fine. I'm sure you know the format.'

Justin's eyes let him down, as did the lump in his throat as he swallowed down the nerves. I'd been much the same on my first show, apart from being late that is. I'm never late. Revelling in the sure knowledge the arrogant tosser was to make his mark in the world of radio by not preparing himself in the slightest, I was filled with a sense of overwhelming gratification. Justin Parks thought he could stroll in and be a hit with the listening public. Fool. Insincerity would get him nowhere on radio.

The red lights came on in the studio. We were live on air.

'Welcome, welcome, welcome, happy BBC Valley listeners everywhere. What a brilliant lifestyle show we have for you on this drizzly Saturday morning. You'll be overjoyed to hear that today's medical panel is devoted to our young people. If previous ones are anything to go by, we shall be busy, busy, busy.' Talbot Howkins played to the microphone, very much at home, smiling across at his panel members as he introduced us.

'The amazing panellists are here and raring to go. In the studio with me today, on this grey summer morn, we have the dashing and encyclopaedic Dr Emile Prasad, a local GP. Great to see you, Doc. Huge thanks for giving up your Saturday morning to be here.'

'A pleasure as always,' Emile Prasad replied with a voice as warm and reassuring as a cosy jumper on a winter's day.

'With him, to answer your mental health questions, we have the one and only Dr Gabriella Dixon, clinical psychologist, looking gorgeous as ever. We know you love her common sense and her razor-sharp mind.'

'Great to be here. Thanks, Talbot.'

Talbot turned to Justin. 'But lovely listeners, today we have a guest panellist joining us. We have double bubble in the camp. For the price of one highly qualified mental health specialist... we have two. Give a big welcome to Justin Parks.' Cutting him off before his guest said one word, Talbot flicked a switch and slid tabs up and down the mixer desk, sending another catchy jingle over the airwaves.

During this brief interlude, he collared his new arrival. 'If you had the decency to turn up on time, I would have had a few minutes to confirm your title and your outstanding qualifications, Mr Parks. We run to time. We're never late on my show. Here's how this works... I put a question to you, you answer it by making use of the caller's name to personalise the advice. If you recommend a product, be careful to balance this with the statement that other such products are available or to seek advice from a pharmacist. Got it?'

Again, he didn't allow time for Justin to answer.

'So, ladies, gentlemen, young people, mums, dads, grandparents and the rest of the family... you have surpassed yourselves with your questions this month. Let's go to our first caller. Lorraine from Swandale. Your son has a problem with repeated ear infections. Tell us all about it and we'll see what Dr Emile Prasad can help with.'

The first question was simple enough to answer, as was the next, both in the remit of the GP. I chipped in with some helpful advice about how to persuade an unwilling child to take much needed antibiotic medicine.

'Super tip for anyone. Thanks, Gabriella,' Talbot enthused. 'And now to a problem with anxiety, a regular topic of discussion on this programme. The caller wishes to be known as Sally, to protect her son's anonymity. Time to hear from Justin Parks. Anxiety seems very prevalent in our young people, Justin. What advice can you give to Sally?'

'Well, hello there, Sally,' Justin began, oozing charm. 'Thanks for being brave enough to bring this important subject to our attention. It's not to be taken lightly.' As he launched into a lecture about stress being helpful and some anxiety being normal, I shuddered. He'd made a basic schoolboy error; one a medical student would be ashamed of. Because he'd failed to undertake any form of assessment, I had no choice other than to step in.

'That's helpful, Justin, but I wonder if Sally could tell us in a little more detail about her son's problems. When did this start? How does she know it's anxiety? What's changed to make her so worried?' I meant it as a helpful hint, but his thunderous expression and narrowed eyes told me Justin hadn't taken it that way. Emile Prasad compounded his hurt when he cut across him.

'Quite right to mention that, Gabriella. Sometimes anxiety symptoms can indicate a physical health problem as well as a mental health one, so it's vital we gather the clues before dishing out solutions.'

Talbot topped it all off by miming a slap on the wrist towards Justin. I wanted to kiss him for that.

14

MYSTERY CALLER

*O*nce the panel had answered Sally's query with sage advice, it was on to the next question on the Life-style Show, and before long it was time for a travel update and another jingle or two.

'Getting in the swing of it now, Justin?' Emile asked while Justin was taking a gulp of water. 'It's like being in clinic only you can't see the patient, which puts us at a distinct disadvantage.'

'I didn't realise we all chipped in so freely. It's not at all helpful.' Justin's obvious discomfort was like a tonic to me. I sat back and soaked it up.

'Maybe not to you, but it is helpful to our listeners, Justin,' Talbot said. 'They love it and it makes for good radio.' He paused for a moment, checked his screen and winked at me. 'Here's one for you, Justin. Night-time enuresis. Did you ever wet the bed as a child?'

'Certainly not.'

With a finger in the air, Talbot silenced him as the red lights reignited. 'Welcome back, listeners. We are halfway through our medical phone-in already. Doesn't it fly by? Right. Another caller needs our help.'

Justin had at least learnt from his first unforced error, and he asked a series of questions to get more information from the caller whose son was a regular bed wetter. Unfortunately, he didn't listen carefully enough to the replies, and tied himself in knots. He then committed the ultimate gaff by saying, '...then there's the possibility of sexual abuse...'

Launching his arms into the air as the lady caller became instantly irate, Talbot intervened. 'No one is suggesting any such thing in your household, Chantelle, but it is a consideration in rare cases, if I'm right. Gabriella, what do you make of this?'

While Talbot made a fist at a red-faced Justin, I tried to be kind to my thoughtless colleague by confirming the relevance of his questions, even if carelessly put. 'There are a number of possible causes, Chantelle, and it's highly likely that your little boy hasn't really reached the stage of maturity for having dry nights. Please be reassured, this is perfectly normal and nothing to worry about.' Going on to suggest a useful website, I brought the discussion to a peaceful close, handing over to Emile for a question about a mystery skin condition.

Off air and during a travel update, Talbot looked across at me. 'I think you should take the next call.' Inclining his head, he said, 'Teenage pregnancy question. Potentially explosive.' He snubbed Justin, who was relegated to the role of additional listener for the final twenty minutes of the show.

Pleased to have a chance to contribute, I readily agreed. 'No problem. Go for it.'

The voice was strangely detached. A man calling himself John was on the line. 'What would you do if you discovered your teenage son had fathered a child and kept it a secret?' the man asked.

'How old is your son?' I enquired in return.

'I'm phoning on behalf of the teenager.'

'Oh, I see. I misunderstood.' Shrugging a query at Talbot, he merely returned it, so I ploughed on. 'You want to know how best to advise the young man, is that right?'

'I'm interested to hear what *you* have to say, yes.' By strongly phrasing the sentence in that way, John insinuated that he sought my advice in particular.

'Can we clarify the age of the mother?'

'Don't worry, she was old enough.'

Struck by the answer being given in the past tense, I wasn't sure if the child had already been born. 'Do you know the stage of the pregnancy? Has she hidden it for long?'

'Too long.'

'And can I ask about the father of the baby?'

'He had a life ahead of him, like she did.'

There it was again. The past tense. He was in the present, talking about the past. Something was off kilter with this call. 'That's so true,' I said. 'Being a teenager is very young to make decisions for the long term. Who else is involved? Are relatives of these young people providing support?'

'Someone had to take control.' The bitter edge to John's voice was unmissable. 'The boy was the one to be punished.'

'Did he deserve punishment? Is that's what's worrying him?' With such a direct question, I hoped to get closer to John's concerns.

'No, he's not worried, not now.' The caller's voice took on a hollow quality. 'He faced the consequences, and they showed no pity.'

Perplexed, I looked across at Emile for help who made a rolling motion using his forearms, encouraging me to continue.

'How do you mean?' I asked, floundering.

'Chance predictions,' John replied. 'They let fate decide. The girl and the boy played a dangerous game and lost.'

'Did she keep the baby?' Emile asked, taking his cue from the scribbled phrase "help me out here!" on my writing pad.

'I guess so,' John responded.

Listening intently, heart pattering, I forced myself to continue with another question. 'Has the father of the baby tried to find out what happened?' I asked, suspecting that John wasn't a friend of the child's father at all. His haunting voice convinced me he was the father desperately searching for answers. Was his child alive? If it was, then was it a girl or a boy? Where was his child?

'He did nothing else but try to find out what happened, Gabriella. For years he tried to forget, but it's so very hard to forgive, isn't it? So hard not to know your own child. Don't you think so, Gabriella?'

'I can only imagine how hard that must be,' I said, reddening with the guilt of lying to Phil for years and denying him the child he craved. Was John deliberately baiting me, I wondered.

Emile came to my rescue again. 'There are some helpful organisations where he may find guidance on how best to proceed.' Dr Prasad was about to launch into advice and details when John spoke across him.

'I found the guidance I needed. It's in the bible.' There was a momentary pause during which Justin tapped against the side of his head and mouthed 'mad,' at me. I ignored him.

'What does the bible say?' I asked, trying to find a suitable ending to this bizarre call.

'Deuteronomy says to show no pity to the guilty. A life for a life. You know how the rest of it goes.'

'So why are you phoning—?'

The line went dead and the atmosphere in the studio became so tense nobody spoke for a second or two until Talbot coughed and pulled himself together. 'That was someone called John.'

15

WHERE DID THE TIME GO?

I looked across from the passenger seat of a luxurious car. Dr Emile Prasad was talking to me as he was driving. We were approaching the outskirts of Bosworth Bishops, and I did not understand how I'd got there.

'You've gone silent all of a sudden, did I hit a raw nerve?' Emile Prasad asked, giving me a quick sideways glance.

I didn't know. I hadn't heard the question. The last thing I remembered hearing was Talbot's voice in the studio. Staring wildly around me, trying to get a handle on things, I could only rustle up a breathy non-committal response. 'Have I?'

'You all right, Gabriella? Listen. Don't let it get to you. The bloke was an attention seeker. A religious nutcase, like I said.'

He was talking about the mystifying caller; the man calling himself John, whose words seeped back into my conscious mind as we weaved through the wet streets. A life for a life. Had John killed his girlfriend? Had she had an abortion without him knowing? It was a terrible scenario.

'Gabriella? You've gone so pale. Should I pull over?'

'No, I'm just not feeling quite myself. You see I forgot breakfast, moved house this week, had a calamity with the bank, ballsed up my own divorce and now I've attracted a nutcase. Not bad for someone who's dead.'

'You're not dead, silly woman. What are you talking about?' Being forced to stop at a set of traffic lights, he play-acted taking my pulse, and grinned. 'You're peaky looking, but very much alive.'

'On paper I'm dead,' I explained. 'The mess at the bank is because someone has managed to register me as dead when I'm not. You couldn't make it up, could you? Now some wacko has targeted me on the radio.'

'Come on, we've been through this once already. He wasn't being personal, merely weird. It sounded totally fabricated to me.' Handing me a tin of travel sweets retrieved from a slot near the handbrake, Emile said, 'Have some sugar.'

Taking one and dusting the fine coating with a fingertip, I saw the time on my watch. Forty whole minutes were unaccounted for. Missing. Absent. When did I agree to Emile giving me this lift? How did he know where I lived?

'Here we are. Derwent Drive. Number six, you said?' The car slowed and came to a gentle halt at the bottom of the driveway. Emile looked across the road to number seven. 'Do you see much of your neighbour?' he asked, raising an eyebrow à la Roger Moore.

'Very rarely.'

'I can tell why you call it the murder house. What has he got wrapped up on those shelves?'

Stunned, I said nothing. I didn't remember mentioning a

single thing to Emile about Kenny, or about the bungalow. When did I have that conversation? And what else had I talked about during the journey? Pulling at the door handle, I thanked Emile for his trouble in returning me home safely and for his professional support.

'My pleasure, see you next month.' He produced a kindly wave as I stood on the pavement, a pasted on confidence masking my dread at what had been unleashed by John's words.

16

THE REGISTER OFFICES

'*A*ngela Gibbs is expecting me,' Peddyr Quirk told the lady at the reception desk as he brushed raindrops from the shoulders of his waxed jacket. 'Is she about?' The receptionist instructed him to take a seat, but preferring to stand, he amused himself by reading the marriage banns posted on a central column in the waiting area. Some Eastern European names were unpronounceable. Not a proper vowel in sight.

A rounded face appeared at the doorway of an office marked "Deputy Registrar". 'Mr Quirk, do come through.' He entered a plain office. 'We don't want any eavesdroppers,' a softly spoken Angela said, closing the door gently behind him. As she moved across to her office chair, the lining of her knee-length skirt made a swishing noise, reminding Peddyr of his old English teacher at school. Now he came to think about it, Angela Gibbs bore an uncanny resemblance to old Mrs Knotting – she of the withering looks and stunning criticism. Mercifully, Angela Gibbs was far more kindly.

'Thanks for fitting me in on a Saturday morning, Angela. I know how busy you are. And please call me Peddyr.'

'I'm as keen to sort this out as you are,' Angela replied, opening a file. 'I've made some urgent enquiries since we spoke on the phone.' She licked a finger to aid in her search for the notes she'd compiled. 'Now then... We have received no medical certification pertaining to the death of a Josephine Dank of Worthington Court; that much I'm sure of, beyond any doubt.' Laying both puffy hands flat on the desk, she held his gaze. 'However, if as you say Mrs Gabriella Louise Dixon is alive and well, we have to investigate whether there's been a deliberate falsification of records. To that end, Mr Quirk, I examined the medical certification of her death. There are no errors, crossings out, or evidence of tampering.'

'Just like you said. Clean as a whistle.' He looked across at her. 'What about the person who registered the death?'

'Ah, yes.' Her apple-pip eyes lit up. 'Mr Arthur Bird.'

'Can I hazard a guess? Tall, pale, glasses, wore a black woollen beanie hat and never took it off.'

Shaking her head, Angela surprised him with her rejection. 'No. He didn't look like that. The man was rather bent over. He did have a hat, a tweed cap, but he held it in his hands. Long overcoat, beige mac type thing. Leather gloves and a paisley print scarf at his neck. Greying wavy hair. Thick square frames to his glasses. Black they were.'

'How come you remember him so vividly?' Peddyr asked, quite taken aback at the level of detail.

'We found him on CCTV,' she announced proudly before handing Peddyr a printed A5 copy of a colour picture.

'Digital. Very clear,' he said with a gentle smile. 'Mighty.'

'We had the date and a timeframe to work with because

he phoned to make an appointment for the fourteenth at twelve forty-five. So here he is... Arthur Bird.'

Knowing this was not the Arthur Bird he'd met at Worthington Court, Peddyr asked to see copies of the ID papers the man used to convince the registrar he was genuine. Sadly, this produced nothing new. Arthur Bird's passport and the telephone bill had been used, as predicted. Peddyr looked again at the picture of the man pretending to be Arthur Bird. 'He bears more than a passing resemblance to the photo in the passport.' Peddyr didn't say so, but he thought Dave Smith was pushing his luck pretending to be someone in his early seventies.

'He produced the required documentation and answered our usual questions without reservation,' Angela said. 'Once the formalities were complete, we went through registration for the Tell Us Once scheme.'

'Which is?'

Angela bestowed a good-natured smile on Peddyr. 'When the death is officially registered by us, we issue a unique reference number. Using that, the family member or whoever is acting on their behalf, can record the death with local and central government services, cancelling things such as state pension, DVLA, passport, national insurance and so on and so forth.'

'Very handy.' This must be a new service, Peddyr thought. He wasn't familiar with the ability to complete these important things online. 'Did Arthur Bird take the green form and the death certificate with him or leave it for relatives to collect?'

'No, he took the forms with him.'

'Any copy certificates?'

With eyebrows knitted together, the registrar consulted the file. 'Yes. He paid cash for three copy certificates.'

'Castle and Wyckes were taking on the arrangements. Is that correct?' Peddyr asked.

Angela's face took on a keen expression. 'Yes, but there was some confusion. We made a note in the file. The deceased was moved to Bright's and after that to Clouds. County Hall had an enquiry from Bright's on the seventeenth of May because no green form had arrived with them. Bright's are the new funeral service for eco-burials and all things less traditional, shall we say.'

Making a note, Peddyr thought about this. 'Bright's? Haven't dealt with them before. Any good?'

'Too soon to say one way or the other. But I expect they were none too pleased to have to refer the matter to the local authority. Very costly for a small business, dealing with a body nobody takes responsibility for.' Tapping her pen on the paperwork, Angela Gibbs sighed. 'If Gabriella Dixon is alive as you say, then this is worth following up, Mr Quirk.'

'It certainly is, Angela, and please call me Peddyr. I feel we've known each other long enough to drop the formalities.' He shot her a warm smile and rose from his seat. 'Can I keep this photo?'

'It's yours to keep. If this becomes an official police matter or needs referring to the Coroner, then we've got the original safe and sound too.' She stood and shook his hand. 'I hope, for Mrs Dixon's sake, she gets this matter cleared up. It must be most alarming to be walking around dead.'

Without losing too much time on niceties and polite farewells to the register office staff, Peddyr made his way to Bright's where he discovered an alternative world of funeral ethics but no straightforward answer to his question.

Walking toward the door he was humming *All Things*

Bright and Beautiful and looking up at the elegant sign-writing on the shop front, he recognised what had prompted this musical moment. He chuckled. The gaudy tree of life design, on the outside window, was followed up by an earthy smelling plant-filled experience once inside.

'Good morning, sir, I'm Steve. How can I be of help today?'

To Peddyr's mind, the man who appeared to be sitting alone in the jungle of greenery, wasn't your everyday funeral arranger. The neatly trimmed beard and herbal tea being supped from a jam jar, one with a handle, gave him away as a hipster. Not that Peddyr understood what being a hipster really entailed. When he last checked into the world of the trendy types, hipsters were a style of jeans. This charming fellow was dressed in cream cotton chinos, deck shoes and a polo shirt with the tree emblem embroidered over his heart. Looking for all the world like a yacht salesman at the Southampton Boat Show, there was no solemnity in how he addressed Peddyr, and no simpering either.

'Do you have the necessary paperwork with you?'

'No, no paperwork, I'm afraid. I'm making enquiries about a body.' Peddyr's explanation didn't take long, and neither did the corresponding reply.

'At last,' Steve said, pumping his arms. 'Somebody starts asking questions about Gabriella Dixon. Yes, we had her remains for a short while. It was a terrible time for us here at Bright's. What do you know about green burials, Mr Quirk?'

Leaning forward in the wicker chair to commune with bearded Steve, Peddyr picked up a glossy pamphlet, one of many left neatly displayed on a bamboo stand. 'Pretty much nothing,' he said, leafing through the first three pages. 'I'm familiar with a number of funeral service providers locally but can't say I've ever gone green.'

The illustrations in the leaflet were of wooded glades and wild coastlines. Picking out the salient remarks in the marketing blurb, it seemed that green meant no embalming, no robust coffin, no official plot, and even cremation wasn't considered green enough for these purists. They've lost the plot completely, Peddyr thought. 'Is this right?' he asked. 'No embalming?'

Steve nodded. 'We revile embalming. A total no-no.'

'What did you do when the relatives of Mrs Dixon failed to appear?' He stopped himself. 'Hang on. How did you end up with the body, anyway? I thought the family would have to request a change of funeral directors. This lady was originally in the hands of Castle and Wyckes.'

'She was,' said Steve. 'And the family requested a transfer to us. At least we thought they did.'

'Oh yes?'

'We had a call from a man calling himself Dave Smith, who said he was her brother and next of kin.'

Peddyr allowed himself a brief smile. 'Ah, the mysterious Dave Smith.'

'So, he *is* her brother?'

'I doubt it. The last I heard, he was her cousin. Still, what do I know?'

Steve looked puzzled.

'His name has come up in the course of my investigation,' Peddyr explained. 'But I've nothing to confirm his actual identity. It's a relief to know I haven't lost the trail though. What did he sound like? Young? Old?'

'Difficult to tell. He sounded upset, like they all do. Said he'd been abroad. According to Mr Smith, his sister wanted a green burial. Adamant he was. The chap blathered on about her eco-credentials and membership of Greenpeace.'

'Nothing about a religious ceremony?'

'Far from it,' Steve said emphatically. 'We phoned Castle and Wyckes and made the transfer immediately. That was on... the fifteenth of May,' he said, nodding at his laptop.

'And the paperwork was in order?'

'Everything tallied with the information we received. Personal details form, list of valuables, identity tags on the deceased are always cross-referenced and carefully checked, we signed the handover forms and booked her into our system.'

Peddyr fished for more. 'And when did Dave Smith put in an appearance?'

Steve stroked his beard. 'Mr Dave Smith told me he was driving from Scotland, that he would be collecting the green form and death certificate from the registrars and planned to be with us before closing.'

Peddyr picked up on the inconsistency straight away. 'He definitely said he was going to collect the green form from the registrars. Are you certain?'

Steve gave a deliberate nod. 'Positive. The devious knob even promised to pay the deposit as soon as he set foot through the door.'

'He never lied about that then...'

'No, I suppose not,' Steve said through gritted teeth.

'So, what happened?'

'Had any dealings with Castle and Wyckes?' As he pursed his lips, Steve's beard lifted.

'Many,' Peddyr replied. 'Can't give details, you understand.'

With a bob of his head, Steve continued. 'They're too big, too impersonal and awkward to deal with,' he said, scratching at the side of his nose. 'Don't get me wrong, they were quick enough to let us have her body, but useless with help in tracing relatives. Downright obstructive when we asked them to take her back.'

Peddyr was tickled by this. 'You didn't really ask them to take her back, did you?'

'Had to. First the cold storage compressor shorted out, then it packed up altogether.'

'I see, and you don't do embalming here, so you got someone else to do it?'

Steve baulked. 'Certainly not. We are a specialist green funeral service, Mr Quirk. It's our ethos to have as minimal an impact on the environment as possible. No chemicals, no plastics.'

'What did you do with a decomposing body on your premises? Sprinkle some pot-pourri about the place?'

Waiting for the reply, Peddyr assessed the likelihood of the business model being successful in a place like Bosworth Bishops, and concluded Bright's might last a year if they were lucky. The only people destined to use the facilities would be the group of new age eco-warriors on the outskirts of town, building hobbit houses for themselves. They eked out a living from honey and vegetables grown on the smallholding advertised as an organic farm. None of them were old enough to need Bright's services for a good number of years. 'Where did the body go next?' he asked.

It had taken Steve a while to recover from Peddyr's pot-pourri jibe, and he was still bristling when he did respond. 'If you must know, we persuaded Clouds to take her, for a financial sweetener.'

'As in...?'

'As in what it cost for extended storage, plus extra for

administration fees and to keep quiet about it. We had three bodies here at the time. It was a case of farming them out.'

The look on Steve's face was enough to make Peddyr forget himself and laugh out loud.

'Please don't let that become common knowledge, Mr Quirk. It won't be good for business if people knew.'

'You have my word.' Peddyr looked again at the glossy brochures. 'What happened to the other two bodies?'

'We buried them as planned. No delay. Collected them from Clouds on the day.'

'And how come you never collected Gabriella Dixon when your cold storage was fixed?'

An embarrassed look passed across Steve's face. 'I wish you hadn't asked me that.' Closing the lid of his laptop, he then placed both palms on top and slowly raised his eyes to meet Peddyr's. 'After we made a few enquiries about Dave Smith, we had to admit defeat. Clouds did the necessary.'

'And what would they do differently to you?'

'They don't provide a green burial, Mr Quirk. They do *everything* differently.'

With a shrug of one arm, Peddyr freed his wristwatch to check the time. 'I'm pretty certain Clouds is open until one.'

'Want me to give them a ring, let them know you're coming?'

'No, don't worry, it's on my way home. I'll wing it.'

'But what about Gabriella Dixon? You'll be recovering costs from the family, I take it?'

One hand on the door handle, Peddyr turned his head. 'Steve, I'd love to tell you something positive about this case, but at the moment I'm trying to trace the movements and whereabouts of a body and a mystery man. To be frank, I've never before been given such a run-around by a dead person.'

17

PEDDYR AND CONNIE

'It's a good job you took the car. The rain never stopped. It was cats and frogs all morning,' Connie said as she flipped an omelette onto a warm plate.

Peddyr smiled at her malapropism but chose not to correct her. He never did. 'I could have walked it and saved a few pennies. But my bloody knee is playing up something chronic.' Marvelling at her ability to produce food from whatever she found in the fridge, he tucked in to the first mouthful of cheesy fluffiness and let out a satisfied purr. 'Delicious. Just what I fancied.' Barely stopping to take a drink, Peddyr ploughed through late lunch in a matter of minutes and only then did he pick up conversation with Connie.

'Tell me,' she asked, 'Did Angela at the register office say anything interesting?'

After giving her the ins and outs of his morning's work, Peddyr summed up. 'It looks like our mystery man is using Arthur Bird as an alias, as well as the uninventive name Dave Smith. The only thing I can be clear about is his height, weight, and the colour of his hair, unless it's a wig.' He shrugged, before throwing one of his riskier terms of endearment her way. 'How did you get on with your side of things, Lao Ban Yang?'

'Hilarious, but true. I am the boss lady, and don't you forget it, Lao Gong.'

He was expecting an insult from her, one of her cheeky references to his slightly doughy midriff or thinning hair, but she surprised him and stuck to the standard informal term for husband before correcting herself and reminding him of his age and his place in the family. 'Make yourself comfortable, Ye Ye, and I'll tell you, if you can stay awake long enough after such a trying morning.'

'Oi, madam. I'd like to remind you we're not grandparents until Hannah pops one out, so until then hold your tongue, Lao Po, or would you prefer Nai Nai?'

The ease with which they shared their excitement about becoming grandparents wasn't hard to discern. With only a matter of a fortnight until their son Marshall became a father for the first time, the anticipation was building and the telephone calls to Scotland more frequent. Peddyr had overheard Connie tell Hannah how excited she was to become a Nai Nai. Personally, he couldn't quite believe either of them were heading for such a dramatic change in their lives. Being referred to as "Ye Ye" would not do his street cred any good, although it was still preferable to "Grandad".

The years seemed to have whizzed by since the children had grown up, but he had to admit, he looked all of his fifty-six years and then some. Conversely, Connie retained her youthfulness, barely seeming to age much apart from a streak of grey hair at her temples and few more laughter lines adding to the warmth of her smile.

'I don't think Hannah would thank you for describing the agony of childbirth as if she were a chicken… Pop one out. She is producing a baby, not an egg.'

'She's got childbearing hips. She'll be fine.'

'Goodness me, Peddyr, where's your sense of decorum?' Connie shook her head as she cleared away the plates. 'Now grab a tea towel and give me a hand before you slope off to your office. I've heard the excuses about your gammy knee and your wonky wrist before.'

Knowing she had beaten him, he followed her into the kitchen. 'Your wish is my command, Lao Po. While I dry, you can tell me what you know about Gabriella Dixon's life and I'll tell you what I've found out about her death. Deal?'

He was very slow as a kitchen assistant, and Connie was soon buzzing around putting cutlery, crockery and utensils back in their rightful places before Peddyr had finished drying the last item, a wooden chopping board. He reviewed what she'd said while at the sink. 'So, her sister Laura was born here, but Gabriella was uprooted from Bedford, leaving her friends behind, and expected to settle into the upper school in town. What a rotten trick at that age.'

Connie muttered her agreement and added, 'I got a bit of background from Tina at Lily Fields. She and Gabriella were at school together.'

'And how did you discover that little gem?'

'Easy-squeezy Japanesey,' Connie said with a theatrical wink, gathering up a handful of knives, forks and spoons. 'I checked Zoopla for house prices in Derwent Drive. It gives the prices for the year a house was last sold. That gave me the year the family moved in. Then I searched the school on-line archives and recognised Tina in the class of ninety-six photograph. Not hard to do, given her flaming head of hair.'

'Impressive, Lao Po.'

'Thanks.' Connie gave a smug grin. 'She remembers Gabby Brady as being very wary of making friends, sitting at the back of the class, reading during breaks rather than joining in the usual gossip about boys. More avoidant than shy, but the type of girl who didn't want to become part of a social group, preferring to keep herself to herself and study instead of getting mixed up with parties, smoking...'

'Bit of a geek then.'

'I'm not so sure,' Connie said. Having sorted the cutlery, she was standing on a stool, her head inside a kitchen cupboard as she stacked plates with precision. 'Did you catch any of the medical phone-in on BBC Valley Radio while you were out?'

'Yes, I did,' Peddyr said with slow emphasis. 'I snatched a few minutes between appointments and calls. Our Gabriella sounded like she knew what she was talking about. And so did Dr Prasad. I didn't see him at his surgery yesterday, but he came across like an all-round decent fella.'

'I thought so too,' Connie said, moving him with a nudge of her hip as she wiped down the work surface he was resting against. 'Unlike the other plonker.'

Hanging the tea towel on a radiator to dry, Peddyr nodded. 'Justin Parks. I need to find out more about him. There's jealousy in the air between the two of them.'

'I think Mr Parks is too stupid to worry about. It was the last caller I'd be more interested in.'

'Oh? I missed that bit. What's the skeet?'

'Listen to it on the radio app later. It's fascinating. After the phone in, Talbot Howkins had to field loads of texts and emails from listeners. The comments were... well, you'll find out. Now give the table a wipe over and I'll tell you what else I found out.'

Begrudgingly he did as he was ordered while Connie returned the condiments to an overhead cupboard near the stove. 'Tina gave me the name of Gabriella's best friend in the sixth form,' she said, raising her voice so her husband could hear her from beyond the kitchen doorway. 'I'm waiting for her to get back to me, but she's moved to Spain. Did you hear me, Lao Gong, or are you going deaf in your old age?'

'Hey, less of the old, if you don't mind.'

'Well, try acknowledging me when I'm telling you important things.'

'Yes, Lao Ban Yang.' As Connie poked her head around the door, he bowed with a flourish of one hand.

Once he'd completed the chores to his wife's satisfaction, Peddyr suggested they put their feet up. 'I'll make us a cup of tea. Your brains are required. Something isn't making sense. In fact, pretty much all of it isn't making sense.'

*H*e'd made it to Clouds in Dyer Street with fifteen minutes to spare, according to his watch. The opening hours so clearly displayed on the door said they were open until one pm on a Saturday, so he held them to their word.

'We're closing,' the woman inside said, a hand hovering over light switches on the back wall.

Peddyr regarded her with some amusement because he'd met no one who so precisely fulfilled the brief for the expression "mutton dressed as lamb". Stuck in a time warp, she sported a hideous beehive hair-do created from what looked like black candy floss, and on her crusty lined face, caked with foundation and powder, she wore thick kohl make-up in the style of Elizabeth Taylor's Cleopatra. An orange nylon blouse topped off a navy miniskirt entirely unsuitable for a chapel of rest.

'Good day to you,' Peddyr said with a warm smile. 'I don't think we've met before. I usually deal with Trevor Shaw; I take it he's not in on a Saturday.'

'No. He's not. It's just me.' The woman sighed as she moved closer to the counter, linking her fingers and resting her hands on the smooth surface. 'What do you want?'

'I shalln't keep you long, only I'm investigating an important matter regarding one of your recent...' With the words fading, because he couldn't think how best to describe a dead body without being disrespectful, he handed over his business card.

'Was it a burial or cremation?'

'That's just the point, Mrs...?'

'Evans, Nora Evans. What's the name?'

'Peddyr Quirk, like it says.' He directed a finger at the card he'd given her and caught sight of chipped ruby-red nail varnish. This finally convinced him she must be a clapped-out call-girl doing a few hours of legitimate work as cover for the seedier side of her life.

'Not you. The deceased,' she said, with a husky snarl.

Peddyr judged her graveside manner to be appalling and pitied any grieving family who had need of her sympathy. 'Gabriella Dixon. It would have been back in May, beginning of June,' he said.

'I'll have to look it up. I only work Saturdays.'

Congratulating himself on the accuracy of his observations about her employment status, Peddyr said, 'Then you won't mind staying on to help resolve matters. It'll save me

119

popping back in to see your boss on Monday.' Bright enough to catch the inference about working the hours she was being paid for, Nora confined herself to an indignant pout of protest while she pulled a hefty leather-bound diary from beneath the countertop. She let it fall open with a slap.

'I can't find it.'

'She was in your mortuary. Brought here by arrangement with Bright's.'

Face-plaster cracked when Nora Evans put together the details and recalled the name. 'I know her now. We called her Dead Loss Flossy. Unclaimed baggage, you see. Those plonkers at Bright's couldn't look after a cadaver properly, anyway. Their coffins aren't designed to seal like proper ones and they're only in business to rip off vegetarians.'

'Is that so?' Mildly bemused by her turn of phrase and outstanding customer service, Peddyr allowed Nora to keep up the stream of complaints and irritations caused by the dead Gabriella Dixon.

'You don't understand what a rumpus that body created.' Nora folded her arms, causing her blouse to gape, exposing the crinkly elephant skin of her chest. 'It sat here for a week before some bloke arrived with the green form and paid a deposit. There was a letter on file to say the husband refused to accept responsibility for funeral expenses because they were in the middle of a divorce.'

'What was the name of this fella, was it Dave Smith?' The look he received from Nora was one of disdain.

'Are you trying to be funny? If you give me a minute, I'll check our records.' Her unmanicured fingers tapped information onto a keyboard. When she read the screen, her wrinkles headed south as her face fell. 'Apologies. It was a Mr David Smith. He was acting for the family. We have consent signed by a Dr Philip Dixon, nearest relative, giving him permission to do so. Mr Smith brought in the correct documentation including the Form 1 for cremation.' With another scroll of the mouse, she flashed her mascara-caked lashes and looked up from the screen. 'All present and correct. I took a grand as deposit, paid by cash, which is unheard of. You'll have to speak to your pal Trevor Shaw about anything else, he'll be back in on Monday wearing his usual hangover.'

18

THE MAGIC 8-BALL

*J*ourneying to work on public transport was an unpleasant revelation. Being a Monday morning commuter again was bad enough, but having to catch a bus to the railway station was quite another matter. There was no choice. A taxi to Crewsthorpe and back every day would have been too expensive. Having paid out for a cab ride to BBC Valley Radio on Saturday, I knew exactly how much it would round up to after five days, and it wouldn't be feasible with what little cash remained at my disposal.

Three hundred and fifty-six pounds and ninepence was the grand sum of my cash assets, augmented by an unexpected find in an old overcoat of two pounds thirty-five pence. Yippee and hooray for minor miracles.

There wasn't much money to live on, and buying a return train ticket to Crewsthorpe that morning made a dent in the dwindling coffers which couldn't be repeated. I stared at the ticket. Twenty-one pounds seventy for a return journey each day was beyond my current means. In future I would have to catch the much slower bus to work and back, or face starvation.

The entire trip on Monday was awful. When the great unwashed sat next to me on the bus I couldn't believe my rotten luck. And when I finally made it to the station, the train was so tightly packed that at one stage my nose ended up rammed into a man's armpit. The smelly oik didn't even have the good grace to apologise for treading on my toes. How I longed to be in my car listening to the radio in a protective, fragrant air-conditioned cocoon.

Adding insult to injury, things didn't improve when I finally made it into the office.

'Ingrid wants to see you and Justin in her office as soon as he gets here.'

'And good morning to you too,' I said smoothly. The team administrator was an insensitive agency temp by the name of Olga. With eyes like ice and a personality to match, she consistently rubbed me up the wrong way. 'Yes, thanks, I had a very fruitful time away from work, moving house, dealing with my mother's estate. Very refreshing.' My satire was lost on Olga who returned to opening the post. I left her and her sour face to it.

Caffeine was a top priority, so after hanging my bag and jacket from the back of an office chair, I headed for the kitchenette. 'No milk. Great.'

'Olga says, because she's a vegan, she won't supply dairy products for the team and it's not in her job description.'

'Hello, Bridget, didn't see you creep in behind me.' I was standing at the fridge, willing a bottle of milk to appear as if by magic. An out-of-date yoghurt, some dry-looking cheddar cheese, a Tupperware box with the sad remnants of someone's forgotten lunch, and a can of Pepsi, were the only items on the shelves. Closing the door, I smiled, genuinely pleased to see Bridget; she was always so good-natured.

'You look knackered, Gabby. What happened?'

'Moving house, that's what happened, Bridge. I'm sick to death of packing and unpacking and too much of a control freak to cope with the chaos I'm living in now.' I hedged around the actual reasons for looking so ashen. Instead, I filled the kettle and prepared to drink black coffee. 'To cap it all, I did the radio phone-in on Saturday and Justin rocked up. He told the producer I was unavailable.'

'I heard about that.' Holding her hands up she said, 'Not anything to do with me, I hasten to add. By the way, where's your lovely new car? It's not in the car park.'

'Out of action,' I said, searching the one and only kitchen unit for my secret stash of decent ground coffee. 'It's a long story. And where the hell is my—?'

'Gabby?' Ingrid, the department's senior manager, was calling to me, and if I say she sounded a tad irked it would be a massive understatement. 'Come through to my office straight away.'

Bridget made an oh-dear-you're-in-for-it face and shuffled round me to store a snack in the fridge. 'See you later. Lunchtime? Perhaps a quick stroll to the corner shop to pick up some milk. If Rosa Klebb can't be arsed to, we'll get our own. And lots of meat to piss her off.'

Replying to the irreverent Bridget with a conspiratorial thumbs up as I left, I then knocked and entered Ingrid's rather pokey office. It was the best the NHS could offer. Space was at a premium and the rest of the team were having to hot desk, which I found intolerable. Preferring my own familiar space, a sanctuary from some of the stress, it was one of the many reasons I'd decided to leave.

'What the hell were you and Justin playing at on Saturday morning?'

Taken off balance at the sharp tone, I faltered in the doorway before replying. 'Has everyone in the office taken a vow not to say good morning to each other since I've been away? Bridget's the only one with a smile on her face this morning.'

Ingrid Jacobs was heading for retirement and not a day too soon in my view. She'd lost her enthusiasm for the job long ago. Going through the motions, she was burnt out and resentful of the hours spent slogging herself to a standstill because every system was designed to make life difficult. Pouring herself coffee from a flask, she didn't offer me one. 'Sit. Is Justin here yet?'

With a flash of my eyes to the clock on the wall above Ingrid's head, I was happy to confirm my colleague's late arrival. 'I haven't heard his car pull up. I'm sure we would have noticed.' Taking advantage of an audience with Ingrid to make my case before Justin put in an appearance, I got in a quick jibe at his expense. 'Poor bloke, he should have thought through what he was saying. Radio audiences can be unforgiving, and he made himself sound... supercilious, if I'm being honest.'

'And you had to make it worse by belittling him, did you?' Ingrid bridled. 'Don't you think it would have been a better idea to support your replacement rather than make him look stupid, and with it the whole of our service?'

'What?' I couldn't believe Ingrid was taking Justin's side. 'He practically accused a mother of not protecting her child from sexual abuse. He failed to listen properly to the questions, and it serves him right if he came across like a blithering berk, because he behaved like one.' With nothing to lose, I thought honesty would be the best policy.

Ingrid stood to retrieve a document from a small printer that lived on top of a filing cabinet behind her desk. 'I can't accept what you say, Gabriella. Justin is a fine asset to the team and, as you are leaving us shortly, I'd thank you to remember that.' She tapped the screen of her desktop computer as she sat down again. 'You may want to make amends with him. HR emailed me; no patient contact for you until your registration and police checks via DBS are reinstated. He'll be running your clinics until then.'

In disbelief, I stared silently back at Ingrid.

'Actually, he may as well take them on permanently,' she said, dismissive in her manner. 'There's no reason not to.'

There wasn't much chance of me holding back my outrage after her last comment. With a matter of weeks to go before starting a fresh job, the pent-up frustrations of perpetually being told how to work and what to do came spilling out. 'I can think of several excellent reasons why Justin Parks shouldn't take my clients on for the next six weeks. Firstly, I have several families tying up endings to their therapy sessions. Secondly, changing therapists at this stage without a proper dovetailed handover would be detrimental, and thirdly, Justin has so far declined to consider carrying out any home assessments which are a vital part of gathering sound collateral information. Fourthly, Justin does not understand community work, he makes everyone see him in a safe clinic environment and he talks to the parents instead of the child. Need I say more?'

'No, you need not,' Ingrid replied. The steely look was not open to misinterpretation. 'I'll hear no more of this jealousy. Enough.' There was a whack as she slapped the desk. It made me flinch, but ultimately triggered more unfettered annoyance.

'Jealousy? I could never be jealous of a jumped-up overinflated wanker like Justin.' The rumbling noise of a finely tuned engine stopped my train of thought. 'He even drives a dick-head's car,' I said, throwing a thumb toward the open window and the noisy car engine. 'And you want my clients to have *him* as a replacement?'

Ingrid glowered back at me, shaking her head in disapproval at the unsavoury outburst. I don't know why, but the resentment dissipated like a retreating tidal wave. Beaten, I glanced to the floor, stood up from my chair and blew out through dry lips. 'I give up. Do what you like. I'll be in my office. The one I share with four other people, even though there are only three chairs and three docking stations for a laptop. I'll start packing my things, and Justin can tell me what he'd like me to cover for him. How about that?'

'I suggest you plan to work from home if you feel you can't work together,' Ingrid said flatly.

Normally this offer would have been a Godsend. 'I would if I could, but as I've just moved house, I have no broadband, no WIFI, no agreed access from IT for my new address, and no bloody office space to work from. So, I guess you must put up with my presence.'

Closing the door behind me, I could feel the sting of angry tears, and battled to keep them at bay. The few yards to my shared office didn't give me long enough to compose myself, requiring a pause at the door where, in a case of bad timing, Olga collared me.

'You have a parcel. It came just now.' She thrust a square box wrapped in plain brown paper at my chest.

Everyone else may have lost their manners, but for me it was automatic to say, 'Thanks,' while giving 007's arch enemy a reluctant smile. It wasn't mirrored. There were no dagger blades shooting out from the pointed ends of her shoes, but there might as well have been.

'What have you got there?' Bridget asked. 'Leaving present from Ingrid?'

That brought my humour back. 'If it was... it'd be a bomb... I don't think I'm flavour of the month with her.'

'Really? I thought you'd get a pat on the back for saving Justin's neck on the radio.'

'You must be joking,' I said, eyes widening. 'Apparently what I said on air was underhand and uncalled for. She's giving him my caseload and I have to lump it.' Pulling at the Sellotape, keen to see what the parcel contained, I wondered if it would be a welcome addition to my new home; perhaps a gift from a grateful family. Accepting the scissors passed to me from Bridget, I snipped the ends free and unravelled the brown paper to reveal purple and pink packaging containing a black ball.

'Is that a Magic 8-Ball?' Bridget asked with an amused twitch of her lips. 'Who on earth sent you that?'

'I haven't seen one of these for years,' I said, turning the box in my hands. 'Not since I was...'

'Ask it something,' Bridget said.

In the mood for a full rebellion, and to amuse ourselves while putting off the demands of endless work emails, we freed the ball and placed it on the desk where I'd staked a claim that day.

'Don't let Olga see the plastic packaging, we'll never hear the end of it.'

'My sister is exactly the bloody same,' I said, throwing the wastepaper and plastic into the bin under another table. 'Right then, what shall we ask it?'

'Who sent the ball?'

'No, it can't answer that. How about... is the person who sent me this ball a close friend?' Shaking the shiny black globe, I shared an impish grin with Bridget. I then turned the ball so the answer would appear in the circular window. A small glowing triangle floated upwards.

'"Outlook not so good",' we read out in unison.

'Is the person an enemy then?' Bridget asked, taking the ball, rolling it around in her palms, then waiting for the oracle's reply. 'Oh Lordy, this says "It is certain".' During this comment, we heard a cursory knock and Justin's voice as he entered Ingrid's office. His haughty tones drifted through the doorway as he blithely besmirched my character to Ingrid.

'The ice queen will give me a meaningless apology, will she?' he said loud enough for me and Bridget to hear. 'No one likes her. She puts on that act, brings in food for us all to share and be grateful to her—' The door closed, cutting off the rest of the assassination.

Bridget glanced at me and then at the corridor. 'You don't think...?'

'Don't be daft. He's an enemy, sure enough, but why would he send me a Magic 8-Ball? I must have missed a little card or something.' I trotted over to the bin, pulled out the brown paper so carelessly tossed aside minutes before, and inspected it. There was a note tucked away which I looked at quickly, then rumpled up the paper in my hand. 'Nothing, a delivery note.' Throwing the paper back in the bin, the impact of what I'd read sucked the air from my lungs.

'Jesus, Gabby. You look like you're about to faint.'

Which was precisely how I felt. 'Lack of coffee, probably. I do feel lightheaded. Could you get me some water please, Bridge? I don't feel right.' That was an understatement, and the request for water was the only way I could think of to keep Bridget busy while I retrieved the note from the bin a second time to read the words again.

'It's not a receipt, or a delivery note, Gabby. What does it say?' With my mind so preoccupied, I had stood there longer than I realised and hadn't heard Bridget return. She held her hand out. 'Show me.'

The creased slither of paper vibrated in my fingers as I passed it over. She lowered her head to study the note closely. 'I don't know about you, but I think it has to be from weird John, the one from the phone-in. "What will fate decide, Gabriella?" That's plain wacko.'

'Oh, yes, that would explain it,' I said, my tongue sticking to the roof of my mouth. 'It could be John. Apart from the fact that he wouldn't know where I work. Not this office, at any rate. He could find out the address of Trust HQ, but…' Making random statements to calm my own fears didn't work, and I couldn't resist checking the window to see who else was in the car park or lurking in the bushes. When I turned back again Bridget was giving me a quizzical look.

'Why, who did you think it was from?'

'I'm not really sure.'

'You didn't think it was John then?'

'Yes, I did, but then I thought maybe it was Justin after all. He was there for the weird John thing.'

'Yes, it's possible.'

'Or Laura.'

'Your sister Laura?'

'We had a bust up. So, it might be her husband Curtis. He's a vengeful shit, it could easily be him.'

I picked up the 8-Ball again. 'A list of possible suspects.' In my head I was wondering which one of them despised me enough to declare me dead. And which one was calling themselves John?

'Is someone out to get me?' I asked the ball.

"It is decidedly so," the ball replied.

19

ABSENT AGAIN

A train pulled into the station, and I became aware of standing on the platform, a briefcase in one hand, a bottle of water in the other. People pushed past me to get on the train, but I couldn't move. Why was I at the station in Crewsthorpe? Why wasn't I at work where I'd been a moment ago?

With my heart rate escalating to dangerous levels, I forced heavy legs to move me towards a metal bench seat being vacated by a sweaty middle-aged man in cargo shorts and a Grateful Dead tee-shirt. Dropping the water bottle into my lap, I clamped clammy fingers to the flaking paint on the edge of the seat. I rocked gently. The woman next to me shuffled to her right, widening the gap between us.

'The train now standing at platform two is the sixteen thirty-five to Marsworth, calling at Hollberry, Lensham, Swandale and Bosworth Bishops.'

According to the announcement over the speakers on the platform, it was gone half past four in the afternoon. 'That can't possibly be right,' I muttered, shakily checking my phone for confirmation. But it was correct, and it scared me. I massaged both temples and breathed slowly and steadily, trying to recall how I'd got through the day knowing nothing about it. My last memory was of being with Bridget, messing about with a Magic 8-Ball.

'Are you all right, love?' the woman on the bench asked, picking up a voluminous shoulder bag.

'Not really, no,' I replied, barely looking in her direction. 'But I'll live.' With trembling hands, I sent a text to Stella in Spain asking her to call urgently, then took a few sips of water as suggested by my good Samaritan who stayed with me for a few seconds longer before dashing off to catch her train home.

I rubbed hard at my forehead, trying to free myself from the tunnel vision which compounded the sensation of falling. Too scared to move, I remained resolutely where I was; a lone figure on an uncomfortable bench, waiting for Stella to phone, needing desperately to hear a familiar voice, speak to a friend, one who I didn't have to explain much to. There was no reason to stay on the station platform, other than not trusting myself to get on a train.

20

PICK UP A PEBBLE

*I*n a bid to look like any other frustrated commuter, I thumbed through my mobile phone searching for clues about the missing parts of my day. Within seconds I found a series of messages between me and Laura apologising to each other for the angry words several days earlier. This made my absence from the planet so much worse. *When the hell did I write that load of sickly sweet hog wash?*

More frustrating was the discovery that I'd agreed to attend a peace-making dinner at Revival Farm on Wednesday evening at seven-thirty. It wasn't much to look forward to after a hard day in the office. By the time I'd made it home from work and changed, I would be cutting it fine to catch a bus and get to Laura's in time, and when I did, dinner would be a disappointment for my stomach. With the likes of vegetarian goulash, or nasturtium salad to look forward to, I wasn't overly thrilled at the prospect. And then there was Curtis. He'd put in an appearance for the sake of it, simply to wind me up because he knew he could. I looked again at the messages. 'Huh, she must be feeling guilty,' I said. I was being offered a lift there and back, so that was my excuse out of the window. Now I'd have to go, like it or not.

The phone rang in my hand, startling me. It wasn't Stella; it was Bridget, and I stalled not knowing what to say and what not to say.

'Hi, Gabby.' The tone was wary. 'I know you're upset, but I wanted to make sure you're okay. You left in such a hurry I didn't have time to ask if you want me to drop your things off this evening, and if you do, then I need your new address.'

With my mind scrabbling around trying to slot together pieces of a riddle, the tannoy system sparked into life again to inform passengers of a delay. It gave me a much-needed reprieve.

'Gabby? Are you at the station?'

'Yes, I'm on my way home. I'm fine.' It was a pathetic answer.

'Of course you're not fine. What happened was a disgrace, and I've already made my views known to Ingrid and to Justin. It was disgusting the way they ganged up on you. Anyway, why have you taken so long to get to the station?'

There was no answer to that one. I had no idea what time I'd left the office. Indeed, what happened and where I'd been before finding myself on the platform was a complete blank, but from what Bridget said, it sounded very much as if I'd been sent home early with suspension an actual possibility. This was earth shattering, and a painful lump rose in my throat.

'Gabby, do you want me to come and get you?'

Being professionally disgraced was devastating, to such

an extent that a huge part of me wanted Bridget to collect me and drive me home. But how was I supposed to explain myself without sounding like I'd become totally unhinged? – which I had.

'It's a lovely offer, Bridge, but I need to be on my own for a while. I'll text you my address. Really kind of you. I'll have a shower, crack a bottle of wine and see you later if that's all right with you.' Bridget didn't sound satisfied by my pitiful assurances, but she relented and ended the call, promising to see me well before eight o'clock that evening.

Almost as soon as the call from Bridget ended, the phone pinged. Checking the screen, I saw a message from Andy, Talbot's producer at BBC Valley Radio.

'"Talbot says, thanks for coming in today, he hopes you reconsider his offer and says to write this in your tatty little notepad. I checked what you asked him, and I can 100% confirm John's call had number withheld. He must have dialled 141. Cheers. Randy Andy".'

This was mind-boggling; not only had I apparently left work early, having perhaps been sacked, I'd also made up with Laura and walked to the station without being aware of these things. Astonishingly, I'd also visited the BBC studios and had a conversation with Talbot. With hands too pumped full of adrenalin to function effectively, I struggled to unfasten my briefcase and wade through the contents to find my notepad. Almost every page was dog-eared and doodled upon, except the last one I turned to. The writing there was in my usual neat hand, but, considering the subject matter, a little too controlled. 'What the hell have I done?'

Reading the bullet points on the page, I squirmed. 'One. Justin walked out without speaking to me. Oh, did he now?' I mumbled. 'Two. Texts from listeners after John's call. Had he committed a crime, question mark. Either sex offence or murder. Three. Police called the studio. Not about John, but to confirm my identity.' At this last item I swore and looked up to check who was around. My agitation and talking to myself seemed to have deterred anyone else from sitting beside me on the grubby bench. The platform was mostly thronging with tired and hot workers jostling for position. They paid me scant attention.

It was plain from the words on the page of my notebook, Talbot was armed with the knowledge about my reported death and that the police were making overtures. I could well imagine what Talbot's offer was. He would be desperate for the story. 'Shit,' I said, as the phone buzzed into life once more.

'Stella? Scooby? Thank God. I'm in a proper pickle.' I gulped down the storm of emotion. 'I've been time travelling.' It had been years, decades, since I'd even mentioned the term. It was our secret; mine and Stella's.

Her voice brought me immense comfort that day on the station platform.

'I expect it's the stress of the move,' she said. 'Have you got your pebble with you?' My wonderful friend hadn't fallen into the trap of asking why my memory was playing tricks or why it was happening again after all this time. She instinctively seemed to know better.

I spotted a raised flowerbed a few yards away. 'No, but I can get one.' Stuffing the notepad inside the briefcase again, I gathered it up and raced to the flower border. Wedging the case between my knees to free up a hand, I scratched about to find what I was looking for, not caring what onlookers might make of my incongruous behaviour.

Holding the rounded stone was strikingly reassuring. Feeling the weight of it in my palm, I smoothed the rounded contours with my thumb. 'Stella? Are you still there?'

'Yes, I'm right here. Do you need me to come?'

'What? No, don't be silly. It's a temporary blip. You're right. Stress with the move, the mix-up at the bank, being dead. Nothing I can't handle.' Plunging a hand into my pocket, I kept a tight grip on the pebble. 'Besides, it's only been a matter of weeks since you left. Carlos would be furious if you abandoned him now.' More than anything I wanted her to catch the next flight back to the UK, but how could I be so selfish? I could manage as long as she kept talking me through.

'Are you any closer to finding out who's responsible for registering you as dead?' she asked.

In my anxious state, I couldn't recall how far I'd updated her on recent events. 'No, not really, but my solicitor, not the divorce one, the other one with the massive ears, has applied to the court for a hearing to have my death registration overturned, but the date could be months away.'

'I know that, I meant how's your personal detective getting on? The last time we spoke, the conversation was taken up with Laura.'

So it was. I remembered the discussion had been lengthy, and I'd been guzzling gin and tonic to take the edge off my fury at Laura's bitterness and envy. I was grateful for the prompt and tried to answer Stella's question as best I could. 'Pretty good. He's turning out to be my best hope. He's on the trail of the body. She's called Josephine Dank. Great name, isn't it? I keep wondering what she was like and whether she looked like me.'

'What a shame they cremated her. Has he worked out how it was done? Has he spoken to Hugh Ingles at Castle and Wyckes?'

'I've no idea. But he's getting closer to finding the man responsible, and he's coming over to meet me later this evening.' I paused. 'The thing is... he wants to get a better idea of my personal history, relationships, work, family, that sort of thing. What do I tell him?'

'Tell him what you can. Tell him the truth.'

'But if I don't know half of it, then how do I explain without him thinking I've got something to hide?'

'Which one of us is the therapist? Gabby just tell him. Look how much damage you did by not being honest with Phil. Your detective man needs all the help he can get, and you need to get this resolved before you lose everything you've worked for. By the way, have you made it up with Laura?'

Another station announcement interrupted our conversation.

'Stella, I'm getting on the next train, so if I lose signal when I go through the tunnel, don't panic. I feel much better having spoken to you, and I have the pebble in my pocket.'

It was true, I really felt more grounded since talking with my best friend, tinged with sadness though it was. Exhausted, I rested my head against the cool glass of the train window and allowed the scenery to whoosh by in a blur, holding on to the pebble to keep me in the here and now. Whatever anyone said about FaceTime, Skype and telephone calls, I still missed Stella's physical presence so badly it hurt like an ache. Phone calls weren't the same as having a hug, or laughing until we nearly wet ourselves, then laughing some more about the delights of bladder weakness. But holding that pebble as the train trundled me back to Bosworth Bishops provided much needed comfort.

No other friend came close to Stella, apart from Phil,

who'd been a delightful companion and a lover, a husband and a champion of my cause to reduce the number of teenage suicides. Why I never admitted to not wanting his children, I couldn't say. I didn't want to hurt his feelings, I suppose. But whatever the reason, I'd lied and kept up the pretence for years.

Sitting on the train back to Bosworth Bishops, I came to the same unerring conclusion that haunted me night after night since discovering my death. Someone out there knew all about me and was exacting their revenge. For what?

21

AN UNPLEASANT DISCOVERY

*S*niffing at the cotton sleeve of my blouse, I alighted from the oppressive atmosphere of the number sixteen bus. I was still trying to fathom how some people lacked the decency to check their personal hygiene levels before setting out.

I required a hot shower to restore me and wash away the reek of fellow passengers and the sweat of my own escalating fears. So, despite the heat, I marched the last few hundred yards back to number six Derwent Drive. My only aim at that moment was to get clean and make sense of this absurd day before Bridget arrived.

The grimy air seemed to stick to me as another passing vehicle picked up dust and spewed out smoky exhaust fumes, and it heartened me to see the bend in the road ahead with the ramp to the driveway where my Nissan once sat. The thought of its loss added to the ever-increasing pile of woes in my weary head.

To my right I spotted movement and a flash of turquoise. Kenny was back at the murder house. His car was on the drive and he was shuffling items wrapped in black plastic bin liners onto the back seat. With anxiety levels more manageable since talking to Stella, curiosity got the better of me, and rather than pretending I hadn't seen him, this was my chance to confront him. If he had anything to do with my death, then I wanted to know.

'Hello there, Kenny, isn't it?' Making him jump resulted in a squeal followed by a howl of pain as his head hit the internal roof of the car. 'Oh, I'm so sorry, I didn't mean to—'

'What the hell are you doing creeping up on people like that?' Kenny's voice was low pitched. Not what I had imagined, given what he was wearing. Shamefully I had him pegged as camp and effeminate, based on his attire and the way he scurried about. Today, the black satin pyjama trousers were on display, complemented by a shimmering sea-green blouse which tied at the neck with a lavish floppy bow. On his feet he sported a pair of purple coloured flip flops. 'What do you want?' he challenged.

A justifiable question given my approach, but as I'd been hasty in deciding to speak to him, I wasn't clear in my mind how to broach the subject. Assurances that he wasn't John, the mystery caller, would do as a start. As would affirmation of his status as eccentric rather than psychopathic. 'I thought you might like to know you're being watched,' I offered, plucking a fact out of thin air as a conversation starter to get on his good side.

'By whom?' Kenny asked, rubbing at the crown of his skull, before looking up and down the road at the dozen or so cars parked against the kerb. 'Who is watching me?' His bristled jowls quivered.

'A man in a BMW, he's been several times in the last week and he takes photographs of the house,' I replied, taking a sly look at the CSI scene through the glass of

Kenny's front window. The only thing missing was some blue and white tape with the word "police" emblazoned in a repeating pattern. Apart from that it was all there, right down to the ominous-looking stain on the vinyl flooring. With some trepidation, I noted that the shelving inside the room was emptier. Three of the black plastic covered packages were now in residence on the back seat of Kenny's car. 'Perhaps he wants to know what you've been storing,' I ventured.

Much to my surprise, Kenny laughed. 'These?' he asked, opening his hands to the car seat.

'And those,' I said, indicating his row of covered motorbikes.

Resting his back against the car, Kenny looked me up and down. 'And this is why you've decided to talk to me, is it, ducky? My new neighbour wants to know what this is about.' Spreading his arms wide, he swung left and right.

'Yes, please. If you don't mind.'

Folding his arms once more, Kenny gave an exaggerated sigh. 'All these years and you're the only person willing to come over and have a chat. I wonder what happened to "good evening, how are you today?" or perhaps "lovely weather for the time of year". No, sadly these days the world is full of paranoid suspicions. "What's he hiding?" "Why doesn't he live in the bungalow?" "Why all the bikes?".'

Having given a valid and damning opinion on the state of social etiquette, Kenny rubbed at one eye with a fist. His hands were tiny for a man of his stature, I noticed, and he bit his nails to the quick.

'Well, you must admit, keeping that many motorcycles under cover isn't standard practice for Derwent Drive. And the lounge could do with some curtains.' I tried a gentle smile, which seemed to have the desired effect.

His face melted and reciprocated my smile. 'It could… but then the Nosey Parkers would suspect I had something else to hide. Wouldn't they?'

I didn't contest the statement. 'What are they?' I asked, aiming a hand towards the window and beyond it to the Dexion shelving where the body parts were stacked.

'Bolts of cloth.'

'Bolts of cloth?' I repeated, a little too loudly. "Body parts" wasn't what I was expecting to hear, but neither was this. 'What on Earth for?'

'I collect them.'

'No shit? How many do you have in your collection?' Kenny stared deeply into my eyes and I let him, assuming he was checking for levels of mockery. But when he found me to be genuinely interested in his story, he seemed to soften. 'I'm Gabby. We have seen each other before. My parents used to live across the road at number six. You probably know my younger sister Laura. She lived here a lot longer than me.'

At this Kenny snorted. 'Oh, I know her all right, the jumped-up madam who thinks, now she's a saviour of the planet, I'll forget her spitefulness and her nasty comments to her friends. It's a disgrace what the police did.'

I took a step back, not knowing precisely what Kenny was referring to, although it didn't take a degree in psychology to take a good guess. 'I'm sorry to hear that.'

'Are you?' he sneered. 'They gave her and her gaggle of vile friends a ticking off. That's all the police could be bothered to do in response to months and years of harassment by your darling sister and your snotty parents. Did the police give two hoots about me? Did they fuck.' There was no apology for the swearing.

'Sorry, I didn't know. I haven't lived here for decades,' I

said, suddenly wanting to distance myself from my family. 'Left when I had the chance and never came back.'

Much to my short-lived relief, Kenny awarded me with an understanding wrinkle of his nose. 'I know, ducky. I've seen you come and go.' He nodded at my overgrown front garden. 'Not your fault your sister has a vicious tongue... you were always more subtle in your disapproval of me,' he said as he angled his head like an inquisitive crow. 'But it doesn't matter, I know who you are, anyway. Dr Gabriella Dixon from the radio show. I listened in on Saturday. I never miss one. What a shame you couldn't bring yourself to speak to me nicely before now, we could have made better acquaintance.'

The residual heat of the day bounced up from the tarmac and unease crept its way up my arms in the form of goosebumps. It was plain that, over the years, Kenny *had* noticed how I evaded him. Ever since he'd moved into the neighbourhood, he'd been the sinister man to avoid, the oddball, the eccentric. Not that it had bothered me before now, because I'd only seen him on the rare occasion when his visits to number seven coincided with me dropping by to see one or both of my parents. He wasn't a frequent visitor, and neither was I.

'You're a hotshot shrink these days,' Kenny said, turning to pat one of the plastic packages on the back seat of his car. Reassured by its presence, he faced me again. 'You'll want to know why I buy yards and yards of material then. Most of it's satin, some brocade, a lot of Indian silks.'

I couldn't help noticing how he stroked his chest and fiddled with the floppy bow at his neck while he described the feel of the fabrics. Prompted by this observation, the timbre of his voice, his faraway look, his need to share and shock, came a nagging thought Kenny might be weird John, the mystery caller from Saturday's phone-in. And even though I was desperate for a shower and time was running short, I held my ground, determined to find out if he was. Had he called the show before? It would make sense; he fitted the profile.

'The feel is the most important thing, then the colour,' he was saying. 'I require smoothness next to my skin.' Lowering his hands, he somewhat enthusiastically stroked his thighs and, without intending to, I stared momentarily at his crotch. Horrified, I realised his unfettered genitals were being gyrated beneath the satin material. Each time Kenny moved, so did his unrestricted manhood and friends. It was too much for me. I changed the direction of my gaze faster than I changed the subject.

'And the motorbikes?'

'Same problem. I have to buy Hondas. They're all Hondas, every single one of them. I have more in a lock-up garage and I never ride one of them. Not one.'

'So, you hoard.' It was ingrained in me to delve, to assess, to find out about other people's lives in order to make sense of their actions. Often, I did it without thinking, but on this occasion it was part of a fact-finding mission to explain my predicament. If Kenny made it his business to know what went on, then he would know Laura and I had inherited the house. And, as it wasn't on the market, it wouldn't be a gigantic leap to predict that one of us would live here.

'I used to hoard, but I'm gradually getting on top of things now,' he replied. 'When my partner died, I couldn't deal with any of it.'

'And when was that?'

'He died three years ago. I moved in with him in 2001. We lived in Kent, so I kept this place on for storage.' He looked wistfully at the front door. 'I never knew I was gay until we met. Would you believe it, ducky?'

I didn't believe it. Not about the discovery of homosexuality at such a late stage. 'And you're moving out. Selling up?' I asked.

Giving an evil grin, Kenny laughed so loudly I jerked backwards with the force of it, barely having time to remind myself not to look at his undulating satin trousers. 'What?' he boomed, 'And give my darling neighbours the satisfaction of seeing this place restored to something resembling suburban tranquillity. No such luck for you lot, ducky. As soon as I've cleared the rooms in the house, I'm moving back in. I'll pop round for a cup of sugar…'

With that appalling possibility in the offing, and without lying, I made my excuses. 'Which reminds me,' I said, pivoting and stepping onto the pavement. 'I have a friend arriving shortly and I must get cleaned up. So goodbye.'

'Goodbye for now, Dr Gabriella Dixon.' I was halfway across the road when he spoke to me again. 'Out of interest, shower or bath?'

'Pardon?' There was no need to wait for an answer, as I faced him from the other side of the street it was written large on Kenny's lascivious face and in the way he was rubbing his hands in circular movements over his body. Laura had been right; he was a pervert and the disgusting willy-waving creature would soon be permanently living across the road; a terrifying thought by anyone's standards.

22

WHAT NOW?

_T_hankfully, it was a little before seven thirty when Bridget rang the front doorbell, well before Peddyr Quirk was due to arrive. In the meantime, I'd convinced myself that Kenny, the perv across the road, was the burglar who'd broken in and taken my laptop. He was the man ruining my life because me and my family had ruined his. In our prejudiced and vindictive way, we had forced him out of his home, and therefore it was reasonable to assume he was doing the same to me. But how was I going to prove it was him?

I couldn't afford any fancy alarms or cameras to protect myself from his intrusions, but there were items of use in the shed; perhaps old hasp and staple fixings or a sliding bolt I could use inside the front and back door to make them safer. Frightened to admit how easy it had been for Kenny to stroll in and take what he liked, I vowed to be more security conscious. Kenny made my flesh crawl and unsettled me so much I'd closed the vertical blinds over the opaque bathroom window and even locked the door, to feel safer. With his performance earlier, Kenny achieved the top spot on my list of suspects, Phil was in second place, and Justin Parks held third.

While I was in the bathroom, I made an unscientific inventory of stores, discovering to my consternation that stocks of toilet rolls were low, as were tampons. There was probably enough shampoo to last a week, and with a little ingenuity I could make the liquid hand soap last much longer than expected by diluting it. Deliberately, I'd run such items down to the minimum to make packing and moving easier, a decision I would come to regret.

*W*restling once again with the bothersome front door, I let Bridget in, apologising for the state of the house. The folds of the maxi skirt I wore hid shaking legs and enabled me surreptitiously to hold on to the pebble in one pocket. It would be a tough job having a conversation with Bridget about events at work that day.

'No need to apologise,' Bridget said, handing over a cardboard box not filled to overflowing with personal effects. The NHS obsession with hot-desking put paid to the days when we would personalise our utilitarian work domains with novelty pencil sharpeners, beanbag toys, family photographs and humorous calendars. 'I don't know how you've unpacked so much in the time. Anyway, here's the stuff from your locker.'

'Oh, I gave you my key.' It was a good guess on my part and a correct one. 'Thanks, Bridget.' All the benefits of a scrub in the shower evaporated as I again grappled with the conundrum of what I'd done at work without being conscious of my actions. It took considerable concentration to formulate questions which wouldn't arouse suspicion. 'I suppose I got what I deserved,' I said, lifting a typed letter from the top of the box. Opening it gave me an opportunity to construct the basics of the missing hours. The letter inside the envelope was standard fare for a suspension on full pay while management investigated the complaint against me.

'What have they done you for?'

'Professional misconduct of a nature likely to reflect poorly on the NHS Trust for which I work,' I replied, barely able to comprehend the lines on the page. 'Otherwise known as insubordination in the ranks.' I looked at Bridget who remained stiffly in the doorway, trying to avoid direct eye contact. 'Come in,' I said. 'I need you to remind me of exactly what happened while I write it down. The-powers-that-be will demand a report, and I was so cross I can't even remember what I said.' Amazed at my inventiveness, I led Bridget into the lounge and offered her a drink.

'Just a glass of water, Gabby. I can't stay long. It's my turn to pick up the kids from drama class. Bedsides, theoretically I'm not supposed to fraternise with you while you're suspended, but bollocks to that, eh? You're leaving anyway, so what does it matter?' Celebrating her rebelliousness, Bridget gave a short-lived fist pump as she laughed nervously.

'What's brought this on?' Having worked with her for several years, I wasn't used to my colleague blatantly breaking rules, or refusing to tow the NHS line. Trying to read her, I stared for a few seconds before excusing myself to fetch the water requested.

'I'm sick to death of the way Justin undermines anyone who gets in his way,' Bridget said, when I reappeared. 'He's a weasel. I can't believe he left the door open so everyone in the office could hear what was being said.'

This was illuminating. I carefully sought an appropriate response without blowing my cover as a rational human being, as opposed to a neurotic amnesiac. Then it came to me. 'You're in a hurry. Give me your version and I'll record it on my phone, how about that?'

'No need, I recorded most of it on mine when it was all kicking off,' Bridget said with a cheeky smile on her freckled face. 'Well, it serves the numpty right for making the entire thing so public. I'll ping it to you on WhatsApp.'

'Bridge. You bloody marvellous woman. What would I do without you?'

It didn't take long to transfer the audio file, after which Bridget stood in the hallway, holding her car keys. She appeared unusually self-conscious. 'It seems so unfair. I don't want to part like this and leave you to deal with the horrible situation on your own, Gabby. How about we meet up at the weekend for a few glasses of something?'

I didn't have the heart to say 'no,' but as I didn't have the money to say 'yes,' I made a non-committal noise and directed her towards the front door, bidding her a half-hearted farewell. Bridget was offering friendship and support, but I'm not the sort to trouble others with my private life. I wasn't ready to share stories of my missing hours, my death, my perverted neighbour, and until I listened to the recording she'd made, I didn't know which way to turn next.

Barely waiting for Bridget to start her car, I rested against the inside of the temperamental front door and pressed the play button on my phone.

23

PULLING TOGETHER

*K*nowing Monday would be Gabriella's first day back at work, Peddyr had taken this into consideration when suggesting they meet. He wanted to see her in her natural habitat, gauge how she was coping, and spy on who was watching her. He followed her for the day, and it was a real eye opener.

By the time he knocked on the door of number six Derwent Drive at eight o'clock that evening, he'd gleaned a fair whack of information about the woman he was being paid to help. Understanding her was the key to finding out who was so determined to make her life fall apart. Through the glass panels in the door, he saw Gabriella Dixon's outline appear as if she was waiting for him behind the door that refused to budge until he pushed against it. 'That was quick,' he said, taking in her bewildered expression, her wet and unbrushed hair. 'You look like you've had more unwelcome news, Mrs Dixon. What's up?'

'Everything. Everything is up,' she replied with a squawk. And as she stood before him, she dissolved into tears, great wracking sobs. Dashing off to hide her emotions, she fetched a much-needed box of tissues.

While he waited for her to regain self-control, he stared around him at the forlorn decor and drab furnishings in the hall and lounge. Patterns were everywhere; the wallpaper was Regency stripes, the upholstery was a swirling homage to the eighties, and the carpet was reminiscent of the one in Peddyr's local pub. Not only an insult to the eye, the place smelled unhappily of neglect and appeared to be nothing short of a monument to her parents' mundane lives. The exception to this were a few more modern items, which announced the recent arrival of a younger, more affluent resident. The glossy flat-screen television was on, talking to itself.

With her chest still spasming, Gabby apologised for her outburst and asked Peddyr to sit. 'The whole thing is beyond me,' she finally managed as she turned off the television using the remote. 'And please call me Gabby.'

'Well, there's no good blubbing about it, Gabby,' Peddyr said as he meandered across the worn Axminster carpet. 'Pull yourself together and tell me what's going on. I'm not a mind reader.' It was plain to see how poorly Gabriella Dixon was holding up under the strain, but her distress didn't garner any compassion. Peddyr was more interested in how truthful she would be with him. Without her honesty there was little chance of getting to the crux of the problem, and besides, being over-sympathetic wasn't his style. Hitching up the legs of his jeans, he sat down. 'Tell me about your day. Let's start with that.' He rocked forward, placed elbows on knees and intertwined his fingers.

'Why? Why is my day important?' Making use of a mirror mounted on the wall nearby, his client blotted at her eyes before perching cautiously on the arm of an upholstered chair.

'Because by the state of you I'd say it's been uncommonly stressful,' he said. Despite best efforts, her face signalled panic around the next corner. 'You caught the train to work. What happened when you got there?' Peddyr asked. He didn't react as she visibly squirmed and slid into the cushioned seat of the chair.

'How do you know I caught the train?'

'I just do. Now tell me about your day. How did it start?'

'I can remember the first half an hour in the office,' she said, reddened eyes darting around the room and eventually settling on her own hands. She was holding something tightly clasped between them and it wasn't her phone, which was lying on the arm of the chair within easy reach.

'Right, so why not recall the rest of the morning?' He coughed, clearing his throat.

In an obvious attempt to avoid answering his direct questions, Gabby offered him a drink, which he declined and forced her back on track. 'What time did you leave work?' he asked.

Her face crumpled as the tears began again. 'I don't know,' she gushed with ever-increasing anguish. 'I don't remember leaving work, I don't know what time I left, and I only know I went to BBC Valley because I got a message telling me I did... and then I ended up on the station platform at about half past four.' Her eyes were wild now, scared. With a quick look towards her phone, she said, 'Before you arrived, I was listening to a recording of an argument at work and I can hear myself, but I don't recall saying any of those things.'

In sharp contrast to her agitation, Peddyr rested against

the back of the sofa, comforted by the veracity of her answer. 'Thank you for telling me. It explains a lot.'

'It does?' Gabby sought his eyes, blowing her nose into a handful of tissues,

'Yes, I followed you today. Not the entire time, only some of it. I cheated and drove to the station. Then I hopped on your train and saw your confrontation with that bloke's armpit. If I may say so, I thought you handled it in a very British way.'

Gabby shot him a horrified look. 'You followed me? What on earth for? Aren't you supposed to be on the trail of the culprit here, not the bloody victim? How fucking insensitive of you?' Infuriated, she hammered a fist on the arm of the chair, releasing a cloud of dust. This made Peddyr smirk. Connie once told him dust was made up of old skin cells, and he couldn't shake the thought that the remains of Gabriella's parents were now floating in his direction.

'Now, now, there you go getting all uppity again without thinking,' he said, raising a hand in defence. 'Whoever is doing this to you will want to watch what happens – it's human nature. So, if I watch you, I might spot them watching you too. Do you see?'

Folding her arms, Gabby frowned. 'And did you?'

This was where Peddyr should have confessed to coming up empty-handed. However, he'd learnt much about Gabriella Dixon that day and blinded her with facts instead of disappointment. 'You've not made a friend out of Justin Parks or your boss. You've been suspended or sacked, I'm not sure which. Talbot Howkins is after a story, but you don't trust him. Your friend Stella is worried about your mental state and Kenny Eversholt is a sex offender, like you suspected. He's possibly under surveillance by the man you've seen in a BMW parked in the street, although I'm not convinced on that one. I need to check it out. And finally, just so you know... your work friend Bridget is a good egg.'

'Holy moly. How the hell...?' Gabby gave a slow shake of her head, and as she did so she relaxed her hands to reveal a rounded grey pebble with streaks of quartz running through it.

Getting up from his position among the skin cells on the tatty sofa, Peddyr walked to the mantlepiece above a tasteless gas fire. He drummed his fingers. 'I watch, I listen, and I learn.' He turned to face her as she followed his every move and hung on each word. 'Nice photograph,' he said, picking up a silver frame. 'You look very much like your mother. Is this your Christening?'

Gabby nodded. 'She was very young when she had me.'

'And she fell for an older man, I see.' Peddyr touched fingertips to the glass before placing the frame back on the mantlepiece. 'Shotgun wedding was it?'

'What?'

'Your parents. She must have been no more than a teenager. Plenty of lead in his pencil though, eh?' The disdain from Gabriella in response to his personal remarks was not unexpected. Plainly he'd strayed into risky territory, so he decided it was worth pursuing, if only briefly.

'What'd he do for a living?' The man in the photograph, Grenville Brady, was at least a decade and a half older than his very glamorous wife, Eileen. He wore a double-breasted suit and the countenance of an educated, affluent man.

'A civil servant. Something big in Whitehall. Defence contracts, I think. It's why we moved here. Dad said he had no choice in the matter, he had to be somewhere between London and Cheltenham.'

'GCHQ,' Peddyr said, pursing his lips. He received a shrug in reply. 'And your mother? Where did they meet?'

'On the train, would you believe? A commuter love story, she was a secretary for some law firm in the city and they often caught the same train into town. He adored her, and she fell for his lifestyle; posh dinners, London shows, plenty of money.' Gabby's voice drifted off slightly. 'I think my arrival put paid to a lot of that.' Her lips twitched with the beginnings of a smile as Peddyr moved along to look at more family portraits.

'I would suggest the opposite,' he said. 'This is like a shrine to your achievements. What were you being presented with here?'

With a self-deprecating grimace, Gabby replied, 'Oh that. The school prize for a short story I wrote. Nothing spectacular.'

'But this is,' Peddyr said, poking a forefinger at a family photo. 'You with a mortarboard on your head, arm in arm with your dad. And this must be little sister Laura looking very neat and cheery in her best dress, and your mother... she could be mistaken for your sister, you know. She's a fine-looking woman. Shame she isn't smiling.'

'She rarely did unless it was at Laura.'

That was a telling statement, thought Peddyr, but rather than pursue it, he returned to the subject of the previous conversation, determined to answer a puzzling question.

'I would have said that, as a psychologist, you'd have effective observation skills.'

Much calmer now, Gabby nodded. 'I would say so, yes.'

'And yet...' Peddyr said, strolling towards a bay window overlooking the back of the house. 'This afternoon, when I was trailing you around town, you didn't notice me, even when I was within feet of you at Crewsthorpe station. Nor did you see me when I followed you from your office to the BBC studios. Nor when I drove up the street this evening, turned, parked my car and spotted a bloke in a silver BMW taking photographs of you talking with your neighbour Kenny Eversholt.'

Gabby stared at him, speechless. 'I had Kenny checked out,' Peddyr added. 'And my friendly neighbourhood police force confirmed that he *is* on the sex offenders register and *is* being kept tabs on because his habits have changed recently.'

'You did? All that?' It was clear Gabby was having some difficulty in assimilating the details of Peddyr's report. 'I don't suppose you know what I said to Talbot, do you? Talbot Howkins at the BBC studios...'

Inclining his head to where he'd left his small rucksack next to the sofa, Peddyr said, 'Er, no. I waited outside, eating my sandwiches in the sunshine while you were gassing with your broadcasting mates. When you came out, I could tell you weren't too chuffed. You goose-stepped to the cafe next door, ordered a drink, sat outside and made some notes. You did a lot of pen-sucking and scribbling.'

From the blank expression he was faced with, Peddyr surmised his client had no recollection of that part of her day. 'When you got the notebook out again at the station, it was as if you'd never seen the words before.' He drew in a lungful of air. 'You're going to have to explain the memory loss thing.'

24

EXPLAIN YOURSELF

hen he'd first met Gabriella Dixon, Peddyr hadn't been enamoured of her starchy aloofness, but he knew now it was a front, a protective wall she hid behind; like Connie had said. Sitting hunched in a chair, pebble clutched tightly in her hand, she looked like a child about to confess an embarrassing secret; which is what she did.

'It used to happen a lot, years ago' Looking down at her lap, she took uneven breaths, trying to control the tears brimming her eyes. 'As a teenager, they referred me for various tests, but it wasn't fully explained at the time. When I grew out of the problem, the amnesia was never mentioned again.' Sadness pulled at the corners of her mouth.

Without giving her statement more than a slight acknowledgement, Peddyr limped over to a cardboard box on the coffee table. 'What do your medical records say?'

'Not much. The doctors investigated me for a head injury, but despite scarring from a bash on the head that I don't remember, they never found obvious brain damage. One doctor put it put down to a severe stress reaction: Moving house, moving school, big changes and a couple of bereavements. Coming slap bang in the middle of adolescence, I couldn't handle the psychological stress. It eased up over time. Until Saturday.' Gabby then explained to Peddyr about the strange journey with Dr Prasad. 'John, the mystery caller, must have set me off.'

'And what set you off at work today?'

'I'm not sure, but I think it was a present I received,' she replied. 'There was a parcel waiting for me.'

Delving into the box, Peddyr produced the Magic 8-Ball. 'Was it this?' He gave the glossy sphere a shake and placed it carefully back in the box. 'What's the relevance, I wonder? Could it be that John – your so-called mystery caller – knows something you don't?'

'Why do you say that?'

'Because I've listened to his performance over and over again. It was very deliberate, if I may say so.' Weighing up whether he should join the dots for Gabby, he gave her a few seconds to think about what John had said. 'He mentioned fate. Chance predictions. That's what the ball does.'

Gabby spread out her hands, allowing the pebble to rest on her skirt. 'Yes, I know that.'

'Who else knows about your amnesia?' he asked, taking up position on a chintz-covered window seat overlooking the garden. By not addressing her face on, Peddyr hoped she would speak more freely, so he lounged back to listen.

'Stella is the only one still alive who knows as much as I do. My parents knew everything of course.'

'You and Stella were at school together, am I right?'

Gabby smiled, looking into the middle distance. 'Yes, we

met on my first day at upper school. She was the one person who picked up on my occasional visits to amnesia-land. Everyone else, including teaching staff, thought I was either forgetful or being deliberately obnoxious.'

From the periphery of Peddyr's vision he saw her give an involuntary shiver, curling her toes into the carpet.

'Why?' Pausing briefly, Peddyr corrected himself. 'Why does the amnesia happen?'

'It's a dissociative response which may or may not be connected with banging my head and shaking up the insides. The head injury was one of those fluke accidents where a clumsy trip resulted in wiping out a chunk of my memory. I don't remember the precise moment it happened, so I only know what I've been told. Hardly a scar to be seen.' She raised one hand and patted the crown of her damp hair, which was twisted and piled into a large clip at the back of her head. 'Ever since, in times of extreme stress, I can suffer episodes of memory loss – at its worst, just half an hour or so goes missing but sometimes it's longer.'

'What happened when your parents twigged something had messed up your head?'

Gabby sighed. 'They went into meltdown and dragged me along to endless appointments with GPs, neurologists, psychiatrists and finally psychologists. Stella never once let slip to our bitchy classmates about my trips to various clinics. If she had, I would have been even more of a target for the school bullies. It's not easy turning up at a new school halfway through a term.'

Gabriella Dixon had a way of skirting around a subject and Peddyr recognised this. There had to be more to her story than a bump on the head, but he couldn't force her to tell him any more than she was prepared to. The details would come if he asked the right questions in the right way.

'You don't sound convinced about the head injury causing your amnesia.'

Gabby shrugged with one shoulder. 'I'm not. I believe I reached breaking point, and we all have one, Mr Quirk. That year was the worst one in my life.'

'Worse than this?'

'On a par.' Gabby looked down at the pebble in her lap and began stroking it as if it were a small mammal. 'Do you remember being fifteen years old? It's hard working out where you fit in the world; wanting to be part of a group and be an individual at the same time. I went to a posh girls' school and my boyfriend Kit went to the local state-run comprehensive, although it's probably an academy by now, everywhere seems to have one.'

'Daddy wasn't happy about that, I dare say,' Peddyr said, twiddling the rope of the sash window.

'Neither of my parents were. The Willis family lived two streets away. Dad called them a bunch of bohemian layabouts and Mum said Shana Willis was a four-by-four. Four children by four different fathers, although that was an exaggeration. I couldn't have picked a more unsuitable boy to knock about with, in their eyes. There was a gang of us: me, Kit, Ben and Camille. The Magic 8-Ball, and something wacko John said about chance, made me think immediately of Kit.'

There was a lengthy pause before she let out the truth she'd been hiding from Peddyr. 'Kit killed himself shortly after we moved here. It was the most appalling emotional pain I have ever felt, before or since. The impact on the teenage me was horrendous.'

'You poor kid. The funeral must have been harrowing.'

'I didn't go. My mother had taken me away to Wales to stay with her sister there before we moved from Bedford.

Mum says it's where I fell and walloped my head. My sister Laura was born then. We heard about Kit shortly after we moved here. I was in a bad way for months after he died and the doctor said I wasn't in a fit state to cope with the funeral, so I didn't get to say my goodbyes.'

'Ouch. And was he the reason your memory problems became worse?'

Raising her eyebrows, Gabriella sighed. 'I would say so. Like a complex grief reaction. Mum, Dad and Stella were the only ones who believed me about my absences. Eventually the professionals labelled me with Factitious Disorder thanks to one jumped up psychiatrist who said I was jealous of my sister's arrival in the family and angry with my parents for the upheaval. How's that for pulling the rug out from under a teenage girl's self-esteem? When I left school, I vowed to right my own wrongs and work it out for myself.'

'That's why you became a psychologist.'

'Got it in one, Sherlock.' Gabby remained impassive. 'I am two people, one who lived my life to the age of fifteen and the other one who subsequently took over – the me I am now, career driven and obsessed with reducing teenage suicides. I'm only this normal thanks to the friendship of a certain scatter-brained Stella Archibald. Two loonies who found each other and stuck like glue.'

'I know that name,' Peddyr said. 'Do you mean Estelle Archibald?'

'Yes, I do.' Gabby sounded surprised.

'Did she used to work for Castle and Wyckes?'

The astonishment on Gabby's face stretched wider. 'Good grief, how do you know that? Yes, she worked there. She always had a morbid curiosity, that girl… about bodies, dead animals, Halloween. She got a Saturday job at Castle and Wyckes when we were in the sixth form – cleaning the mortuary or something dreadful. After college she went full time on an apprenticeship scheme. She loved it. I think she was with them for about four years before she transferred to their newest branch in Oxford when they expanded.'

Swinging his legs to the floor from his comfortable perch propped against the window frame, Peddyr patrolled the room. When he'd previously asked about her upbringing, Gabriella Dixon had reeled off the usual twaddle about joyous holidays, tough times at school because she was academic and not at all sporty, etcetera, etcetera. But she never mentioned the death of her childhood sweetheart or the uncomfortable relationship with her parents and younger sister. 'How do you know if the story your parents told you is the truth?'

Her eyes betrayed her well before her lips moved. 'Story about what? About banging my head?'

'No, I meant about Kit. Are you certain he died? Could they have told you that story to make sure you never saw him again?'

The shocked expression on Gabby's face was immediate. The tears flowed freely, like raindrops down a windowpane in a storm. 'What the hell are you suggesting? Of course he really died. I saw the order of service, I wrote to his mother, I spoke to Ben.'

'How did he die?'

'Alcohol and a cocktail of pills. There was a Coroner's Inquiry.'

Feeling ashamed, Peddyr apologised. 'I had to ask.' He tugged at an earlobe, pausing to examine the family photographs once more. 'I take it your sister Laura knows nothing about this?'

Gabby shook her head. 'And neither does Phil, my nearly

ex-husband. I lied to him for years... He knew about Kit but not about the mess I got into when he died.' She looked to the ceiling. 'Phil is a good man, and I loved him in my own way. The best I could. But he wasn't Kit.'

An internal door swung in a ghost-like breeze, and the house seemed to creak, prompting Gabby to get up from the chair and head into the kitchen. When she returned with two tumblers of iced water, a thoughtful silence continued as they sipped down the drinks, not looking at one another. 'Shall I put in a request for my medical records? See if there is anything useful from years ago?' Gabby asked eventually.

'I doubt it will tell us anything you don't already know. Quite how, I'm not sure, but this business has to relate to your younger years,' Peddyr said, thinking aloud, as he often did. 'Leave it with me. I'll come up with a good lead soon enough. In the meantime, we should meet up with Bernie Kershaw and get our heads together. The three of us need to regroup and get cracking on this before...' He tailed off, not daring to speculate on the intended outcome of these events.

'How is the investigation going overall?' Gabby asked, obviously relieved at the chance to change the focus away from herself.

For several minutes Peddyr updated her on his progress, which wasn't much more than he'd told her in his most recent phone call. 'I've accounted for the funeral services in town, apart from one. The register office is dealt with, and I've spoken to the local authority on several occasions. There was a letter on file outlining your husband's refusal to pay for your funeral expenses, and a consent form giving a man called Dave Smith the right to act on behalf of the family. It records him as a cousin.'

Gabby sat pale and immobilised, as if her remaining energy had finally ebbed away.

'My one lead is the man in the picture captured at the register office, but without something from you I can't move much further forward.'

'I have to fill in the gaps?'

'I believe so, Mrs Dixon. Can I call you tomorrow with the arrangements for a meeting with Bernie?'

'Feel free. I won't be at work,' she replied, melancholy deflating her.

'In that case, can you do me a favour and write a time-line of your life to date instead? Give me what you can. Note down all the significant events starting as far back as you can recall. I could do with guidance in formulating a list of suspects and with your help we could generate some new leads.'

'Who do you have so far?' Gabby asked. In a rapid change of mood, she appeared to have livened up at the suggestion. Looking in the street's direction she said, 'I have Kenny, my soon to be ex-husband Phil, and Justin Parks. Mind you, if my dinner with Laura and her loser husband goes badly on Wednesday night, I may add to it.' She caught Peddyr's eye. 'The Magic 8-Ball may be a coincidence, but if this isn't Kenny wanting retribution, or Phil, or Justin... then someone I can't remember is responsible, and that someone wants me dead.'

'If they wanted you dead, then you'd be dead by now,' Peddyr said, stating what he considered to be the obvious. 'Remember what John said? He quoted from the bible, an eye for an eye, a life for a life. It strikes me he's taking away your life. That's not the same as wanting to kill you.'

'Hell on earth, is what he's putting me through.'

'I agree, but what we need is the motive behind it. Why this course of action and why now?'

Raising a fake smile, his exhausted client led him to the front door where she struggled to pull it free and kicked at the bottom panel in irritation. He laughed at her efforts and stepped in to help, keen to get home for a well-earned dinner with Connie. He had much to tell her.

25

CLOSE, CLOSER, CLOSEST

*P*eddyr pushed at the handle, and as the door widened a bell rang, letting out a jingle above his head. Castle and Wyckes was one of the largest funeral directors in the area. They had several branches, mostly modern and purpose-built. However, the one in Bosworth Bishops remained on the site of the original family undertakers, first establishing itself as a funeral home in the Victorian era. The building was a red brick monstrosity with a vast courtyard to the rear where the vehicles were stored. The frontage was a resplendent show of gold leaf signwriting on black gloss, with tasteful flower displays in the two large windows either side of the half-glazed entrance.

'Ah, excellent timing.' The chirpy greeting came from Hugh Ingles, managing director of the company and great-great-grandson of the Castle side of the business. 'Paddy, I'd like you to meet Owen Fox. We recruited him to our Hollberry branch, but he was wasted there. I don't think you've had the pleasure.' Standing beside the hunched figure of Hugh Ingles was a much younger man, tall and slender in his charcoal-coloured suit. Instantly forgettable.

'I don't believe I have,' Peddyr answered, holding out his hand and being mildly surprised by the firmness of Owen Fox's grip. Hugh's handshake was more feeble, as was he.

'Paddy Quirk has served us well over many years,' warbled the older man. 'He's our secret weapon in balancing the books. You may have heard how instrumental he was in catching a vandal here two years ago, Owen. A dreadful business. It cost us an absolute fortune in paint jobs.'

It was hard for Peddyr to forget the nights spent staking out the courtyard at Castle and Wyckes, ready to pounce on the misguided reprobate who wilfully damaged the limousines and hearses. Peddyr secreted himself away in a body bag in the back of a hearse and waited to catch the guilty party, who he filmed in the act before petrifying him with his Lazarus impersonation. The motive turned out to be that of bitter revenge for parking outside the offender's house, which Castle and Wyckes occasionally did when shuffling vehicles around. When caught, the man was fined heavily, charged with wilful damage, bound over to keep the peace and humiliated in the local papers. He subsequently and sensibly moved house.

Spending lonely hours in the back of a hearse wasn't the worst thing he'd ever had to do, but when it came down to it Peddyr much preferred tracing families via more modern means and reuniting them with deceased relatives. Mostly this was to ensure someone paid the funeral expenses, but now and again family members turned out to be grateful, especially when they realised they may be beneficiaries in a will.

'What can we do for you, Mr Quirk?' Owen asked. 'Business or personal?'

'Good question, Owen, I hadn't thought of that,' Hugh Ingles said, looking at his protege with pride.

A grin from Peddyr soon told them it was business. 'I'm tracing a dead body,' he said. 'Does the name Gabriella Dixon mean anything to either of you? She died back in May and I'm trying to track her down.'

Hugh Ingles raised a wizened hand. 'I'm sure she can't have got far. The dead have a habit of lying about and being generally inactive.' He laughed at his own comment before adding an apology. 'I'm afraid I shall have to leave you in the capable hands of Owen here. I've only popped in to cast an eye over the books, although why I bother these days beats me. Habit, I suppose.' He threw his hand outwards. 'Good to see you again, Paddy. Keep up the outstanding work.' With that, he turned on his heels and left Owen to deal with Peddyr's request.

'The name is familiar, but I can't say I remember anything about her funeral,' Owen said, scratching at his chin with a forefinger. 'Come through to the office, Mr Quirk. Let's see what we can dig up, if you pardon the pun. I've got about fifteen minutes before my next appointment. I'm all yours until then.'

'Please call me Peddyr – but you can call me Paddy if it's easier. I've given up correcting Mr Ingles and besides it's a common mistake and mine is an uncommon name.'

Whether it was his walk, his confident manner, or an intuitive hunch, Peddyr couldn't decide, but Owen Fox intrigued him. He was fairly sure he wasn't ex-forces, but there was a hint of it somehow. Making a mental note to find out, Peddyr duly followed Owen through the centre of a stuffy office where he caught inquisitive looks between two ladies sitting in front of computer screens. Desk fans made a constant whirring to keep the place cool in the summer heat. 'Don't mind us,' Owen said, glancing at them. 'We're only passing through.'

One of the two ladies extended her neck and caught Peddyr's eye. 'Haven't seen you in ages, Mr Quirk. How are you?'

'Very well thanks, Marjorie. How are you these days? You and Diane keeping Mr Fox here on his toes?' There was a polite exchange of smiles and nods before Marjorie raised a finger. 'Oh. Before I forget,' she said to Owen. 'Dr Godfrey collected his diary yesterday afternoon.' She rolled her eyes and threw her hands in the air. 'He'll forget his head next. Did you know there were blank prescriptions inside? Honestly... someone should tell him it's time to retire. That's the second time in as many months. I swear he's getting worse.'

Peddyr smiled sympathetically. He thought the old GP had retired years ago. 'He's never still locuming, is he?' he asked.

'Yep,' Diane clucked. 'The silly old twerp can't say no.'

'Well, he should,' Marjorie added firmly. 'He's a menace. He forgets his bag, his hat, his glasses... and Saturday morning he left his precious appointments diary on the counter in reception. We couldn't get hold of him until yesterday morning.' She looked again at Owen. 'And did you find out who's been messing with the make-up? Only Cressida is furious. She says there's an entire pot of powder missing. She's on the warpath.'

'Thanks for the warning. I'll prepare for battle,' he replied with a wink. He led Peddyr into a side room where they could discuss matters in private. 'Cressida is our free-lance embalmer,' he explained. 'She's quite fearsome. Excuse the mess. I had all the files out for Mr Ingles to see.' He placed his jacket on the back of a chair.

'No problem. Anyway, they say a tidy desk is the sign of a sick mind, don't they?'

'Do they?' Owen took a seat in front of his desktop screen. 'What name was it again?' Having punched in the required letters, he thoughtfully swivelled the screen around for Peddyr to see. 'Here you are. That's why I don't recall the service arrangements. Bright's collected the deceased the day after we transported her from her home address. There'll be a record of the on-call information.'

It was all there. The call from Arthur Bird, the time, the confirmation that death had been pronounced, the address. 'Did the bearers report anything unusual about the job?' Peddyr asked.

Owen shrugged. 'Not that I recall. She was young, all things considered. About my age, come to think of it. I can give you the names of the two lads who collected the body if you want to talk to them.'

'Thanks. I might take you up on that if I get stuck. Can I ask, is it unusual for another funeral service to take over?'

'Not at all. The neighbour chose us because we'd handled a funeral for one of his relatives and he didn't know who else to call. Bright's were contacted by a member of Mrs Dixon's family and Bright's collected the body from us soon as.'

'Do you have a hard-copy of the paperwork signed by the neighbour?'

'Yes, we do.' It took only minutes before Marjorie produced a file and handed it to Owen. 'There you are, Owen. The on-call paperwork signed by Mr Arthur Bird. The registration into our safekeeping, and the transfer paperwork to Bright's.'

It stumped Peddyr. Gabriella's name appeared on all the paperwork and the dates and times tallied exactly. 'Oh, well. Looks like I must get on to the local authority again. I'm running out of ideas.'

'You tried Bright's?'

With a simple 'yes,' Peddyr answered the question, followed by one of his own. 'Have you always been in the funeral business?'

'Me? No, not always. Why do you ask?'

'Just curious how a man ends up in this job. How old are you, forty odd?'

'I was a late starter. Only been in this game for three years.' If that were true it didn't rule out time in the armed forces, Peddyr thought. Most ex-servicemen saw death in their careers, this could be a natural continuation; uniform, structure, death.

'What did you do before comforting the bereaved?'

An ironic laugh escaped Owen's lips. 'I worked for a housing authority in Oxford, fulfilling the maintenance contract for a group of care homes. Not very glamorous, and difficult to progress, which is why I left. Before that, the retail trade. Splendid job title, crap money.'

Owen Fox came across as likeable and reassuring, which is exactly what would be expected, given his career choice. The employment history had a ring of truth to it, Peddyr thought. Even so, it was worth delving deeper into Owen's past because he didn't yet have the measure of this man. 'Hugh Ingles knows his stuff. And from what I hear, he looks after his employees well. How long have you been at this branch?'

'Coming up for a year next month,' Owen replied, shuffling documents and returning them to lever arch files. 'It was a sensible career move. I get to experience most parts of the industry, apart from embalming. That doesn't appeal, to be honest.'

'I can see why.'

'How about you?' Owen asked.

'No, embalming's not for me either,' Peddyr replied, evading the actual question.

'Did you find the information you needed?' Owen asked, shutting down the screen.

'Not entirely, but it's nothing for you to worry about. An administrative issue at County Hall is causing some difficulty, but I'll get it sorted in no time. Some slap-dash secretary seems to have put the wrong information on their database. Pay peanuts, get monkeys as they say.'

With a smile, Owen stood up. 'Were you hoping we'd made the error?'

Peddyr shook his hand, registering the firm grip as before. 'As a matter of fact, I was. It would have made my life a heck of a lot simpler.'

26

DINNER WITH THE DOGS

*S*ome things are better left unsaid, and I decided not to let on to my sister about my suspension from work, preferring a more palatable version of events. 'I'm working from home this week until HR sort out the muddle with my registration,' I told her when she called to confirm arrangements for our reconciliation dinner. Laura was well aware of the financial constraints I was facing and the problems in accessing my salary. But I had to be careful, I didn't want her getting wind of the true extent of the mess, the drastic level of debt I was getting into, or the deeper, more sinister goings on.

It had come as a horrible shock to discover that the coffee I'd unknowingly consumed on Monday had cost three pounds twenty and was in fact tea. An extortionate amount of money for a hot drink. The receipt in my purse boldly informed me I'd ordered a Chai Latte Massimo. It was a puzzler, I couldn't recall ever having such an extravagant cup of tea before, so why order one when I'd never even heard of a Chai Latte Massimo?

As a penance for such reckless spending on one drink, I opened a tin of tuna which I thought would have to last the whole of Tuesday. However, salvation came in the form of a Big Mac and use of the free WIFI when I found two pound coins and a few coppers on the floor of a wardrobe. The joy was momentary. More unpleasant news confronted me when I checked my pile of redirected post while living it up in Macky D's.

Blue Box Storage wanted immediate payment for my monthly bill. My bulky furniture, what there was of it, was placed in secure storage waiting for me to get the house up to scratch. With the direct debits not being paid, this was to be the first of many requests for settlement of bills. Blue Box Storage were forthright; pay or we sell off your furniture. If I failed to pay within thirty days, my goods and chattels could end up on one of those awful reality TV programmes where so-called traders bid for unseen contents of a container.

The rest of Tuesday and much of Wednesday I spent making a list of food stocks, searching the house, garage and shed for useful items, and noting potentially saleable goods. There was increasing likelihood of me lowering the tone of Derwent Drive by holding a garage sale if I were forced to survive for much longer on cash alone.

When I completed the physical chores, I sat down to make a chronology of my life, for Peddyr's benefit. Stirring up partial memories of my adolescence, I still experienced painful emotions. Not as raw as they were when Kit had died, but they were there, gnawing away, as were niggles about the time when Laura had arrived in our family. Even as a selfish teenager I had been aware of something going horribly wrong between my parents. Their once strong bond and mutual respect had vanished. In came Laura, out went the happiness in my father's eyes. Now as I tried to write down those events in a sensible order, there were several gaps and one or two glaring inconsistencies. I tapped my temple. 'Come on out. I know you're in there somewhere.'

The events of Wednesday evening didn't improve things. Laura dispatched Curtis to collect me, but I consoled myself knowing that it would be a one-way ticket. He wouldn't be driving me back home again because he drank too much on any day with a 'y' in it. When he quaffed the usual umpteen pints, he excelled at behaving like an insufferable prick, but was at least sensible enough not to get behind the steering wheel of a car.

Laura had been too nice on the phone earlier, putting me immediately on alert. So, when Curtis drew up in his builder's van, I was ready for him. The door of the Ford flatbed clanged shut and my hackles rose on hearing my brother-in-law's whistle, undoing my determination to smile in a welcoming manner. Why couldn't he use the doorbell like any other adult? I scrabbled to prise the front door from its default position; wedged against the frame like a limpet to a rock.

'I'll take a plane to that tomorrow. No need for you to battle with a door. I've got a new lock for it too. Keep those thieving bastards at bay, eh?' This was very suspicious. A grinning Curtis was wearing his best shirt for the occasion, and the introduction of a hair product had tamed his wild sandy mop. He even appeared untainted by his usual farmer-cum-builder whiff of wood shavings and manure. Temporarily disarmed, I thanked him for the offer and made to pick up my handbag from the hall table. 'Mind if I look down the garden while I'm here? Laura tells me you're planning on building a three-bed.'

And there it was, the real reason for tonight's invitation and my brother-in-law's chivalrous offer of a lift. Money.

As Bernard had said, crime is invariably about money, so when Curtis made his move, I immediately ramped up my defences. A death often resulted in spectacular fallouts over inheritance, and I wondered if Laura had been civil since our mother's death for that reason alone. Was she all sweetness and light because she was hoping to get her hands on the cash much sooner than if we'd marketed number six with an estate agent? Was she mercenary enough to send Curtis along to lay claim to more than they were entitled to?

I didn't have the answers because I hadn't as yet spent enough time with my own sister to know one way or the other.

Staring at me, expecting a response, Curtis stood, chest out, hands shoved in the back pockets of his Levi's. 'Sure, let's have a little wander down through the brambles and see what you think,' I said. 'Your expertise would be most helpful. I've no idea what to do for the best.' It was a better-the-devil-you-know strategy, mixed with a keep-your-friends-close-and-your-enemies-closer approach with a smattering of Socratic irony thrown in for good measure. He seemed to fall for the flattery and launched into a thinly disguised sales pitch in his best Devonshire drawl.

'Have you thought about the benefits of building an eco-house on this plot?'

'You've got me there, Curtis,' I replied, unsurprised by the suggestion. 'What sort of thing would you recommend?'

'A cob house,' he answered, hands now on hips, nodding sagely. 'This spot is perfect. What a stunning setting for a unique building of quality materials and balanced proportions. Exactly the sort of project I like to get my teeth into.'

Not allowing myself even to blink, I concealed the amusement I felt as he delivered his carefully memorised lines. I wasn't intending to cave in to his persuasion, far from it, but it would be interesting to see how much planning and forethought had gone into Curtis's pitch.

'I've been perfecting the technique back at the farm,' he continued. 'And the results are astounding so far as sustainability and insulation go.' If he'd been wearing medals on his chest, he would have been giving them a quick self-congratulatory polish by now.

Holding back from a sarcastic comment about troglodytes or termite mounds, I urged him on with a warm smile. 'Goodness, that sounds worth considering. I can't wait to see what you've done at the farm.' He beamed back at me while I inwardly reflected there was no way planning permission would be granted to put a bloody great pile of mud, cow shit and straw in a middle-class suburban street. What was the ignoramus thinking?

Less than thirty minutes later, I found out what sort of construction he had in mind as we approached Revival Farm via a rutted track. The one and only time I'd been there was some years ago for their wedding knees-up. It was much scruffier then, with a ramshackle bungalow taking centre stage. Nearby were a series of stables, an open barn and a wooden workshop to one side of the bungalow, with a paddock and a pond to the other. Bouncing along in the passenger seat of the truck, I was shocked to see the scale of the change before me.

Gone was the soulless bungalow, replaced by something resembling a Medieval dwelling used in historical re-enactments. The house was a great dollop of ochre-coloured walls, with a thatched roof, wooden beams set at peculiar angles and arched windows. However, what could loosely have been described as an artisan construction, finished to a high level of rustic charm, was let down badly by the unholy mess surrounding it.

Building materials, chickens, a kennel, free-roaming dogs and a heap of logs in need of stacking surrounded the cottage. A poly-tunnel took up a good third of what passed for a garden space. The paddock was divided into different areas for livestock, mostly goats from what I could see, separated by post and rail fencing from the vegetables beyond. I shuddered to see the disorder, the stinking manure seeping and steaming right next to where Curtis parked. Looking down, I blessed my own common sense for choosing to wear a much-loved pair of Swedish clogs.

'Hi, so glad you could make it.' To my ears Laura's chirpy welcome seemed forced and false. Another prepared act of the play. My role was to be equally charming, I decided.

'I'm so pleased you asked me. I felt rotten about having that silly argument. The stress of everything and lack of sleep has turned me into an old grouch,' I said, sliding carefully from the passenger seat onto the mucky concrete of the yard.

'Like what we've done with the place?'

'Stunned.' This wasn't a lie, and allowed me to add, truthfully, 'I can't wait to see inside the house.' I only hoped my eyes didn't betray the real thoughts about the midden she and Curtis were so proud of.

It wasn't nearly as foul-smelling inside, and not as dark as I'd imagined. The walls being nearly two feet thick, I'd expected the place would feel claustrophobic, but with some thoughtful use of arched windows, open-plan room design and a large skylight, I found myself in an unusual and well thought out property. The only thing letting it down was the general chaos and uncleanliness everywhere I looked.

Treading carefully over and around the toys left scattered on the flagstone floor, Laura led me through the higgledy-piggledy living area to the back of the property where a wooden lean-to log cabin added a substantial dining room. On the scrubbed pine refectory table was a veritable feast of salad and vegetables, a loaf of homemade bread and some goat's cheese. Gone were the mean-spirited thoughts about unappetising vegetarian options, I was so hungry my response was genuinely enthusiastic. 'Looks wonderful. Thanks, Laura.'

Halfway through the meal, with the children in bed, fast asleep, Curtis was slugging back cider as if it were available on tap. Something about his loutish behaviour prompted me to ask about why he wanted the contract to build on what was to be my land.

'Well, if you're struggling for money, I could fund the materials and start the build straight away. No delay. And because you and Lar own the place between you, we could share the profits on the sale.'

He always called her "Lar". Luckily, he'd never thought to name me "Gab".

'If you get your money sorted before then...' Curtis sloshed his cloudy drink to the rim of his glass tankard '...all well and good, but if you don't, where are you going to get the funds to start the build?' He was slurring his words, but what he said did at least make some sort of sense. He knew I couldn't pay a contractor to complete the build, but Curtis could finish the job using his own money and take the costs from the proceeds of sale. It was an option.

'I doubt we'll get planning,' I said, coming to my senses. 'A cob house would look out of place in Derwent Drive.'

'Not if I design it to blend in. The planning department is screaming out for green projects. They'll bite my hand off and, what's more, we could get a grant for putting in a ground-source heat pump.'

Apparently Curtis had already done some planning of his own, in anticipation of my response. How very obvious of him.

After we'd stuffed ourselves with summer pudding and yoghurt, he retreated to a more comfortable chair and I cleared the dishes with Laura, happy to stay out of his way. Her chatter was all of the proposed building project. 'It's for the best, Gabby,' she assured me. 'Because if this being dead business drags on for too long, you'll be in debt up to your eyeballs. All those bills not being paid. And I notice your car is still missing, so you'll be facing a massive charge to have that released from the compound. My mate Henry paid a small fortune to get his Range Rover back.'

I flung the soggy tea towel over my left shoulder. 'And your mate Henry could provide ID and proof of ownership, which I can't. Thanks for the cheery words of encouragement.' Tired of her prodding at me to agree to Curtis's grand plan, I raised the thorny question of privacy. 'If you noticed my car was still absent from the driveway, then you've been round the house again, I assume.' A trip to Derwent Drive took her well out of her way, so she couldn't have been passing by.

'Who do you think has been doing the gardening since Mum died?'

If this statement was designed to make me feel guilty, it didn't work for one reason; namely the notable absence of any gardening having been carried out. 'But I've moved in now, Laura. There's no need for you to keep the weeds under control. You've enough to do.' We were heading for another disagreement, which wasn't on the agenda for the evening. I backed off with an apology for under-appreciating her invisible efforts to maintain number six in reasonable order. 'Especially with the kids in tow. You did an amazing job. I can't thank you enough.'

'Then you'll consider our offer?' Detergent bubbles covered her hands as she pulled the last spoon from the sink. 'It's cheaper than owing rent.'

'Rent? For what?' Aghast, I froze, waiting for an indication this was just a joke made at my expense.

'For Laura's half of number six. By rights you should be paying to occupy it... but only until the sale completes.' Curtis was standing in the kitchen archway, a glass in his hand, a smirk on his greedy face. 'It's only fair.'

'You instruct Bernard Kershaw to transfer six months' rent in advance to our account and we'll say no more about it.' Laura was wiping her dishpan hands on a towel as she spoke. The passive aggression was textbook.

It had taken considerable negotiation for Bernard to persuade NHS Finance to pay my salary into an account he would set up. The only way I could access money would be through him, and so far the cogs of the NHS machine had failed to turn because I no longer had a valid National Insurance number. No number, no money. I could pay no bills. I wished to God I hadn't told Laura about the arrangement. It was supposed to have pacified her.

'Or else?' I asked.

They exchanged a look of victory. 'We're only trying to help,' Laura said, sidling up to her husband. 'It could be months before you're able to buy me out and you are still earning money...'

It was like a slap in the face. Where was the family loyalty in this?

I answered my own question as I stared at this pair of New Age eco-extortionists. There was no family loyalty. They were strangers to me. People with whom I had nothing in common – people I chose to spend minimal time with and wouldn't wish to seek out as friends.

'Take your time to think about what works best for you,' Curtis said. 'Lar will drop you home. I'll be round tomorrow with new door locks and to plane that sticky front door.'

He slurped at his glass of cider with gusto, dribbling some from one corner of his mouth before wiping it away with the back of his hand. The alcohol inspired one more insult. 'Can't say we're not good landlords, now can you?'

27

WHO'S THERE?

I woke up to hear the front door rattling and the bell being sounded repeatedly. My first depressing thought was that Curtis had kept to his drunken promise and was about to invade my life with his toolbox and insensitivity. Stumbling out of bed, I grabbed my mobile phone to check the time. Six forty-five, too early for Curtis. 'Who the…?' Opening the window, I thrust my head out and yelled for the thoughtless individual to show themselves.

There was movement below as next door's cat appeared. It was rubbing against a large Barbie-pink suitcase, curling its tail into a question mark. 'I said… who are you and what do you want?' For an instant I thought it might be Kenny the Perv, but his car wasn't outside number seven and someone had parked a Mini on my drive.

'That's no way to welcome your best friend, you rude bitch,' came the salty response. On hearing the most welcome of voices, I burst into cries of unbridled joy. 'Stella? Don't move an inch. I'll be right down.' In my haste to get to her, I tripped over the muddy clogs I'd abandoned in the hall the night before, then swore and blasphemed loudly when the front door refused to budge.

'Calm down. I'll go round the side,' Stella said. Through the frosted glass I could see her grab the telescopic handle of her case and wheel it behind her to the side of the house. I beat her to it and had the backdoor wide open before she even reached it. Practically jumping on her, I launched myself into her arms and we stood together, cry-laughing in the brisk morning air. I kept touching her to make sure she wasn't a cruel apparition.

'I told you not to come. Carlos will be furious... and what the hell have you done to your hair?'

Stella and I were about the same age, but that was where the similarities ended. She was a tall slender creature with glowing skin, giant eyes and a luscious Debbie Harry smile. Unlike me, she bounced through life like Tigger on amphetamines, not caring what the latest fashion trend was. Stella had her own well-groomed and always expensive style. When we'd said our tearful farewells at the airport, she'd left as the newly married Stella Cortez, a sleek brunette. When she popped back to the UK for Mum's funeral she'd gone blonde; today, she sported a spiky grey elfin cut with a pink rinse. It suited her.

'Like it? Thought I'd get hair to match my suitcase.' There was a logic to her thinking; a bonkers logic that no-one else seemed to possess. 'Carlos is in Nice at a stag do for some oil magnate. He won't miss me while there's gambling, drinking and lechery to keep him occupied. Now stop gawping and get me a coffee.'

When we were kids, Stella Archibald, as she was back then, was the ugly duckling whose acne refused to abate, naturally gauche and clumsy. As she matured, she developed a sharp wit and a streetwise charm. Alongside her engaging personality, new physical attributes emerged and by the time she reached eighteen the boys came sniffing round in packs. Not blessed with an academic brain, she was intelligent in a different way and made very best use of whatever assets she had at her disposal.

'I had a phone call from Connie Quirk,' she said, trundling her oversized luggage into the kitchen. 'It was much easier for me to catch a plane back to the UK than to answer all her questions by email. Anyway, I want to meet her. She sounds hilarious.' Watching me spoon instant coffee into a mug, she tutted. 'Your standards have slipped. Where's the proper stuff?'

'Ran out yesterday,' I said. 'MacDonald's is open, they do excellent coffee.' This made her laugh and reach out for me again.

'Come here, you silly biddy.' With a warm, tight hug, she apologised. 'I'm such a dimwit, that was bloody thoughtless of me. Instant will do fine for now. How about I stay here with you for a few days and in return you let me stock your larder?'

For a so-called dimwit, she was more shrewd when it came to practicalities than I ever could be. 'It's a deal.'

'Good, then get showered and put on your slap, we will get to the bottom of this problem. What time is your meeting with Mister Private Dick and your solicitor bloke?'

It had almost slipped my mind, Peddyr Quirk had arranged a meeting for this morning. I was certain having Stella with me would make it more fruitful. 'Ten o'clock. We've got loads of time. Pick a bedroom.' As I padded upstairs, Stella commented freely on my new home. To her it was my old home, the place she would come for tea as a teenager because my mother made delicious coffee and walnut cake. My parents always had a soft spot for Stella.

'Love what you've done to the place,' she said. I could hear the mockery in her voice. 'It's like stepping back in time. I'm waiting for your dad to come in from the potting shed and moan about slugs. The amount of time he spent pricking out seedlings and grouching about aphids, it's hardly surprising he died in there. Anything to avoid spending time with your mother...'

Minutes later, standing under the hot stream of the shower, I thought about my parents. Dear old Dad had a heart attack the weekend before my PhD graduation. I wasn't too upset to miss the ceremony, but I was sad when he died, very sad. He was a gentle soul, and I felt cheated because I hadn't spent as much time with him as I'd wished. He was always at work when I was a child. Four years at Derwent Drive and then fewer and fewer visits home as I made my way in life, and time slipped by. I thought when he retired that he'd be around forever.

After his death, Mum dwindled away in tiny increments. Cancer got hold of her and never let go. My sister was seventeen when Dad died, out of control, and rebelling for all she was worth. Her defiance fizzled out when she stupidly got herself pregnant by the moronic Curtis. Where was I all this time? Enjoying married life with Phil, saving adolescents from self-destruction by working long hours and making excuses not to visit my parents unless I had to.

Although Mum and I looked very much alike, we never found the bond we were supposed to have as mother and daughter. For some reason, it was as if she couldn't spread her love between her two daughters in equal measure. From the moment we moved from Bedford she kept her emotional distance from me, preferring to see to Laura's needs. I was Daddy's girl. The year I turned fifteen changed our family forever, and since returning to Derwent Drive it had been playing on my mind. We should never have come here, I thought.

'Stella? Did Mum or Dad ever mention our old house in Bedford to you?' Wrapping a towel around my head as I emerged from the bathroom, I found her unpacking in Laura's old room. 'Why did you choose this one?' I asked.

'Because it felt too weird to sleep in either of your parents' rooms.' She was right. It was the same reason I'd chosen the spare bedroom. Mum and Dad hadn't slept together, not since we'd lived in Bedford. That was one of the most telling signs of a marriage under strain, although at fifteen I hadn't properly registered the fact.

At the time, I was in turmoil and despair at leaving my friends, being dragged away from the places I knew so well. After that, I had to confront Kit's loss and start at a new school. With my memory playing cruel tricks into the bargain, I gave little thought to anyone else but myself. Moping, sobbing, declining to eat properly, I barely acknowledged the animosity between my parents, which soon became the norm.

I trotted into my bedroom and sat at the dressing table. Stella and I shouted to each other from our respective bedrooms.

'Why do you ask about Bedford?' she enquired.

'Because Peddyr asked me to write a chronology of life events and I thought I might go back to see if there are any old neighbours there who might remember me and who stayed in touch with Mum or Dad. Maybe Kit's parents are still around.'

'What about your aunty Wynn, is she still alive?'

'God, no, she popped off years ago. Anyway, she was in

Wales, not Bedford.'

'Yes, I realise that, but you lived with her for a while before you came here, didn't you? Maybe she has neighbours or relatives who would know about your accident from talking to her. It was always pretty mysterious, wasn't it? Your Mum said you slipped and fell against the caravan door, but it would be good to know if that was the case or not. Surely someone must know how seriously you were injured.'

'It's worth considering,' I said. The hum of the hairdryer drowned out any further conversation and gave me time to mull over these suggestions. Until Peddyr Quirk asked me to write my autobiography, Aunty Wynn was someone I hadn't thought about in years. She was my mother's elder sister and had run a camping and caravan site near Tenby where Laura was born unexpectedly early. Apparently, I'd been there numerous times as a child, but those holidays were archived in a jumble of very similar photographs, leaving me with only snatches of memories involving sand, striped windbreaks and rainy days spent cooped up in a caravan.

What I did have was a powerful physical memory of Aunty Wynn; the lilting way she spoke and how she smelt like fresh bread whenever she crushed me against her enormous chest. I could recall vividly the way she waddled when she walked, and how she smiled benignly all the time. Aunty Wynn was the one who gave me stamps so I could write to Kit and slipped me a few coins, allowing me to make a call from the phone box in the village when Mum was otherwise occupied.

There was such a stark contrast between her and my mother, who became utterly miserable the moment we left Bedford that year. If it made her feel depressed to move so far away, then she should have understood why I was bereft without Kit, but she seemed not to care about my feelings. She should have told Dad we would not move to Bosworth Bishops, miles and miles from home. But she never did.

'I think you're right, Stella. If I'm going to fill in the gaps, then I have to go to Wales and see if anything there jogs my memory. And...' I said, thinking out loud '...I want to work out why Mum was so determined to keep me from staying in touch with Kit.'

'Yeah, makes no sense, does it? Unless she knew it would have to end eventually. You were so young, maybe she thought it was for the best.'

'Well, she was wrong. And it doesn't explain why she became so critical of me when I was the one at her side when Laura was born. And where was Dad then, for goodness' sake? He should have been there.' Taking my frustration out on my hair, I brushed and tugged it into submission. 'I really wish I could work out why someone from so long ago wants to shit on me now.'

'It's over twenty years ago, Gabby, nobody remembers every single thing that happens in their life.'

'But that time in Wales was so...' I scrabbled for the right word '...life-changing. Not everyone delivers their own sister in a sodding caravan in the middle of a field, for God's sake. So why is it all so vague to me?'

By the time I'd put on a monochrome wrap dress and strappy sandals, I felt more human. Make-up applied with a practised hand made my reflection more recognisable to me than it had been of late. The tell-tale dark rings were still there beneath my eyes and so was the tension-knotted muscle in my shoulder, which caught me unawares whenever I reached upwards, but I felt brighter in myself and so thankful for my best friend's unexpected arrival.

'Come on,' she demanded. 'I'll treat us both to breakfast, then we'll hit the shops after the meeting.'

When we thundered down the stairs, I couldn't fail to notice a letter lying in the centre of the doormat. It was a note folded in two.

'Friendly milkman?' Stella asked. 'Wants his bill paying too, does he?'

I unfolded the sheet of paper and read it before sharing the contents with her. 'No, this is from *him*.' She stepped closer to read for herself, holding the edge of the paper to stop it from quivering.

'This is a quote,' she said. '"To regret deeply is to live afresh". Bloody hell, Gabby, you've got yourself a nutcase here. "Ask for forgiveness and you shall live your life".'

Sheer relief at having my friend around must have led me to react in the way I did. Not stopping to wrestle with the front door, I zoomed through the house, out the back and onto the drive. Seeing the familiar sight of a silver BMW as it drove off, I shouted towards number seven, assuming Kenny was there: 'I don't know what I've done to offend you and I don't care. So just fuck off to Pervyville where you belong and leave me alone!'

Stella was right behind me. 'Who was in that car?'

'The police, they have Kenny the Perv under surveillance. He must be here somewhere even though his car isn't.'

I was about to suggest we could ask Peddyr Quirk to chase this up when Curtis barrelled into Derwent Drive at the wheel of his mucky truck, forcing us to run for safety at the side of the drive. 'Not a word to twatface over there. Nothing. Ever.'

'Schtum!' Stella replied, sliding a finger across her lilac-painted lips, winking at me.

MISS HOITY-TOITY

*P*eddyr carried the teapot, following Connie out onto the balcony to have breakfast in the cool morning air. The clear sky was promising another sultry summer's day. He watched as she chose the most anaemic slice from the toast rack and slathered it with butter. Scientists would have shuddered at the number of calories and saturated fats she put away each day and yet she never put on so much as a pound in weight. He supposed she was gifted with a fast metabolism because with her natural energy for life, she never seemed to tire.

Conversely, he was feeling weary and unrefreshed after what should be deemed a good night's sleep, considering the number of hours spent in bed. He stifled a yawn.

'You should take up Tai Chi,' Connie said, smiling at him as she twisted the top from a jar of marmalade. 'The meditation effects are phenomenal.'

'We've been through this. I don't want to waft about like Kung Fu Panda with a load of octogenarians down the local community centre, thank you. And you can forget about Pilates, the same applies.'

'The physio said it would help.'

'Stuff what the physio said. I only get acute pain if I overdo it. Anyway, things are improving, I can walk a lot further these days.'

'Rubbish, Lao Gong.' Giving a dismissive wave of her knife, Connie scooped out a glob of marmalade and smeared this on her toast. 'Tell me about Miss Hoity-Toity's younger sister. You were so exhausted last night, I barely got much out of you after dinner.'

Peddyr approved of his wife's nickname for Gabby Dixon, because it was precisely the first impression she gave. The barriers put up to avoid anyone getting near the person beneath were once steel-plated, but when he'd seen her on Monday, after her disastrous day at work, he knew they'd been breached. Severely.

Despite the posed family photographs at the house, Gabby's younger sister Laura wasn't at all what he was expecting when he met her in the flesh. He was shocked to discover she and her husband were the eco-warriors who lived at Revival Farm; the place of organic honey and hobbit dwellings on the outskirts of town. Given its position at the end of a farm track, he couldn't easily nose around without being mauled by dogs or hounded by the guard geese. However, he could see into the farm from the lay-by where he parked on Wednesday morning.

'When did she venture out?'

'About mid-morning. An older lady, I'm assuming it was her mother-in-law, arrived in a little runabout, a Toyota Aygo. Then Laura left in the same car. I tailed her to Derwent Drive where she parked within sight of number six. She sat there, made a phone call and didn't move until

Miss Hoity-Toity went out, dressed to the nines, as she does.'

'Black trouser-suit, pricey white shirt? Or was it a black skirt with black shirt?' As usual, Connie had guessed correctly. Gabriella Dixon, with her life unravelling around her, had behaved as if she were leaving to attend a business meeting, keeping up appearances. 'I feel for that woman,' Connie sighed. 'Where is the colour in her life?'

For one awful moment Peddyr thought his wife was about to launch into some alternative therapy discussion about the healing qualities of colour, but when she didn't he pressed on, eager to tell her his findings. 'Laura then gets out of her car, skitters along the pavement, up the drive and tries the front door, which won't give. So she dashes through the gate into the back garden. That was the first chance I had to get a good look at her.'

'Well?'

'Nothing like her sister. Although, I say that…' He mused a while. 'They both have the same thick mass of hair, same facial features, same bright eyes, both shortish, but Laura is a throwback to the sixties and seventies flower-power thing. Unlike her big sister, she wore plenty of colour and a bandana doodah in her dreadlocks.'

'Dreadlocks?

'Picture this: Sideshow Bob – only female – with dark long dreads held away from her face by a red and orange tasselled scarf, pale skin, piercings, tattoos up one arm, loads of bangles and beads, skinny, athletic, patchwork pantaloons and a strappy top. Got it?'

Nodding her vehement appreciation of his descriptive talents, Connie took another slice of toast and beckoned for him to deliver more of his story. There wasn't much to tell about Laura's visit to Derwent Drive. From what he could see, she went into the house for only a few minutes before emerging again with a couple of sheets of paper, which she folded as she stepped out of the backdoor. She looked around the garden, picked up a few weeds lining the path to the garage, tossed them onto a compost heap and made her way out again.

'My morning only became interesting when I followed her into town. She did some shopping. Nothing extravagant: washing powder, shampoo, one or two other household items and some fresh yeast from the local bakery. Barely enough to fill her shoulder bag.'

Peddyr had followed Laura into a charity shop, but instead of buying clothes, as he thought she would, she spent several minutes leafing through the second-hand books, settling on a thick paperback by Martina Cole. After this, she had traipsed around as if wasting time, window-shopping, checking each clock she passed by.

'And?' Connie asked.

'And then she met a man for an early lunch, and it wasn't her husband.'

Connie smiled in delight. 'Go on,' she demanded, wriggling forward on the patio chair. 'Who was it, did you find out?'

'I recognised him, though I could hardly believe it. My first thought was, he's too old for her and not her type. But when I'd watched for a while, it didn't look like an affair. It wasn't intimate, not in that way.' Gazing distractedly at the trees in the park beyond, he played back the scene in his mind. 'They had their heads together. He was telling her something and she was shaking her head, cross with him, upset. She showed him a document of some sort, I couldn't see what and I daren't go any nearer in case he saw me. It rattled him, whatever it was.'

'Peddyr! Who was it?' Connie demanded, banging the handle of her knife onto the table.

'It was Owen Fox.'

His wife frowned, struggling to recall the name.

'From Castle and Wyckes? The man who arranged her mother's funeral?'

A small gasp escaped Connie as she reached across the table to touch his hand. 'No wonder you were tossing and turning in bed last night.'

29

ARE FOUR HEADS BETTER
THAN ONE?

*S*tella was the odd one out, but then she always was. Her pink tinged hair, bold patterned maxi dress, and jangling jewellery lit up the dowdy wooden panelling of Bernard Kershaw's office. I smiled patiently as his secretary Fiona delivered a tray of lemon barley waters, evoking memories of Wimbledon and television adverts. She winked at me as she set the tray down. 'How are you holding up, dear?' she asked, patting me on the shoulder. It wasn't patronising or in any way intrusive, Fiona was just being her kindly self. 'I'm glad your friend got here in time.'

An intervention had evidently been planned between Bernard Kershaw, Peddyr Quirk and my friend Stella. It appeared that she had been told of my dire need for an emotional prop and arranged her surprise visit accordingly. Some self-reliant types would have been annoyed by that but I couldn't have been more relieved to have her with me, no matter how it came about. Looking around, it occurred to me with sorrow that these three people were the only ones on whom I could rely to any degree, and I was paying two of them – or at least I would do when I regained access to my money.

Peddyr Quirk was a dignified sight in a suit, even when he dispensed with his jacket. He wore a shirt and braces with authority, as did Bernard Kershaw. The two men had an easy way about them, comfortable with each other. I watched them with interest, still not able to decide what their connection was. They were wearing the same ties as each other.

'Were you two at school together?' I asked.

Both men dropped their heads, touched their ties and laughed with embarrassment. 'No,' said Bernard. 'Same rugby club.' That explained a lot. He and Peddyr exchanged knowing winks. What goes on tour, stays on tour – as Phil used to say.

'Where to start,' Bernard said as he reached for his drink. 'The situation seems to become more complex by the day, so let's recap for our mutual benefit.'

Not the man for using three words when one would do, Bernard gave a rundown of my current position. 'Registered as deceased by person or persons unknown, bank accounts frozen, bills piling up at an alarming rate, suspended from work, no access to pay because of NHS red-tape, no car, and no divorce.' Then he lightened the mood. 'But the good news is, I have a court hearing date of September the twelfth.' He stabbed his expensive ball-point pen at an open desk diary.

At this I choked, unable to swallow a mouthful of barley water without spluttering. Stella spoke my thoughts. 'The middle of September? But that's weeks away,' she shrieked, shooting me a horrified look.

'That's damned quick,' Peddyr chipped in. 'Bernie pulled strings at the old boys' club. Count yourself bloody lucky.'

An admonishment for being ungrateful wasn't unexpected, but, in my defence, remaining dead for that long was likely to bankrupt me.

'I'm sorry to react so negatively,' I said with a rasp, my throat still in spasm. 'I thought getting a court hearing was just a formality. Didn't realise there was a queue.' Staring hard at Bernard, I willed him to ease my pain.

'It would have been a lot more straightforward if your persecutor hadn't stolen your most important personal documents.' Bernard turned stiffly to Peddyr, who was resting against a cold radiator near an open window. 'But we have made progress elsewhere, I understand.'

Swivelling our heads in synchronised trepidation, Stella and I turned to lock eyes on Peddyr Quirk. There was a weariness about him that hadn't been evident on Monday.

'I've been up into the early hours with this,' he began, and the ominous note to his announcement must have struck Stella in the same way it did me. She reached out, touched my knee and whispered 'Pebble'. I didn't require a second prompt. My right hand slid easily into the pocket of my dress and I wrapped clammy fingers around the cool stone. With the other, I held onto Stella's hand.

'Owen Fox. He dealt with your mother's funeral arrangements.'

'Right.' I knew who he was talking about, but didn't know why. 'The chap Laura made the arrangements with?'

'What do you know about him?'

The answer was straightforward. I knew nothing about Owen Fox other than he worked for Castle and Wyckes and he'd made a passable job of respecting Mum's wishes.

'Only passable?'

'I'm probably being unfair,' I said. 'Perhaps I shouldn't have left things to Laura like I did. The caterers were a let-down, but actually I can't complain about Castle and Wyckes. They were expensive, but then Laura did order the most costly coffin in the catalogue because Mum said she wanted solid wood and brass handles.'

'But when you met Owen Fox, what did you make of him?'

'Not a lot, I barely took much notice of the man… why are we talking about a funeral director all of a sudden?'

Peddyr cleared his throat and threw a look at my solicitor. 'He knows your sister well enough to meet her in town for lunch.' Peddyr folded his arms decisively. 'What the heck… you may as well find out now,' he said, apparently deciding against a subtle approach. 'I saw him with your sister yesterday, they seemed very close. More than casual friends, shall we say.'

'Excellent,' said Stella animatedly. 'She's having a fling behind brick-head-the-dickhead's back. About time she woke up and got herself a decent man.'

I wasn't so enthusiastic. From what I'd seen the evening before, Curtis and Laura were as tight as ever. Affectionate and scheming together to get hold of my money. Peddyr was watching my reaction. 'Laura – having an affair with Mister Mournful? There's no way,' I said.

'No, you're right,' Peddyr confirmed, swivelling his gaze and winking at Stella. 'You've jumped the gun, Mrs Cortez. Although it crossed my mind at first, I'll grant you. Let me explain my interest in Owen Fox,' he said, before striding across the room where he took up position next to a flip chart set ready on an easel. On the plain sheet of paper, he wrote three words in capitals. 'Means, motive and opportunity. The holy trinity of guilt, ladies.'

He aimed the marker pen at Stella. 'Hear me out if you would. Owen Fox works at the local undertakers, Castle and Wyckes, your old stomping ground Mrs Cortez. Did you come across him before you took early retirement?'

'No. I don't think so. He must be relatively new,' Stella said. 'We didn't cross paths until Eileen's funeral.'

'That's a shame. Never mind,' Peddyr shrugged. 'Anyway, we do know he was the one on call the night Josephine Dank died. He therefore has the means to arrange removal of a body.' Peddyr wrote Owen's name and Josie's on the flip chart paper. He then drew an arrow to the name Castle and Wyckes, which he circled.

'Here is my best guess. Owen Fox takes the details, knows the deceased is female, is about the same age as Gabriella and has no known relatives, because the neighbour, Mr Arthur Bird, tells him so. Knowing the doctor has been and gone, Owen waits until the pallbearers collect the body before presenting himself at Worthington Court pretending to be Josie's cousin Dave Smith. Not a very inventive name, I might add.'

I could feel Stella becoming increasingly enthralled by this and was expecting her to say something fatuous about Hercule Poirot or Inspector Barnaby. But she seemed stunned into silence.

Dave Smith's name went next to that of Owen Fox with AKA scrawled beside it. Peddyr's handwriting deteriorated as he speeded up his explanation. 'Owen then makes certain he takes information and certain documents from Arthur Bird, the neighbour, and from Josie's flat. Then he trots along to register the death of Gabriella Dixon, *not* Josephine Dank. He pretends to be Arthur Bird, another alias to add to the collection. After that, using the name Dave Smith again, he arranges for Josie's body to be transferred to another funeral service, distancing him from his crime. He changes all the documentation and creates body ID tags in

Gabriella's name. No one takes responsibility for funeral arrangements because a letter is received, ostensibly from Dr Philip Dixon, refusing to accept liability for the funeral. Owen Fox could easily have produced that letter. Are you with me?'

I nod once, barely able to comprehend the lengths to which Fox has gone. A man I don't even know.

'There is the opportunity,' Peddyr says with satisfaction. 'Well, almost all of it. Correct me if I'm wrong, Mrs Cortez. You know all about these things.' Putting the lid back on the pen, he turned to Bernard Kershaw. 'It's taken me a friggin' long time to work out how anyone would get hold of a medical cause of death certificate. Dr Prasad wrote the original dea—'

'Emile? Emile Prasad wrote my death certificate?' The words left my mouth as I shot to my feet. 'How could he do such a thing? Is he in on this?'

Peddyr's reaction told me I was wide of the mark, which is why he's a private detective and I'm not. He flapped his hand.

'Sit down. Let me finish.' Turning to Bernard he declared, 'This was an awful idea. I told you, she's in no fit state to take this on board.'

Looking towards Stella and me, Bernard Kershaw asked for our response by cocking one bushy eyebrow.

'She's fine,' Stella said firmly.

'I'm fine,' I reiterated. 'It's my death and I want to find out *who* killed me off, *how* they killed me off and *why* they did it. Especially if my sister has something to do with it. So please continue. I won't interrupt again.' Contrite, I sat back down.

Facing the flip chart, Peddyr released the nib of the pen and circled Owen Fox's name again. 'I believe this man laid his hands on a blank certificate some weeks earlier, courtesy of a forgetful and elderly GP who is prone to leaving significant items lying around when he has cause to visit Castle and Wyckes. I can't prove this because I haven't had time to make the necessary enquiries as yet… but it is possible.' He looked at me with a steady gaze, tapping on the corresponding words written boldly on the chart next to him. 'If I'm right, Owen Fox had the means and the opportunity. He planned your death carefully and went to great lengths to forge cremation certificates. The local authority had no cause for concern over their validity and the independent mediating doctor assigned to the crem signed off cremation form five.' Peddyr stared into my eyes.

'That is the "how". As far as the "who" is concerned, he is currently manifesting himself. Owen Fox wants you to identify him. He sent personal messages and gifts signposting who he is. Hence the latest note from this morning.' Peddyr smiled thinly. 'Now you can speak, Gabby.'

And I would have done if my mouth and brain had made a better connection, but I had so many questions they ran into one another, creating a nonsensical pile-up. 'I… Er… I … why? How?'

'I've explained how. No other possible suspect, barring your husband Dr Philip Dixon, had the means to access a cause of death certificate, but the man in the photograph at the register office isn't Philip Dixon. And I understand from Bernie that your husband is about to transfer the financial settlement from your divorce, now he knows you're not dead.'

'Is he?' I asked, almost winded by this incredible news.

'According to his solicitor, he's transferring the full amount to my holding account.'

'Wow! I guess that rules him out then,' Stella interjected.

'Correct,' Peddyr affirmed. 'It would be totally wrong to keep him on any list of suspects. I spoke to Dr Dixon and he's as keen as you are to reach a formal conclusion to your marriage.'

'I doubt he used such diplomatic words,' I said.

Peddyr shook his head. 'He didn't.'

'So why is Owen Fox doing this?' I asked. 'And who's to say Phil didn't pay him to do it? And you're sure it's not creepy Kenny doing this in revenge for our so-called harassment of him?'

'I'm as certain as I can be that it's neither of them. Philip Dixon is as clean as a whistle,' Peddyr replied. 'Granted, he closed your email account, but then again he believed you to be dead. He wasn't the one who closed your bank accounts because he never laid hands on any copy death certificate. I've spoken to him and, trust me, he's not your man. Too straight. And Justin Parkes hates the sight of you but is too thick, before you ask...'

'Well, what about Kenny then? The police have him under surveillance. There's a detective watching him,' I countered.

'Yes, they have him on their radar, but the police haven't got the manpower for a detective to sit watching your perverted neighbour all hours of the day and night. The bloke you assumed to be a detective... what does he look like and how often is he there?'

'I've only seen him either early morning or in the evening. Seven p.m. onwards. Although he was there on the Monday I moved in. Lunchtime-ish.'

'Monday. Owen Fox has a day off then to compensate him for working Saturdays or on-call,' Peddyr said, rubbing palms together.

Giving this more thought, I saw the pattern. 'So BMW

man is monitoring *me*, not Kenny Eversholt. That was just a way of putting me off the scent?'

'Oh, shit,' Stella said, raising a hand to her mouth. 'He's stalking you, and Laura has something to do with it. This is terrible.'

Walking forward, Peddyr hooked thumbs into his elasticated braces and fixed Stella with a serious expression. 'Yes, it is fairly terrible, but no one has died, unless you count Josephine Dank. No crime has been committed that we can prove. Nothing stolen other than Gabby's ability to function. If the plan is to ruin her life, then it's been a successful campaign. But the question remains: why?'

'But I don't know Owen Fox,' I blurted. 'What has he got to do with me?'

Peddyr remained deadpan. 'If you don't have a connection to him then, as Mrs Cortez implied, we have to ask if Owen Fox is acting for himself or for your sister?'

Dismayed to hear of Laura's likely betrayal, I released a sigh. 'She and Curtis are after my money, that's for sure. Laura is resentful. She thinks I shouldn't have an equal share in the inheritance, because she was the one who remained at home to care for our mother. If I agree to their demands for rent and the building project, then they win. And by the time this mess gets sorted, I'll owe money to all and sundry.' With my stomach in one big painful knot, I resigned myself to being cornered. 'Either way, I lose.'

Bernard hadn't spoken for a while, but it was his turn. 'Peddyr will keep researching Owen Fox's background, he may well find a link to you, but I'd like to know if Laura is aware of Peddyr's involvement in this. Does she know there's a private investigation going on?'

'Yes,' I replied weakly. 'Was I wrong to tell her?'

30

DIVIDE AND CONQUER

*I*n the supermarket car park, Stella filled the boot and the back seat of the hired Mini with bags of shopping and boxes of necessities. 'I still don't think six bottles will see us through the weekend,' she said, oblivious to my zombie-like state. I was going through the motions, numbed by the possibility my sister had gone to such convoluted lengths to discredit and destroy me.

This turned to a simmering rage when we pulled up on the driveway of number six Derwent Drive. There was no sign of Curtis, just a new lock and a note tacked to the front door with a nail, instructing me to collect a set of keys from Revival Farm. 'Keys to my own fucking house!' I yelled at an undeserving Stella while I ripped the sheet of paper from the door and screwed it into a tight ball. 'She can have this back and recycle it from where the sun doesn't shine.'

'Now, now, calm yourself. We have to play this carefully,' Stella said. 'We mustn't let on what we suspect. But we do need to squeeze the truth out about why she met with Owen whatsisname for lunch.' On our short drive to the farm Stella shared with me what she had in mind and I had to admit it was admirable. 'Just go with me,' she advised as we drew into the courtyard, sending geese honking and dusty dogs into a frenzy.

'And you think she'll believe you want to buy number six?'

'I'm rich enough.' Stella winked at me. Millionaire husband or no millionaire husband, I had no way of knowing if she personally was wealthy enough to purchase my house outright, and Laura wouldn't know either.

Curtis's van wasn't anywhere in sight, but a livid Laura soon appeared at the open oak door, I could have sworn she'd been crying. She held a set of glistening house keys in her hand and with a wide stance filled the doorway, clearly not intending to invite us in.

'Curtis said there was a visitor at the house this morning. I didn't know you were coming to stay, Stella.' There was no eye contact coming my way, Laura kept her gaze fixed on Stella as she got out of the driver's seat, doing a good job of ignoring me. Shrugging out of the seat belt, I stood with the Mini between me and my seething sister.

'She doesn't need permission from you, does she?' I countered, feeling my resolve not to antagonise her, slipping dangerously away.

'Me an' Curtis want a private chat. We want to review our offer... without an audience.' What a scornful smirk my sister produced as she forced home how unwelcome my friend was.

Plainly, Stella had chosen the wrong career. Given her performance over the next quarter of an hour, she should have applied to RADA. I'd never seen such acting skills. Sounding as sincere as Mother Teresa, she said, 'I couldn't stay away when my best mate was in such a terrible situation, now could I? What sort of friend would I be?'

The response from Laura was a sickly grin. 'Someone has to be on her side.' She'd never liked Stella.

'It's such a shame you two have to fall out over money,' my friend continued. 'Shall I tell your sister the wonderful news?' she asked me.

'Please be my guest,' I replied. While I hung grimly on to my composure, what there was left of it, Stella rested folded arms on top of the car door. 'It isn't nearly as difficult to settle as you would think,' she said. 'And I may have the perfect solution.'

'Oh, yes?' Laura ventured, angling her head to one side.

'You'll be getting your money within the next week.'

'What?'

'Your money.' Stella pronounced each syllable slowly and deliberately. 'I'm buying number six outright so you can soon be paid for your half share. You won't have to wait for Gabby to sort out her little problem.'

Even though I knew what Stella was doing, and that it was a downright lie, I couldn't quite credit what I was hearing. The house keys fell from Laura's hand.

'One less thing for you and Curtis to worry about.' Stella made certain to turn and smile at me as she said this. 'And you can save the money you would have to pay your accountant fellow.'

'What accountant?' Laura asked, brushing dirt from the bunch of keys as she picked them out of the dust.

'The one you met with in town yesterday. My brother Graham says he saw you in The Salad Box having a spot of lunch.' Stella stopped smiling and took on a more sober tone. 'Oh, I'm so sorry. Did he get that wrong? He could have sworn it was Freddie Cook, the accountant. Was he mistaken?' Avoiding any exaggeration, Stella's body language was subtle enough to look authentic.

Taken aback, the thunderous look on Laura's face seemed to worsen. 'No, it wasn't an accountant. It was... it was none of your business.' Flinging her hand outward, she aimed the keys in Stella's direction. 'Gabriella can let me know when she's moving out. I'll be glad to see the back of her and her endless lies.'

Without warning, the confrontation had notched up a gear and for a second I couldn't fathom why.

'I'm not ready to discuss this any further until *she...*' Laura said, uncoiling an arm in my direction '...can be honest about what she did.'

Suddenly everything fell into place for me. Owen Fox knew about me, about my past, and had told Laura. The trouble was, I hadn't a clue what that secret might be. I let rip: 'So it *is* you behind all this. You and that wanker Owen Fox, whoever the hell he is!' I gripped the car door handle and pulled. 'Stella, get in, we're going. The house is yours if you want it. Bernard Kershaw and the police can deal with everything. I'm off. I should never have come back.'

Laura held fists up to the colourful bandana on her head, crying angry tears. 'Fuck you!' she shrieked. 'I don't need you in my life, Gabby. I never did.'

31

TIME FOR SOME PERSPECTIVE

We put the shopping away in record time. Once we had placed the tins and dry goods in cupboards, Stella handed me items for the fridge, which I subsequently lobbed onto shelves without my usual orderliness. She insisted I reconsider my hasty decision to sell Derwent Drive, but I was hearing none of it.

'No, that's it, I am not staying in this house any longer than I have to. That fucking girl is riddled with envy, jealousy and now greed. She'll get only what she's due and I'm changing my will. When I die, you can have the lot. She can bloody swivel.' It wasn't strictly necessary for me to raise a middle finger, but it made me feel better and stopped me punching a wall. 'How could she be so downright devious?'

'Now hold on. We don't know for sure–'

'Yes, we do. She didn't deny meeting Owen Fox. She was here when my laptop and documents were stolen. The bloody girl comes and goes as she pleases. And what's more, she told me to fuck right off. So I shall.'

We fell quiet for a while, putting rubbish in the bin and

deliberately not sorting out any recyclable materials, filling the kettle and busying ourselves with mundane tasks. 'What did you and Laura talk about on your way home last night? Bet you wish you'd caught the bus,' Stella prompted me.

*T*he journey from Revival Farm to Derwent Drive had taken no longer than fifteen minutes. Laura drove me to my door at her insistence. I was a captive audience, and she made the most of the trip to grill me about my decision not to have children. 'Phil said you had an abortion,' she said as we pulled out from the farm track and onto smooth tarmac.

'He had no right to talk to you about that,' I replied, rubbing at my left upper arm in a subconscious defensive gesture.

She took aim again. 'Never liked kids, have you?'

'It's not a case of disliking them, it's my choice not to be a mother.'

Taking her time, Laura pushed a well-directed lunge with her spiteful word sword. 'Why, because your own mother didn't love you? Because you were a mistake?'

'Charming. And you weren't exactly planned,' I parried. 'We were doing fine until you came along.'

*A*s I relayed the scene back to Stella, she stood with her mouth widening in disbelief. 'The vicious little cow,' she said, rocking back against the kitchen work surface, her rosy hair clashing with the pea-soup green of the kitchen cupboards.

'I wasn't much better,' I confessed. 'I shouldn't have been lured into a bitch fight, but she kept on and on about how

I'd abandoned her, went off without a care, didn't think about her from one week to the next. Me, me, me…'

'Vicious and selfish. What happened when she dropped you off?'

'Not a lot. She said I was getting what I deserved and drove away at top speed, looking like she would explode.'

In a rapid change of subject, or so I thought, Stella said, 'It all seems to connect back to your younger days. Laura's obviously resented you for a long time and there's something in your childhood we still haven't got to the bottom of. Shall we go to Wales tomorrow? Get away from Laura and try to reboot your memory about the night you banged your head?'

'Wales is tempting, and I could do with a break from this ludicrous pressure, but personally I think our time could be better spent confronting Owen Fox. I want to know what he has to say for himself.' I stared her out. 'Then we declare the game over. Get Laura to return my ID, to confess to the bank, the registrar and the police, and Bob's your sodding uncle.'

'And what are you going to say to him? "Hi, I think you are the nutter who is spying on me even though I don't know you. Give yourself up."' She grabbed me by my shoulders and gave a gentle yet firm shake. 'Get a grip. Let's run this past your personal detective before you make a fool of yourself. Give him a ring.'

*W*hen Stella and I mounted the stairs to P.Q. Investigations, we heard Connie's high-pitched chatter coming from above. Peddyr's wife sounded more excitable than when I'd first met her. Rushing to greet us, she was hopping from one foot to the other barely long enough to close the door behind us.

'Hannah went into labour last night. My daughter-in-law.' Without pausing she introduced herself to Stella, declared how delighted she was to meet her and then zipped around at top speed, putting a purse into her handbag, followed by a sheaf of paper from the printer. 'Pedd!' she shouted. 'Pedd, the ladies are here. There are enough meals in the freezer for you. Don't do what you did last time.'

The door to Peddyr Quirk's office swung open, and he sauntered into the whirlwind created by his hyperactive wife. 'Connie, slow down. There's plenty of time, your flight doesn't leave for hours.'

'Going back to Hong Kong?' I asked, trying to make sense of the mayhem.

'No, Glasgow. Marshall and Hannah moved there after they got married. It's our first grandchild,' Connie squeaked. 'A boy. A lovely boy. Eight pounds six. A good healthy weight.'

'What wonderful news,' Stella said, greatly entertained by these antics.

Connie tapped her oversized leather handbag. 'Tickets, passport, money. Presents are in the car, suitcase packed. You have food, Ye Ye. I'll phone you as soon as I get to Bristol Airport.' Without another word, Connie stretched up onto her toes and kissed her husband on the cheek and did the same to me and Stella. We returned her hugs with equal enthusiasm. The glee was infectious.

This must have been normal behaviour in the Quirk household because Peddyr absorbed the chaos and waved her through the door into their flat, releasing a lengthy sigh once relative peace descended.

'Sorry about that,' he said.

'No need to apologise, you must be thrilled,' Stella said as we followed him into his Sam Spade office. 'Oh, I like this,' she declared, immediately making for his leather captain's chair. 'May I?'

'Be my guest,' he replied taking up residence on the corner of the desk while I avoided doing battle again with the soggy armchair by choosing instead to wedge myself onto one of two hardback chairs opposite Stella. I wasn't falling for the-chair-that-eats-you trick a second time.

'That accent of yours,' I said, feeling rather pleased with myself. 'I finally worked it out.'

'Oh?'

'The name Peddyr was so unusual I looked it up and put two and two together. You're a Manx man.'

'He's a what?' Stella asked, her eyebrows shooting towards her fringe.

Clapping his hands in an exaggerated manner, Peddyr Quirk grinned. 'What took you so long?'

'I've been a bit dead lately. Tends to interfere with the functioning of the brain,' I replied, tapping a finger to my temple.

'Well, now that it's working better, I'm glad you called,' he said. 'I have an update on this morning.' Patting a buff folder lying on the desk next to him, he sucked in his lips. 'I've been searching the electoral register and Owen Fox's name comes up with his previous two addresses. One where he lived with his ex-wife until recently and before that when he lived in a flat for a few years on De Pary's Avenue in Bedford.' He looked at me expectantly.

'No. Still a blank from me, I'm afraid. The name means nothing. I don't remember the man.' I stared back at him, waiting for more.

'Your old school friends in Bedford, Ben and Camille, do you have surnames and any idea where I might find them?'

'Camille is with her parents in Bedford Cemetery up on Norse Road. They died in a tragic house fire about six days before Kit died. Needless to say, I never went to that funeral either.'

It had been a long time since I'd thought about Camille and I'd filed her death under a section in my mind which remained closed most of the time. But as I spoke about her to Peddyr Quirk, I could almost see her as she was when we used to meet at Ben's house; a lively soul with an infectious laugh and sleek hair. 'Where Ben's concerned, I *can* help. His full name is Ben Harmer, he's an actor. We haven't stayed in touch, but I keep tabs on his career. He's been on telly several times. Bit parts mostly. He was in one episode of *'Death in Surbiton'* as the victim. He's doing a play right now in Swindon.'

I was rewarded with a grin from Peddyr. 'Not too far away, I could get a bike out and meet him there. Would he speak to me? I need some background information and he may know who Owen Fox is.' He looked pensively across at Stella before directing his gaze at me again.

'Probably,' I said. 'He'll take all the attention he can get; he revels in it.'

I noticed Peddyr rubbing at his wrist, which made me question what he'd just said. 'If Connie is taking the car... you said you would go to Swindon on your bike. Your motorbike?'

'Yes, I'm looking forward to it. Any chance to see if my leathers still fit me,' he replied, and I caught Stella licking her lips, which earned my disapproval. This wasn't the time for flirting.

'But Connie said you shouldn't.'

A cheeky grin appeared on his face. 'Ah, no, she was referring to when I snapped my cruciate, broke an ankle and my wrist. These aren't any old war wounds, you know.'

'That's what I mean. You might have another crash.'

'What crash?' Looking perplexed for a second, Peddyr then suddenly threw back his head and let rip a splendid belly laugh. 'I didn't fall off a bike. No, no. The last time she went to Glasgow without me, I went to the pub with Bernie. We got hammered and tried to walk home carrying a take-away curry without opening our eyes.'

I'd never seen this playful side of Peddyr Quirk. 'What happened?' I asked, agog.

He chortled at the memory. 'I veered too far left, bounced off the side of a building and tripped over a road-works sign. One of those damn' great metal triangles. Landed in a heap, then Bernie landed on top of me. Curry everywhere. Ambulance job. All those years in the Force and I end up broken in several places thanks to a fat solici-tor. I still haven't recovered.'

'Bernie, as in Bernard Kershaw, dead posh, slightly obnoxious, law-abiding solicitor Bernie?' Stella asked, giggling along with the story.

'The very same,' Peddyr said with pride. 'Connie banned me from going out drinking with Bernie, not banned me from my bikes. That would never do.'

32

A JOURNEY OF DISCOVERY

*W*hen we got back to Derwent Drive, I made a quick call to Bernard. 'I'd like you to take whatever you're owed from my financial settlement when it arrives from Phil,' I said. 'Then I want you to pay whatever I owe Mr Quirk.'

'These things can wait, Gabriella.'

'No, I want to pay what I owe up to now, because I want you to transfer the balance into Stella's account. I'll email you her bank details. She's going to buy Laura's half of Derwent Drive with the money. I can't do it because I'm dead and I want to make a clean break from Laura and Curtis as soon as possible.'

'Are you sure you can trust Mrs Cortez?'

'With my life,' I replied.

'In that case, I shall see your instructions are carried out.'

Feeling more at ease now that at least some of my debts were to be paid, I thanked him. 'Once I'm declared alive again, I'll put the house on the market, complete the divorce, pay whatever else I owe and settle down some-where far away from here. I can't wait.'

*W*hat a shame Stella hadn't thought to hire a more spacious car when she flew in from Spain. However, with only the two of us to cater for during our trip to Wales, we had enough room for luggage and a supply of alcohol without feeling overly cramped. It was a while before we were ready to set off on the Friday morning.

'Got waterproofs and wellies in?' Stella asked. Convinced it would rain for the entire weekend, I'd resorted to rooting around until I found spare wet weather gear for her to borrow. Mum's old gardening jacket and a pair of Laura's floral wellies would suffice.

For conceding to her requirements, Stella made me promise to wear jeans. 'No more stupid suits and blouses. It's time to chill out and leave your starchy psychologist persona behind. It doesn't fool me and no one else cares.' Harsh but true. 'Oh, and that bun on top of your noggin can go. Ponytail or plaits only. Stella rules now apply.' I complied without argument. It was time for me to change, inside and out.

Neither of us attempted to load the car until we were certain Owen Fox wasn't spying on us from his BMW. He would get his comeuppance once Peddyr had the evidence to take to the police about failure to properly register a death, deliberate falsification of records pertaining to medical certification of death, and anything else he could think of that would stack up. Owen Fox would be looking for a new job very shortly, and I would get my life back.

Stella scanned the road. 'No sign of the creep. All clear. Time to vamoose.'

We weren't so lucky with Kenny the Perv. Squeezed behind the wheel of his car, he pootled onto his driveway as I was ramming the final holdall into the boot of the Mini, wedging the Magic 8-Ball on top of it. I'd intended to give a polite wave and ignore him, but Stella had other ideas. 'Hi,' she said as he emerged from his car. 'You must be Kenny. I'm Gabriella's friend from Spain. I used to live here in Bosworth years ago. You local originally?'

Not expecting a friendly greeting, Kenny appeared shocked. He looked around him before replying. 'Me? Yes, I'm Kenny, and no, I hail from Winchester. Who did you say you are again, ducky?'

'Stella. I'm Gabriella's friend from Spain. Can I ask a favour? While you're here, can you keep an eye out for uninvited visitors. We're going away for a couple of nights and...' She left this request unfinished, not because of the astonishment on my face, but to appeal to Kenny's inquisitive nature.

'Going somewhere nice?'

'Wales. Tenby.'

With a loud cough, I distracted Stella long enough for her to pay me some heed. This was madness. 'What the absolute fuck are you doing?' I stage-whispered.

Turning away from me, she beamed at Kenny. 'We had a strange note through the door yesterday morning, and after that peculiar phone-in on last Saturday's radio show... well.' To my horror, Stella was practically begging the man to house-sit. 'Gabby said you're an avid fan of the show, so you must realise how freaky it is to have a stalker. Would you mind watching the place if you're around? We'll be back on Sunday evening.'

Only then did I twig what she was up to. A pervert he may be but, to ingratiate himself, Kenny would watch the place like a hawk and if Laura bowled up, he'd have the perfect excuse to challenge her. It could make for interesting viewing for a fly on the wall, if it happened.

'I'll do better than that,' Kenny said with a leer. 'There's a security camera covering my porch, I'll aim it in your direction. It's digital.'

Selling up would be a pleasure, I decided. The sooner I could put a healthy distance between Kenny and me, the better. In the future, he could lech at someone else. Homosexual, my arse.

'That's amazingly kind of you, see you on Sunday then,' I said, bringing the conversation to an end and directing Stella to do the same. 'We must get cracking, or we'll never get there in time to book in.'

We were barely out of town when I realised there was a flaw in her plan. 'If Kenny tells Laura we've gone to Wales, she'll tell Owen Fox.'

'Shit. I didn't think of that. Still, what's the worst that can happen? You're already dead, aren't you?'

Not existing any more does tend to lend a unique perspective to life.

*O*nce we'd left the M50 heading past Ross on Wye, I had a call from Peddyr Quirk. Via Bluetooth, his voice filled the car. He was about to leave for Swindon and wanted to let me know Ben Harmer had agreed to meet with him. 'I won't be able to phone you again until afterwards. Have a safe trip and keep in touch.'

'Do they really talk like that in the Isle of Man?' Stella queried.

'It's further north than you think. You're not confusing it with the Isle of Wight, are you?' Geography was never her strong subject.

'No, I'm not that stupid. I should have realised. The ferries run from Liverpool to the Isle of Man, don't they?' Glancing across at me fleetingly she asked, 'What's our plan of action for this trip down Memory Lane then?'

Strangely enough, I'd been thinking about the exact same thing. 'With my psychologist's head on, I've realised something very important,' I said, keeping my eyes on the road ahead. 'My memory lapses occur when I'm particularly stressed. Things seem to improve when I'm with you.'

'And?'

'And therefore, even though it happened years ago, you will make me relive what happened on the night Laura was born and what happened when I bumped my head and ended up in hospital. We are going to the caravan site at the farm and I want to remember everything, and that way I will uncover why it was Kit took his own life rather than find a way to be with me.'

The stab of emotional pain in my gut jolted me forward. 'And I will work out why my parents really wanted to keep our move from Bedford so secretive.'

'You don't believe their story?' For a change she was serious. Her hands tightened on the steering wheel. 'It would be good to find out why Kit killed himself. And I know you think your death is connected to his, but–'

'They have to be connected and Owen bloody Fox has to know about me and Kit. He knew about the Magic 8-Ball. He knew what games we used to play. He blames me for Kit's death, and I don't have the slightest idea who he is or how he fits in with this. If he and Laura are in cahoots, then it's because he instigated it, not the other way around.'

33

PEDDYR MEETS BEN

*B*en Harmer was appearing in *"Dust after Destruction"* at a small regional theatre on the outskirts of Swindon. According to the posters outside, he was playing the part of George Lansdowne, a misguided scientist who initiated a nuclear holocaust. Peddyr much preferred a musical.

'Hi there, Paddy. Come on in. Great to meet you. You're the first Dick I've ever had in my dressing room.'

Based on some of the creative types he'd met on his way through the stage door entrance, Peddyr wasn't convinced on that score. He managed a polite shake of the hand before correcting Ben. 'It's Peddyr, not Paddy. Like Peter rather than Patrick.'

'Excellent. Take a seat and put that crash helmet on the floor. Right, what can I do for you, Pete?' As he sat in his uninspiring dressing room with his legs wide apart in the way arrogant men do, the body language said, *Look at me, I'm showing you my genitals to prove how masculine I am. I'm not one of those camp thespians. I'm all testosterone and testicles...*

It was only when he looked more closely did Peddyr realise that Ben's lower left leg was missing. He would have to reassess his first impression of the man, because sitting in the way he did was more a matter of balance than arrogance.

Casting around the cluttered dressing room, Peddyr spied a metal prosthetic leg propped against the wall to his right. Next to it was a wooden crutch with a leather-bound armpit pad. Ben followed his gaze.

'After three weeks of this tripe, I'm sick and tired of that crutch. It's like playing Long John Silver, but without the parrot.' Ben Harmer spoke in a mellow, measured voice. Unfortunately, with bits of his face flaking off, being cast as a post-apocalyptic scientist did nothing for his credibility.

'Joined the army when I left school. Lost my virginity, my innocence and a leg,' he said, tapping his knee. 'Desk job for a while then ended up as part of the SSVC mostly in Combined Services Entertainment, which led to my fine acting career. Mustn't grumble, I never would have met Sean Connery if it wasn't for getting my leg blown off.'

After listening to the man give a rundown of his acting career to date, dropping famous names left right and centre, Peddyr held up a hand. 'It's been fascinating, but, as I said on the phone, I'm after specific information about the Willis family and about Gabriella Brady.'

'Such as?' Not being able to talk about himself, Ben Harmer soon became more interested in touching up his ghastly make-up than supplying Peddyr with much-needed information.

'You said on the phone that the four of you usually hung around together after school.'

'That's right... I was the gang leader. We met at my house, then there was Camille Bullimore, Kit and Gabby.' As he said this, Ben placed a hand on his right knee and rubbed at it gently.

'Gabby wasn't supposed to hang around with us,' he continued. 'She went to the posh public girls' school. We weren't good enough for the likes of her father, but as he wasn't around much, she could do what she liked as long as he didn't find out.'

'What about her mother?'

'Too busy to notice. She spent hours at the hairdressers, getting her nails done, shopping. Gabby was nothing like her.'

'She looked just like her.'

Ben shook his head. 'That's not what I meant. Gabby didn't behave like her mother. She was a proper tearaway that one, jeans and a tee-shirt, getting into fights, hell of a left hook.'

'Are we talking about the same girl? Gabriella Brady liked a bit of rough and tumble?' Peddyr found he couldn't keep the surprise from his voice.

Prodding at a slice of grey-painted flesh with a tissue, Ben grinned into an oval mirror, elbows resting on his dressing table. 'You could challenge that girl to do almost anything, she never backed away from it. Never chickened out from an eight-ball decision. Not once.'

'Are you referring to a Magic 8-Ball?' Peddyr asked.

Ben dipped his head. 'Yep, we always let the ball decide anyone's fate. That was the game. Bloody hilarious at times it was too. Gabby once cut off Kit's hair while he was asleep… classic.'

'What about the other members of the Willis family?'

Ben thought about this for a second before giving the uncensored version of Willis family life. 'Shana was the mum. A fat lazy slag, you know the sort, fag in her mouth, didn't dress until lunchtime when it was time to go to the pub.' Clearly beginning to enjoy the drama, Ben Harmer turned away from titivating in the mirror and faced Peddyr to give a personal performance. 'Their house was a fucking mess with kids everywhere and stinky nappies left strewn about the place, clothes drying and beds unmade.

'Mickie Willis was the dad; Kit looked just like him. Everyone knew Mickie Willis; one of those larger-than-life characters with a Transit shagging waggon, tight jeans and a reputation with the ladies.' Ben nodded approvingly. 'I wanted to be Mickie Willis when I grew up.'

'What did he do for a living?'

'A builder, plumber, handyman. Odd jobs, here and there. Servicing boilers and other people's wives mostly, which was probably why Shana threw him out. After that she shacked up with a Sri Lankan called Hank who spent most of the time lying on the sofa in their front room sipping from a can of Tenant's Super. Shana and Hank had a coffee-coloured kid called Castro.'

Peddyr's imagination conjured up a small horde of feral children living in a hovel, largely ignored by a slovenly woman with badly dyed hair. 'Castro? After Fidel?'

'Who knows? They all had weird names in that family.'

'Does the name Owen Fox mean anything to you?'

'Should it?'

'I was hoping so... he lived in Bedford although he's maybe a couple of years older than you.'

When Ben shook his head, a random flake of scaly earlobe drifted to the floor unnoticed. 'No. Means nothing to me. Sorry.' Pausing, he looked again at Peddyr through bloodshot contact lenses. 'You said this had to do with

Gabby and Kit. You know Kit topped himself, right? And that Camille died in a fire?'

'Gabby told me, but I don't know the details, other than Kit took a load of pills and alcohol. Do you know why he killed himself?'

'The coroner gave an open verdict. There was no note so they couldn't prove Kit wanted to die. There were rumours…'

'Such as?' Peddyr tried to sound nonchalant.

'A week or two before he died, Gabby phoned Kit from a call box somewhere in Wales. He was gutted. Probably because she made up this mad story about how she and her mum had to leave in a hurry because of something to do with her father's secret work for the Government and she wasn't allowed to talk about it. Why she thought he'd fall for that, I don't know. She obviously lied to him.'

'But that can't have been it,' Peddyr countered. 'It's sad, but not enough to make someone commit suicide.'

'She didn't tell you about the baby then?'

'Yes, she did. I know about Laura. She was born when Mrs Brady and Gabby were staying with a relative in Wales. Is there something else I should be aware of?'

Several crevasses appeared in Ben's prosthetic flesh as he raised his eyebrows. 'Oh, so she admitted it – finally,' he said, standing up on his left leg and checking the clock over the doorway. 'Must dash. Nearly curtain call.'

Being pushed for time, Peddyr couldn't afford to hedge. 'Admitted what? Gabby admitted what?'

Ben was flapping, keen to end the conversation and return to the backstage area with his fellow apocalypse survivors. The reply arrived in a torrent as he hopped from his seat and lunged for the crutch against the wall.

'Admitted she was pregnant and they had to move because of the scandal, and that Gabby lied to Kit to stop him from finding out, but when Mickie discovered the truth, he told Kit, and Kit killed himself.'

Peddyr scooped up his jacket and crash helmet and followed Ben out through the door of his dressing room into a corridor where they were jostled into a wall by a stream of passing actors. 'I'm not with you. Why would Eileen Brady having a baby lead to Kit's suicide?'

'Not her mum,' Ben snapped. 'Not Mrs Brady. When Mickie found them, Gabby was being taken in an ambulance with a baby. Mickie was there.'

'I need to speak to him,' Peddyr shouted above the sounds of nervous chattering cast members and loud instructions coming from the stage manager.

'You'll have a job,' Ben barked. 'Mickie drank himself to death last year. He hit the bottle hard years ago. After the court hearing.'

Swept away by the tide of other actors heading to the stage, Ben Harmer disappeared from view. Not to be beaten, Peddyr forced his way forward until he grabbed hold of Ben's upper right arm and hoped it was a genuine one. 'What court hearing? Do you mean the coroner's?' His voice was lost in the hubbub. They stumbled on and after a few more hard yards Peddyr bumped into Ben's back, nearly knocking the crutch from under his arm. 'Was anyone called Owen Fox called to give evidence before the Coroner in Bedford?' The way was barred by the stage manager's assistant, who demanded they stop talking. This left Peddyr only moments to get an answer.

'Look, Pete. I can't remember anyone called Owen Fox...'

Peddyr whispered as loud as he dare. 'Call me if you remember.' But with howling music starting up front of house, Ben's reply was drowned out. All Peddyr could discern was the phrase 'I wish you luck…'

He waved. 'Thanks, I'll work it out. Break a leg.'

34

HOME ALONE

*O*utside the theatre, Peddyr sat astride his motorbike and waited for Gabby to answer her mobile phone. It rang out five times before she responded. 'I'm about to head back to Bosworth Bishops, but I have one or two important questions to ask you,' he said.

'Go ahead.'

'Is Laura your daughter?'

He'd expected a shocked reaction, but given the excessive period of silence, Peddyr thought he'd lost the signal and he pulled the phone from his ear to check. 'Gabby? Are you there?'

'Of course I'm here, I'm just speechless. Why on earth would you think Laura was my child? Is that what Ben told you?'

'Pretty much.' He repeated what Ben Harmer had said, leaving Gabby to explain.

'Dad went into hiding because of some Government leak. Or that's what Mum told me then. She said we had to disappear in order to keep safe. We weren't allowed to contact anyone, especially not Dad, and no one from home, not even Kit. I fell for it at the time, but not anymore. It makes no sense. As for Laura being my daughter, that is complete and utter nonsense. I was there when she was born. From an angle no child should ever have to witness, I saw my mother giving birth. That is the one hideous moment etched permanently into my memory.'

Tapping his gloved fingers on the petrol tank of his favourite Yamaha, Peddyr said, 'Then the gossipmongers got it badly wrong.' He had his own rapidly forming hypothesis and wasn't persuaded by Gabriella Dixon's story. 'Did you know that a man called Mickie Willis saw you being carted off in an ambulance on the night Laura was born?'

This statement resulted in an eruption at the end of the phone. 'Whaaaat?' Gabby screeched. 'Ben told you that?' Her voice drifted off as if something had occurred to her.

'Are you at the caravan site now?' Peddyr asked.

'No, but we're heading there soon. We're about to re-enact the fateful night I allegedly whacked my bonce on the side of a caravan, but you might have saved me the trouble.' Her tone became muffled as Peddyr listened to Gabby relay the news to Stella. 'The man who came to our caravan that night wasn't my dad making a secret visit. It turns out to be Mickie fucking Willis! Christ-all-bloody-mighty. Now it makes perfect sense.'

It was a while before he heard her address him again. 'Mr Quirk. Based on the information you have given me and the obvious clues, which as a teenager I completely missed, it is a distinct possibility my mother had been shagging around with Mickie Willis and, just so you know, he answered the phone when I called Kit from a telephone box two days before Laura was born.'

The pennies were lining up ready to drop into place for Peddyr. 'Listen, I need a timeline of the events as they happened that night. Apart from not having a clue how Owen Fox fits in with all this, I think we've about cracked it. Speak to you soon.' He didn't have time to debate this with his client. There was work to do.

Riding his bike required concentration and the sheer joy of accelerating out of the sweeping bends on the journey home provided a special form of therapeutic mindfulness, allowing Peddyr to switch off from the case and free up his thinking. If Connie had been at home, he would have asked her to search the databases but as she was miles away, gawping at a miniature Winston Churchill, he was resigned to doing the donkey work once he arrived home. He didn't think about any of Gabby Dixon's problems until he had put his bike back in the garage and stripped off his helmet, gloves and jacket.

Peddyr rubbed at his head and pulled earplugs from his ears as he stepped into the flat. With no Connie around to clear up behind him, the place was as he'd left it, and he put the breakfast dishes into the dishwasher before making any more mess. After that, he stood at the fridge door holding it open, indecisive about which snack he could treat himself to. A pork pie and a tomato won his attention, but only because they were finger-food and wouldn't create dirty dishes. A quick change of clothes saw him arrive at his computer monitor within the next five minutes.

In less time than it took for his bike to cool down, he sought assistance and reached for the phone to call Connie. 'That's nice, Lao Po. I'm glad they're doing well. Is that the baby I can hear screaming his lungs out?' Peddyr squirmed at the sound, glad he wasn't in Glasgow with his wife. 'Sounds like you're having a splendid time. Listen, I need your help with some background stuff.' He briefly outlined what he'd learned from Ben. Straining to hear a reply over the wailing of his grandson, he sighed, 'OK, you're busy. Stupid of me.'

In her usual direct way, Connie steered him right above the noise of the baby exercising his lungs. 'Search the marriage records for Shana and Michael Willis, then the birth records of their children.'

'Gotcha!' he said triumphantly only thirty minutes later. It was time to enlighten Bernard Kershaw. 'Bernie. Still on for tonight?' Connie had forbidden him from going out for a beer with Bernie while she was away, but she had said nothing to suggest Peddyr couldn't invite him round for a drink or two. A business meeting was a perfectly legitimate reason, and Connie need never find out.

'Looking forward to it, Pedd. How's the case going?'

'I'll tell you about it when I see you. In the meantime, I'm chasing up on some fascinating history involving a disabled actor, a girl killed in a house fire and an apparent suicide, all of which are inextricably linked to a certain Gabriella Dixon.'

35

NOTHING LEFT WORTH KEEPING

*S*tella and I hadn't got as far as unpacking bags when we arrived in Tenby. After the long, cramped drive we couldn't be bothered, and besides the place didn't exactly encourage relaxing in the afternoon sun. There was a small concrete yard at the back of the premises, and a larger one at the front where we parked.

Stella liberated the keys from a hook behind a downpipe at the side of the cottage and we entered with our expectations set low. We were not disappointed. It was as bad as we had imagined.

'My mother-in-law does that,' Stella said, nodding toward a three-piece suite covered in thick see-through plastic protection. 'What you get in the Cortez household is a sweaty backside in the summer and a cold bum in the winter.'

The table in the open-plan room wore a wipe clean tablecloth and, in an effort to save the rest of the furniture from wayward guests, there were coasters and table mats evenly distributed on any flat surface. 'God, this is hideous,'

I said. 'Shall we go out for a late lunch? Maybe a stroll to the beach for an ice cream after?' I had the Magic 8-Ball in my hands, and I gave it a shake. The answer was a puzzling "Ask again later".

A waitress had already taken our food order when the call from Peddyr Quirk came and, as a result, our plans changed. If Ben Harmer was right, then Mickie Willis had driven from Bedford to Wales to see my mother the night Laura was born. That could mean one of two things – if there were rumours about me being pregnant, he could have assumed Kit was the father and was checking it out for himself. Alternatively, my first reaction to Peddyr earlier had been correct; Mother had been the one in hiding, and Mickie Willis had something to do with it.

'I think we should go to Manorbier after we've eaten,' I said, still reeling from the second possibility.

Stella asked the ball to decide for us. 'It is certain,' she said in a robotic voice. 'That's it then. We go to the caravan site after lunch. No prosecco for us 'til later.'

I could hear the disappointment in her voice and completely understood. It would have been so easy to wallow in wine. Instead, we talked through the news from Peddyr Quirk as we drove towards the farm. 'I knew it was a man with Mum. I heard his voice. I smelt him.'

'Mickie Willis was a bit of a ponger then, was he?' asked Stella.

'No, Kit's old man was the type who splashed on the aftershave.'

The lady at the farm, a Mrs Price, was incredibly under-standing when we arrived shortly before four o'clock. After at least three cups of tea, a guided tour, and half an hour of small talk, she led us to an ancient static caravan relegated to use as a henhouse.

'This would have been the type of van you stayed in when your Aunty Wynn ran the place. We've upgraded since then, a couple of times.' The spritely old lady waved towards the modern chalet-style statics neatly parked around the main site. 'Do you remember much about the place?'

'Quite a lot, actually,' I said. 'Our caravan was on the far corner facing the farmhouse. The gate for the footpath to the beach was behind it.'

'It still is,' said Mrs Price, blinking against the summer sun. 'People in the village often talk about the night your sister was born.'

This surprised me. 'They do?'

'Alma at the Post Office said you were the bravest little girl she'd ever come across. You didn't panic but ran to call for help when your mother went into labour and then ran back to stay with her. You'd delivered the tiny mite minutes before the ambulance turned up. Such a shame you fell and hurt yourself somewhere along the way.'

'Mum told me I did, but I can't remember that bit of the drama.'

According to Mrs Price, the story made the regional papers the week after the event, but it amused me to hear I had become a local legend. 'Off you went in the ambulance, you, the baby and your mum,' Mrs Price added, clasping at her chest. 'Such a dreadful night it was too. Rain lashing down and howling winds.' Stella and I smiled politely, letting her finish the tale.

'We won't be long,' my friend said when she had the chance. 'As I said over tea, we're researching for a documentary film about that night and want to get our facts in the right order, so we thought jogging Gabby's memory by coming here was the best way to achieve that.' She was in her element again, fabricating a background that didn't exist.

'I never knew you TV producers went to so much trouble. I'll leave you to it then,' Mrs Price said. 'Now don't forget, if you get stuck – ask Alma at the Post Office.'

'Will do,' I replied, thanking her for her time and declining the offer of more tea, I was awash with the stuff. We waited until she was out of earshot before we began. Stella took notes on her phone. 'I might as well use it for something,' she said. 'It's no bloody good as a phone.' The signal had disappeared as soon as we'd turned off the main road and headed towards the village of Manorbier. 'Are you ready? Then let's begin. Tell me about the night Laura was born.'

'It was raining.'

'Enormous surprise there…'

Staring into the henhouse, I ran through the story Stella had heard many times before. Now we had a location to give it context and credence, my emotions seemed more engaged with the memories. 'We'd left home with the bare minimum in suitcases and caught a train, Whitsun week I think it was. School half-term holidays. Aunty Wynn sent someone to collect us from the nearest station and I thought we were having a holiday like before and my father would join us when he could.

'I can still remember the conversation me and Mum had a few days later, when she broke the news about us never going back. She was crying… I was sobbing and shouting, and she shouted back, demanding I do as I was told or risk our lives by being selfish.' It was difficult for me even now, as an adult, to accept what she did. She'd left my father. We weren't fugitives from enemy spies or fleeing for our lives. We were there because she'd run away from my dad while she was pregnant. Could Laura really be Mickie Willis's child?

'Mum kept herself busy by knitting items to sell in the village, from local wool. She asked me to take a jumper to Aunty Wynn at the farmhouse, so I borrowed her mac and stuffed the jumper down the front. I took a brolly. I wasn't gone long. About an hour.'

'Took your time then.'

'I liked Aunty Wynn. She was having a late supper, about eight-ish. It wasn't dark, just dull because of the weather. I dragged out the visit. It was better than being cooped up with Mum. She was driving me to distraction with her misery.'

'Moaning about your dad.'

'She barely mentioned him.'

Thinking back, I should have realised what was going on, but I was so torn apart by having to leave Kit and my friends and my life in Bedford, I didn't give my mother much thought, ignoring her most of the time. I spewed out my grief and anguish in my diary several times a day. Although I blamed Mum to her face, I was angrier with my dad for putting us in this position. Back then, I was ignorant of my mother's ability to conceal awkward facts from him – such as an unplanned pregnancy.

'I noticed a scruffy van had arrived when I made my way back to the caravan in the rain. It was parked nearby, but not in our allocated space. I walked right past it but couldn't see inside because the windows were steamed up. When I got close to the front door of the caravan, I heard voices from inside. A man talking to my mother.'

'Mickie Willis.'

'I guess so. The voices were muffled and even though I wanted it to be, I knew it wasn't my dad. I hid the other side of the caravan, under the trees, sheltering beneath my umbrella, and tried to listen in. Mum was sobbing, and I heard the man come out and say something about not wanting anything to do with her. So, then I assumed it was someone Dad had sent, and she was being warned to stay away from him for even longer.'

'Did Kit know your mother was pregnant?'

I shook my head vehemently. 'I never told him about the baby, just where we were staying and that I wasn't allowed to see him again.' Looking across to where our old caravan had once stood, I said, 'Because of the storm I was soaked through, but I waited to hear the van start up before I left my hiding place.'

'Who did your mum say it was?'

'She didn't. There was a chair pulled out as if someone had been sitting at the table and muddy footprints on the floor. I asked her if she'd had a visitor, but she denied it. Flatly. Right to my face. Told me not to make up stories. She was blubbing again, so I went to lie on my bunk. I was so sick of her.' Repeating those words made me feel the same nausea I had then.

'And the van left the site,' Stella said, needing confirmation of the precise turn of events.

'I don't know. I assume so.' I searched her eyes. 'But perhaps not... which means Mickie will have seen quite a lot of what happened next.'

The henhouse stank of ammonia, so I withdrew and turned my attention to the full site, recalling how it had looked on that dark, rainy night my mother gave birth there. I began to wonder in that moment if my subsequent amnesia was in fact a form of PTSD. Witnessing

Laura's birth was traumatic, without a doubt. Had it tainted my whole life? Was it the core reason I rejected motherhood – because I feared childbirth?

Stella tapped away on her phone while I continued with my story. 'The sequence of events is hazy. This is the bit I find so frustrating. I knew when Mum had gone into labour, she was giving the odd moan, sucking in air through her teeth, and rubbing her lower back with both hands.'

'Well, at fifteen I would expect you to have guessed that one. What happened next?'

'That's just it.' I looked at my friend despairingly. 'I just can't bloody remember.'

Stella gave this some thought, searching for a prompt. 'You were a sensible well-educated young teenager. Your reaction would have been to seek help. What did you say to her?'

The memory eluded me. It would not come.

'You're trying too hard,' Stella said. 'Close your eyes and breath it through, slow and steady. Picture yourself back then. Who was on your mind when you saw your mother in labour?'

'Dad,' I said, without thinking. 'I wanted my dad to be there to make decisions to take control.' I opened my eyes and stared at Stella in shock. 'She threw me out.'

'What?'

*I*n a flood, the scene poured back into my conscious mind from wherever it had been hiding. 'Mum was leaning forward, one hand on her bump, one arm propping her up over the table. I told her I was going to get help and ring Dad. Her reaction was terrifying. She screamed like a madwoman and said she would never speak to me again if I rang my father. I argued with her, crying, scared, saying he had a right to know. The look on her face was of pure hate. She said everything was my fault, that the truth had come out and she would never forgive me and Kit for what we had done to her.'

'And how did you react? What did she mean by that? Keep going, keep breathing.'

'She sounded bloody delirious. I can only think she needed to vent her anger at someone and that someone was me. The truth was, she'd left Dad and now the father of her baby had dumped her. She was alone; I suppose I took the brunt.' I shrugged at Stella, trying to make psychological sense of the hurtful words my own mother had hurled at me.

'She screamed at me to get out. Then there is a gap of time. Perhaps I really did trip and fall like she said. When I came to, I was outside in a heap near the door in my pyjamas and a coat I'd put on intending to get help. The umbrella was on the ground a few feet away, unopened. I hadn't got far. Soaking wet from the rain, cold and shivering, I dragged myself back in. Mum was sitting on the floor, a towel under her, her nightie pulled over her knees. She was in agony and so was my head. I put my fingers to where it hurt and there was blood. But still, I ran back into the dark and headed for Aunty Wynn's. It took an age for her to come to the door. She said she would phone for an ambulance and meet me back at the caravan.'

Another recollection poked its head through the fog of recall. 'I told her to phone my dad. I needed my dad.'

Stella held my hand, abandoning the idea of making notes on her phone. 'And when you went back to your mum?'

I knew the answer to that one. When I went back to my

mum, nothing was ever the same again between us. I was no clearer who Owen Fox was and what he had to do with any of this, but at last I understood why motherhood was something I avoided at all costs. Trauma and stress were part of it but the reality was that I didn't want to end up like my own mother.

36

RAIN STOPS PLAY

*H*anding Bernard a glass filled to the brim with a fine Burgundy, Peddyr said, 'I've just heard from Gabby. She and Stella are driving back tomorrow morning.'

'Cutting the weekend short?' his companion asked, moving the wine to his lips with a steady hand.

Peddyr sat down in his favourite armchair and swung his feet onto a leather footstool before reaching for his own glass. 'Buckets of rain are on the way, the tail end of Storm Eustace according to the BBC forecast this morning, so it'll be blowing a hoolie. Anyway, I can't blame them. Their accommodation sounded basic and they already have the answers they were looking for, or so Gabby tells me.'

'And what are they?'

Drawing in a deep breath, Peddyr tried to summarise them. 'Laura Churchill is not Gabby's daughter, as Ben Harmer believes. The circumstances of Laura's birth made the papers in West Wales and Eileen Brady is most definitely her mother, no question. However, what the media didn't know was that back in 1993, Mrs Eileen Brady, who was a stunner when she was younger, may have had a fling with the local handyman, a certain Michael Willis, father of her daughter's boyfriend Kit, and may have conceived Mickie's child. Possibly to hide the scandalous truth, Eileen did a flit to her sister's caravan site in West Wales.'

Bernard placed his glass delicately on the coffee table, exchanging it for a handful of peanuts from a bowl. 'And how does this link with Owen Fox?'

'That, my friend, is the most important question.'

'And are you going to answer it?'

Peddyr laughed at Bernard's belligerent tone. 'Kit Willis had an elder brother. His surname was Fox – the maiden name of Shana Willis.' Peddyr was loath to confess how much time Connie's expertise had saved him in his attempts to unravel this piece of the puzzle.

'Ah, so now we get to the interesting part of the story,' Bernard said. 'And the motive for Owen Fox wanting to destroy Gabriella's comfortable existence?'

'I'm still not sure. It goes back to those teenage years before Laura was born. Kit Willis, young Gabby's boyfriend, was thought to have killed himself in the misguided belief she was having his child. This was hearsay and a gross inaccuracy, fuelled by Ben Harmer's tendency to embellish stories.' Peddyr rubbed the rim of his wine glass with the tip of his forefinger. 'I asked myself why Kit would do such a thing. With his family background, no one would have turned a hair at a teenage pregnancy. It doesn't fit.

'Then there's the fact that a mutual friend of Kit and Gabby's called Camille Bullimore was killed in a house fire, along with her parents, only days before Kit Willis took his own life, leaving us with the likelihood of a more complex back story.'

Elbows on knees, Bernard was staring hard at him. 'You're surmising that Owen Fox is guilty of murder, covering something up for his father? Two sets of murders? Surely not...' Rolling his thumbs, Bernard shook his head reprovingly.

'No,' Peddyr admitted reluctantly. 'And I'm not accusing him of anything specific, or not without more evidence. I'm speculating here, that's all.' Intrigued by the possibility of Owen Fox being implicated in these deaths, Peddyr had become engrossed in related news stories on the internet, swallowing up hours of his time.

'There was an investigation into the fire at the Bullimores' but, despite a strong whiff of arson, no-one was ever charged in connection with their deaths.' He sighed. 'Secondly, there was a Coroner's Inquiry into Kit Willis's untimely death, but an open verdict was returned because of lack of conclusive evidence for suicide.' Peddyr's facial expression tightened. 'Decades later, when her mother died, Gabriella came back into Owen Fox's life and – wham!' He brushed his palms together as if removing dust from his hands.

'A serial killer on the loose, eh?' Bernard raised one eyebrow to show he remained unconvinced.

'Don't take the piss, fella. I'm serious enough to take what I've got to the police as soon as I can tie some loose ends together.'

'And the motive?'

The doorbell rang, cutting through a heavy silence.

'Ah, that'll be the pizzas,' Peddyr said, rising from his chair. 'Back in a tick. Hold that thought, whatever it was...'

He could almost hear Bernard's brain whirring as he passed by, wallet in hand.

Sniffing the air, Bernard grinned his thanks as he accepted the pizza box from Peddyr on his return to the lounge.

'I ordered us the same – loads of pepperoni and mushrooms.' Taking up a comfortable position in his chair, Peddyr flipped open the lid on his box and wafted the steam towards his nose. 'Just the job,' he said. 'Now, where were we?'

'Accusing Owen Fox of murder, I believe,' Bernard muttered through a mouthful of stuffed crust. He chewed and swallowed. 'One thing is bothering me though. Why does Owen Fox wait until now to take revenge on Gabriella Dixon?'

With a heavily laden slice of pizza drooping from his fingers, Peddyr nodded. 'I've not figured that out yet. The reason will reveal itself, eventually. By the time he possibly, allegedly, perhaps killed Kit and Camille, Gabby had done a moonlight flit with her mother, Laura was born, and Grenville Brady had stepped forward to act as the baby's father. Maybe there was no need to bump her off. We must ask her, though, what she and her friends did to make Owen Fox angry enough to want them dead.'

'But not to kill Ben Harmer.'

Twitching his nose, Peddyr shook his head slowly. 'Yes, old mate, he wasn't targeted, which is suspicious.'

Dabbing his lips with a sheet of paper kitchen towel, Bernard scowled. 'One has to be curious about that. Has the truth been stretched here?' he asked, eyeing a long string of warm mozzarella cheese as he pulled it free from the pizza base.

'Ben Harmer is unreliable, that's for sure, so I've no way of knowing what the facts are,' Peddyr said, still peeved about the tall tale Harmer had spun.

Bernard, ever one for getting to the nub of the matter, asked, 'What happened at the time Laura was born?'

'After my long chat with Gabby on the phone earlier, I can give you the basic rundown. Picture the scene; a caravan in Wales. Eileen Brady goes into labour. There's an argument between mother and daughter. Gabby recalls a searing pain to the back of her head and blacks out. When she came to, her mother was in the late stages of labour and Gabriella runs into a stormy night to call an ambulance. Bloodied and battered, young Gabby somehow helps her mother give birth. Then – hey presto – the ambulance arrives and takes them all to hospital.'

'And why didn't she knock on her aunt's door?'

Such an incisive question from Bernard was exactly the reason Peddyr needed him. 'Good point, maybe she did just that. I forgot to ask her to clarify.'

'Very sloppy of you, dear boy.'

Sloshing more wine into both glasses, Peddyr stared at a photograph of Connie on the wall. 'If we assume that Owen Fox phoned BBC Valley Radio and left clues for Gabby about his identity, then she must realise who he is by now.' By sharing his ideas, he hoped Bernard would add a useful perspective, something Connie would normally do. 'Why deny knowing who he is?' A thought suddenly occurred to him. '"An eye for an eye…" That quote from the bible, how does it go?'

Reaching for their Smartphones in unison, both men scrolled through search engines to find the relevant verses. 'Got it,' said Bernard, a smile widening his chubby jowls. 'Deuteronomy. "Show no pity to the guilty. Your rule should be life for life, eye for eye, tooth for tooth, hand for hand, foot for foot".' He looked up. 'Doesn't quite fit the facts, does it?'

'Looks like he stuck with a version of the first suggestion, a life for a life,' Peddyr said, puffing out his cheeks.

37

A LIFE FOR A LIFE

*A*fter the trip to the caravan site, sleep eluded me and although the bed hadn't been wholly uncomfortable, the room was fusty and unwelcoming. I couldn't relax enough to stay asleep for long, there were too many conflicting thoughts whirring around in my head.

Not wanting to disturb Stella, I crept downstairs to make a cup of coffee. The lounge remained as it was the night before, three empty bottles standing in a row on the occasional table. 'I don't remember getting through that lot,' I commented, knowing I wasn't the one who would be suffering that morning. My head felt tired and confused, but not banging with alcohol poisoning. I wasn't the one who'd made the dent in the Prosecco supplies and the gin, and I was shocked to see so many empties.

The decision to head home early was easily made. Neither Stella nor I wanted to stay longer. The weather had turned unfavourable, and I had a confession to make to Peddyr Quirk which couldn't wait and needed to be made face to face. The smell of the coffee perked me up well before the effects of the caffeine took hold. I sank two cups of it and ate a slice of buttered toast before heading for the bathroom.

Time was getting on, and Stella hadn't surfaced, so I knocked on her bedroom door. 'Get up, you old soak. Time to pack the car and get going.' There was no verbal response other than a groan from beyond. My bag was re-packed, and I'd tidied up the plastic-covered lounge, removing the empty bottles and washing glasses in the sink, before I heard movement from upstairs.

'You look shocking,' I said, as a fragile Stella tiptoed into the kitchen, silently hugging herself. This inability to communicate continued for some time and I watched in mild fascination as she forced herself to gather belongings and hand them to me. 'You pack. You drive,' she said. 'I can't. If you need me, I'll be asleep.' Leaving me to force our bags back into the Mini, lock up the house and return the key to its hiding place, she sat in the passenger seat, head propped against the window, puffy eyes closed.

Settling into the driver's side, I handed her a bottle of water. 'Keep drinking. You'll feel better soon. Another fifteen minutes and the paracetamol will kick in.' I was hopeful of a smooth journey as I turned the ignition on, but Stella was less convinced she would survive the trip home.

'I'll let you know if I'm going to throw up,' she said, her voice hoarse from last night's drunken laughter and wild confessions.

'Well, make sure you do it before we get to the motorway,' I begged, handing her a carrier bag as a precaution. 'We can't have the police asking for my driving licence when they already have it.'

Despite an unscheduled stop for Stella to retch onto a grass verge, the journey was otherwise uneventful and, with everyone else travelling in the opposite direction, we made it back to Bosworth Bishops in record time. I parked on the driveway and pulled Stella from the passenger seat, allowing her to lean on me as she staggered gratefully towards the front door. 'I feel dreadful,' she muttered. 'I'm going for a lie down.'

Abandoned once more, I unloaded the car and took her suitcase up to her room. 'Stella, do you want some chicken soup for lunch?' I asked, putting a freshly refilled bottle of water on the bedside cabinet. 'I'll have a bowlful, then I'm going out. There's something I need to do. I'll be back later.'

Stirring, she turned towards me. Her hair was a matted mess and without make-up she looked washed out, charcoal-coloured smudges under her dulled eyes. 'Nothing for me. My stomach can't handle anything right now. Later.' She raised a semi-smile. 'Thanks.'

'What for? It should be me thanking you, not the other way around.'

In our inebriated state the night before, Stella and I had revisited my teenage years and I'd told her about how Ben, Camille, Kit and I had used a Magic 8-Ball to decide on childish pranks. How we dared each other and how those dares became wilder and more inventive as time went on.

Ben's parents had gone ballistic when we'd tattooed his name on his thigh, using ordinary ink and a sewing needle, a week before his sixteenth birthday. It was a rainy Saturday and Ben phoned me at home to say he was bored, which to me was a call for our gang's brand of entertainment services. I called round for Kit and Camille and we met Ben in the summerhouse at the bottom of his garden, like we always did when we needed a place to shelter.

The challenge was agreed, and the Magic 8-Ball said, "Signs point to yes". Camille did a passable job; she used a biro to draw out the template and the cursive script looked almost professional. When Ben winced with the pain, she gave him short shrift, reminding him to be grateful his name wasn't Christopher. She had such a quick tongue in her head that girl.

For a short while we became obsessed with needles in one form or another. On one memorable occasion Kit pierced my ears, using an ice cube to freeze the lobes first and a cork to push an embroidery needle against. It hurt like hell. Unfortunately, the piercings became infected, and I told my parents I'd used a local hairdressers', on a whim. Not for the last time, my deceit was exposed when my mother confronted the manager of the salon about poor standards of hygiene.

Sometimes the ball would allow a reprieve and the dare couldn't go ahead, but more often than not it would give a positive response. None of us wanted to lose face and back down; least of all me, the posh girl with everything to prove.

*O*n my second large glass of fizzy stuff the previous night, I'd snatched a memory from the back of my head. 'Owen Fox,' I said to Stella, hand flying to my chest. 'I know who he is!'

'You do?'

My stomach lurched. 'I'd forgotten all about him.'

'Obviously,' Stella replied. She wobbled to her feet. 'Must go for a wee-wee.'

When she returned, and because she'd been gone so long, she seemed to have lost the thread of our conversation and focussed on a confession of her own. 'I only married Carlos for his money,' she said. 'Oh, and the size of his cock,' she added with relish. She didn't seem to notice my unease, for which I was grateful. It gave me time to think. As she rambled on about her bedroom antics, I glazed over. The prospect of alcohol no longer appealed because I wanted a clear head, so I left Stella to finish the second bottle, although I don't remember her starting on the next she must have done. There were definitely three empty bottles the next morning.

By sipping at my glass now and again, I gave the impression I was joining in the fun. I laughed when she laughed, and nodded along, but inside I was fighting deeply buried doubts.

The weight of disquiet stayed with me through the drive back from Wales. I couldn't bear to keep it to myself much longer. Given the nature of the problem, there was only one person in whom I could confide before going to see Owen Fox and finding out for myself. Peddyr Quirk would help me work this out.

Tilting my head back, I held onto the newel post at the bottom of the stairs and shouted. 'Stella? I'm taking the Mini. I won't be long.'

38

WHAT IS GOING ON?

*C*ongratulations were in order, Peddyr had removed any trace of pizza, wine, beer and whisky by being meticulous in his wiping of surfaces. With judicious use of next door's rubbish skip he could dispose of evidence. The dishwasher had taken care of everything else apart from the giveaway red wine stain in the middle of the lounge carpet.

'I'll sort it later,' Peddyr said to himself, staring forlornly at the stubborn stain. As he stood rubbing at the stubble on his cheek, he recalled something about soda water being useful in such unfortunate circumstances. 'Or maybe it was salt... or perhaps vinegar.' Dealing with the spillage when it happened would have been the best approach, but neither he nor Bernie were capable of rational thought when the glass tumbled from the table sometime after midnight. They were more upset by the waste of alcohol and only made perfunctory efforts to dab at the stain with one of Peddyr's socks. 'Cheese and wine,' Bernard Kershaw had said. 'How apt.'

Peddyr was about to head out of the door when his

mobile phone rang out from his back pocket. The noise was far too shrill for his sensitive head to tolerate, and instead of answering the call from Connie, he accidentally rejected it. Hoping her exuberance and volume were toned down today, he returned the call once he was out in the fresh air. In a nearby driveway he leant against a wooden gatepost holding his splitting forehead in his free hand while Connie regaled him with the latest grandparental news.

'I can't talk for long; I'm following up an important lead,' he replied when she asked what his plans were for the day. 'And before you ask, I have kept the flat tidy, I have eaten, and yes, I do miss you.' She checked in with him at least twice a day and always made the same enquiries. This time he saved her the bother, and himself from more ear-piercing chatter. 'Connie, I must go. I'll speak to you later.'

The brisk walk to Revival Farm across the fields allowed time to gather his wits before speaking to Laura Churchill. The geese in the yard gave away his approach and made menacing lunges for his legs as the dogs joined in with ferocious barking. They were safely behind metal fencing, but even so Peddyr stood still, not wanting to antagonise them further. 'Hello. Anyone home?' he called.

Curtis Churchill's van was outside the rambling house and the man himself emerged from behind the open barn doors, wiping sweaty hands down his heavily stained jeans. A few stern words and the dogs retreated into a corner of their compound.

'Can I help you, mate?' Curtis had a soft West Country accent, elongating the vowels further than even the local accent allowed for.

'Is your wife at home?' Peddyr asked, offering a hand to shake.

'And you are?'

'My name is Quirk.' The two men exchanged competitive handshakes and eyed each other warily.

'Oh-ar, the investigator bloke. What do you want with Lar?'

'I need her help.'

'Do you now, and why would that be?'

Surprisingly, he invited Peddyr into the house and, in response to her name, Laura soon put in an appearance, patting her hands with a damp tea towel. A baby on her hip, a toddler hung on to one of her legs, eyeing Peddyr with suspicion. 'The detective bloke wants to speak to you,' Curtis explained, taking his place at his wife's side, picking up the small boy and holding him on the crook of one arm. 'You'd better tell him everything.' Placing a grubby, callused hand on her waist, he gave it a squeeze.

Peddyr was asked to take a seat and after negotiating a child's dumper truck and a threadbare teddy, chose an upright wooden wheel-back chair. He scanned the couple, taking in their uncomfortable poses and sidelong glances at each other.

'You want to know what Owen Fox told me,' Laura began, her voice devoid of inflection.

'I do,' Peddyr replied, grateful for her apparent willingness to engage with him. 'To be honest, I was expecting this to be a tough conversation.'

'My wife has been recovering from the shock of it all,' Curtis interjected, cutting Laura off as she opened her mouth. 'It's not every day you find out who your actual father is.'

'Michael Willis was a builder from Bedford,' Peddyr said, wanting them to know he was up to speed with the case and nearing a conclusion. 'I think your mother was lonely when your dad was away a lot. These things happen.'

Laura tensed. 'Who the hell is Michael Willis and what has he got to do with my real father?'

The thick walls and low ceiling of the cottage seemed to grow evermore claustrophobic as Peddyr realised he had been wrong in his assumptions. 'I'm sorry, I thought you said you knew…'

Curtis and Laura stared at each other and then turned on Peddyr. 'Explain yourself, detective,' Curtis said curtly.

Shuffling in his seat, Peddyr cleared his throat. 'My investigations lead me to believe that Mrs Eileen Brady had an extramarital affair with a man called Michael Willis. When Mr Brady found out and discovered Michael Willis's rejection of the child… that is, you, Laura… he stepped in and registered himself as the father, resuming his marriage to Eileen. No one else was any the wiser.'

'And why would you be interested in my wife's parentage?' Curtis said jutting out his lower jaw. 'We thought you were investigating a case of fraud and identity theft. You're supposed to be getting Gabby's money back for—'

'Never mind that,' Laura said, taking a step forward. 'Who is Michael Willis?'

Confounded, Peddyr backtracked to work out where his hypothesis had fallen flat. 'I'm trying to unravel why Owen Fox from Castle and Wyckes was so upset by his father's affair with your mother that he took it out on your sister. You see, Owen Fox is Michael Willis's eldest son. He's your half-brother.'

'No,' Laura said. 'Owen Fox is my real father. He told me so himself.'

39

GABBY GETS A SHOCK

he door to P.Q. Investigations was locked and there was no sign of life when I rang the bell. With no other option open to me, I tried Peddyr's mobile. I knew something was up by the way he spoke. 'P.Q. Investigations, how may I help?'

He knew my number; he knew it was me on the end of the line, and yet he persisted with the new customer charade to the point of muffling the phone with his hand and apologising to whoever he was with. 'If you could send me an email with some limited details of your enquiry, I'll get back to you as soon as I return to the office,' he said.

I rolled my eyes. 'If you could get back to me with some urgency, I'd appreciate it.' There was little to be gained from making a fuss. Peddyr was clearly tied up, so I went back to the Mini and waited for him to become free. Killing time, I tried Stella, but the call went straight to answerphone. She'd most likely forgotten to put her mobile on charge or switched it off to prevent thoughtless friends like me from waking her up. Fifteen minutes dragged by like an eternity before Peddyr returned my call.

'Gabby, are you still near the office? Can you wait there for me? We need to talk and I'm on Shanks's pony this afternoon.'

'I can do better than that, I'm in Stella's hire car. I'll pick you up.' This was fortuitous. With Peddyr in the car, we could confront Owen Fox together. The mud was at last beginning to settle in the puddle of confusion. Owen Fox must have listened to rumours about me being pregnant by Kit, blamed me for Kit's death and was meting out a slow dripping revenge for the loss of his brother. And to think, I'd almost erased Kit's older brother from my memory.

Peddyr was waiting for me by the public footpath sign as arranged and, as far as prizes for the worst hangovers went, it was a close-run thing between him and Stella.

'You look–'

'As rough as a badger's arse. Yes, I know. And there's no need to gawp at me all holier-than-thou. Not looking so hot yourself as it happens.'

Checking for traffic in the mirrors I pulled away from the kerb, heading back towards Dyer Street. 'You and Bernard fall into a pub, did you?'

He frowned. 'Certainly not, I'd never break a promise to my wife. Bernie and I had a long business meeting last night which may have involved alcohol to free up lateral think-ing.' He glanced around him. 'Got any water? I'm parched.'

I passed an unopened bottle from the door pocket on the driver's side. 'I know who Owen Fox is,' I said. 'It came to me last night, courtesy of some lateral thinking... although not as lateral as you and Bernard managed, by the looks of you.'

A hesitant 'Oh?' was the reply, and I spotted a change in

body language from my passenger. He was on his guard. 'You mean apart from being Kit Willis's older brother. What took you so long to find out when you could have asked Laura?'

This comment from Peddyr must have resulted from dehydration, because Laura knew Owen Fox as far as funerals went, but she knew nothing about Kit or my old friends. I took a guess at what Owen had disclosed to Laura in The Salad Box over lunch a few days ago. 'Can you imagine… "Hi, Laura. I'm your half-brother Owen". So… he told her about Mickie Willis then.' With a sardonic smile, I tilted my head upwards and huffed. 'Cor, I bet that took the wind out of her sails; Mum having a romp with a bit of rough. Fancy finding out just how much of a mistake you really are.'

I'll freely admit to gloating. As far as I was concerned it was poetic justice for Laura's hurtful words to me recently. 'The daughter of a rogue builder, eh? No wonder she and Curtis were attracted to each other, it's in the genes.' I could feel pensive tension from the passenger seat where Peddyr slumped over the bottle of water held in both hands as he strangled it.

'What?' I asked, bracing myself.

'Pull over.'

'I'll thank you not to spew in my friend's car,' I said sharply, swerving into a convenient lay-by.

'I was going to tell you when we got back to the office, but while you have wheels at your disposal, legal or otherwise, we might as well make some use of them with a trip to the police station.' Peddyr shifted in his seat, facing me as best he could in the confined space of the Mini. 'I've been to see your sister today, and she tells me Owen Fox insists *he* is her real father.'

'Blow me down with a feather' was an expression my dear old dad often used, and it fitted my reaction all too well at that moment. I could practically feel the blood draining to my feet as my vision narrowed to the shining logo on the steering wheel.

'*T*ake another sip when you're ready,' Peddyr said, resting his hand on my shoulder. My shaking fingers interlocked around a green plastic beaker and I was engulfed by a familiar leather chair in his office. 'Are you back with me yet?' His voice was unusually kind; not at all his normal brusque self. I looked into his concerned eyes, struck once again by how triangular they were.

My mouth declined to speak the words dictated by my brain and only a gurgle escaped, making me sound more disorientated than I was. Somehow, we had arrived at Dyer Street and I was in Peddyr's office once again, with no recollection at all of the journey. The cold drink helped a little, and after taking another minute to calm rampaging thoughts and emotions, I said, 'No, he can't be. Owen Fox can't be Laura's father. I'm sure it was Mickie Willis at the caravan that night. I heard him.' But what if I was wrong about that too? What if I'd seen Mickie's Transit van, but heard his son's voice coming from inside the caravan?

Being unable to explain myself fully, all I could do was listen to what Peddyr had to tell me about his research of the registers for births, deaths and marriages. I confirmed Owen's status as eldest son of Shana and Michael Willis and mumbled a few words about how I'd known him only by his nickname – Carny. 'Carny. Everyone knew him as Carny.'

'Not Canny?'

'No. Carny. Don't ask me why… I've not a clue. I thought he was a Willis, the same as the others.'

Peddyr addressed me sternly. 'Before we involve the police and put matters to bed, I must understand what drove Owen Fox to take such drastic action to keep his affair with your mother a secret.'

'What drastic action? You mean abandoning her and leaving her to deal with the shame of having another man's child? I don't see what's so drastic about that as a course of action. There must be hundreds of cases of infidelity and children brought up by men who aren't their real fathers…' For an intelligent woman, I had failed to acknowledge what I knew to be possible. I had dug a pit so deep in my mind and buried unsavoury fears there so long ago, this rush to unearth them created a physical shock wave.

'Tell me,' Peddyr ordered, seeing me shudder.

'Oh, God… It was so long ago.'

'Start with Ben Harmer, you, Camille and Kit. What did you and your group of friends do to Owen Fox to piss him off so much?'

'Ben had nothing to do with it,' I began. 'He contracted meningitis and was hospitalised. That's how he lost his leg.' Peddyr looked askance at me. 'Surely you noticed his amputation,' I said.

'Of course I friggin' well noticed. But he told me he lost it in combat.'

I didn't have it in me to laugh. 'Christ! He's still so full of shit.' Ben Harmer evidently hadn't changed. Making things up to sound more exciting, more interesting, was his favourite pastime. 'Ben Harmer was never in the army,' I scoffed at the very thought. 'I'm telling you, he lost a leg because of meningitis. Me and Camille visited him in hospital, for God's sake. He was ill for months, failed his exams, and his mother sent him to drama classes to keep him occupied. Carny was the one who wanted to join the army, that's why he never did drugs.'

It was Peddyr's turn to look ashamed. 'I've been taken for a mug.'

'Yes, you have. But you're not the first.'

'Are you saying he never knew Owen Fox?'

'Yes and no. Ben didn't move in the same circles; he was right about that. Carny was known to him, but Ben never had reason to spend time in his company, Carny was a few years older. Let me explain. We didn't see Ben for weeks on end when he was poorly, so if it was raining or cold, we had nowhere to meet like we normally would. Instead, we used Kit's bedroom, doing what teenagers do, gossiping, listening to crappy music, having a crafty smoke. But there was a downside; the Willis household was overcrowded, in a disgusting state generally, and Kit shared a musty bedroom with his big brother.'

'Owen.'

I nodded. 'Carny. Nobody ever called him Owen. Me and Camille made it our business to stay out of his way. He was so much older, and, quite frankly, he was intimidating. And although he wasn't there often, with foul weather he sometimes came home early from the building sites where he was working with Mickie. He made a nuisance of himself. Taking the piss, winding Kit up, flashing porn magazines at us girls. None of us liked him, not even Kit.'

Creepy Carny had once declared an interest in joining our gang to educate us about proper music and show us how grown-ups played nicely together. They were almost his exact words. He'd thrust his hips at us, making sure we understood his meaning. 'He had a filthy way about him,' I said, shuddering.

'I know it probably sounds perfectly normal for a lad of nineteen to be obsessed with sex, but we were at least four years behind, remember. A good kiss with tongues and a fumble were as far as it went with us. My father would have crucified me if I'd allowed Kit any more than that.'

It didn't take me long to tell the rest. Kit had joked along with his bullying brother's demands by suggesting there was a special initiation ceremony before we permitted anyone to join our tiny gang. Kit, Camille and I huddled together to come up with something so unlikely he'd never agree to it.

'Which was?' Peddyr asked.

'It was stupid,' I said, closing my eyes in deep embarrassment at the recollection. 'Camille dared him to snog my mother, to prove how adult he truly was.'

'That was the dare?'

'Yes, and he had to do it in front of witnesses. Not a peck on the cheek, it had to be a full-on French kiss.'

'So what the hell happened? Got out the old Magic 8-Ball, did you?'

'No, Kit said we couldn't use it as this would defeat the object of an initiation test. Carny never mentioned joining the gang after that, so for a while I thought he'd let it drop. We never thought he'd do it, anyway. It was too farfetched. But...' The memory got stuck in my head. 'I... something happened. Everything went sour about two weeks later. The challenges stopped, and Kit said we should do something more constructive. Instead of spending time at the Willises', we joined a youth club.'

'The three of you?'

'No, Camille found a boyfriend and drifted off. When I bumped into her anywhere in town, she pretended she hadn't seen me, or couldn't meet my eye. It had to be something to do with the photographs she and Kit had taken the night Carny kissed my mother.'

'He went ahead with the dare then?'

'Seems so. Roughly a week after it was proposed, on my way back from the bathroom at the Willises', I overheard Camille and Kit whispering about what they should do. They were afraid of Carny's reaction and had lied to him about something.'

It was a long time ago, but as I talked, the memories came spilling out from their corners. 'When we left the Willises' house that day, Carny pulled up in Mickie Willis's battered old pickup. He launched himself out of the driver's side and grabbed Kit by the throat, slamming him into the side of the truck. "What did you see?" he yelled. I didn't even know what he was referring to then.'

This was true. It had been a whirlwind of aggression, and anger loosed without warning. Like watching television, I'd looked on as Carny throttled my defenceless boyfriend and, despite being sickened by the level of violence, I did nothing. I stood there rooted to the spot. Petrified.

'And Kit denied any wrongdoing?'

'Yep, he and Camille both submissively held their hands in the air and asked what Carny was talking about. Kit didn't fight back when his brother started to thump him. He took the beating until Carny stopped. Then he poked Kit in the chest and had a verbal dig at him about keeping his word. Said he'd never wanted to be a part of our stupid gang, anyway. Like a kid.'

Then and there I knew Carny had carried out the dare. What a dreadful moment. The thought of my mother kissing a boy half her age had repelled me.

'But what you overheard later made you think differently about Kit and Camille's involvement. Something about photographs, you said?'

'That's all I know. Camille had them, she said to Kit they were evidence, and she would keep them hidden "in case".'

'In case of what?'

'That's just it, I never found out, never asked. I didn't want them to discover I'd been eavesdropping, and I guess they didn't want Carny to know they'd spied on him. Secrets and lies all round. Over the next few weeks, we let the incident fade into the past. We were young and naïve.'

The gaping hole in this story yawned before me. I needed answers as badly as Peddyr did, and the only person who had them was the man determined to ruin me. Owen Fox.

There was so much I needed to know from him.

Why and how was my mother tempted into having sex with a teenage boy? This was a stomach-churning thought, as was the one that came directly after it. Had Kit and Camille witnessed Carny in the act, taken pictures and threatened to expose him for his affair with a married woman? Did he think I'd seen those pictures?

Peddyr Quirk must have been reading my mind. 'Very Mrs Robinson,' he said.

'How could she have done such a thing?' My own mother. What a disgrace. I stopped short. 'But what if it wasn't like that? What if he raped her?' The horrendous alternative resulted in a sick feeling. What we as teenagers put in motion had ended up ruining my mother's life. She had been right. It was all my fault.

Peddyr handed me the keys to the Mini. 'I parked it round the back. You weren't safe behind the wheel and I was barely sober enough to drive, but there you go… Needs must.'

40

LET FATE DECIDE

*T*he local newspaper was spread over the Formica table in the kitchen of number six Derwent Drive when I arrived back, at least an hour later than I'd anticipated. By some miracle of sleep, paracetamol and cosmetics, Stella was back to her usual self but with an added frisson of excitement in her eyes. She sat with one shoulder resting against the wall.

'I've been to see Peddyr.'

'I thought that might be the case,' she replied, smoothing the newspaper with the flat of both hands. 'How is he?'

'I left him scrubbing a nasty stain from his lounge carpet.'

'While the wife's away… Any update on your case?'

Too tired to go into sordid details, I spoke in short snappy sentences. 'Owen Fox. I remembered who he was. I mean is.'

'Yes, you said last night. I was pissed, but that little bombshell came back to me this afternoon. Kit's elder brother. I can't understand what took you so long.'

'Probably because everyone knew him as Carny. His surname was different to the other Willis kids because Shana and Mickie Willis didn't get married until she was pregnant with Kit. I never heard anyone call him Owen, not once. He was always Carny. Carny Willis.' I spoke stiffly. 'He told Laura he was her real father. How about that? He had sex with my mother and left her to deal with the consequences.'

The tale came out of my mouth with no frills attached. 'At the time he spread rumours about me being pregnant, to take the heat away from himself. Which leads me to wonder what possible reason he could have for reappearing in my life and screwing it up now?' I swung my handbag onto the floor beside the table leg. 'It should be the other way around. I haven't done anything to him. I never did. So what the fuck am I supposed to be begging his forgiveness for?' I grabbed the back of a kitchen chair to steady myself. 'I want to hear it from his lips.'

'I was counting on this reaction,' Stella said without hesitation. 'I have a cunning scheme to get him where we want him. If I'm right, he's on call again this weekend, which is why we haven't seen him lurking around since Thursday morning.'

'And how do you propose we confirm those suspicions?' I enquired.

She finished dialling a number into her mobile and beamed at me. 'Like this,' she said. When the call was answered she winked and gave a thumbs up sign before making an apology for calling the wrong number in a voice scarily reminiscent of Aunty Wynn.

'It was him,' Stella said. 'So polite. "Castle and Wyckes Funeral Services, Owen Fox speaking, how can I help you?". Beautifully done. So far so good.'

Stella had a plan; one she'd been working on in the time I was absent. 'We arrange to meet Owen Fox at Castle and Wyckes, the Bosworth branch. You request your ID in return for silence about his part in the illegal cremation of a body, falsification of records and anything else you can think of. He agrees and you get to hear what he has to say for himself.'

A cold sensation snaked its way between my shoulder blades and up the back of my neck into my hairline. 'Peddyr said he would report Owen to the police on Monday and they would ask him in for questioning. Shouldn't we wait? Do this legally?'

Stella banged a fist on the table. 'Where's your backbone, Gabby? You think that'll happen in time for you to avoid bankruptcy, do you? He'll deny everything, and there's no proof apart from a digital photograph and some cranky handwritten notes, which you can bet won't have his fingerprints on them. There's no case to answer, no massive fraud, no nothing; zero, zilch, nada, niente.'

I dragged the chair I was holding towards me and plonked myself down on it. With shoulders rounded, I allowed my head to loll forward until it rested on the table. Curled over like a shy toddler, I explained Peddyr's theory to Stella.

'...it's distinctly possible that Kit and Camille photographed Owen Fox having sexual intercourse with my mother. Months later, one way or another, he became aware of Laura's imminent arrival in the world. Covering his tracks, he destroys the photographs by setting a house on fire and inadvertently kills three people. He's in deep now. Kit becomes suspicious, perhaps challenges him, and is killed for his trouble.' I raise my head an inch or two before letting it drop back heavily onto the tabletop. 'Oh, I don't know.'

Stella hoisted her phone in the air, and I sat up to listen to her next suggestion. I could feel it coming and welcomed it. 'But you want to find out,' she said. 'And if we get a full confession, record it on a phone and send it to the police, we'll have resolved everything much quicker than two detectives ever could. It's comeuppance time for Mr Fox.'

With fascination, I witnessed Stella's next Oscar-winning performance. 'Don't panic,' she said to me. 'Call divert at his end means the number doesn't show on his phone.' Having pressed redial, she used her posh telephone voice as she spoke.

'Hi, Owen, this is Moira Liggins from the Broadstairs branch. Can I ask a massive favour? You should be expecting a transfer from us, an out of area death.' There was a pause. 'That's the one. What a sad story... fancy dying while visiting your own sister in a care home... Heart attack. Yes, the Coroner's paperwork is done. The body needs transferring to you.' There was a delay before she spoke again. 'That's my dilemma, Owen, the server's gone down at this end, so can I give you the gentleman's details over the phone? We'd like to transfer tomorrow.'

She rolled her eyes as if this was a real business transaction taking place between two colleagues. 'I know... so much simpler to do it on a Sunday. You'll be there to accept? Brilliant, what time suits you? The boys can be with you late morning at the earliest, barring any difficulties. Super. We'll say anytime from eleven thirty then. Smashing.' Stella let out a flirtatious giggle. 'I'll return the favour; you only have to ask.'

She reeled off an unfamiliar name, an address in

Bosworth Bishops, and the place of death as being Sunny-dale Villa Care Home in Broadstairs. Stella gave the date and time of death and contact details for the relatives as if quoting from a bus timetable. She ended with more teasing. 'That's right, the Broadstairs branch... Off the High Street... The one on the latest brochure. Huge, modern and normally highly efficient.' She grinned widely. 'Oh, cheeky! If you want to see how large my frontage is, you must drop by and have a look. You're a star. Lovely to talk to you. Thanks again. Phone the branch number if you need anything.'

By the time she pressed the red button, I was running low on oxygen. I sucked in lungfuls of air, glad to breathe freely. 'Oh, my good God, what have you done?' I gasped.

'I've made certain that Mr Owen Fox is played at his own game. He will be at Castle and Wyckes tomorrow morning. In a while you will phone him and demand to meet with him at eleven o'clock. He will insist you have to meet at his workplace.'

'What if he checks up on you and finds out there's no Moira from Broadstairs?'

Moira Liggins, it turned out, was the actual manager at the Castle and Wykes branch in Broadstairs. Moira used to work with Stella at the Oxford branch before a well-deserved promotion. She and many other colleagues had remained friends and stayed in touch when Stella moved to Spain. An old hand, Stella knew the systems inside and out, and was putting her knowledge to good use.

'But what if he rings back?'

'Then Moira will answer, and all will be well.'

'Oh, will it now?' I said, pessimistic about the whole idea.

In sharp contrast, Stella's expression was determined. 'After the deed is done, this mobile phone lands in the hands of the police. They can keep it for evidence, I've got another one. I'm flying back to Spain on Monday. This is our last chance.'

A timetable had been set. 'But why will he agree to meet with me?' It wasn't cowardice making me err on the side of caution so much as uncertainty. Owen Fox held the winning cards in his devious hands. He held my identity to ransom and had made his intentions clear; my life was to be ruined, to pay for what he thought I'd done, though I still had no inkling what that was.

'You call his bluff. Pretend you know what he did. Tell him that, in return for your silence, he gives you your life back and all will be forgiven. Even stevens.'

'And he'll go for that?'

'Wouldn't you? He keeps his job. Gets to know the daughter he missed out on. Doesn't have to fear exposure anymore. A life for a life. Just as he wanted.'

Standing upright, propped against the kitchen work surface, I felt strangely disembodied as I waited for Owen Fox to pick up. My heartbeat pounded in my chest. Stella forced me to keep looking at her, grabbing my shoulders as I eased her mobile phone away from my ear enough for her to hear both sides of the conversation. 'You can do this,' she whispered.

My voice quavered dramatically. 'Owen, this is Gabriella Dixon. We need to talk.'

The volume of the reply was low, the rate steady, the tone perfunctory. 'Yes, we need to finish this. It's time for you to hear what I have to say. Bring your pink-haired friend with you as a witness, for your safety and for mine. No mobile phones. We each say our piece then go our separate ways. Can you meet me tomorrow at Castle and Wyckes? The chapel of rest would seem an appropriate place.'

Caught completely off guard, I stumbled over my response. 'Wh-What t-time?'

When I ended the call somewhat prematurely, Stella slumped. I'd let the side down. 'Should we even go with no phones to record what happens?' I asked.

There was a holdall behind me on the work surface containing the unused waterproofs from our trip to Wales. I hadn't mustered the enthusiasm to hang them back up in the under-stairs cupboard. Lying ominously on top of the bag was the black glossy sphere of the Magic 8-Ball. 'Shall I?'

'Well, it's more exciting than flipping a coin,' Stella replied, staring at me with a look of disappointment in her eyes. It would seal our fate one way or the other, but was merely a delaying tactic. I rolled the ball in my hands and waited for the floating triangle to become visible.

'Hang on,' Stella intervened. 'What question did you ask it?'

'I asked if I should meet Owen Fox tomorrow.' And the ball obliged with an unequivocal "YES". My need to prevaricate persisted, and I invented more reasons for not following through. 'But what about Peddyr Quirk? Aren't I paying him to do this?'

'And you think Owen Fox will tell him anything? No, he wants to free up his conscience and confess to you. He said as much on the phone.'

She was right. The end was beginning.

41

WHO'S DEAD?

I was awake with the dawn chorus, lying in bed dreading the day ahead. Grey clouds filled the sky. A night of sweaty oppression had heralded a summer storm. The ominous weather reflected my mood perfectly. By ten o'clock that morning I could hear the thunder rolling in the distant hills.

'Got a decent-sized umbrella anywhere?' Stella shouted from the kitchen.

'Aren't we taking the car?'

'No, we're walking. Leave the car on the drive. Let Kenny the Perv think we're still at home and if Owen Fox is watching, he won't know we've already left. Catch him on the hop.' What a calculating mind Stella possessed, I thought admiringly.

'But we'll get struck by lightning.' Not relishing the prospect of a thorough drenching, I took hold of a dusty black umbrella from a stand by the front door. Stella was pulling on my mother's Wellington boots, standing on the backdoor mat as if dressed for a trip to the compost heap.

Apart from her hair, she was unrecognisable. The sight was so disarming I allowed a chuckle to escape, despite my creeping anxiety. I reached to a hook behind the door and passed her a tweed cap. 'Go on. I can pretend I've adopted a tramp.'

We made for a fine pair as we huddled beneath the large umbrella and dashed for the back gate. I wore a long trench coat which wasn't as waterproof as it should have been, but as the summer rain wasn't cold, I didn't concern myself to any degree. I'd been more interested in whether or not the pockets were deep enough to conceal my trusty pebble.

Rainwater cascaded down lanes and alleyways into the town centre and we splashed across the road, reaching Castle and Wyckes at five minutes to eleven. The closed sign was on show, and no lights were on inside. Stella rapped on the door.

Within a minute, a besuited Owen Fox appeared. He pulled the door wide and a brass bell rang out above my head. I stepped over the threshold to wipe my feet, leaving Stella to lower the umbrella and follow behind me. Neither of us had taken handbags. We travelled light in the hope Owen wouldn't feel the need to pat us down for hidden mobile phones. If he did, all he'd find on me was a pebble.

Only as I braved catching his eye did I see the Owen Fox of my youth. Carny was there if I looked hard enough. He had more of his mother's features than the physicality of his father. Wiry and tall, exterior charm was on display, but coldness lurked not far beneath the surface. When he returned my assessment, by scanning me, wet toes to soggy head, I barely flinched. Gone were my business suits, the chic updo, the emotional defence strategies. I stood before him as myself, Gabriella Dixon, scared but very much alive.

He locked the door. 'Come this way,' he said formally, as

if escorting bereaved relatives. 'I have what you want in my office. If you wouldn't mind waiting in the next room, I'll fetch it.'

I shared an anxious look with Stella who shrugged and stepped forward, taking my mother's old raincoat from her shoulders, shaking it gently, and removing her borrowed cap. The pink hair on her head was flat and elfin like. She pushed me in the small of my back. I moved hesitantly into a discreet area where two coffins, an array of small caskets and several urns were on show. Owen turned on the lights, to compensate for the sunless day, and their reflections bounced back from a sleek marble tiled floor. The decor of the room was thoughtful, the quality of the displays a testament to the high standards on which Castle and Wyckes had built their reputation.

In silent accord Stella and I sat at a table. We glanced at the catalogues lying there. Stella lay the tweed cap upturned on the table top, satin lining illuminated by the bright lighting. I was pretending to look closely at a page illustrating the wide variety of brass coffin handles available when Owen Fox re-emerged carrying a shoe box, looking for all the world as if he were delivering someone's cremated remains. 'This is you,' he said to me. 'Your life in a box. It's all here. Certificates, passport, registration documents. Everything.'

I can't define what I was expecting from this meeting, but it wasn't to see all the official documentation of my existence gathered together and neatly presented to me. Was I supposed to thank him and walk away? His demeanour was hard to interpret. He spoke again. 'Well? You'll want to know why I did this to you.'

His thinly veiled conceit sparked something in my core and I stiffened, holding the box close to my ribs. 'I've come here to listen to what you have to say, yes.' I drew in a deep breath to steady myself. 'Because, no matter how hard I try, I can't find any reason for you to want me to suffer in this way, so please... tell me.' Stella reached out and took the shoebox from me, sliding it across the table.

Owen Fox walked to a window which overlooked the courtyard at the rear of the property. His silver BMW was parked there. He did an about-face and leant against the windowsill.

'When Laura came in to organise your mother's funeral, I was in two minds about whether or not to declare an interest. Then you appeared on the scene and it was too late to change my decision to proceed as if I knew none of you. Anyway, I needn't have worried, you barely acknowledged my presence.'

'There's no need to drag this out, Carny.' I deliberately used his old nickname. 'You told Laura you are her real father, which means you had sex with my mother, to put it bluntly. I already know that.' Checking my progress required a surreptitious glance in Stella's direction. She was willing me on. I could tell.

'I want to know why you chose this particular year, this crappy year, to take a swipe at me. What have I ever done to you?'

There was no explosion of rage, no furious repercussion. 'In the eulogy you gave at your mother's funeral you really upset me,' he said.

Aghast, I could hardly speak. 'My eulogy upset you so much you decided to destroy my life as a punishment?' Opening my hands wide, I invited him to explain.

'You stood in front of the mourners and told them there was only one man in your mother's life. You said your father protected and loved her and Eileen was never happier than when she could spend time with her family.'

'What's wrong with that?' Stella chimed in. 'Cheesy and heartfelt are the order of the day at a good funeral, surely? Nobody speaks ill of the dead.'

'I'm sorry, we haven't been introduced,' Owen said, holding out his hand.

'I'm an old friend. I grew up around here. I knew Gabby's parents well.'

Stella accepted his handshake politely, but she was holding back and suddenly I realised why. She'd been at the funeral too. Not only that, but she'd come with me to see my mother in the chapel of rest and been accosted by Hugh Ingles, her old boss, who'd made a rare fuss of her. Owen would have seen that. Stella had worked in another branch of Castle and Wyckes before she left for Spain, but all the same if he recognised her, beneath the pink hair and wellies, we were done for. He would never trust her to keep silent if he realised who she was.

'If you knew the Bradys, then you'll know that Eileen was an unhappy woman. She should never have gone back to her husband. He was too old, too controlling.' Owen Fox pulled back his shoulders and spoke directly to me again. 'At the funeral you said she didn't deserve what happened to her, so I assumed you knew. You looked straight at me.' He thrust his head forward accusingly.

Affronted at his insensitivity, I got to my feet. 'My mother had cancer. It was a long, painful and protracted illness, and no matter how bad our relationship was, I wouldn't have wished such a death on my worst enemy. Why would you take that statement so personally?'

Owen Fox tensed. 'I loved your mother. We were going to be together.'

'And what stopped you, Casanova?' A bitterness arrived with a metallic taste in my mouth from where I'd bitten the inside of my cheek.

'You did, Gabby. *You* stopped me. Think about it. Eileen was in her prime when I knew her, voluptuous and lonely. Your old dad was off with his establishment buddies turning the wheels of government politics, and she needed more than he could give her. She called me Owen and treated me like a man. But she couldn't bear to go through with it. She chose you over me. She chose a stable home with her stuffy husband and lived a sad life so her two daughters could have the security they needed. Your father was persuaded to take her back because of *you* and she broke my heart because of *you*.' He poked a forefinger in my direction.

Before replying, I considered carefully what he'd said, studying his body language.

'That makes sense, I suppose,' I said, noting the suffering, loss and grief reflected in his face. 'But tell me, am I supposed to be asking your forgiveness for my ignorance? You see, I have a brain, Carny. So why don't you try telling the truth instead of pretending there was a romantic love story behind this. Or is that what you've convinced yourself?'

Owen Fox shook his head slowly and clasped his hands together. 'We loved each other, your mum and me. And I know it's wrong to feel jealous after all this time, but it was hard to see her again. Such a wasted life. I wanted you to know how it felt to lose the life you were supposed to have. Like I did.'

I can tell a liar when I see and hear one. This story was first-class poppycock, and it annoyed the hell out of me. 'Well, congratulations, you did an outstanding job of screwing up my life. So, what happens now? You and Laura get to know one another, make up for years apart, and I shake you warmly by the hand and welcome you into the fold. Is that what I'm expected to do?'

He crossed his arms. Classic defensive posture. Interesting. 'Look, I didn't know she was pregnant. She ran off to Wales to hide the pregnancy, from me and from her husband. But when I found out I vowed to provide for her and the baby.'

I'd heard enough. I clapped sarcastically several times. 'Credit where credit's due, Carny. In itself, the story is plausible but you're only giving me my life back because I don't know what really happened. Putting me under this much strain and making sure I worked out who you were was a test to see what I knew. Well, listen up, sunshine. I know nothing.'

A crack of thunder exploded outside and a second later the lights flickered as sheet lightening flashed across the sky. Like a strobe, it lit up Owen Fox's face – impassive, unreadable.

Stella stooped down and picked up the shoe box. 'Let's go,' she said. 'We've heard enough.' She was right. It was the most sensible course of action to leave while we still had the advantage and I had the documents necessary to restart my life, but without all the answers I'd come for, I was left feeling desperately unsatisfied with this outcome.

'We'll say no more about it then,' Owen Fox concluded. 'You give Laura her money for the house and move on.'

Stella was prodding me towards the archway and the front entrance beyond. We couldn't get out without the door being unlocked, and unfortunately Owen Fox had the keys. He was right behind me. 'Don't you worry, Señor. She won't be hanging around,' Stella said, flashing Owen a fake smile over her shoulder. 'What this girl needs is a holiday.'

That brief interlude gave me enough of a window to analyse what had been said since we arrived at Castle and Wyckes. I slid to an abrupt halt on the shiny flooring. My spell of being officially dead seemed to have produced atrophy of the brain, most likely caused by panic and stress overload, but safe in Stella's company I had nothing left to fear and reason returned in the nick of time.

'Ha!' I said, laughing with a rush of enlightenment, a warped sensation of joy. 'So Bernard Kershaw was right.'

I felt the instant when Stella released me from her grip and turned to stare at me, doubt etched on her face. As I relaxed, she tensed.

'This is about money,' I announced. The slap I landed on my forehead sounded shockingly loud in these hushed surroundings. 'Pah! You nearly had me there, Carny. Nearly, but not quite.'

Owen Fox didn't seem to have a response. He glanced past me to a bewildered and sodden Stella, who was shaking her head. While he was distracted, I threw out thoughts like a mad Evangelist. 'You were a bully, and all bullies are cowards. You would never have had the guts to kiss my mother, let alone seduce her or worse...'

'What are you accusing me of?'

'Nothing,' I shot back. 'In fact, I doubt you went anywhere near her.' I laughed, properly this time. 'I was going to ask you about the photographs that Kit took. I thought they were of you and my mother, but they weren't, were they?'

42

OOPS

I waited for Owen Fox's answer to my question, knowing this was dangerous territory.

'There are no photographs,' he said, standing firm.

'Not of you with my mother, no. But several incriminating photographs existed, and if I'm right...' I stopped myself mid-flow. Happiness and sadness mingled to form a heady mixture. I ran my fingers through my tangled hair and rested them on the crown of my head, holding them there for a moment. 'Carny worked with his dad, walked like his dad and wanted to be his dad, but he didn't have looks or the magnetic sexuality of Mickie Willis.' Resting my arms, I put my hands in the pockets of my trench coat and fingered the pebble there as I spoke.

'Kit and Camille went to my house thinking they would be taking pictures of you snogging the lips off my mother, but you never turned up. Most likely, what they saw was your dad having a sexual encounter with my mother, and probably not for the first time.' Fleetingly I met Stella's eyes.

'With Dad away so often, Mickie Willis did jobs around the house for my parents. He became a regular visitor and usually called when I was at school, strangely enough. "Mickie fixed the boiler... Mickie mended your wardrobe door, darling.'

Owen Fox capitulated. His shoulders sagged; his chin dipped towards his shirt collar. 'You don't know,' he said. 'You weren't there. Did you see the photos?' he asked, tilting his head.

I stepped to the side and Stella moved with me as if attached by an invisible shackle. 'So you know about them then? The photos did exist; you've just said so.'

'*T*hat Camille girl couldn't keep her mouth shut. My dad found out what she and Kit did,' Owen replied, barely moving his lips.

'Only because you told him...' I half turned to go. I had my answers. It must have been Mickie Willis in the photographs Kit took. Before I could work through the permutations in my head, Owen Fox bared his teeth and spoke again with such venom I took a step back and faced him square on. Something told me not to turn my back on him.

'Dad gave my brother a good hiding and told him to sort it.'

'What?'

'You heard me. Dad went off on one, Kit was told to destroy the evidence. *He* set light to the Bullimores' place. Not my dad and not me, if that's what you were thinking. It was Kit. He did it. They were supposed to be on holiday. Kit killed the lot of them and afterwards he couldn't live with it.'

Somehow the air felt thicker. I struggled to inhale. The dreadful puzzle was solved. Carny hadn't changed, he was always a coward and a sneak. Carny would do anything to please his father...

'You were there with your dad when he visited my mum in Wales, weren't you?' I said. 'You saw me hiding alongside the caravan while he was inside and you knew everything. Did you come back later that night?'

'You'll never prove any of it,' he said, his lip curling.

'You did. Mickie was in the nearest pub drowning his sorrows and you came back in his van. I didn't slip and fall. I was on my way to get help and you hit me. It was you, not an accident.'

'As I said... prove it.' I didn't have to, I could see the guilt in his face.

It was a while before I spoke again, and when I did, it sounded like the summary of a seedy story on a daytime TV show. 'Well, there we have it. You ratted on your brother, your father gave him his orders and when it went wrong, Kit unsurprisingly committed suicide. To stop me from telling people that your dad visited my mother when she was on the point of giving birth to his child, you hit me hard enough to kill me, but you couldn't even get that right. As a result of the mess, Mickie Willis took to drinking himself to death, and you joined the sodding army. My mother had Laura to dote on, I gained a sister I've never liked, my father another daughter... And we all lived unhappily ever after.'

Owen Fox didn't contradict me. He undid his tie, pulled it free from his shirt collar and stuffed it into a pocket.

'Are you going to tell Laura you're not her real father or shall I?' I said, hooking an arm through Stella's and marching over to the entrance door where I collected my wet umbrella.

'You won't tell her anything,' Owen growled. He retrieved the tie from his pocket and wound an end around each fist. In response, I raised the tip of the umbrella from the floor, holding it steady, ready to defend myself.

'If we keep quiet about what you did, you can walk away from this, disappear back where you came from,' Stella added. The shoebox was under one arm and she had me tightly gripped by a handful of trench coat.

Bile rose in my throat. 'Do you know something, Carny? If you hadn't stirred it all up and registered me as dead, I would never have worked out that Mickie was Laura's father.'

'It was time you did. You and Laura have more money than you know what to do with. And I'm a relative, don't forget. I have a right to my share.' There was the confession and admission of guilt, delivered with not one ounce of shame or remorse.

'I see it now: you make certain she and I fall out, you make a claim by pretending to be her father and eventually get to share in Laura's wealth. Meanwhile, I end up destitute as a perverse punishment.' I shook the umbrella at him. 'Today you were to feed me a line about a love affair with my mother. I was to accept your fanciful story and gratefully take my life back. Embarrassed by the scandal, I would say nothing. Isn't that what you expected?'

There wasn't much left to say. Now I'd exposed the truth, the blue touch paper had been lit. Owen Fox was heading for ignition and blast off. I could feel it and Stella must have sensed it too. I felt her become almost rigid. He stepped towards us and we scuttled like human crabs towards the coffin display area, making space to move, to dodge, to head for the rear exit. 'Pay me what I'm owed,' Owen said. 'Then I'll go, leave you alone...'

I jinked to my right and the link between me and Stella broke as she went the other way. We stood either side of a display coffin.

'What do you mean?'

'You transfer £50,000 to me now. Today. And I let you live. You can have your life back.'

'And what if I don't? Kill me off and make a claim on my estate, will you? You'll make it look like an accident, I expect,' I blurted out.

Owen Fox gave a shrug, his eyes narrowing. 'Self-defence. Mad woman comes here accusing me of things I've never done. Things get out of hand.'

Stella was looking about her for a means of escape. Inadvertently, we'd backed ourselves into a corner. She allowed the shoebox to fall from her hands.

'Just one problem,' I squawked. 'You closed my bank account.'

It was Owen's turn to laugh. 'Pull the other one, love,' he sniggered. 'I'll get my money from her.' He jabbed a fist in Stella's direction. 'She has plenty of it.'

Never taking his eyes from me, he sprang forward as I staggered into reverse, trying to get nearer to Stella again. It didn't take many seconds to work out that Laura must have told him about the deal made with rich Stella Cortez. Owen Fox knew she'd bail me out and pay the ransom.

I raised the umbrella like a sword to save myself as I collided with the wall. 'She'll pay if there's no other way,' he said, his voice bitter. Unravelling one end of his tie, a murderous-looking Owen Fox balled his right hand into a fist and, cowering, I shut my eyes tight, expecting in the next second to feel a lot of pain.

Instead, there was a scream from Stella, 'Owen!' then a garbled shout, more bangs, a crash and a boom. Opening my eyes, I watched in slow-motion horror as the fully lined, ornate coffin left its carved trestles and crashed down on top of Owen Fox's head.

'What happened?' I called to Stella.

'He slipped on the wet floor.'

I looked down at the umbrella in my hands and the cascade of drips running from the metal tip. As I checked along the marble floor, I could see the skid marks made by Owen Fox's highly polished shoes. He lay motionless in a crumpled heap beside the overturned coffin, Stella standing over him.

'How the hell did he end up like that?' I asked.

Speaking like an automaton, she gawped at Owen Fox's shattered head. 'He put his arms out. I think he hit his head on the hard floor before the coffin fell on him.' Beside his dented head lay a stone urn, used for cremation ashes. 'I hate to say this, but he's not breathing.'

Neither Stella nor I made a move to help the stricken man. We both knew he was dead.

It was Stella who spoke first. She looked at her watch and licked dry lips. 'We might not have long. Broadstairs will be dropping off Mr Hubbard any time now.'

I shook my head and blinked rapidly. 'What the hell are you on about?'

'The body, the transfer from Broadstairs, the one I arranged over the phone. Snap out of it and start thinking how we're going to deal with this!' Her Spanish suntan had turned a peculiar grey colour and yet she remained oddly composed.

'There is no bloody transfer from Broadstairs. You made it up,' I said, panting in short bursts.

'No, I didn't,' Stella responded. 'I phoned and spoke to Moira yesterday, just for a catch up, a friendly chat, like you do. She told me about a problem at work and asked my advice. Her computers had crashed before she could arrange an urgent transfer for Edward John Hubbard. He was a Bosworth sporting hero, so he warranted a few column inches in the local newspaper. Hugh Ingles owed me a favour, so I told Moira I'd pull some strings and get the transfer done today, which I did. Perfect timing for us and for her. I'd have done the same even if it wasn't Owen Fox on call.'

Stupefied, I looked at Owen's lifeless form under the coffin, lying on the glassy marble tiles of the floor. There wasn't much blood. 'Perhaps he broke his neck in the fall,' I said.

Stella took me by the shoulders, just as she had done when I'd made a fateful call to Owen Fox the day before. 'Look, you're not getting this are you? How he died is irrelevant. He's dead and you have the best motive in the world for killing him. Who will believe it's an accident, eh?'

'But it was. You're my witness.'

She pulled me up onto my toes by the lapels of the trench coat. 'Peddyr Quirk believes that Owen Fox was a prime suspect in your friends' unexplained deaths. He thinks Owen Fox was out to ruin your life to keep a tragic secret about being the father of your mother's illegitimate child. You even suggested he'd raped her. I'm an accomplice. We left our mobile phones behind, so we can't be traced. We hid our faces from any cameras in town. We left the Mini on the drive and used the back door...' Her vehemence was undeniable, as was her argument. On that set of facts alone they would judge us guilty of manslaughter, perhaps even murder. 'Gabby! Do you understand how serious this is?' She shook me hard and my head flopped back and forth. I was laughing again, this time hysterically, loud and long and hard, and an invisible hand reached into my world and pressed the pause button.

43

PADDY QUIRK GETS A PHONE CALL
FROM HUGH INGLES

*P*eddyr resorted to buying a pot of expensive stain remover from the local supermarket first thing on Tuesday morning and was reading the instructions for use when his mobile phone rang. It wasn't Connie; he knew that much; she'd already checked up on him and enquired about whether he'd had fruit and yogurt for breakfast.

With only a couple more days to make sure the stain on the lounge carpet would be invisible to her hawk eyes, he was under pressure to keep the flat and offices neat and ready for his wife's return from Scotland. After his dawn trip to the shops, he made a start on the hillock of dirty laundry and called the washing machine into action. He was waiting for the spin cycle to finish when his phone distracted him.

'P.Q. Investigations, Peddyr Quirk speaking.' He hadn't recognised the caller's number. It wasn't one stored into the phone's directory.

'Paddy, this is Hugh Ingles,' said a querulous voice. 'I

require your discreet assistance with a most unfortunate matter.'

'You have my full attention, Mr Ingles. How can I be of assistance?' Peddyr rested on the arm of a chair and placed the pot of stain remover down on a side table, listening attentively. There was a mystery to be solved.

'You remember Owen Fox?' This seemingly innocent opening was laden with concern. 'He was on call this weekend. Marjorie opened up yesterday morning as usual and there was nothing to suggest anything was wrong, apart from the fact that Owen's car was still in the courtyard. It's his day off on a Monday.'

Peddyr waited for the full explanation.

'But he hasn't turned up for work today and we can't get hold of him. He hasn't contacted us to say he's sick, which is most unlike the fellow. You won't be surprised to hear Marjorie got her underwear in a tangle and sent Diane to his home to see if he needed a doctor. No sign of him there either and the fellow lives alone. Any ideas?'

This put Peddyr in a delicate position because of what he'd done the previous day. Before going to the police station on Monday, he had tried to contact Gabby to see how she wanted him to proceed. But with her phone switched off, he could only assume she was with Stella, seeing her off at the airport. Knowing how emotionally hard this would be for her, he didn't want to interrupt, so he left a simple message instead.

With only supposition and circumstantial evidence to back him up, Peddyr appeared at the police station. As he outlined his suspicions, a sceptical young officer took the details. In Peddyr's opinion Owen Fox was guilty of fraudulently registering Gabriella Dixon's death, if nothing else, and it wouldn't be long before irrefutable evidence came to light to implicate him in other crimes.

He turned his mind back to the present. 'When was Owen last seen?'

'You have me there, Paddy,' Hugh Ingles said. 'According to computer records, he took delivery of a body from our Broadstairs branch at 12.20 on Sunday. However, the driver said they didn't see him in person as t'were. They were buzzed in. He apologised over the intercom for not helping, said he was on a call to a hysterical relative but had opened up for them. They waved to him as they left.'

'And where was he when they waved to him?'

'At a window overlooking the courtyard. I couldn't say which one precisely.'

There were two possibilities running through Peddyr's mind. One, that Owen Fox had done a runner on Monday before the police had caught up with him, or two, the police had taken Peddyr seriously and had pulled Fox in for questioning.

'And his car's still there, you say?' Peddyr asked Hugh Ingles. This was the one thing that didn't make much sense. 'Leave it with me. I'll do some scouting around. See what I can come up with. I'll come down to the Bosworth branch, there's bound to be a simple explanation.'

He phoned the police station and quoted the reference number they had given him the day before.

'There's been no update,' the call handler said. The police force in Bosworth Bishops had gone the way of so many others. A central number was used to filter calls other than for an emergency on 999. Reports were inputted and updated on a central database and the call centre referenced anything written there. 'Who's handling the case?' Peddyr asked.

'It's not allocated to an officer yet, Mr Quirk. It's not a priority case.'

There was little point in pursuing this. The police didn't have the time or the manpower, and they were never interested in Gabriella's story about a person or persons unknown deliberately and falsely registering her as deceased. To them, she was a nuisance, and Peddyr was on the same list.

Leaving the carpet stain untouched, he grabbed a jacket in case of more rain and headed out to Castle and Wyckes on foot. The roads were too slippery to take the motorbike, and besides, he enjoyed the exercise. It wasn't far.

Marjorie was on edge; her nerves got the better of her as she fumbled with the keys, flicking each one on the keyring, unable to locate the one she was looking for. 'Owen still has his with him, but fortunately there's a spare set for this office. Diane uses his desk on a Monday to book in relatives for funeral arrangement appointments and visits to the chapel of rest. We have access if we need somewhere quiet to work.'

'Any sign of his car keys?'

'Er, no.' Marjorie looked across the office to where Diane was sitting. Her colleague shook her head in confirmation.

'Anyone looked inside his car?'

The suggestion was too much for Marjorie. Her hands rocketed up to her cheeks. 'You don't think…'

'I don't know what to think, Marjorie. For all I know he could have run off with a barmaid on Sunday night and disappeared into the sunset never to be seen again.' Peddyr cast his eyes over the tidy desk in Owen Fox's office. 'Do you have a key for the drawer?' he asked pulling at the brass handle to his left.

On the desk, next to the monitor, a wooden box caught Peddyr's eye. He lifted the lid to reveal pens, pencils and a pencil sharpener. With a flick of his hand, he turned the lid over. Stuck to the underside by a blob of Blu Tack was a key. 'No matter, I think I've found the little fella.'

It fitted the lock and turned with ease. 'Diane? Do you know what Owen keeps in this desk drawer?' he shouted loud enough for her to hear from outside the confines of the smaller office.

'No,' she replied, apparently taken aback at the implication. 'It's private.'

The drawer itself was deep and had a number of containers within. Some plastic ones, and a cardboard shoe box. Peddyr sat in the office chair and, pulling the drawer out to its fullest extent, began a thorough investigation of the contents.

'I'll leave you to it,' Marjorie said. 'We have a family coming in to settle an account, so I'll be with Diane in the main reception for a while. Make yourself at home.'

'I could do with access to the CCTV recordings for the weekend, before you go,' Peddyr said.

'No problem, I'll get them up on my screen. You know how it all works.'

He did. Peddyr had been the one to suggest use of security cameras after Castle and Wyckes had their run-in with the vehicle slasher next door. The cameras only covered the rear entrance gates and the courtyard, not the front door; that was felt to be too intrusive for grieving relatives. With any luck, Peddyr would see the arrival of Owen Fox's car and the delivery of the body from Broadstairs. He hoped for more.

However, there were boxes to be examined before he sat down to filter through hours of CCTV footage. He pulled the first one from the drawer and laid it carefully on the desktop. Within were spare glasses stored safely in a leather case. These had thick black rims whereas Fox's everyday pair were sleek and more suited to his face. Apart from spectacles, there was a printer cable surplus to require-ments, breath-freshening mints in a plastic pot, indigestion tablets, a packet of tissues, a copy of Castle and Wyckes' human resources handbook for employees, and a multi-tool penknife. Peddyr repacked the box and placed it to one side on the floor before reaching for the next box, a cardboard one. A shoebox.

'Well, strike a bloody light!' he said as he lifted the lid and picked up the first item. It was Gabriella Louise Dixon's passport.

44

WHERE HAS SHE GONE?

*T*he CCTV footage showed Owen Fox's arrival at ten twenty-seven on Sunday morning. He drove into the courtyard at Castle and Wyckes, the automatic gates closed behind his BMW, which he parked nose on to the building. Wearing a dark-grey suit, he dashed inside, a newspaper held over his head to shelter him from the rain. 'Smartly dressed,' Peddyr commented for his own benefit. Diane and Marjorie had not reappeared, although he could hear them having an in-depth discussion with two people, a man and a woman. It sounded positive, which was more than could be said of his own efforts to locate Owen Fox.

'You devious bugger,' he muttered, deciding by process of elimination that Owen must have left by the front door. He checked his phone. Still no response from Gabby, which was frustrating as he wanted to talk to her directly, not leave a message to say he'd recovered her documents and proved Owen Fox's guilt.

He'd found a black woolly hat in the desk drawer, and a tweed cap with talcum powder on the inside, most likely from when Owen had pretended to be Arthur Bird, Peddyr thought. Everything fitted with his theory, everything was here, apart from Owen Fox.

The bell of the front door jangled and, before long, Peddyr heard the return of Castle and Wyckes' remaining staff members. 'Another very satisfied customer,' Diane said. 'Any news on Owen?'

'I've tried the hospitals, the police, his neighbours, looked through the windows of his car, checked the rest of the premises, the CCTV... and in short, the answer is no, nothing. We must wait a day or so before police will consider him a missing person, but I could try the railway station to see if anyone saw him buying a ticket recently. Can I have another wander around to see if I might have missed something?' Peddyr asked.

'Like what?'

'I won't know until I see it.' Nothing had appeared out of place or untoward when he'd arrived that day and a more thorough appraisal of Owen's office, the main office, the chapel of rest, the mortuary area and reception, revealed precisely zero. It wasn't until he moved through to the display area for coffins, cremation receptacles and their various accessories that he spied anything of interest. He hunkered down next to a fine walnut coffin to examine a chip in the marble-tiled floor. Some clumsy Nellie had dropped a heavy object, he guessed. To the side of his head, there was a corresponding dent in the wood on the corner of the casket.

The coffin was open to show the satin lining, a section of which was cut away to expose the zinc panel below that. Standing upright, Peddyr pivoted on his heels. The other display coffin, some six feet away, had its lid in place. 'Now then, I wonder...' He sniffed and approached the closed casket quietly, not appreciating the slightly irrational thought which crept into his head. He had to check inside. Circling the coffin, he examined it externally before locating the sealing key at the foot. He turned it and lifted the lid, breaking the rubber gasket seal as he did so. It was empty.

Peddyr laughed at himself and was about to leave the room when he spotted something against the leg of one trestle which made him shiver.

An anomaly. A pebble. A pebble he recognised.

Gabriella Dixon had been here.

Wasting no time, he dialled her number once more. Still dead. Calling out to Diane and Marjorie, he made an excuse about needing to speak to the ticket office at Bosworth Bishops' station and left.

The station would wait. The shortest route to Derwent Drive was through the maze of interconnecting alleyways and back lanes, then across a park. As he rounded the penultimate corner, his destination in sight, he saw Kenny Eversholt pushing the doorbell to number six. As Peddyr approached unnoticed, Kenny looked up at the bedroom windows and then tip-toed close to a front window, cupping his hands to see in.

'Nobody home?' Peddyr enquired, startling Kenny who leapt back, losing a purple flip-flop among the weeds. He bent down to retrieve it before replying.

'God save us!' he wheezed, placing a hand to his silken shirt. 'Who are you?'

'I'm looking for Gabriella. Have you seen her recently?'

'What's it to you, ducky?' Kenny scoured Peddyr with suspicious eyes. 'You're not local plod. But you are plod.'

Individuals of a criminal disposition had an uncanny knack of spotting a policeman, retired or otherwise. 'Not for many years, Mr Eversholt. I've been trying to get hold of Mrs Dixon by phone since yesterday, but she's not returning my calls. Have you seen her today?'

Kenny puckered his lips as if unsure how best to reply. He swayed side to side like a punch bag at the end of a boxer's training session. 'She was here yesterday. I saw her leave with that Spanish friend of hers. They drove off in a Mini.'

'Together in a Mini, you're sure about that?'

'Look, ducky, I know a Mini when I see one. It's been on the drive since Saturday when they came back from an aborted trip to sunny Wales. The friend must have taken ill. She looked as sick as a dog when I saw them get out of the car.' After some hesitation he explained to Peddyr how he'd kept an eye on number six while the women were away. 'I popped over to tell Gabriella that I've repositioned the camera. Wouldn't want her to think I was... you know... spying on her.'

'And she didn't come back on Monday?'

'Yes, she did. It was evening time, I waved and shouted across the road at her as she was opening the front door. I thought she should know there were no unwanted visitors during the day. She was polite enough, said it was a hell of a long train journey from Gatwick and she wouldn't recommend it.'

'And how did she seem?'

'Tired, a bit rushed. Can't say I blame her.' Kenny sighed quietly.

'I'll try her sister's place,' Peddyr said. It was the logical next option.

Kenny tutted and flicked his head back. 'She won't be there, that Laura is a bitch and they've had a major wobbly. Shouldn't bother if I were you, ducky.'

.   .   .

*J*t was a fair trek to Revival Farm and Peddyr himself could have done with reviving by the time he got there. A drink of water would have been most welcome. Unfortunately, he wasn't greeted with the offer of one and had to ask.

'Like I said, she's not here,' Laura said sharply.

Peddyr couldn't go into detail, but after some diplomatic wrangling, and a tall glass of iced water, he persuaded Laura to drive him back to Derwent Drive on the pretext of ensuring the property was secure and to ensure Gabby hadn't had an unfortunate accident. Laura escorted him and held on to the house keys at all times.

The windows were closed, the house pretty much as Peddyr had last seen it; packing cases stacked in a corner of the lounge, still awaiting disposal, cushions on the sofa plumped up, and everywhere was clean. Kitchen cupboards contained a few tins, and the fridge had cheese, milk, butter substitute and half a bottle of Cava within. 'Like the Marie Celeste,' Peddyr offered.

They went upstairs, Laura huffing about wasting her time. 'What's all the fuss for? She's gone into a super-sized sulk because I have a father and hers is dead, her mate Stella's left her in the lurch, and we asked her to pay some rent. She'll get over it.'

It wasn't Peddyr's place to argue, and he was almost inclined to agree

…If it hadn't been for that pebble. It placed Gabby at Castle and Wyckes, but he didn't know when or why she went there other than to meet Owen Fox who was now missing. He prayed she hadn't been so rash.

The bedrooms were untouched, but on closer inspection

there was no hairbrush or make-up bag on the dressing table – something picked up by Laura. In the bathroom there was another helpful sign. 'No toothbrush… I told you, she's gone to lick her wounds. Try some of her mates from work.'

'Know any?'

Laura laughed. 'No, I don't know any of her friends apart from Stella and I can't stand her, the manipulative cow.'

Apart from Justin Parks, Bridget was the only person Peddyr knew as far as Gabby's work colleagues went. He would track her down. Gabby would be somewhere local. He and Laura gave up the search and made their way downstairs and into the front hall. Laura was on a roll. 'And when you find Gabby, tell her to ask Stella for my money. She promised I'd have it this week. I'm expecting a bank transfer by Thursday at the latest.'

Peddyr made the right noises, bade Laura farewell and retreated through the streets of Bosworth Bishops to his own office. It was time to call Bernie Kershaw for advice.

45

TWO FOR THE PRICE OF ONE

*T*he next day Peddyr was at Castle and Wyckes again. He knew the answer to Gabriella Dixon's pseudo death and subsequent disappearance had to be there. He'd been in contact with Bridget Ryan, who hadn't heard anything of Gabby since the day she dropped off her belongings from work. Texts had gone unanswered.

'Strictly I'm not permitted to have any contact with her,' Bridget had said. 'She's under suspension from work. It's against policy. But you know how it is, I didn't want her to think I'd forgotten about her, so I dropped her a few messages asking how she was coping. It worried me. She lives for her job. Being suspended will have rocked her world completely.'

Peddyr asked if Bridget could think of anywhere Gabby might be, other than at her sister's. The reply was illuminating. 'Mr Quirk, Gabby keeps herself to herself. She's generous with her professional help and with biscuits, but she's very private. Ask anyone in the team about Gabby's personal life and you'll come up with a blank. I know she has a sister and I know she got divorced recently and that her ex-husband is a GP, but I don't know her favourite colour, what she does for fun, or who she mixes with at the weekend. She gives out very little and rarely socialises with any of us. If she does, she remains stone cold sober. I wouldn't have a clue where she might be.'

With nothing else to go on, Peddyr looked for inspiration to explain the pebble he found at Castle and Wyckes. There were now direct orders from Bernie to find Gabriella Dixon. Mrs Estelle Cortez had phoned the offices of Bagshot and Laker's from Spain, asking to speak to him. She was 'beside herself with worry,' according to his secretary Fiona. Since saying goodbye to her at Gatwick Airport, Stella Cortez had not been able to contact Gabby and was now instructing dear old Bernie to enlist Peddyr's help in locating her. Bernie was asked to report Gabby to the police as a missing person, but as she wasn't considered vulnerable in any way, no action was taken.

Gabriella Dixon was seen on Monday evening by her peculiar neighbour Kenny Eversholt and that was the last known sighting of her. Peddyr automatically discounted Kenny as a suspect, abduction wasn't his style. Grooming perhaps, but not kidnap, and he had no motive to speak of.

Then there was the disappearance of Owen Fox. On the Sunday he was last seen, Owen would have had his mobile with him. The main enquiry number for Castle and Wyckes was diverted to it, allowing him to receive out of hours calls, day or night. He had a bunch of keys in his possession, ones that locked the doors at Castle and Wyckes, and would have kept his car keys with him and his wallet. But why leave without his car?

He was going around in ever decreasing circles. If Owen Fox was Laura's real father and had covered up the fact for years because of incriminating photographs, then perhaps, as Gabby had feared, he'd raped Eileen Brady.

Talking to himself, Peddyr said, 'Gabby disappeared sometime late Monday night, or in the early hours of Tuesday morning. Could Owen Fox have disappeared at the same time?' His head was aching with the strain. He blew out, deflating his lungs until there was no more air left in them before taking in a fresh lungful.

'If Owen Fox was not seen leaving Castle and Wyckes on Sunday, then maybe he never left at all. What if Gabby killed him and dumped his body in the boot of his own car some time much later on Sunday than I was looking for on CCTV?' Something else occurred to him. 'Or vice versa... what if Owen had killed Gabby late on Monday, on his day off?' He shivered. Owen would know how to dispose of a body. He would know not to use his own car.

The day of Edward John Hubbard's funeral had arrived and along with it much activity at the Bosworth branch. Peddyr became distracted by the comings and goings. Flowers were delivered from the florist's, itineraries checked, hearse and limousines given a final polish. He couldn't interrupt and would have to wait to examine Owen Fox's car again. This time more thoroughly.

As the hour of the funeral service approached, Peddyr watched from the administration office window as a coffin was handled carefully by four pallbearers. With great solemnity and respect, they transferred the heavy casket from a trolley onto a sliding mechanism in the back of the hearse. The scene made for fascinating viewing and set Peddyr thinking about the tasks required of an undertaker.

What a strange title to describe a person who buried the dead; undertaker.

'Shifting bodies must create physical wear and tear. Bad backs and all that,' he said.

Marjorie was at his side. 'We do regular moving and handling training. Keeps us in line with health and safety procedures.' She hummed. 'There he goes, right on time.'

'Church?'

'No... crematorium, it's what the family wanted. His son and a niece made the arrangements. I think they've shared the costs.'

Pondering on the decisions made by people to take up a job which involved disposing of the dead, he wondered how he'd cope with the reality of a decomposing body if he happened to find a rotting Owen Fox in the back of a BMW.

'How come he doesn't smell bad?' Peddyr said, nodding in the hearse's direction outside.

'It's amazing how effective embalming can be. The embalmer usually takes a few extra precautions, like sealing the nose and putting incontinence pads inside the clothing. If the deceased is in a poor state to start with, we might use a plastic body suit first before dressing it. Then they're wrapped in a shroud.'

The words of Steve the hipster at Bright's came back to him. 'Yes, I knew about plastic shrouds. Like shrink wrapping.'

'Almost. We use sealed bags and refrigeration to store the body until we dress the deceased for viewing or the funeral. In Mr Hubbard's case, the Broadstairs branch did the hard work.'

'And how do they know they've got the right body in there?' Peddyr asked.

Marjorie looked askance at him. 'Mr Quirk. These things are checked and double-checked. The deceased is carefully labelled. There are failsafe procedures to ensure we send the right body to the right funeral service. And the application process for cremation is very rigorous these days.'

When the cortege left through the automatic gates, the courtyard seemed so much larger. Owen Fox's BMW was the one remaining vehicle, and the sight of it nudged Peddyr's conscience.

'Oh, shit. Flies,' he said, pressing his nose to the tinted rear windows. Peddyr checked both sides of the car again before building up enough courage to take a long, hard sniff at the boot. He resembled a mad dog, its nose pushed hard against the joins where the boot met the bodywork, seeking the tell-tale sickly odour of decomposition. He wouldn't look much of a detective if, when opened, it revealed the decaying corpse of the man he was looking for.

'Found anything, Paddy?' The familiar voice of Hugh Ingles came from behind him.

'Not that I can smell,' Peddyr replied. 'I was clutching at straws, anyway.'

'Time to report him as an official missing person then, shall I do the honours?'

Peddyr was grateful for the offer, Hugh Ingles making a statement to the police was far more likely to get a result than if he rocked up at the local nick to add to an already unlikely story.

Hugh was using a walking stick and winced whenever his weight moved unevenly through his right hip. He hobbled back to the building. Peddyr matched his slow pace and opened the door for him.

Facing the possibility of an unsolved case, he decided to

focus on clarifying Gabby's last movements, prompted by something Connie had said during her daily call first thing that morning. 'Could Stella Cortez have an ulterior motive?' his wife had asked.

Working it through, Peddyr reasoned that Stella was not in the country when Gabby had gone missing. She could be after Gabby's money, he supposed, but had no need for it because she was loaded. Bernie had checked her financial status before he transferred his client's money to Stella's personal bank account. It was very prudent of Gabby to have such a paranoid solicitor.

'I doubt it,' Peddyr had told his wife. 'In fact, Stella would be the person most likely to help Gabby.'

'Yes, Lao Gong, which is my main argument for considering her a suspect. She's the person Gabriella calls in a crisis. There is nobody else she can rely on. And because you said there was no connection between Stella Cortez and Owen Fox... when professionally speaking there is.'

Connie was correct. Peddyr reflected on her words as he walked back inside, carefully closing the door to the courtyard behind him, waiting patiently while Hugh Ingles shuffled arthritically along the corridor.

'Mr Ingles? Would Stella Cortez have known Owen Fox? Would she have had reason to come across him before she left to live in Spain?'

Hugh Ingles limped to a standstill. 'Who?'

'Estelle Cortez. Used to be Estelle Archibald when she first started work here part time, and after that when she left school. Stella Archibald.' The woman had married several times, and for the life of him Peddyr couldn't bring to mind any of her previous surnames.

'Ah, yes, my most experienced and greatly missed employee. Young Archie. I miss that woman. She was mistress of my domain.' These were lavish compliments indeed, thought Peddyr. 'There won't be anyone in the whole organisation who hasn't heard of Stella or participated in one of her legendary training days. She always knew how to keep the audience enthralled. From the cleaners to the funeral directors in each branch, she generated a sense of pride in the service we provide. I'll never replace her.' Hugh Ingles spoke with such energy he lost balance and tipped against the wall. 'If Owen hasn't come across her, I'll eat my hat.'

And she'd been present for Eileen Brady's funeral. There had always been a link between the two of them. 'Curiouser and curiouser,' Peddyr exclaimed, thanking Hugh for his time before encouraging him on his way. 'I'd better not hold you up. The sooner you can prod the police into action, the sooner they can begin looking for him, eh?'

Hugh readily agreed and resumed his unsteady progress toward his sparkling Jaguar saloon parked at the front of the premises in one of the spaces reserved for customers.

Standing next to the sealed display coffin, Peddyr tapped his fingers rhythmically on the lid. It was an undeniable fact that Owen, Gabriella and Stella were all linked to Castle and Wyckes. Stella knew the processes and procedures here better than Owen.

If the pebble was here, so was Gabby. And if Gabby was here to confront Owen, she wouldn't have been brave enough to do so on her own. There was a fair chance Stella was with her too, on Sunday when he was taking delivery of a body from Broadstairs... but whose side was Stella on?

Connie's observations were solid. Stella and Gabby had been inseparable. Stella was the strong one, she knew everything about Gabby. She was the only person who did. They must have been together.

'If Owen wasn't seen anywhere after Sunday and the two ladies were both seen on Monday, then the chances are he never left this building.'

Peddyr folded his and frowned.

'Gabby Dixon, what the hell have you done?'

46

ANY PROBLEMS?

I'd been alone throughout my journey, exhausted and drained, and there was no one to meet me at the airport. It was undoubtedly the loneliest I'd felt in my entire life. The address I needed to find was written on a piece of paper clasped firmly in my sweaty right hand as I slumped into the nearest taxi. Converting cash at the port in Plymouth, the exchange rate hadn't done my finances any favours. But staying in a crusty back-street hostel in Santander the previous night meant I had easily enough Euros to get me from Girona Airport to El Castallet on Avenida 11 Setembre.

The road-weary taxi driver who picked me up spoke much better English than I could have hoped for, and in some small way this helped to settle my frayed nerves. His name was Juan, a very common name in Catalonia, he told me.

'I know at least seven Juans, two of them are my cousins,' he said, reeling off the occupations of the other Juans. For the whole trip so far, I'd felt sick at what I'd put in motion in the previous seventy-two hours and had hardly slept. I'm sure I wasn't pleasant company for Juan the taxi driver.

'I'm Josephine. Pleased to meet you, Juan.'

'You come from England?' he asked.

'Er, no, I've been in Northern Spain. Walking.' Then I did the classic tourist schtick, peeling myself from the sticky vinyl seat as I leaned forward and spoke louder and more slowly than necessary. 'The pilgrimage... Camino de Santiago.' This wasn't an outright lie; I had walked along the route running through Santander. Less than two miles of it, mind you. What's more, I still looked the part; walking boots battered and dusty on my feet, crumpled sun hat, and an old rucksack filled to the brim with essentials for my onward journey. I'd stayed in the hostel for one fitful night before traipsing to Santander Airport the following day. In by boat, out by plane.

The taxi driver nodded sagely. 'Ah, yes, and now you go for a relaxing holiday. Palamos is a nice place, I live in Palamos,' he said proudly. 'Rest your feet by the sea, very nice, Miss Josephine.'

'No, not this time, Juan. I'm starting a new job. Working.'

'At El Castallet?' he raised a quizzical look, his leathery winkles deepened.

Despite the jitters, I had to laugh. El Castellet was a bar, and clearly my Spanish wasn't up to any hospitality career. 'No, I'm meeting a friend there. I'll be working for a charity.' That wasn't far from the truth either. I'd be relying on handouts for a while.

I spotted her as soon as we pulled up. There was Stella, reading a newspaper at an outside table, under the shade of an umbrella with a glass of cold beer to hand. A welcome sight in sunglasses, a green shift dress and wide-brimmed hat, I could see from her shimmering chestnut fringe that she'd wasted no time in treating herself to another trip to the hairdressers. Something I craved.

Juan the taxi driver wished me luck as he passed me my bulging rucksack. 'If you ever need my services, the taxi office is near the bus station.' Not necessarily helpful information for a complete stranger to the town, but it made me feel more welcome than Stella's greeting.

'Good God! Don't you think you've overdone the bedraggled traveller look?' She stood to greet me, keeping it deliberately low key. 'Made it then,' she said as we kissed cheeks.

I pushed the burdensome rucksack under the table and stood defeated and exhausted. 'Obviously.'

The look I received from her then was scathing. 'Are those your mother's clothes?' she asked, indicating a seat opposite her and sliding elegantly back into the rattan chair she'd been occupying up to the point of my arrival. 'I usually expect a better standard of dress and personal hygiene from the people I have lunch with. I think we may have to go shopping.' Finally, a grin crept across her face. 'I honestly wasn't sure you'd have the guts to go through with it,' she said, reaching out for my hand and patting it gently.

'All for one, and one for all,' I replied. We both knew that if either of us backed out, we'd both face dire consequences. It was all or nothing, shit or bust. She'd been there for me since the day we first met and never once let me down. Stella was the only family I had left. Not in the true sense of the word, but she was the sister I wanted, rather than the one foisted upon me. My parents had treated her like one of the family too.

'Any problems?' she asked.

'Are you kidding? I'm a wreck.' I held out my hands, which were shaking uncontrollably, as they had done since

Sunday. 'I'm crippled with anxiety most of the time, but by some miracle I'm here. Your instructions were great, although I free-wheeled a bit, improvising now and again.' I tugged at the front of my tee-shirt. 'I thought this was ironic.' There was a faded green iron-on transfer emblazoned in bold letters across my grubby top which read, "God loves a trier…" I'd found it in a bag of clothing while searching the loft for a suitable travel bag. 'It's a few years old and stinks to high heaven, but it fitted the bill nicely. Must have come from Mum's church fundraising days,' I said.

Stella ordered two beers when the waiter appeared. He was back in record time and I gulped down a good inch of the refreshing lager, falling silent.

'The new hair cut is…'

'Shoddy,' I said, helping Stella to find the right description. 'It was a rush job with a pair of kitchen scissors.'

'Must have been good enough, and those reading glasses are very fetching.'

The most nerve-wracking part of the deception was the border controls at ports and airports. Each time I approached one my guts cramped, and my legs went jelly-like with fear. It was excruciatingly tense, requiring the use of a new pebble. I'd lost the other one. When Girona security handed my passport back and said, 'Thank you, Miss Dank, have a nice trip,' I could hardly raise a smile in response. Given my attire, I can only assume they thought I was a complete flake and not worth their time. My passport was authentic, but I wasn't.

Stella raised her glass. 'To Josie.' She sipped, her eyes glinting over the rim at me. 'And God bless Gabriella's last will and testament, and her generosity in bequeathing me half her estate after taxes. Here's to the day it arrives.'

The newspaper lying on the table was an English tabloid

with an unsubtle headline on show. 'I checked the papers on the plane,' I said.

Stella shrugged briefly. 'I don't suppose there's anything to report, but I confess, I've been scanning the BBC local online news. Nothing happening in Bosworth Bishops and nothing has come to light regarding any disappearances, yours or Owen Fox's. But I've started making noises, I phoned Bernard Kershaw's secretary to say I can't seem to contact my friend Gabby. I told dear Fiona that I'm worried about your state of mind – I mean, Gabby's state of mind. By the way, what did you do with your phone?'

Explaining how thorough I'd been in covering my tracks, I sounded like a spy from a Hollywood film. 'I fired up the old barbecue and burnt the SIM along with my chopped-off hair, the notebook you gave me, apart from the pages with addresses on them, and Josie's medical certification of death. The phone handset landed in the drink about ten miles off the coast of England. My clothes from Sunday went into the charity clothes bank on the way to Bosworth station.'

'Good girl.' Stella looked serene. Her long, manicured nails wavered over her open handbag. 'I have something for you,' she said, and passed me a cheque written out to Miss Josephine Dank for the exact amount I'd asked to be transferred into her account only days before.

I jiggled my legs and picked at my fingernails. 'Thanks. Enough for a small apartment and...' The words caught in my throat when the enormity of what I'd left behind struck me; a career with a decent pension, a professional reputation, qualifications, Bridget and a dozen work colleagues. I already missed Phil, even though our marriage was at an end. I wouldn't see Laura, little Alice and stroppy Leo ever again. I'd abandoned my clothes, old photographs, furniture, my name and my past. My future with a new name depended on one thing – getting away with the death of another human being. Stella and I had deliberately concealed that fact and the ramifications were potentially catastrophic. She insisted it was an accident, but I still wasn't so sure, nagging doubts eroding my acceptance of her story about Owen slipping on a wet floor. Tales of slipping on floors had been told to me before.

The thought of it became overwhelming. 'I shan't be able to sleep until I know it's been done.'

Stella smiled and winked at me. 'It's all in hand. The service is today. Soon he'll be a pile of unrecognisable ash.'

My mouth dried. 'How can you be so fucking calm about it?' I reached for more alcohol, needing both hands to steady the glass.

'Now then, Josie, use of profanity is not very becoming in a pilgrim, is it?'

'But I've only got your word for it,' I objected. My last clear recollection of the events of Sunday morning had been seeing Owen Fox lying on a cold marble floor, dead as the proverbial dodo. After that I dipped in and out of tunnel vision and waves of abject panic. That level of intense dread and dismay resulted in a very unreliable set of flashbacks.

Stella had taken charge, and I relied on her version of events to fill in the missing hours. According to her, she spoke on the intercom to the drivers from Broadstairs in her best deep and throaty voice and even waved to them through a window while wearing my dad's old cap. After they'd left, she decided it would be sensible to return my documents to Owen's office, as if we'd never been there. Apparently, we found the drawer where he'd kept them along with various other items. The decision to take Josephine Dank's papers and passport, instead of my own, was the catalyst for our ultimate plan for me to disappear. I had no recollection whatsoever of what we did with Owen's body. It remained a complete blank.

A whole day and some hours later, on a train heading back to Bosworth Bishops from Gatwick, I had a brand-new reporter's notebook on my lap and was reading the lines written there in Stella's hand.

If I know you well enough, I'm guessing you won't remember everything we agreed. In the following notes, I've outlined details of what to do next. Once you have read this and are up to speed, please destroy the notebook but keep hold of the information about the travel arrangements we made while waiting for my flight. Time well spent, I think you'll agree.

And now I'd made it to Palamos, there was no going back. Stella leant towards me. 'You've only got my word for it? I can't believe you said that. My word not good enough all of a sudden?'

'Sorry, I'm overwrought. I can't think straight, everything is so...'

She pulled a face. 'I understand. Finish your beer, we'll order a snack then get you cleaned up. Tomorrow you can relax.'

My lips formed a stiff smile, but privately I wondered if I could ever relax again after what we'd done. I checked my watch, Gabriella's watch, and said a small prayer for Owen Fox.

47

A MORAL DILEMMA

*C*onnie bounced through the door and jumped into Peddyr's arms. 'Hello, Ye Ye. Miss me?' Not giving him a chance to answer, she kissed him full on the lips and ruffled his spiky hair. 'You need a trim. Very scruffy.' He lowered her gently to the floor and took hold of the car keys.

'I'll fetch the luggage, shall I? Please tell me you brought back less than you went with.' He risked a glance through the doorway at the lounge carpet. It appeared perfectly clean and stain-free to his eyes. The ultimate test of his domestic abilities would come soon enough.

On his return, puffing with exertion at carrying bags up the rear stairs to the flat, he found Connie preparing a pot of tea. 'I'm so glad to be home. The thrill of a grandchild soon wears off when the wee might won't stop crying.'

'A very Scottish expression I notice, Lao Po,' said Peddyr, trundling the hefty suitcase through to their bedroom. 'Learn any others?'

'Aye, I did, hen.' Connie giggled. 'I also learnt a bit about

Estelle and Carlos Cortez on my way home. The wait for my flight was long enough for me to gather some vital data for you. Shall we sit on the balcony, it's such a lovely day?' She rummaged around in one of the bags Peddyr had deposited in the kitchen. 'Shortbread. Yummy.' Placing a tartan packet on a tray with mugs and a teapot, Connie announced all was ready.

Once settled on their familiar seats opposite each other Peddyr slid an arm forward to stroke her hand. 'While we wait for it to brew, I need your advice.'

'Oh, dear, it must be serious.'

'It is.'

'You've found Owen Fox and Gabriella Dixon in a secret love shack.'

'No, I think neither of them will be seen again.'

'Dead?'

'One almost certainly is, the other… I'm not sure.'

Connie sat back in her chair. For an inveterate chatterbox, she was sensitive enough to know when to keep quiet and listen. This was one such time.

'I think Gabby killed Owen Fox in revenge for raping her mother, for ruining her life, and for the death of her first love Kit Willis. Maybe she momentarily lost control. Whatever, he is killed at Castle and Wyckes. He never leaves. He's not in the mortuary, nor in the empty coffin on display near reception, and he wasn't seen on any CCTV in town or at the train station.'

'Right. I'm with you so far.' Connie lifted the lid of the teapot and stirred musically with a teaspoon.

'I think the original plan was to retrieve Gabby's documents from Owen Fox and force him into leaving town forever. But things went horribly wrong when he died. Once the panic was over and his body was dealt with, instead of taking the box of Gabby's documents away with her, she put it back in Owen's drawer, making it seem as if she'd never been there.'

'Genius,' Connie said, rewarding him with an approving smile.

'Gabby and her friend Stella then left the area. Stella went first, back to sunny Spain as planned. Gabby disappeared in the early hours of Tuesday and I truly fear what she may have been contemplating...'

'Suicide?'

'It's possible.'

'And the body? What did they do with Owen Fox?'

'My best guess is they put him in the same coffin as Edward John Hubbard, who was cremated yesterday. Stella would have known exactly what to do to get him in there, with Gabby's help, and reseal it. She would have checked the computer system to confirm arrangements. By now he's a pile of ashes, all mixed up with another man's remains.'

Connie gasped, then touched her hands to her lips. She held them there, not moving for a second or two, before grabbing hold of Peddyr's forearm. 'Oh my God! Can you prove this?'

'No.'

'Have you told the police?'

'Not yet. They say as he's an adult he has every right to disappear.'

Connie sat back. 'Wouldn't someone notice two bodies in one coffin?'

This was a consideration Peddyr had been mulling over during the night. 'They were both slim. I wondered if one could have been placed below the other.'

'And doesn't the funeral director have to do a final check

before the coffin is put in the hearse? You may have to think about this again. Where else could he be?'

'Wrapped in plastic, sealed and placed in the boot of his own car… Who knows?'

'Does Bernie know about all this?'

'I'm meeting him in an hour.'

*A*fter a cup of tea and a change of clothes, both Connie and Peddyr arrived in good time for an appointment with Bernard Kershaw.

'Sorry about spilling wine on your nice carpet, Connie. There's no excuse, I'm a clumsy oaf at ti—.' It was too late to redeem himself. By confessing, Bernard had undone all Peddyr's hard work to keep their boozy night a secret.

Fortunately, Connie's response was tinged with humour. 'I knew it!' she said to her husband. 'I knew things couldn't be as perfect as you made them out to be. There's always a disaster when I'm away, and invariably it involves the two of you. Last time it was a drunken caper with a trip to hospital as a result. This time the carpet gets wine sloshed over it. Honestly…'

Bernie coughed to cover his embarrassment. 'To business then.' He took out his pen to make notes. 'I'll keep Fiona out of this,' he said, 'until I know what we're dealing with. So far, we have assumed that Owen Fox forged all the paperwork pertaining to Gabriella's cremation and subsequent registration as deceased, the body in fact being that of Josephine Dank.'

Peddyr nodded. 'He would have previous forms to copy. He knows the requirements.'

'You say the CCTV recording, showing Castle and Wyckes' rear courtyard, stops for several hours on Sunday, but the police still say they require evidence of a crime being committed before they'll act. In which case, may I suggest you go back to Castle and Wyckes and pop the boot of Fox's car open. Then we'll know. He's either dead and concealed there or he left the premises under his own steam.'

With a shrug, Peddyr agreed. 'It might be the only way.' He glanced at his wife, who signalled her agreement with a slight nod.

'Gabriella was seen on Monday so she can't be the body in the boot of the car if it was put there when the CCTV wasn't recording,' Connie suggested. 'But if Owen Fox is in there, then she's in real trouble.'

Bernard stopped writing. 'Go on.'

Connie's investigation into Estelle and Carlos Cortez had led her through a maze of financial dealings to discover they were fast heading for insolvency. Carlos looked good in terms of assets, but recently had played fast and loose with his investments.

'Stella is driven by money,' Connie explained. 'Her personal wealth is substantial, although when you look back, she lived well beyond her means for years. Previous marriages resulted in financial gain and this one was supposed to do the same, but it seems Carlos is a gambler and his winning streak has ended. Perhaps Gabriella was her way out of the mess Carlos has landed them in.'

'What are you saying?' Bernard asked, tugging at his tie.

'I'm saying you need to dig deeper into Stella's financial history. She earned good money at Castle and Wyckes, and, if Laura is to be believed, had decent enough settlements from previous divorce proceedings. Not enough, however, to explain her extravagant spending on cars, clothes, jewellery, holiday homes abroad and the rest.

There has to be another source of income, other bank accounts.'

Peddyr looked at his wife with pride. 'We follow the money, because there's a chance Stella is not the friend she pretends to be. Gabby thinks Stella is her saviour, but what if she isn't?' He rolled his shoulders. 'Who benefits most from helping Gabriella? Remember, folks, there's a lot of Gabby's money in Stella's account.'

Connie looked at Bernie, who in turn looked at Peddyr. Nobody spoke for a while.

'Good grief, and buckets of blood!' exclaimed Bernard, rising from his seat and making for a filing cabinet in the corner of his office. 'She was a beneficiary in Eileen Brady's will... not a large amount, a few grand, but if I'm right Thomas Moreton bequeathed her a decent sum too, several years ago.' He pulled out a slender file and returned to his desk.

'Who's he?' Connie asked.

'An old client. Died a couple of years ago.' Looking agitated, Bernard picked up the phone to call Fiona McFarland into the room.

'Can you circulate a highly confidential memo to all the partners, asking for information on any cases where an Estelle Cortez, nee Archibald, has been bequeathed money or items in a will. I need responses as a matter of urgency.'

Fiona took the details down and raised a fine eyebrow at the mention of Stella's name. With a nod, she left the office.

'If I'm right, Mrs Cortez benefitted from her time at Castle and Wyckes in more ways than one,' Bernard said, a vein beginning to throb on his forehead. 'After I've checked out my own law firm, I shall be making enquiries of our colleagues in other local practices and notifying the police of my findings.'

'A Harold Shipman manoeuvre?' Connie asked.

'I fear that may well be the case,' Bernard replied. 'Cultivating rich clients, doing them a special favour, perhaps marrying one or two… It's high time undertakers were better regulated.' He stared hard at Peddyr. 'I agree, Connie. Mrs Gabriella Dixon may be in hot water.'

Peddyr let out a low moan. 'Christ, what if it was Stella's intention to kill her all along and she used Owen Fox to get what she wanted?'

'Explain yourself, man,' Bernard barked.

Peddyr didn't know quite where to begin. 'Way back when Owen arranged Eileen Brady's funeral, say he knew exactly who Eileen was because of the intimate relationship they'd had in the past.'

'If he was Laura's father,' Bernard stated flatly.

'Or even if he wasn't, he knew the family. And at a wild guess, I reckon Stella and Owen have known each other for a while too. He worked in Oxford, so did she. He worked in care homes for the elderly where residents only moved out wearing wooden overcoats. She was a funeral director. See the links?'

Bernard was thoughtful, Connie silenced by the possibilities.

'If she set this whole thing up,' Peddyr continued, 'Owen gets the chance to fleece Laura, and Stella profits from Gabby's situation in the longer term. But they take it one step further and arrange to kill her, to get a quick pay out. They jointly plan to get her to Castle and Wyckes on Sunday, murder and dispose of her, but…'

Connie carried on where Peddyr stopped. 'Perhaps Stella killed Owen for double-crossing her.'

Bernard slapped his flattened hands on the table. 'Come, come. This is unacceptable speculation. I will confer again with the Coroner's Office in respect of Josephine Dank's cremation and the fraudulent registration of Gabriella's death. Connie, you set your sights on Owen Fox's previous employment record. I want to know if he and Stella Cortez were working in tandem or in competition. Pedd, crack open Owen Fox's car, then if necessary get hold of the police. Tell them I sent you.'

Peddyr slung an arm round his wife's shoulders and squeezed. 'Fancy a trip to the undertakers, then the local police station?'

'You take me to the nicest places,' she replied.

48

WHO AM I?

I thought I'd feel a sense of relief at meeting Stella again, but the incessant niggles in the back of my mind had swollen to a chorus imploring me to pay attention. Stubbornly, I drowned them out.

We didn't go to her house, as I'd assumed we would. Instead, we travelled by taxi and she booked me into a hotel on the outskirts of town where I showered before we embarked upon a shopping trip. 'Keep the sunglasses and that dreadful hat on whenever we're out in the street,' Stella insisted.

'But the police won't come here. They're not looking for Josephine Dank. Nobody is. I mean, Gabriella doesn't have a passport. They'll be looking for her in England.'

'Yes, you're right. I know it sounds like I'm getting paranoid in my old age, but nevertheless we'd better not take any chances for a while. First things first. You need fresh clothes, a suitcase, a better haircut and a new colour.'

'A suitcase?'

'You can't stay here in Palamos. It's too obvious. Why do

you think we met at a bar and not my villa? We must be careful.'

This was devastating news. I felt numbed by rejection. 'But where will I go? I thought I would rent an apartment here in Palamos to be near you for support, help me find my feet, learn the language. You said perhaps I could work for Carlos.'

Fear brings a special sensation with it; a chill swept over me, starting at my legs and slowly encompassing my heart.

'What I said was that Carlos could pull some strings, and he will. You have money, I gave you a cheque. It's your safety net. But you must be patient.' Stella reached for my shoulders like she always did when she needed me to be brave. 'It's too soon for us to be seen together. On Monday we head to Perpignan, over the border in France. There's a big ex-pat community there, and the marina is always looking for English-speaking workers. Your French is passable... and Carlos knows loads of people from the yacht club at Canet. We'll sort some lodgings. Once your residency is in order, you can open a French bank account.'

The muscles in my neck were so taut I could barely nod. The precautions advised by my best friend were commendable, things I would never have considered. She'd left her flashy car at home and used a taxi today. Also, I noticed her usual flamboyance was toned down; she'd dressed demurely so as not to be recognised readily. In short, she'd thought through my disappearance far more thoroughly than I had.

We left the hotel and walked through the back streets of Palamos, coming to a hesitant stop outside a ladies' hairdressers. It wasn't Stella's usual type of establishment; this one catered for the mature women of the town and sorely required a facelift if it were to attract the younger wealthier customer.

'You're kidding,' I said as she pushed against the door. The air-conditioning was a welcome relief from the heat of the day but hairspray filled the air, as did the whiff of ammonia from old-fashioned perm lotion being liberally applied to an elderly lady's head of tight rollers.

A petite woman who jabbered at me excitedly ushered me to a seat. My Spanish was minimal, my understanding of Catalan non-existent. All I gathered in those first few minutes was her name, Rita. Apart from that, she may as well have been speaking Martian with a Saturn accent.

Stella made a show of requesting a cut and colour, and I went much lighter than my usual rich conker brown. I was looking like the real Josephine Dank. In the two hours I was there, I barely understood a word being said and got by using sign language and a form of Esperanto, thus providing highly entertaining moments for the other customers. For me, the experience served to emphasise how alien I felt. More than homesickness, the emotions were raw and petrifying. I wanted desperately to go home but didn't know where that was anymore.

Stella left me inhaling flammable gases, only returning in time to see Rita putting the finishing touches to a 1960s Jackie Onassis bouffant hairdo. It was bloody dreadful. With no way of communicating my preference for a sleek head of hair, I'd given up and succumbed to whatever came my way. I did the same with Stella, who'd purchased clothes on my behalf.

When we returned to my hotel room, she pulled items one by one from various shopping bags. Cropped denim, striped shirts, tee-shirts, plain sundresses and two skirts. The general colour scheme appeared to be blue and white. Very nautical.

'What happened to black?' I asked.

'This is Spain. Only widows wear black.'

'Please tell me you bought underwear. I've rotated three pairs of knickers since leaving England.' The sooner I could open a bank account, the better. The need for ready cash was becoming chronic. 'How much is the hotel going to cost me?'

Stella screwed up her nose. 'Stop worrying. I've paid up front with cash. Repay me when you can.'

'I will pay you back in cash. We wouldn't want there to be any way of tracing you to Josephine Dank.'

She threw me a curious frown. 'That's right, I'm glad you understand how foolish it would be to go to all this trouble and trip ourselves up by being careless. If we bide our time, they will declare Gabriella missing, assumed dead. And because on paper she's already dead and buried, it won't be long before her estate is settled. In the meantime, you've plenty of money to keep you going because your husband has paid up and I can access it easily enough.'

'But that's Gabriella's money,' I said. 'How long will it be before Bernard Kershaw asks you to return it to her estate? Er... my estate.' Being someone else was becoming confusing. I tried to talk about myself in the third person – "she", "Gabriella" – in the hope I would adjust. Josephine was a lovely name, and I was gradually getting used to the surname Dank. All the same, it was surreal.

Minutes seemed to pass before Stella answered me. She stood at the open door of the wardrobe in my hotel room and took time to hang up my clothes, throwing the old ones into a refuse sack. Her brows were furrowed in concentration. 'Will he ask me to return it? Why would he if I'm a beneficiary?'

'I don't know. It just crossed my mind that he might. You were going to use it to buy Laura's share of Derwent Drive on my behalf with my money. Bernard knew it was my money and Laura is expecting you to buy her out. Whether Gabriella is dead or not, Laura will pester Bernard Kershaw to tap you up, to keep your promise. In which case I'd better not cash that cheque at all.'

Stella faltered; her eyes darted left and right as she considered what I'd said. 'Fuck it.' Her agitation spilled out as she paced towards me. 'If your solicitor screws this up, we're both in the shit. This could take a lot longer than I originally thought.' She seemed angrier with me than with herself.

'Do you want the cheque back?'

'No, tear it up, burn it. Do what you like. If I have to give the money back to Bernard lah-di-dah Kershaw, so be it. We'll wait for probate.' Stella reached into her handbag. 'Here, this should keep you going until Monday.' She handed me a thick wedge of Euros. 'Get some dinner, maybe some deck shoes to go with your clothes. You must make a good impression. There's no holiday for you, my girl. You need a job, and pronto.' She attempted a reassuring smile, but it didn't quite reach her eyes. Apparently, she hadn't considered every contingency. And why would she? I'd brought this on her, and it was expecting a lot to suppose she'd be able to engineer my complete disappearance.

'Aren't we seeing each other over the weekend? I thought at least we'd have dinner; you, me, and Carlos.' Her expression said it all. It was the stupid suggestion of a needy woman, lost and floundering.

'No. We stay away from each other. Enjoy your few days in Palamos. Don't mention you know the Cortez family. Do the touristy stuff and I'll meet you first thing on Monday. Chin up. We'll sort it.'

She closed the door quietly, abandoning me in a back-street hotel, in a place I didn't know.

Not for the first time since leaving Plymouth, I allowed abject fear to swallow me up. I spent hours curled up on the bed, covering my guilty head with the bedclothes. When I surfaced, it was to sip at a glass of water before hiding away again, despairing and grieving for all I'd lost.

I spent a large part of Thursday in my room, wallowing in self-pity, but by late afternoon I'd become exasperated by my own negativity. I stared at myself in the bathroom mirror and ran open fingers through tangled hair. 'Shape up, woman,' I said to my unfamiliar reflection. 'Gabriella Dixon, you no longer have a place in the world, you do not exist. Goodbye.' If I was to thrive and become independent again, then I had to change how I thought about life overall. I could waste away in a hotel room and submit myself to clinical depression or do the opposite.

I closed my eyes for the count of five before I reopened them. 'Josephine Dank, Josie, you've barely made a mark on the world. It's time for you to live.'

49

CARELESS TALK COSTS LIVES

I was as good as my word, to myself and to Stella. The shops in town quickly became boring, which I put down to my most recent persona, Josie, being more interested in other ways of passing the time. Josie had an urge to explore, and I wandered around the sights of Palamos late into Thursday evening, eventually stopping at a bar to indulge in the fine art of people-watching, sipping a coffee.

Investigating the delights of the fish market on Friday morning, newly acquired phrase book at the ready, I enjoyed myself. It was a bit of a shock to my nostrils, true, but the sheer variety of fish and shellfish for sale was splendidly distracting. Such a shame I had nowhere to cook for myself. With the return of my appetite, refreshments were called for. I ended my tour of the seafront in favour of an early lunch while I read Thursday's edition of an English newspaper.

As promised, I'd mentioned no connection with the

Cortez family during my time exploring the streets of Palamos. Someone else did.

Carlos had friends at the yacht club in Perpignan, just like Stella had said. He was also known by the yachting fraternity in the Marina Palamos. Some of them had ventured away from the clubhouse and were eating at the next table in the quaint restaurant I found at the eastern end of town.

The group of men and women on the adjacent table were loud, brash and didn't have a favourable word to say about Carlos Cortez or his business dealings. From my corner table, the conversation going on beside me had me transfixed. One of the diners was Dutch and his wife was Canadian, the others were less open about their country of origin. Out of mutual respect they used English as the preferred international language and because many of the waiters weren't fluent in foreign languages, the Cortez family secrets were relatively safe.

Head buried in my book purchases, I appeared to be learning French as I sat at the table alone. I ordered from the Menu del Día a cheap meal of local fish and patatas bravas. How Mediterranean I felt, sipping sparkling water and eating with the locals. Josie Dank was enjoying herself – myself. I caught the first reference to Carlos Cortez and dismissed it as coincidence; it was a common name. But when the gossip on the next table involved his English wife, and she was referred to by her name, I was radar on.

The restaurant wasn't busy, there was one other couple at a table on the far side of the rowdy yachters. They had their heads together, deep in conversation with their backs to me.

'She's the one,' the lofty Dutchman said. 'He was in fine

shape before her greedy hands became involved. They say Cortez Holdings is haemorrhaging money.'

'Now, Walter, you have no proof,' his wife interjected. 'Bad management is what I've heard, poor accountancy. There are hundreds of thousands of Euros rotating between his business interests, he's playing the international markets. This is nothing new for Carlos, just be sensible and give him a wide berth.'

'I couldn't agree more. Miriam is right, Walter. Carlos Cortez is not to be trusted. If that wife of his has any sense, she'll make sure her money is kept separate from his. I heard he married her for financial reasons, although she's a fine-looking girl.'

I was enjoying my simple but delicious lunch and could only smile at the gossip. The conversation with Stella on Monday would have to include a discussion about whether Carlos was an unscrupulous double-dealer heading for financial ruin. If it was the case, then she should guard her money carefully and perhaps move mine out of her account.

The group changed the topic, and I opened the newspaper. There, on page four, was a picture of a white forensic tent, police in protective overalls, and crime scene tape across the entrance to a familiar courtyard. The headline was unsubtle – "Body found in boot of car." I scanned the columns for details; Peddyr Quirk, private investigator, had called police to Castle and Wyckes undertakers in Bosworth Bishops. The body found in the boot of the BMW was that of Edward John Hubbard. He had been due for cremation the previous day. A body was cremated, and a service had taken place, but not for the right man. Police had launched a full investigation, and the Coroner's Office were involved.

The brief period of respite from anxiety ended abruptly.

I stared around me, and put sunglasses back on for fear of being recognised. I didn't know what to do next other than to find Stella. Leaving the paper on the table, I paid the bill and left to find the taxi rank. I'd found the whereabouts of Stella and Carlos's villa on a street map of Palamos given to me by the owner of the bookshop in town. I knew the address off by heart. Stella and I sent gifts and cards to each other frequently. I had to warn her and plead with her to move my money somewhere neutral and get me to Perpignan today. Monday was too long to wait.

The unfamiliar streets flummoxed me. I thought I was heading to the bus station but, on reviewing my map, found I was several roads in the wrong direction. It was nearly one o'clock, and the lunch hour was gathering momentum with restaurants and bars filling rapidly. Siesta time would arrive soon enough after that, when the whole town closed until much later in the afternoon. I turned around to get my bearings and caught sight of a Scandinavian-looking woman, staring at a street name, then looking through the window of the building in front of her. She spoke happily into a mobile phone, stepped off the pavement and into the front entrance of the Deutsche Bank. As I passed back that way to reach the right road, I couldn't resist glancing in.

I stumbled like a drunkard when I saw Stella at the cashier's desk, hat and dark glasses on, as I'd seen her on Wednesday, unobtrusive-looking. What luck, I thought. Thank God I'd found her. I scooted through the doors and approached from behind, knowing she would spot me easily enough once she turned around. I hovered several feet away from the queue. She slid her hand forward through a gap in the Perspex of the cashier's position, taking hold of a pile of banknotes.

'Thanks, er... gracias,' she said in a sweet whisper, sliding a bank card back into her purse.

'Thank you, Miss Dank,' the cashier said, beaming at her.

The floor became spongy beneath my feet, the walls encroached, and I folded inwardly; there had been no mistake in what I'd seen and heard, but how could it be possible?

Fortunately, Stella moved without turning in my direction and I had enough presence of mind to swivel and face the opposite way. I pretended to be interested in a display of leaflets and I'm sure I would have remained there, mute and stupefied, if someone hadn't taken me by the elbow and asked if I needed help. At least I think that's what he said.

I muttered something about being English, and not feeling well, which was true. In shock, I was whimpering, hyperventilating, and gripping so tightly to the leaflet in my hand, my knuckles turned white. It was a close-run thing, but I nearly made it to the taxi rank before the fishy patatas bravas put in a reappearance at the base of a tree. This vomitous crescendo seemed to bring an end to my state of panic. Breathing more evenly, I leaned against the trunk of the sick-splattered tree.

In through the nose, out through the mouth.

This mantra repeated itself again and again in my head as I evaluated the enormity of my discovery. Blind to Stella's treachery, I'd been taken in by her for years – we all had; me, my parents, Laura, Stella's string of husbands, Bernard Kershaw and even the dependable Peddyr Quirk. None of us had recognised her capacity to deceive with such ruthless efficiency.

When I'd composed myself and swabbed my mouth with a tissue, I approached the first taxi in the line and asked for Juan.

'Which Juan you want?' the driver asked. It would have been funny at any other time, but the pain of Stella's betrayal was cutting into me like a knife and I had a burning desire to throttle the next person who offended me. Me. Josephine Dank.

Dank was a German-sounding name. A name for someone who already had an account with Deutsche Bank, someone who had money in that account. A useful account for Stella to abuse. Bernard Kershaw was right. This was about money. Stella had my money, and she had Josephine Dank's money and goodness knows who else had fallen for her convincing lies.

'Can you take me to the nearest Deutsche Bank that's not in Palamos?' I asked. The taxi driver heaved a giant shrug and pointed back towards the town centre shops. 'No. Not here. Somewhere else.'

Behind me a car horn hooted. A driver stepped out of his taxi and shouted, 'Miss Josephine. Where you want to go?'

*T*he bank in Palafrugell was about six kilometres away and we had to hurry. 'It closes at two, but we will do a good time,' Juan assured me.

I should have been a quivering wreck, I should have been in tears and unable to function, but I wasn't. Instead, I was monumentally furious and intent on protecting what assets Josephine Dank had left. I was out for revenge; a kind of retribution Josie could live with.

The words of my mystery caller on BBC Valley Radio popped into my head. "Show no pity to the guilty, an eye for an eye, a tooth for a tooth, a life for a life." The trouble was, being neither a cold-blooded killer nor a violent person, I couldn't contemplate the ultimate sin, but I could hurt Stella without physically injuring her. She would answer for her crimes if I went about it in the right way.

Every single day since it had happened I'd become increasingly convinced that Stella had a deliberate hand in Owen Fox's death after he became too greedy, planning to con money out of Laura as well as contriving a hefty pay out from me. She wasn't going to stand by meekly and see him snatch the lion's share. He didn't slip on a wet floor; he was bludgeoned from behind with a stone urn, the one that ended up next to him on the tiles. The tumbled coffin was just window dressing. He hadn't reached for the urn; it didn't end up on the floor of its own accord, and I'd been too busy quaking against a wall in a wet trench coat, wielding an umbrella, to reach for it.

Stella had killed Owen Fox.

Killed him to protect herself and get her hands on my money. And then tried to make me believe his death was my fault. If the newspapers were right, she'd hidden his body in the coffin of Edward Hubbard; Owen Fox had then been cremated to hide the evidence of murder. Left with a spare body to dispose of, she'd put Edward Hubbard in the boot of Owen's car. *We* had put the body in the boot, I supposed, grateful for once for my amnesia. Stella and I had done that. She couldn't have done it on her own.

Juan glanced at me in the rear-view mirror of the taxi. 'Don't be worried, Miss Josephine. You are safe.'

I must have looked petrified, and I suppose I was in a way. Once I'd accepted Stella's willingness to kill another human and cover up the deed, I knew she could do the same to me. If she was to keep my divorce settlement money and inherit from my will... I would have to die.

A virtual crossroads presented itself. I could go back to

England, hand myself in to the police, confess all I knew and go back to whatever life I had left – once I'd paid for concealing Owen's murder and preventing another man's funeral.

Or I could do something else.

I drew a piece of paper from my purse and with it a passport. Josephine Dank's passport was at the top of a pile of documents held together with an elastic band. These precious pieces of paper were the reason I was still alive. Stella would need these to access Josie's full bank account.

Within that pile were several household bills and a small prayer book where Josie had scribbled the PINs for her bank cards. Inside an envelope were her birth certificate, a letter from HMRC detailing inheritance tax at 40%, an NHS Medical card, and even an EHIC card, all of which I'd guarded within a tatty leather satchel throughout the whole journey from Bosworth Bishops to Palamos. I'd read them a dozen times trying to piece together what Josie was like, who she was. I had these and a few clues from what Peddyr Quirk disclosed. Apart from that, Josie was an unknown quantity. I had free rein to create Josephine Dank in my own image.

'Do you speak English?' I asked the cashier when I reached the bank. 'I lost my purse somewhere between Palamos and here. I need to cancel my bank cards. Can you help?'

She called Customer Services, who were efficient and polite, as one would expect from a German company. There were understandable concerns about my request. 'Do you have an account with us, Miss Dank?'

While I knew this to be the case, I hadn't any details with me; no account number, no cheque book and no cards.

Maria from customer services wasn't surprised. 'You can cancel on-line from your mobile phone.'

'I'm sorry, but I don't use one.' Having rifled through the paperwork in my bag so many times, I knew Josie rarely used a telephone. Her itemised bill wasn't long. Her life was a frugal one and there was no evidence of broadband or digital television contracts, just a paper copy of her TV licence.

Maria looked at the computer screen, and a faint smile appeared.

'I prefer to use telephone banking from home or face to face with real people in a bank,' I said to her.

'Can you confirm the first line of your home address, please?' This I did without hesitation. I knew it off by heart. 'Do you have any ID with you?'

Out came the passport.

'Thank you, Miss Dank. One moment.' Maria's fingers flashed over the keyboard. 'There we are, all good. I've cancelled your debit and credit cards. It seems you were not quick enough. A sum of eight hundred Euros was withdrawn from the Palamos branch not half an hour ago.'

I must have looked crestfallen because Maria was quick to assure me I would be covered for the full amount on the bank's insurance as soon as the theft was reported to the police.

'I'm not sure my Spanish is quite up to the job,' I said. Nothing to worry about, the bank would see to it, Maria informed me. She looked again at my account.

'How fortunate you have come to see us, Miss Dank. According to our records, we have written to you several times in recent weeks to advise you to consider a financial review.'

'I've been travelling,' I said, cobbling together a reason for not responding.

'You have a lot of money in this one account. It may be safer to transfer it to a premier international current account.'

'Really?' My plan had been to cash the cheque Stella left with me and hang the consequences. It would lead back to her and ultimately to me. But, recalling the letter from the tax office, I was presented with other options. 'I inherited property when my parents died, and I sold it not long ago.' I knew this to be true, making me sound convincing. Acting for Josephine Dank, being her, made it straightforward. I didn't have to lie to the bank. 'A different type of account would protect my money better?' I asked.

'We could set it up and you could have replacement cards by Monday afternoon.' She tilted her head. 'In cases of identity fraud, it is wise to set up a new account, we'll transfer everything.' She showed me a printout of my current balance and recent transactions. Over 300,000 Euros were at my disposal. I didn't gasp aloud because Josie isn't like that. She's very humble and extremely careful with money.

'It looks in order,' I said. During the seconds afforded to me, I noticed Josie's direct debits were still being paid for electricity and council tax, and that someone had with-drawn small amounts of cash from her account in the last month. Owen Fox must have been helping himself since May, and now Stella was pilfering Josie's unprotected assets.

Josie didn't deserve that.

Maria was waiting for a decision. 'Well, it would seem sensible to create a fresh account,' I said, seeing a much better outcome than I'd imagined possible. 'Thank you.'

I signed a consent form using the same signature as on Josie's passport and, as the ink flowed, I mused on how duplicitous Stella had been. She must have taken Josie's bank cards and found the PINs before giving me the rest of the documents in England. Her face would have been a picture when she checked the bank balance at the first opportunity. No wonder she hid me in a cheap hotel, kept me out of Carlos's way, and planned to whisk me to Perpignan. Although on reflection, I don't think I would have lived long enough to see France. I knew too much, and I was worth too much to remain alive.

'Thanks for your custom, Miss Dank.'

I smiled for the first time in a while. 'Thank you, Maria. You've been a lifesaver.'

Nobody was looking for Josephine Dank. As far as Deutsche Bank and the Spanish police knew, she was an innocent victim of fraud who the bank was only too pleased to help. On the other hand, Stella had been impetuous, exposing herself by withdrawing cash directly from the bank in Palamos, instead of taking smaller amounts from ATM's like Owen Fox had done.

She must have read the news. The police would soon be looking for her in connection with Owen's disappearance. She needed money to escape. Carlos's money, my money, and Josie's money.

50

AND FINALLY, THREE MONTHS LATER

*T*he voice of radio presenter Talbot Howkins was blaring out from the kitchen when Peddyr strolled into the flat. It was a Saturday morning and Talbot was in a serious mood as he announced the subject of his regular weekend slot.

'Today, listeners, BBC Valley Radio brings you a special edition of the Saturday Phone-In. We are enlisting your help with the police investigation into the disappearance of our very own Dr Gabriella Dixon, who mysteriously vanished twelve weeks ago tomorrow. This is a desperate situation for her family and friends. Local police are no further forward, despite the arrest of Mrs Estelle Cortez by Spanish police and her subsequent questioning by detectives from the UK.'

Potato peeler in her hand, Connie shouted at the radio. 'Detectives? Not in my book, sweetheart. Useless, all of them. They would have nothing if it wasn't for my Pedd.' Picking up a potato, Connie flashed the peeler back and forth in rapid swipes, peelings littered the work surface.

'Why did they take so long to extradite her? That's what I want to know.'

Talbot Howkins had moved on to thank his listeners for their help in piecing together Owen Fox's role at Castle and Wyckes with his chequered past. 'It's hard to accept that two people in positions of trust should take advantage of the elderly and bereaved to swindle them out of their money. It beggars belief, in fact.'

A peeled potato landed in a saucepan full of salted water with a loud plop, as Connie nodded along in agreement with the radio presenter.

'And where's the investigation into Owen Fox, ladies and gentlemen?' Talbot asked the airwaves. 'Forensics may have proved he was killed at Castle and Wyckes, but, as Estelle Cortez has found out, they don't need a body to charge someone with murder these days. And so what if he's dead? He should still be exposed for what he was: a thief. He stole from those poor old folks in Oxfordshire. He even removed bank cards from dead people, taking money from accounts, knowing they had no one to look after their affairs.'

Connie stabbed the air with the peeler. 'The Cortez woman, she's worse. They should lock her up for a long time for what they both did.' She turned when she sensed Peddyr in the room. He was holding a postcard in his hand. 'Bernard in Italy this year?' she asked, quickly reducing volume and voracity. 'Having a nice time, is he?'

As Talbot Howkins introduced his first guest, she moved towards the radio to turn the sound down. A Detective Inspector Simpkins began to catalogue the efforts of the local force in determining Gabriella's last known move-ments and the forensic searches undertaken at number six Derwent Drive and at Castle and Wyckes. 'The undeniable link between the disappearance of Gabriella Dixon and of

Owen Fox has been reported widely in the national press, but the case is far more complex than first thought.'

Peddyr sat at the kitchen table staring at the postcard, flapping it from front to back. 'It's not from Bernie,' he said. 'He doesn't go on holiday until next week.'

Connie fell silent as her husband made a phone call.

'Bernie, what's the legal position on Gabriella Dixon if she's never found?' The call was relatively short but Peddyr's pensive mood continued as he placed the postcard, picture side up, on the table, fingering the edges.

'What *is* the legal position?' Connie enquired, breaking the strange mood.

'According to Bernie, if Gabriella's body isn't found soon, there could be a case for declaring her dead, given that she's already registered as such. The Coroner is seeking a High Court ruling. After which, Gabby's last will and testament can be openly contested because she names Estelle Cortez as one of the main beneficiaries. That'll set Laura Churchill off like a rocket, she's been driving Bernie mad with her constant badgering. And before you continue yelling at the radio, you should take into consideration that Stella's on remand, and not cooperating with the police investigation in the slightest. She's denying everything they've charged her with; fraud, embezzlement, and suspicion of murder. Yet she isn't saying a word about what happened to Gabby Dixon. Nothing.'

The postcard had drawn Connie's eye, and she stood looking down at the picture. 'Lovely scenery. Who's it from?' It was Connie's turn to examine the words written on the postcard. She picked it up. 'Santiago di Compostela. That's northern Spain.' She read aloud. '"Cousin Juan runs a hotel along the way. I have a job. All found. Live in. Cash in hand. Spanish improving. Don't need much money, just peace of mind. She did what they say she did. I have a new life, a better one. No pebbles needed. Thank you for everything".'

A soft crooning noise came from Connie's throat. 'You must be the one person in this world she trusts,' she said, lowering her voice to a gentle whisper. 'What should we do? Shall we inform the police?'

Peddyr reached around his wife's waist. 'No, she deserves a fresh start. The police had their chance to help her and they failed. So now we must do what we feel is right.' He glanced once more at the card, noting the initials used to sign at the bottom. A smile became a chuckle, and a chuckle became a throaty laugh as the last pieces of the puzzle slid into place for Peddyr. 'Fair exchange is no robbery,' he said. 'A life for a life. Have a good one, Josephine Dank.'

ABOUT THE AUTHOR

Alison Morgan lives in rural Bedfordshire UK with her engineer husband and bonkers dog. She spent several decades working on the front line of NHS Mental Health Services and latterly as a specialist nurse and clinical manager for a dedicated psychosis service across her home county. However, when a heart problem brought her career to a juddering halt, Alison needed to find a way of managing her own sanity. She took up writing. Her intention was to produce a set of clinical guidelines for student nurses but instead a story that had been lurking in her mind for some years came spewing forth onto the pages of what became her first novel.

Since then she has become an established crime writer, unable to stem the flow of ideas. From a writing shack at the top of her garden she creates stories with memorable characters, always with a sprinkling of humour, often drawing on years of experience in the world of psychiatry where the truth can be much stranger than fiction. To find out more about Alison please check her website **www. abmorgan.co.uk**.

ACKNOWLEDGMENTS

To everyone who gave their time and valuable opinion in reading draft versions of this story. Special thanks to Nicky, Simon and to The Bongo of Great Age and Wisdom' (aka my mother). To the team at Hobeck Books for their enthusiasm and professionalism and for gifting me a fabulous editor and cover designer to bring this novel to life. To my husband, 'The Bearded Wonder' for being wonderful and bearded and for listening as I read out loud. To Sadie Waggytail for keeping me company and dragging me out for a walk every day. (I know dogs can't read, but she deserves a mention.) Thanks to you all.

HOBECK BOOKS – THE HOME OF GREAT STORIES

We hope you've enjoyed reading this novel by the brilliant Alison Morgan. To find out more about Alison and her work please visit her website: **www.abmorgan.co.uk**.

This novel is the first of full-length Quirk Files, of which there are many more to come. Alison Morgan has also written a prequel novella to this book *Old Dogs, Old Tricks* which is free as an ebook to subscribers of Hobeck Books.

David Corcoran is dead. Did he die of natural causes, or was he murdered? His daughter seems to think there is more to his sudden death at the sleepy Blackthorne Lakes Retirement Village than a case of another day, another resident meets their maker. Enter Peddyr and Connie Quirk, newly formed PI husband-and-wife team, to 'act' as residents to see if they can sniff out the truth. Can they pull it off? Will Connie convince the Blackthorne golfing set that she's a real resident? Is there more to this story than simply old man dies happy?

To download your free copy please go to the Hobeck Books website **www.hobeck.net**.

Also please visit the Hobeck Books website for details of our other superb authors and their books, and if you would like to get in touch, we would love to hear from you.